"Marilynn Griffith is a fresh voice in Christian fiction. Her funny, breezy style is sure to take the market by storm!"

Tracey Bateman, author, *Leave It to Clare*

"From beginning to end, you can't help but see the hand of God ministering through Marilynn Griffith's work."

Vanessa Davis Griggs, author, *Promises Beyond Jordan* and *Wings of Grace*

"Marilynn Griffith digs deep inside to write a novel about everyday people who love the Lord."

LaShaunda C. Hoffman, editor, *Shades of Romance* magazine

"With poetic description and compelling storytelling, Marilynn Griffith delights readers with every sentence."

Stephanie Perry Moore, author, *A Lova' Like No Otha'*, Payton Sky series, and Carmen Browne series

"Looking for a sassy, engaging read that keeps you turning pages and recalling your faith? Look no further. Marilynn Griffith won't disappoint."

Stacy Hawkins Adams, author, *Speak to My Heart*

"Marilynn Griffith's writing makes the five senses come alive. Her writing makes you taste color, smell love, hear hearts, see purpose, and touch God's truth in every word and phrase. She is a master storyteller!"

Gail M. Hayes, author, *Daughters of the King*

"In a dizzy world of fashion, hard bodies, and romantic tangles, *Pink* exposes a basic truth: when we hide our true selves from others because we don't want to get hurt, we get hurt anyway—and others do too. Author Marilynn Griffith struggles with the risk of vulnerability and its bottom line: learning to be honest with others—and ourselves."

Neta Jackson, author, *The Yada Yada Prayer Group*

Pink

shades of style: book 1

Pink

marilynn griffith

Revell
Grand Rapids, Michigan

Published by Fleming H. Revell
a division of Baker Publishing Group
P.O. Box 6287, Grand Rapids, MI 49516-6287

Printed in the United States of America

Library of Congress Cataloging-in-Publication Data
Griffith, Marilynn.
    Pink / Marilynn Griffith.
        p.   cm. — (Shades of style ; bk. 1)
    ISBN 0-8007-3040-2 (pbk.)
        1. Triangles (Interpersonal relations)—Fiction. 2. Women fashion
    designers—Fiction. 3. Wedding costume—Fiction. I. Title.
    PS3607.R54885P56 2006
    813'.6—dc22   2005019091

For my princesses, Ashlie, Michelle, and Jewell. May each of you find God's happy ending.

1

"Come . . ." Gram fluttered each of her long, slender fingers. It was a motion Raya Joseph knew well. The frowning brow and waving hand meant for Raya to grab her own Bible, fill another cup, and join in the study and prayers as she had so many times before. They'd talk more later. Much later if Raya had anything to do with it.

Looking past Gram's outstretched hand, Raya slipped into the kitchen for a cup of freshly ground coffee syrupy with Splenda. Though she longed to join Gram's fellowship, Raya knew that one second at the table and she'd spill her guts. There was no fooling Gram.

Or God.

So drowning her bitterness with too sweet coffee, she escaped to her room, checked her new do, a flamboyant white-blond afro, in the mirror, and pulled on a little pink something she'd shoveled out of the bargain bin downtown. Before she'd met Darrell, pink had been her favorite color. She loved how fresh it looked on her, a bright flush against her dark skin.

Though Raya's mother had cautioned such bold color choices for someone of her complexion, Gram had taught her early not to listen to folks about what she couldn't wear. "The rainbow is yours," she'd said. And Raya had believed it. Until Darrell came along. Today she was reclaiming the rainbow still somewhere inside her.

When Raya returned to the kitchen, Gram looked up from her Bible. Raya's eyes fixed on the word above her grandmother's thumb.

Enemy.

The older woman raked a hand through her own afro, white from wisdom instead of dye. "One more thing. Miss Man Stealer is coming this way."

Raya gulped for air. "Who, Megan?"

Gram no longer spoke the girl's—woman's—name. To Gram's credit, she never had cared for Megan, not even when Megan was Raya's roommate at Stanford. "Watch that one," she'd said. "She's the devil in a tennis outfit." If only Raya had known how close the words would come to being true.

"Yes, her. She's coming to the city. I heard her say it on TV last night. Watch yourself, Aryanna."

"I doubt she'll look me up." Raya certainly wouldn't go looking for her.

"Oh, but she will look you up, don't you see? Her kind won't stop until we're undone. Did you see the NBA play-offs? Your father took that one and her mother along with him. He had them on the summer Nia special too. I taped it for you."

"I don't watch the network much anymore, Gram. And yes, I saw them at the play-offs. What Daddy does on his time is his business."

His business. That's what everyone had always called it, though Mother's money and Raya's childhood served as the sacrifices that had built the Nia Network. Not so long ago, it had even seemed worth it. Now that Daddy had sold to Allied Media and they'd dropped most of the programs she'd help develop from the lineup, Raya didn't watch. It made her too sad . . . and too angry. "What he does has nothing to do with me."

"It has everything to do with you. Why do you think the Nia ball is in New York this year? You, that's why. Still, watch out. That worthless girl has more mess in mind. I can feel it."

More mess? Where had Gram been? There was nothing left to damage. This summer had flattened Raya like the toothpaste tubes in the bathroom down the hall.

"I will never leave you nor forsake you."

Her racing heart slowed. "I'm not worried about Megan. You shouldn't be either. Like you say, it's God's day. I'd better go out to meet it."

With another kiss on her grandmother's cheek and a mumbled, guilty prayer, Raya left the house, feeling like herself for the first time in almost two years.

Floating on a combination of caffeine and oil sheen, Raya walked easily to the train station instead of grueling down the avenue like on other days. Once on the platform, she took her usual seat to wait for her train, ignoring the coffee curses and urine-stained cement. Ignoring and being ignored, that was her plan, and up until now, she'd enjoyed great success.

Her pink dress, however, had other plans. It refused to be ignored.

"Hey, pretty mama," a man in a hard hat whispered as he passed. He paused for a reply, but she turned away, though a smile replaced the hard line that had been her mouth. He whistled on as if satisfied with her grin.

Another man, smelling of cabbage, stopped in front of her.

"Nice dress. Good cut," he said in a matter-of-fact, whiskey-laced way.

Raya whispered thank you in a pained tone as she recognized the man as a former tailor in the garment district, one whose shop had been orphaned by the sluggish economy.

"Tell your grandmother I said hello," he said as she slipped him her last twenty.

"I will," Raya said, praying for the two men, for the city, for herself. She finished with a hasty amen before she messed around and got comfortable. God wouldn't settle for less than all of her, and that was more than she currently had to give.

A cluster of women who'd smiled at Raya all summer, approving of her taupe demeanor and sensible shoes, frowned now, narrowing their eyes into jealous slits. Raya knew the look well, the shock when other women saw her legs, her crazy hair, her pink thinking. She'd tried to stay beige, be good, but there was enough of that at work.

Ignoring the women's chatter, Raya dragged her eyes toward her lap—but they snagged on a pair of almond eyes focused in her direction. Was he staring at her? She peeked again to be sure.

Definitely staring. And she was too.

Whether it was sleep deprivation or temporary insanity Raya wasn't sure, but for the first time since coming to New York, she'd stared down a guy in the subway.

A very cute guy.

The one thing she'd come to like about New York was the friendly unfriendliness. People were nice enough, with smiles to spare, but there was no chitchat to endure, no looks to deflect. Nothing to explain. Everyone danced to their own music, rushed to their own destinations.

Except for him.

Eye Guy, seated directly across from her, pulled up the *New York Times*, crossed his legs, and left Raya to contemplate the razor-sharp pleats in his buttercream-colored suit pants. "You can tell a lot about a man by his pants," Daddy often said. She was more of a shoe girl, but Eye Guy's buff and cream shoes covered that too.

Though women's design was her passion, Raya admired the crisp lines of his suit, a modern take on a classic Brooksie three-piece, one her grandfather would have worn. The blazer spilled carelessly over the seat like sand spilling off a beach. His tie was perfectly knotted and just the right width to show off the vest, but it was the pants that stole the show.

Whether it was the pleats, the way he bobbed his ankle on his knee, or the three-quarter-inch cuffs young men never wore these days, Raya wasn't sure, but her eyes kept traveling back in the direction of her newspaper-masked neighbor.

A finger tapped her shoulder. Apparently, she'd captured someone else's attention as well. A girl with burgundy braids and dimples pointed at Raya's white-blond curls.

"What color is that?" She leaned in for a closer look.

Raya smiled and considered the girl's cheekbones. Good structure. Dramatic eyes. She'd make a great evening-gown model.

"It's platinum. Got it done at the Dominican shop in Flatbush."

The *Times* jerked down across the aisle. Eye Guy's temples were smooth, and his subtly highlighted hair spiked in places.

All the right places.

Hair Girl should have been questioning him. Wherever he went, they knew just what to do. He lowered the paper farther, revealing the beginnings of a beard, sculpted as though it'd been shaved around the edges. A dime of fuzz, identical to the ones she'd detested on other men, graced his lower lip. What kind of brothah was this? He was Wall Street and round-the-way all wrapped in one. Raya held her breath, taking in his smooth lips, the same nutmeg shade as his skin.

You need to stop. Right now.

Hair Girl helped out by tapping Raya again. "You said the Dominican shop, right? The last time I was there for a color, I came out looking like Pepé Le Pew. They can doobie though—wrap that hair around your head and have you looking oh so fine."

Raya nodded, remembering the times she'd sat in that shop, drinking in the sounds, watching the sway of the women's skirts as they whisked her hair around her head, set her tresses on rollers almost as big as orange juice cans. She was Daddy's little girl then.

"I know that's right. And there's a discount on—"

"Mondays, Tuesdays, and Wednesdays. Girl, you don't have to tell me. I might forget about hair salon discounts if I can get a fierce fro like that."

Fighting the urge to attack the rustling paper across from her and toss it away, Raya chuckled, both at the woman and at herself. After months of enduring New York's gorgeous men at every turn, she would have a breakdown because a guy had a nice suit. It figured.

"Try the shop again. Ask for Monica."

The girl nodded, but her expression remained serious. Obviously, hair was no laughing matter to her. "Thanks, girl. You rockin' that cut. I want it bad, but to tell the truth, I ain't that brave." She said it low, like a treasured secret.

Brave? I'm just tired.

"Thanks." Not knowing what else to say, Raya turned back, but not directly to the front. No point in encouraging him.

Or herself.

Men were trouble. Especially buttercream-suit-wearing men. He had that same upwardly mobile look Darrell had. And studying the *Times* before work? Her father would have loved it. At least she didn't have to wonder if a man wanted her for money anymore.

The train screeched to a stop behind her and opened its doors before she could think. Usually she'd have spent the last few minutes clearing her head for the jam-packed ride. She wrinkled her nose at the morning smells swirling about as she squeezed inside the train—coconut hair grease, fried chicken, Adidas cologne, and Icy Hot. Her stomach knotted. Not the best combination.

Raya compressed her body as the last passenger, no doubt responsible for the menthol part of the scent, shuffled into the car, clinging to a pole with one wrinkled hand and her pocketbook with the other.

Gram, although taller, more confident, and much more dangerous than this gray-haired lady appeared, had taught Raya something about respecting her elders. She stared as a headphoned teen reeking of cologne marched to the last seat before the woman could sit down.

Raya gripped her bag and shook her head. At least she could share the pole with the older lady, make her feel more secure—

"Why, thank you, young man."

Huh?

Raya's heart pounded as Eye Guy lurched forward to the pole beside her. She'd tried her best to ignore him as they'd entered the car and had been relieved when he'd taken a seat. Now he'd given it up. The *Times* neatly tucked under his arm, he assessed her with his eyes, but he remained silent. With a passing glance, she inspected his lips up close. Did he wear lip gloss or what? She nibbled at her own Bonne

15

Bell, suddenly wishing she'd opted for something more grown-up.

What is wrong with me today?

"You're welcome, ma'am."

Raya's shoulders slumped. It was hot enough to swim in the train, but Eye Guy's voice sounded like a cool mist whistling up from Martha's Vineyard, her father's favorite summer getaway. The stranger's earthy timbre and sharp syllables rolled across the short space between them like a morning tide.

She swallowed as he stared down at her one last time, adding a camera-ready smile before a final retreat behind his paper. Raya forced her eyes to the floor. He probably played this game every day. And she'd played enough games.

The train brakes hissed to a stop. Raya tensed, anticipating the press toward the door. The old woman didn't move, and Raya was glad of it. The center of a mass of people probably wasn't the best place for the sweet-looking lady. The corner of a newspaper, neatly folded, brushed her elbow. She looked to get away, to escape, but there was nowhere to go.

Eye Guy leaned over and whispered in her ear. "God loves you. I don't know why, but I feel like he wanted me to tell you that."

She stared back at him as the crowd crushed from behind. The doors opened and spit them both onto the platform. Without looking back, Raya spun on her heels, her legs moving like overcooked spaghetti. Her head ached, both from the sandalwood-lemon something that lingered on her shoulder and from the words that rang in her ears.

Couldn't he at least have been a little more original? And why didn't she feel comforted? Maybe because somehow she still didn't think she deserved the love of God—or anyone else.

There is none righteous. Not one.

Raya ignored the whisper slicing across her bruised heart. She picked up her pace, marched toward another lie—her position at Garments of Praise Fashion Design. Raya didn't belong there, designing practical uniforms instead of her crazy gowns, but for now, for Chenille, she'd have to make it work. Somehow.

"God loves you."

Her legs churned faster as those chiseled cheeks blurred across her mind. And those clothes? Tailor-made. The walking Jesus tract was a good act, but this former Black American Princess knew all the lines.

To make things worse, she'd gotten blown off in her new favorite outfit. She'd actually thought she looked cute this morning, dark circles and all. Instead, she'd looked like exactly what she was—a woman in need of Jesus.

She turned onto the sidewalk and headed for her job, whispering into the morning humidity. "Lord, if you're trying to drive me crazy, you're a little late. I lost my mind three months ago."

2

Choking in a fog of leather, nail polish, and body wax, Flex Dunham couldn't catch his breath or pull his thoughts away from the white hair and pink silkiness he'd just left behind.

Who was that? he wondered, entering Man-O-Cure, the men's salon where he reluctantly had his hands "serviced," as the client who'd complained about his ragged cuticles called it. The whole thing was a little girly for his liking, but the models and actresses he worked with actually noticed such things. His chest tightened. He sagged against the marble counter.

The man across the desk, a member of Flex's church and his personal fashion advisor, adjusted his turquoise spectacles. "You all right, Flex?"

"I'm good, Stan. Just a little out of breath." A lot, actually, but no use making a fuss.

With a skeptical glance, the fellow nodded. "I see you've got your suit on. That one will get you far. Trust me."

Flex tucked both thumbs in his vest, veiling his struggle to inhale. "The suit is growing on me, I must admit." The beauty queen on the train certainly seemed to have liked it.

"Whatever you say. Just don't pass out in here, okay?"

"Nope. I'm good."

Stan let out a concerned sigh. "Highlights still look good. Trying the city slicker package today? Or just the hands?"

Halfway to the soda machine, Flex turned back, trying not to recoil. "Just the hands." Wasn't that bad enough? He punched the Vanilla Coke tab, grabbed the can before it hit bottom, ripped it open, and took a gulp. "Missed you at church Sunday."

Stan nodded. "Hospital visits. They usually call me for the AIDS runs." His fingers flicked across the computer keyboard, finding the appointment menu and sending a message to the appropriate station.

Flex scratched his head. "Yeah. I saw the sign-up for that." Guilt tinged his voice. Working with the AIDS program at church was something he'd like to do, but he'd have to work his way up to it. For now he'd stick with the children's ministry.

A message popped up on the screen between them: "He's late, but I'll take him. Give me ten minutes."

Stan turned the monitor around. "It's okay, man. Other people signed up. I don't mind going. Most of the patients are people who helped start the Coming into Light ministry. They were there for me. I want to be there for them."

"I understand," Flex said.

He didn't really understand, of course, not about being redeemed from an alternative lifestyle, but he did know about struggling every day to be more like Christ. One thing was clear—ogling women on the train was definitely out of bounds. He'd acted like some knucklehead kid, then topped it off with the kicker . . .

19

God loves you.

Why not just spout the whole script? "God loves you, and he has a wonderful plan for your life." In his mind, the words fell flat, both as a tool to share Jesus and as a way to get the phone number of a never-to-be-seen-again beauty. Sheesh. Flex ground his eyes with the heels of his hands as the sugar dumped into his bloodstream.

As his chest expanded, pink paisley and white hair danced before his mind's eye. And . . . those legs. They'd gone on for days, even without the platform shoes. She was more than pretty, and he saw beautiful women every day, plastic bodies built with the finest spare parts. But not this one. Her lean frame boasted no injections or foreign objects. She was all too real, even with that crazy white hair. Sort of like Halle Berry's in that *X-Men* movie but cut short.

You're losing it.

Flex downed the rest of the Coke, blinking as a headache tightened around his skull. He'd been the first one down at the altar call yesterday, pouring his heart out, giving it all up. The prayer of relinquishment, as his prayer partner called it, giving up his own way, giving over every part of himself to Jesus . . . again. Two years plus of celibacy kept him on his knees. All that praying and seeking yesterday . . . and then came her. Flex stared up at the ceiling.

You didn't waste any time, did you?

He crushed the empty can and tossed it in the recycle bin before checking the clock. Fourteen minutes had passed. Roxy was going to chew him out as it was.

A shrill voice agreed as he rounded the corner. "What are you waiting for, a private invitation?" His manicurist's eyes locked on the Coke can protruding from the full recycle bin. "Did you actually drink that?"

"I did." Adjusting his bag, Flex ignored her nagging tone

and followed Roxy to her station. "Sometimes I just need one." He dropped into the chrome chair across from her.

She frowned, surveying his torn cuticles and shivering with disgust. "Caffeine is linked to cancer, you know. And sugar? Don't get me started. I'm making sure they come pick up that pop machine this week."

Flex stared at her in mock disbelief. By now he'd grown used to Roxy spouting tirades about holistic living with a cigarette hanging from her lips.

She dunked his wide fingers into the soaking solution. "What'd you do this time, dig a garden?"

He turned away from the smell of the liquid. "Not exactly."

She shook her head, sending her mop of blue-black twists flying in every direction. "Remodeling at the church again?"

Flex smiled. "Something like that." Expanding the church nursery had been his idea, so doing the work had been his idea too. It was only fair.

She pulled up one of his hands, frowned, and dunked it back in the stinky liquid, the first of many solutions. This one softened or something. He wasn't sure what solution number two did besides burn. He didn't want to know.

Flex watched her shaking fingers, knowing that she'd go for another cigarette if he didn't steer the conversation back onto safe ground. Though she was usually the one to bring it up, any mention of church made Roxy nervous.

And the faintest puff of smoke made him sick. For all Roxy's talk on the perils of caffeine, the dangers of smoking seemed to totally escape her. Typical. She could see the twig in the other guy's eye while overlooking the rotting log in her own. Didn't he do the same thing?

"Sorry about being late."

With a steady hand, she forced back the cuticle on his

thumb. "I was surprised, but at least you called. I count on the rest of the fellas being thirty minutes behind. The salon appointment isn't a male concept, I guess."

Tell me about it.

If Flex's business wasn't built around appointments, he'd never make it either. But it was, and so he made it where he had to go. Early. Except for today. Today he'd been so caught up reading the obituary of a long-ago girlfriend in the *Times* that he'd taken the wrong train, looked at the wrong woman, gotten off at the wrong stop, and said the wrong thing.

His mother had told him about Brooke's diagnosis months before, and he'd even talked to Brooke on the phone, prayed with her in person. She was his last relationship before becoming celibate, and he'd been tested since then, but it was still a scary thing. On days like today, he wondered how he could ever have been so stupid. And then a few seconds later when a chocolate Barbie in pink looked his way, how he could have been so stupid became all too clear.

It'd been a wrong kind of morning, one that should have done everything to solidify his faith and encourage him in his celibacy. Instead, it served as a reminder that there were women like that in the world. The head-turning, heart-stopping kind of woman. The kind he'd convinced himself no longer existed. Still, seeing her didn't mean anything. Without a doubt, if they ever got past hello, it'd end the same way as all the others—badly.

In spite of that, she made him want to go back to the station and re-create the whole messed-up morning every day if it meant seeing her again. And the way her voice squeaked between her Ivy League words. If that wasn't the cutest, craziest thing. Whether she was the buppie she sounded like or the girl from the hood she looked like he wasn't sure. The only thing he did know was that he wanted her.

Bad.

And that scared him. Though he was still man enough to appreciate a nice-looking woman, it'd been a while since somebody made him feel like this. She had it going on in every direction. There was more to her than big earrings and wild hair. Something deep was running underneath all that bling. Not that he was one to talk about being authentic, running around in a tailor-made suit like somebody's granddaddy. At least he'd picked the cuffs.

The memory of his silk-clad warrior woman and her Love's Baby Soft cologne grated at his mind. What grown woman would wear that? And why did it smell so good on her? He smiled, remembering the bottle he'd bought for his mother when he was ten. Maybe the morning wasn't all wrong. Maybe . . .

"Ow!" Flex yanked his hand away.

Roxy smiled as she dropped a hangnail into her cup. She tugged his fingers toward her. "Maybe if I'm a little rough, you'll be a little more gentle with these things. I doubt it, but maybe." Her eyes flashed with their usual suggestion.

He shook his head, chuckling nervously. He'd made it clear from his first appointment that nothing could happen between them, but it didn't stop Roxy from flirting. Every week.

Her voice went down an octave. "What kept you, anyway? God or girl?"

Flex fell back against the chair.

"Both."

Morning heat clung to Raya like a second skin as she walked down the front hall of Garments of Praise. Instead of the receptionist, her girlfriend Chenille sat behind the front desk, her red ringlets piled on top of her head and her pregnant belly curving sweetly underneath a linen sheath.

"Well, if it isn't Raya with the flava!" She slapped the desk, then stared at her hand. "Ouch!"

"Did you hurt yourself, silly?" Raya turned over Chenille's palm for a closer look.

Chenille pulled away and pinched Raya's cheek. "Gotcha. You are so easy to fool."

Tell me about it.

"Before you get started, don't. I've had a rough morning—"

"Already?" Chenille put a hand on her hip. "I don't believe it. Look at you. That dress is cute enough to eat. And that hair? Now, that's the Raya I know." She straightened and did her best imitation of Raya's father, lifted eyebrows and all. "Aryanna Joseph, daughter of black media mogul, has disappeared from Nia studios and reappeared in New York City looking luscious as usual—"

"Stop, nut. Leave Daddy alone. Besides, he only does that with the left eyebrow." Raya tilted her head. "Like this."

Chenille stifled a giggle. "Okay, that's scary. I never thought you looked like him, but you were his eyebrow twin just now. That's just insane."

"And so are you. Now leave me be. I'm going to my spot. See you in the meeting—"

Chenille pulled her back. "Oh, no you don't. These people met the wrong woman. My friend is back, and I have to introduce her around."

Raya froze. "Please don't." The staff didn't seem to have too much love for her as it was. The whole rich girl myth and all. No sense making things worse.

"Nonsense. Lily, Jean, everybody! Come look at our new and improved designer, Raya Joseph!"

Lily Chau, head of the pattern department—if you call three employees a department—arrived first, giving a quick, sharp nod. "Very nice," she said, before disappearing again.

Raya murmured, "Thanks," realizing that was the most Lily had said to her since last week's pattern-cutter accident. Raya could get down with a pencil, pad, even a computer drawing program, but all other implements turned into weapons in her hands. Maybe it was God's way of saying, "Thou shalt not sew." Too bad he hadn't spoken up when she was passing glances with that fool on the train. Sometimes free will had its drawbacks.

A grunt sifted through the claps and catcalls of the other workers. Raya smiled at Jean Guerra, head of Chenille's cutting department and the firm's secret weapon for a perfect fit. It was rumored that Jean had once worked for Yves Saint Laurent. No one knew why she stayed at Garments of Praise, but everybody knew to stay out of her way and to take her malice for what it was—affection.

She frowned at Raya. "A tight dress and white hair? So what? I come to work like that every day. Nobody claps for me." Jean gave her co-worker an undercover wink before shoving her way back to the "threshing floor," as she'd aptly named the cutting room.

Raya sighed with relief as Jean and the others walked away. Perhaps the little run-in with Lily last week was forgotten. She hoped so.

"Don't forget the team meeting, folks," Chenille called out behind them.

Raya stiffened at the mention of the weekly event she both anticipated and dreaded. It was the closest thing to church she'd been to since coming to New York.

"So what's all this about, anyway?" Chenille waved her

hands up and down Raya's body, pausing at the platform sandals. "I haven't seen you pink like this since you arrived."

"It's Katayone Adeli. Can you believe it? Silk. Found in the sale bin at an outlet on Seventeenth. I blew the last of my check on it."

Chenille looked at Raya as if she'd spoken in a foreign language. "Adeli? You've got to be kidding. Were there any of her chiffon fringed tops? Or those skinny Lucy Liu pants?"

Raya eyed her friend's blooming hips, on top of which two fists were now perched. "The tops were too expensive, and the pants? Well, I'll keep an eye out, but Lucy doesn't have all that junk in her trunk, honey."

Their eyes met. Chenille hugged her belly as they both burst out laughing.

Raya recovered first. "As for the hair, I traded a cut and color for drawing a picture of the stylist's little brother. Gram told her about me. He was a cute little thing." Real cute. When he grew up, he'd probably buy three-piece suits with razor-sharp pleats and tease women on the subway. The humor leaked out of the moment. "Anyway, see you at the meeting."

For once eager to get to her makeshift office, formerly known as the back hall, Raya made a quick exit. Three bookcases lined the walls, stuffed to bursting with art books and photo collections for inspiration. A mood board with tigers and cheetahs and swatches of black and gold cloth was propped in the corner, a reminder of the running suit prototype she needed to review this week. An easel with swatches of every texture and hue, a fan, a full-length mirror, and racks of hangers left little room for her desk and files.

Still, her office had a window and an outlet for her power strip, so she couldn't complain, though it was a far cry from her design room back in California. At least Daddy had indulged her with that. His girlfriend was probably in there right now, shoving another shopping bag full of clothes she'd never wear on top of Raya's drawing table.

She blocked the thought. It didn't matter now. This place mattered. It had to. The computer hummed at her command. She shoved her purse into the bottom drawer of the file cabinet. Her back relaxed against the tight fit of her chair. The wheels were a little slippery, but the comfort was unmatched. She could work in this thing for hours.

Chenille had anything but work in mind. "I know you didn't think you got away that easily. What happened this morning? You did the squeak-toy thing with your voice. Cute guy?"

With a jerk, Raya turned to face her childhood friend so determined to marry her off. Too bad her mother didn't give Chenille a chance. They'd be good together. "You don't miss a thing, do you?"

Chenille smiled. "I catch the stuff that matters. Now spill it." She looked at the clock. Her smile faded. It was 8:23. The Monday meeting always started at 8:30 sharp. "Give me the short version."

Raya released the words all at once. "Cute guy on the train. Stared at me. Nice pants. Great eyes. Gave an old lady his seat. Got off at my stop . . ." She paused to see if Chenille was following.

Her boss gave the "I'm with you" nod and leaned in closer, smelling of baby lotion. She'd been sampling again. "And?"

"And he walked up and told me God loved me before we got off at the stop." Raya smoothed her dress and pointed at the clock, grabbing a pad and pen. The less time Chenille had to analyze the story's implications—spiritual and otherwise—the better. "Let's go."

Chenille waddled beside her. "God loves you, huh? And nice pants? My kind of guy. Did you exchange numbers, email addresses, anything?" She whispered the last part as they entered the conference room created by a series of partitions on the warehouse floor.

Raya shook her head and took the first seat she came to, while Chenille made her way to the room's center.

With that, the program began, a short prayer followed by a tone-deaf version of "Leaning on the Everlasting Arms," which everyone belted out except for Raya and Jean. Jean's excuse? Who knew? Raya's voice refused to cooperate with the lyrics, probably because, in some ways, to sing it boldly would have been a lie.

Brushing against the everlasting arms? Resting on the everlasting fingertips? That was more like the reality. Lily's usually quiet voice boomed right over the crowd. Wonders never ceased.

Next came a psalm, a proverb, and an individual blessing on each member of the team by Chenille, the part Raya hated most. Something personal always showed through her friend's words. Today was no different.

"Stir her heart with skill and creativity. Fill her mouth with good things. Guide her hands with compassion and truth. Make her your woman. Delight her with surprises, Jesus, more than she can ask or think, even in the most unexpected places."

Chenille's words torpedoed Raya back to the train. Enough surprises for one day. One look in that man's eyes could last a girl a lifetime . . .

Don't go there.

"Now comes the best part." Chenille walked the circle. "And the worst. The pictures of the children, our children. What this business is all about."

Raya nodded. Chenille's policy of giving 10 percent of the proceeds to clothe and feed children in need ranked almost as high as their friendship in Raya's decision to work at the firm. The children came from all over the world, but most were from New York City. Kids she might have passed on the block or on the subway. Every Monday the staff acknowledged the children's needs, attempting, even for a moment, to provide a garment of praise instead of a spirit of despair.

As always, controlled applause followed Chenille's little speech, hand claps swallowed by silence when the reality of a child's life shrouded their own. Raya gasped as Chenille lifted the enlarged snapshot for this week—a lanky boy with buckteeth and a mouth full of laughter. She covered her mouth, for a minute remembering the problems her braces had corrected. His smile was much like hers had been. Too much so. He could have easily been Raya's little brother.

Nods came from around the room.

"Jay's parents both died from AIDS. Jay has been tested every six months in the five years since their deaths, but no one wants to take a chance on him. His elderly aunt takes care of him the best she can—"

"Wow," one of the salesmen said softly. "How old is he?"

She held up a photo. "He's eleven in this picture but thirteen now. He likes basketball, airplanes, and playing with friends. He lives with an aunt in Bedstuy." Chenille's voice faltered. "This is a little hard for me, because I know this boy. He came in the stack with the others, but he goes to my church. I've even taught him in Sunday school. I'm ashamed to say I didn't realize the depth of his situation . . .

"He's been getting into trouble lately, and both the school and social services are considering taking him from his aunt's care."

Chenille wiped her eyes. "He's a bright kid. Handsome. Alone most times at church, but when I see him on the street, he's with a gang—a bunch of kids. The wrong kind. I'd like to try and encourage his interests. Any suggestions?"

While her co-workers batted around ideas on ways to change Jay's future, Raya sat like a stone. AIDS? Both his parents? She bit down to keep her teeth from chattering.

"Raya? Are you all right?" Jean asked with none of the usual grit in her voice.

"Fine. Just thinking. What did we decide?" Raya stared at the clock and again at the boy's photo. She tried to imagine his parents. The thought of losing her life for a mistake . . .

"I will never leave you nor forsake you."

Chenille tapped the photo on the conference table. "I just remembered that a friend of ours is starting a basketball team for the boys at the church. He mentioned wanting to join some Christian league, but the uniforms and team costs were a couple thousand."

"Thousand?" Lily asked with a shocked expression. "Why so much?"

Raya knew why. The rule of the dollar, the way of keeping certain kinds of people out. She'd grown up on the other side of such rules, though she'd never been proud of it.

"What if we designed the uniforms?" she asked. "Wouldn't that help? Maybe we could partner with the church somehow?"

Someone laughed. "Have you seen Chenille's church?"

Her friend rolled her eyes. "New Man Worship Center isn't rich, but we try and extend ministry to the people some churches would rather not deal with—teen mothers, recovering addicts, broken families, people coming out of alternative lifestyles, and kids like Jay. Our sanctuary may not have all the trimmings, but that's okay. It's not a pew-warming place, but a meeting place before we go back out into the mission field around us. And we do have a gymnasium, thank you very much."

A little amen fluttered in Raya's heart. She still hadn't settled on what to do about church, but wherever she went, she wanted it to be in a place like that. If she never saw another stained-glass window, it would be too soon.

Someone muttered a quick prayer before the clock buzzed, signaling the top of the hour, and Chenille closed the meeting. "I'll work on this and email an update. Thanks for all you do here, for our customers and for the children."

The room cleared a little more slowly than usual until Chenille and Raya were alone once more.

Chenille said, "I think we can do uniforms for the team and get the church to sponsor the league costs. The coach is Lyle's friend. A good guy."

"Sounds like it." Raya started for the door.

If the guy was friends with Chenille's husband, a setup was imminent. No matter how she tried to explain that things were different, that she was different, Chenille just refused to accept that Raya wasn't looking to get married.

Raya picked up Jay's picture on her way out and smoothed her finger across his dancing eyes. Just as part of this little boy had died with his parents, part of her had died back in LA. A part she longed to forget but couldn't. A stretch of night, a few hours of darkness, where she'd left her old self behind.

3

"So what do you think?"

Raya gripped the phone, trying to push enough air into her lungs to speak. Not wanting to have any more powwows with Chenille after yesterday's meeting, she'd had the bright idea to take a run in the prototype tracksuit. She'd done it more to run off her own confusion than anything, but now, a hundred yards from where she'd begun, Jean's expert cutting proved a bit much.

She snapped at the outfit's grip on her thigh and pulled the cell phone to her face. "Chenille, I think any woman who can run in this thing should get a trophy."

Raya's eyes skimmed down the canary yellow and black material draining her breath. It was a twist on the cheetah idea she'd started with; everyone had agreed something simpler would be more suitable.

She set off again, winding through the garment district.

"If we do our job right, any woman who wears this can win a medal. Edge is in the details," Chenille said.

Tugging at another patch of material, Raya agreed. Details. The little things had once been her strength, but now they seemed to go undone.

In the days following her arrival from California, Raya whispered her prayers and flipped aimlessly through her Bible alone on Sunday mornings. Midweek services came and went. Headaches and Saturday night insomnia sabotaged her Sundays. In the past Gram would have ordered her to go to church, but now she dressed in silence, eyes brimming with disappointment, leaving Raya to deal with God—and her guilt—alone.

"How's the wind?" Chenille's voice boomed through the phone.

"Nonexistent."

"No resistance at all?"

Raya sighed. "The only thing working against me is my tired legs and this tight thing." She tugged a final time at the Lycra spandex, which quickly molded back into the same spot. She mopped her brow. "There isn't even a whisper of wind."

"Okay. Keep going. If something comes to you, holler."

"Will do."

Raya's feet pounded rain-slicked Seventh Avenue, splashing over the names on the Fashion Walk of Fame. On other days she'd stopped here to daydream, to wonder if she'd ever find her design niche. Today she ran without even looking down, thinking instead of the email from the AIDS clinic this morning. She should be retested in December just to be sure. How could she have been so stupid?

"I, even I, am he who blots out your transgressions . . . and remembers your sins no more."

She'd joined Gram for tea this morning and copied that verse down into her journal. Spoken it aloud over and over while getting dressed. Whispered it to herself on the train, which had been thankfully devoid of handsome men. God *had* forgiven her. Why couldn't she forgive herself?

If only it was that simple.

It is.

She sighed, moving faster. Simple but not easy. Her body looked the same, but her eyes, the eyes to her soul, refused to keep their flame. She'd come here desperate to ignite her life again, to help her friends, to reunite with family, to capture the joy of her old self. So far most of it had eluded her.

But this was a new day with mercies of its own. Raya was learning to take things in minutes and hours instead of monthly milestones and five-year plans. Today she had Jesus. That was enough. Tomorrow perhaps she'd pour a cup of tea and join Gram for Bible study again. From her grandmother's grunts and nods, Raya knew she'd been in Romans this morning. Chapter 5 or 6. Gram reserved special sounds for those chapters.

For now, though, Raya had to deal with rating this outfit and complying with Chenille's latest memo about "redirecting" her creativity. No matter how much doublespeak her friend spouted, Raya knew what that meant. She'd heard it all her life, even in design school: Get practical. Make it simple.

She tried, but somehow everything ended up swathed in tulle and gathered in satin. Maybe if she went through the motions enough, the flourish in her head would be tamed. The thought pained her, but maybe it was best. Maybe then that good, clean feeling would come back.

"Though your sins are like scarlet, they shall be as white as snow."

Raya slowed to a walk and wiped away the sweat and tears stinging her eyes. Memorizing Isaiah over the phone with Gram the past few summers had given back much more than she could have imagined. The verses popped up in her soul when she least expected it. If only she hadn't silenced those words when she needed them most.

Winded and ready to turn back, Raya looked down at her bumblebee-clad frame and ran through her design questions. Is the garment fun? Check. Fashionable? The jury was still out on that one, but she liked it. Suited to the client's needs? Her mind went blank. Trying to imagine the needs of a runner was harder than she'd thought.

She ran a hand through the tendrils of her afro, which was curling in with the rising temperature, "drawing up," as her grandmother called it. After two years of weaves and wigs to keep Darrell happy, it felt strange to be free again. Strange but wonderful. Not that she wouldn't rock a few of her signature wigs once winter hit.

A runner streaked past, breaking her musings. A woman followed, jerking along behind her male partner, her step landing square in a puddle at Raya's feet. Well, more like a small pond if the splash was any indication. Raya pulled up short as the stinky wetness soaked through her clothes. The runner, a stylishly thin but obviously out of shape beauty with russet curls and a blond streak down the center of her mane, jogged on, not bothering to apologize.

Raya frowned as the woman's rear profile registered in her head. She'd know that skunk anywhere. Megan Arietta, her roommate from college, daughter of her father's girlfriend, and the bridesmaid that got away—with the groom.

Her groom.

And from the looks of things, Megan hadn't had the decency to keep him. Raya watched with horror as the first runner turned and started toward her.

Eye Guy from the train. And if she'd thought him handsome in that suit, the six-pack straining against his meshed shirt told the real story—he'd been sculpted from a block of hazelnut wood. His biceps tensed as he approached. Raya looked away, losing what remained of her breath. She'd know Mr. Four Spiritual Laws anywhere. Unfortunately, no recognition flashed in his eyes.

He grabbed Raya's elbow. "Are you okay?" He released her just as quickly.

She sighed, rubbing the place where he'd touched her. "I'm fine." For someone so strong looking, he had feather fingers. Like Gram's.

He smiled blankly, inventorying the wet spot across her waist. Obviously, she'd been nothing more to him than a possible convert or a trial for a weak pickup line.

Two could play at that game.

He cut his eyes at Megan, who was walking toward them with a shrug. "Sorry about that," he said. "And your shoes too."

Megan trotted up beside him. "Nothing's ruined. It'll wash out, just like that color in your hair, right girl?"

Raya didn't even try to fake a civil response. She stared at Megan, wondering if those highlight stripes had sucked out most of her brain. The girl was messed up.

The guy, who'd looked so penitent seconds earlier, now looked confused as he realized the two women weren't strangers. Raya tried not to laugh. If he was going to hang out with Megan, he'd need to get used to stunts like this.

He rubbed his jaw, which was now bare and flawless, though Raya couldn't decide if it was an improvement on yesterday's shadow. Seeing him at all made her stomach hurt. That suit was one thing, but this? This was unreal. No matter. Megan had him under her evil powers. She'd probably chosen this route to stake out Raya's workplace.

"You know her?" he asked, as if caught between two lines of fire.

"Oh yes. We go way back." Megan painted on her name-brand smile. Medium width. High shine. "That hair. I almost didn't recognize you. You always were *different*." She let the word slide off her tongue. "How are you, anyway? After well, you know . . ." She extended her arms for a hug.

Raya stayed put. "I'm good."

Megan pouted. "You aren't still holding that little thing with Darrell against me, are you?"

Little thing?

"Of course not." Raya was too busy holding another "little thing" against herself.

As if sensing the tension, the guy started jogging in place. "Again, sorry about the splash." He gave his partner a curt nod, then checked the heart-rate monitor on his wrist. "Let's go. We'll have to do another mile to get back in fat burning range."

Fat burning range? Why did that bring up images of a rotisserie chicken with grease dripping into the fire? Raya suddenly wished she hadn't returned that Pilates machine her mother had bought for her birthday.

He stole a glance at her. "And nice to meet you."

Nice? Not really. It was unsettling, same as the first time. "You too."

Megan's feet remained still. "Wait, forgive my rudeness . . ."

Did Megan actually know how to apologize? Wow. First time for everything.

She continued, adjusting the gleam of her smile to full blast, like a toothpaste commercial. "Flex, this is Ary—"

"Raya." She felt her strength gaining as she spoke her New

York summer name, the one choked back by her mother every fall.

Raya smiled, thinking of Gram. "Sometimes it takes more strength to be nothing than to try and be something. It'll cost you, cherie, but just be yourself," her grandmother told her repeatedly.

Eye Guy, or whatever she'd said his name was, narrowed his eyes at Raya, probing with his glance. Did he remember her? She did have a white afro, after all. The brothah could give her some kind of respect. But if he did remember, where would that leave her? Smack-dab in Megan's drama. Again. No thanks. Raya started a stationary jog of her own. She wasn't Aryanna anymore. That girl was last seen in the ink on her unused wedding napkins, in the signature on her parents' divorce decree—both facilitated by Megan. No sense getting fired for wasting time with someone who didn't deserve the courtesy.

Megan smacked her lips. "You should have stuck around Cali instead of coming here. I know you took your parents' split hard, but hey, get over it. More guilt money that way."

Raya stiffened, unable to continue her movement. Gram was right. Megan and her mother had no class. What right did she have to even mention Raya's parents? And she still hadn't bothered to make more than excuses for the thing with Darrell.

"I pay my own way, Megan. My parents' finances are none of my concern. Or yours." Raya lifted her chin. "I've got to get going. Nice seeing you." It wasn't, of course, but years of home training were hard to shake. "And you too, Mr. . . . um . . ." What was that ridiculous name? "Stretch."

The guy stumbled back. He held his rock hard stomach, pressing his hand against the grid of his shirt. "Flex!"

"Sorry." Raya shrugged.

"Yeah. Nice meeting you too." The wave of his ocean voice almost made her teeter off the curb.

He stepped toward her, but Megan pressed a hand against his chest. Flex pushed her hand away. Maybe he had a little sense after all.

"Don't run off Ary—Raya. I did hope to see you today." Megan winked at Flex, whose rigid jaw turned toward the street. "I'd like you to design my wedding dress."

Raya started backpedaling, too stunned to respond. Could she pretend not to have heard? No, they were standing too close for that. She had to be kidding.

"We make uniforms, not gowns." For the first time, Raya was grateful for Chenille's down-to-earth focus.

Megan's can-of-spritz hair stayed stiff as she whipped her head from side to side. Raya bought as much hairspray as the next girl, but that stuff looked bulletproof.

"I think my price will make it worth your boss's while. One million. But you have to do the design."

Flex, who'd managed to remain still, save a jerk at the word *wedding*, couldn't hide his astonishment. With a snort, he jogged off, casting a final wave. Raya couldn't blame him. It'd been a while since she'd heard the world *million* tossed around in conversation herself. She continued walking back, though more slowly now.

"Think about it." Megan cupped her hands around her mouth and shouted the words as she followed Flex up the avenue.

Raya turned and stumbled. Think about it? Sure. Right after she planned her move to the moon.

"You okay?" Megan purred, her voice full of the flirt she wore like a necklace.

"I'm fine." Flex reached for his foot behind him, stretching his quadriceps.

Liar.

To be sure, he was undone. It was her. The girl from the train. The getup was new, but the hair, that squeaky voice . . .

Flex pointed his foot and leaned forward into the burn in his hamstrings, mindful of Megan's presence beside him. She'd done all she could to make Raya look less cultured, all the while showing her own uncouth. And a million dollars for a dress? Come on. Flex studied the markets enough to know her father's company, Arietta Enterprises.

Even with two great quarters behind him, her dad could scarcely afford a million dollars' worth of fabric, could he? And even if he could, why waste the money? People were dying, suffering, both at home and abroad.

The same reason you're getting manicures and live in Bushwick. It's all part of the game.

Flex balled his fists. It might be that way for now, but not forever. One day he'd stop tiptoeing from one paycheck to another. One day soon. He touched his toes, then pulled up, one vertebra at a time.

His client followed suit, or at least she tried. "Raya's attractive, isn't she?" Megan's voice contradicted her words.

Attractive? Flex looked over at his morning running partner, bejeweled and painted like all the other Ashleys, Buffys, Megans, and Brookes he'd known. All of them poured on beauty purchased from the finest cosmetic counters, dressed in clothes with too little fabric, and drenched themselves in too much cologne. New money, as his mother described those who worked hard for their fortunes and worked even harder to show them off.

Until now Flex had considered such thinking snobbery, but after a few minutes in the presence of Raya's unpretentious beauty in contrast to Megan's brazen attempt at the same, he wasn't so sure. Attractive. It was like calling the ocean deep.

"She's beautiful, no doubt."

Megan frowned, creasing her layer of makeup, still miraculously affixed even in this heat. That couldn't be healthy.

"I suppose. If one goes for the minimalist look." She tugged at the straps of her sports bra and took a step toward him. "I like a full package myself."

He liked a real package—inside and out. "Right. Well, it was nice meeting her. And congrats on your wedding. Is that why you signed up? You didn't mention it. We do have a Buff Brides program."

Heavenly Bodies Gym also had a policy that she'd conveniently forgotten, even though Flex had spelled it out clearly, as he did before every first session—no personal physical contact. Or as Flex phrased it, "No nonworkout touching." After a few weeks on the job, he'd learned that the farther he stayed away from his lonely, beautiful, and usually crazy clients, the better. Megan was no exception.

She looked offended at the suggestion. "I won't be needing any special program. As for the wedding, it's a new development. I wanted to talk to Raya about the dress before I send out the invitations. And tell the groom, of course."

Tell the groom? His eyes rolled back before he could catch himself. He thought only his mother came up with such crazy ideas. Flex unfolded Megan's profile from his pocket and started to fill out the information from the session. She'd paid extra to accommodate the route she wanted, but the sooner this was over, the better.

41

"Good luck with that. Same time tomorrow?" He signed his name and held open the door to the gym.

She shook her head. "Not tomorrow. I'll be back when I'm ready."

"But you paid for twelve weeks." He knew already she probably wouldn't be back. The whole morning had been a setup. Her use for him was done, thank God.

"Tell your boss to keep it . . . plus that little tip I put in for you." She traced an airbrushed fingertip across his shoulders, down his bicep. "I'm sure you'll find a way to make it up to me."

Flex let the door slam. He extended a finger of his own. "Don't touch me again. Please." Ice covered his voice.

Megan's nostrils flared. "Don't raise your finger at me." She skirted a glance around the room. "And lower your voice, you little—well, big—"

"Your refund will be mailed to you at the end of the month when we do invoicing. If you need it before then—"

"Whatever, pretty boy. If you treat all your clients like this, you'll need every dime."

If she treated her husband like this, the guy would need medication. "I apologize, but as I pointed out in the orientation, there are rules here. Rules for safety and—"

"Fear, if my guess is right." She pointed to the worn cross around his neck. "Don't worry, preacher man. I won't break you down. Not yet, anyway." With that, Megan turned for the locker room, swinging hair and hips every step of the way. Executives from the morning spinning class filled the aisle between them, craning their necks as she passed.

Flex sat down on a padded bench. Megan had it all wrong. Women like her didn't scare him. His hands-off policy was more to protect himself from scandal and gossip than to restrain his passion, bridled by long hours with silly, shallow women.

It was Raya who worried him. She'd had him thinking about her constantly for forty-eight hours. When he'd seen her this morning, he'd choked, not knowing what to say. After his goofy "God loves you" on the train, she'd walked off like he was a moron. He'd hoped that maybe she would acknowledge their first meeting and then he could apologize, but she hadn't given him a second look.

That was best. If he did try a relationship again, it didn't need to be focused on him. It definitely wouldn't have sex to cloud things either. How exactly a nonphysical relationship worked he wasn't sure, but he wanted the 1 Corinthians 13 kind of love, even if it meant staying single to have it. Still learning to love God that way, Flex didn't have much to offer. And if a man wasn't willing to go all the way—marriage, kids, the whole deal—why bother?

White afros and brown eyes, that's why.

He scratched at his temples, still avoiding what was really bothering him—why hadn't Raya recognized him? Sure, he hadn't stared at her stupidly like the first time, but she'd looked through him today like he wasn't there. And he was wearing an ab shirt even. That could mess with a guy's mind.

Whoa. What's that about? Pride talking?

Pride it was. He offered it up to Christ and started for the locker room, reaching in his pocket for his bag of prayer beads, rubbing them between his fingers as he went. It was a good thing Raya hadn't recognized him. Now all he had to do was forget her.

Mission impossible.

4

"There you are."

Raya snapped around to see Chenille smiling in that charming but annoying way. "I'm here. Sorry about taking so long on the run yesterday. I'm planning to stay late tonight." She smoothed her dress, another pink one, from the same bin as the Adeli. What kind of bubblegum trip had she been on that day?

"More pink! How delightful. And cute shoes. Chunky. Are they from Two Lips?"

"Via Spiga. Mother sent them."

Chenille fanned herself. "Whoa. Now, that's my kind of gift. Good shoes."

"Don't be fooled. They came with a letter from her lawyer. Daddy sent me his little document last week. Sign or starve. That's pretty much how things stand."

Chenille looked worried. "And you chose . . . ?"

"Starve. At least I'll enjoy myself."

Her friend bobbed a little. "Great! And you won't starve. You can always come

44

over to our place. I've got a mac and cheese stash you'd never believe."

Raya shook her head. "I was just kidding. I'll never starve at Gram's."

"Right." Chenille dug out a handful of cheese crackers, also known as lunch, from the box on the corner of Raya's desk. "And don't worry about staying late. You went over last Thursday, remember?"

"I'd forgotten." Raya smiled at her pregnant friend licking nacho cheese from her fingertips. "I bet you and Lyle have stock in Cheez-Its, huh?"

Chenille stared off dreamily as though considering the idea. "Cheez-Its. Cheetos. Cheese something. Every night Lyle pulls away the box, the bag, whatever it is and says, 'It's not yo cheese!' Get it? Nacho cheese?" Chenille doubled over with laughter. Well, maybe quartered over. She bent as much as a mother in her eighth month could.

Raya slapped her forehead in disgust. "You two are so corny. Is this what marriage does?"

Her friend winked. "I'll let you tell me."

Here we go.

"Don't look at me like that. Just listen. Remember the boy from Monday's meeting?"

"Jay?" Raya fingered the manila file with his photo inside.

"Right. Well, I arranged a consult with Jay's coach, and . . ."

"And?" Chenille had that master-plan look in her eyes. It was bad enough that Raya was going to have to explain to her about Megan's million-dollar offer and her plan to regretfully decline. Now this. "You're up to something."

"You know me so well." Her face lit up. "He's coming by

45

for a consult with you on the uniforms. It'll be a blessing to Jay and . . ."

Raya waved her hands in protest. A consult? More like a setup. And a church man? She could smell the trap a mile away. As she swung her arms, the file flipped open. Jay's smiled beamed up at her, almost pleading.

Chenille ignored her objections and plowed ahead. "I've been wanting to introduce you two, but he's always working except on Sunday, and you won't come to church." She paused for effect. "So this will flip two zippers at once." She covered her mouth. "Flip. Zip. I'm just on a roll today."

"I'm going to roll your goofy behind out of here. Did you ever consider that you couldn't hook us up because we weren't meant to be hooked up? I'm really glad you and Lyle are so happy, but I'm not looking for a relationship. With anyone." She was still trying to reconnect with God, let alone man.

Crunching another handful of crackers, Chenille checked her watch. "But you're perfect for each other. I know you're having a faith crisis right now, but—"

"A what? Lyle made that up, didn't he? Is that what he tells people during those counseling sessions? I realize you have a spiritual deficit, but—"

"He'll like that one. Mind if I share it with him?" She snatched the box of crackers.

"You two are impossible."

"That's why you love us. Now fix your face. He's on his way."

Raya stared in horror. "He's coming now?"

Chenille waddled to the exit. "Uh-huh. I'll be in my office so you can thank me after. Oh, and sketch up something real quick to show him." She escaped seconds before a wad of paper flew in her direction.

Jay Andrews. Orphaned by AIDS. Great laugh. Cheery disposi-tion. In need of permanent home.

Raya's heart beat like a drum as she read the Monday's Child card again. This was about Jay, not her or even Chenille. This was about doing something that mattered, something bigger than herself. For too long everything had been about money—how to invest it, spend it, make it, keep it. In a way, money still occupied much of her thoughts, like how much longer Chenille would remain open and how far a million dollars would go to help kids like Jay. Too much to think about. This—one design and a few meetings with some nerdy church guy—she could handle.

As usual, Chenille had left a folder in the conference room with some notes for discussion: price points, colors, tentative delivery schedule. Raya slipped her hasty computer-aided drawing sketch on top of the pile.

A knock sounded at the door.

Raya tapped her papers on the edge of the table. "Come in."

Her throat constricted as he did. If her heart had been pumping before, it raced like a Nascar engine now. Flex. This time in a short-sleeved oxford, a pair of faded jeans, and slip-on loafers.

"It's you." His mouth made a perfect circle, revealing even, straight teeth.

"And it's . . . it's you," she stammered.

He came closer, bringing with him a wonderful mix of Magic Shave and Irish Spring soap. That lemony something from the subway lingered underneath.

Flex smiled like a cover model at a photo shoot. "It's us."

He dropped into the chair across from her, hinging one arm across the back of it. "We meet again."

Raya blinked repeatedly, the way she did when things refused to make sense. Too shocked to speak, she tried to guess the designer of his jeans instead. It was a very London look. Ted Baker probably . . .

He leaned forward, one elbow on the table. "I'm sorry about that bit with Megan. Can we forget that? Start over?"

Raya tapped the table with the folder. Forget about Megan? If only she could. Wasn't he the one marrying Megan? That's what she'd thought after their last encounter. Now he wanted to forget her? The same guy who'd tried to be the voice of God on Monday. Talk about a faith crisis.

"Maybe Megan should join us. I wouldn't want there to be any misunderstanding—"

"Huh? Why would she come here?" He stopped and stroked where that little patch of silky hair under his lip had been. Raya tried to look away. No man should be that fine.

He's a dog too. Don't you see it?

"Wait, do you think there's something between me—" he made a sour-grape face "—and her?"

"Aren't you two getting married?" Raya's voice squeaked like a bath toy. She sank down in her chair.

He coughed into his fist, trying to restrain his laughter, but it escaped low and rich, like the Vermont maple syrup Daddy insisted on. "You've got to be kidding. I just met her last week. I don't know who she's marrying, but it isn't me." He settled back in his chair. "I'm not marrying anybody."

Raya wished the makeshift conference room would swallow her. How stupid was she going to look today? And why was she as sad to hear he wasn't marrying anybody as she'd been angry when she thought he was engaged? "I'm sorry.

I thought . . . well, it doesn't matter. We'd better get down to business."

He licked his lips. "I'd like that."

She swallowed, but the knot in her throat refused to budge.

Chenille poked her red mop of hair inside the door. "Things going okay in here?" She waved to Flex, not waiting for an answer. "I know Raya is taking good care of you."

She dusted nacho cheese from her hands into the trash can and opened the door wide, kicking the stop in place. For once, Raya was thankful for her friend's neurosis. She couldn't be closed up in here with Flex and think straight.

"It's hot in here," Chenille said.

And it was. In more ways than one. Raya hadn't felt like this since a day long ago, walking along the beach. It was a feeling she hadn't had with Darrell even, a feeling she'd thought would never come again. Her stomach flip-flopped in case she wasn't sure. She wanted to run.

Flex reached across the desk and laid his hand on Raya's. She tried not to react as the equivalent of a bolt of electricity sparked through her at his touch. He made no such effort to hide her effect on him, jerking slightly.

"Raya and I have met before. I'm excited about working with her. I'm sure we'll come up with something."

Raya shook her head as Chenille ducked into the hall. A giggle floated behind her. Raya would never hear the end of this one. She pulled her hand from under Flex's and fumbled with the folder.

"Now you've got her started. Let's get this over with." She held up her sketch. "Here's the idea. Tell me what you think." She stared at the table.

When Flex didn't answer, Raya looked up, surprised to find him still scanning the page.

"You drew this? On the computer?"

She nodded. The admiration in his voice surprised her. Aside from Gram, Chenille, and a few teachers at the Fashion Institute of Technology, no one had much respect for her work. Her father thought she'd ruined her life by dropping out of the MBA program at Stanford to attend design school. Then Darrell came along and all her choices suddenly became okay. What better training to be a millionaire's wife than fashion design?

Flex's expression changed from awe to concern. "This is great. Really. But can you make it simpler, maybe? These kids don't have a lot of money."

Simpler. Always simpler.

Raya stared at her sketch, now on the table in front of him. A blue jersey emblazoned with an orange flame down the left side and the player's number on the upper right shoulder. An eagle soared down the right side with Isaiah 40:30.

"I'll try to keep the costs down, but I'd like to keep the design. Build their confidence."

He drew back. "I have a feeling that this meeting is a technicality and you're going to do what you want anyway."

What was that supposed to mean?

"No. This meeting is so you can tell me what you need. I'm willing to compromise."

Flex nodded. "Right." He seemed to lose focus for a second and then find it again a few seconds later . . . on one of Raya's ankles. He lifted his eyes to hers.

"Do what you want, but keep it around twenty or thirty bucks."

"Are you serious?"

On big orders that'd be easy, but there were only twenty boys on the team. For a minute, she considered asking her father to help, maybe feature the boys on the network, but he'd only use them as bait to get her back there. Besides, there weren't any shows left in the lineup that ran human-interest pieces.

Flex dusted off his jeans. "If you can't do it—"

"I can." At least she hoped so.

He stood as if waiting for her to say something else.

What was she supposed to say, "Thank you for dropping by, Your Handsomeness"? Or was it "Your Holiness"? Probably not, from the way he'd been checking out her legs. She'd liked him better as God's messenger or even Megan's boyfriend. The real Flex was disappointing.

He opened his wallet and slid a card across the desk. "Call if you need me."

Heavenly Bodies Gym. Flex Dunham, personal trainer. His cell, fax, and email were listed below.

"That's me. You can reach me on that phone anytime." He took a step toward the door.

Raya blinked, reading the name of his employer again. Too bad his personality seemed to have originated south of glory. "I'll be in touch, Mr. Dunham."

He shrugged. "I can't wait."

Flex ran a hand through his hair, which had been spiked with gel this morning but was now waving with natural curls. Lucky hair—it got to chill while he went nuts. He strode through the narrow corridor of Garments of Praise, away from the buzz of sewing machines, the clack of scissors, the expectation in Chenille's eyes . . . and the scent of bubble-gum lip gloss and Love's Baby Soft cologne.

A few times during the meeting, he'd had to stare at the floor to keep his mind straight. For all her smart mouth one minute and sophistication the next, it was the little girl in

Raya that got to him, made him think about unreasonable things. Things like love.

He grabbed the door handle and swung it back, hoping to leave his thoughts of her behind. In the past, the physical payback had made up for whatever his girlfriends lacked emotionally. Now he understood that sex was something sacred, a wedding gift from God. Commitment required more money, time, and emotion than he could give, more faith than he probably possessed. And that was just for a regular woman. What would it take to love someone like Raya? Another question burned through his mind. What would it be like to *be* loved by her?

He raked a fist through his hair as if trying to drive the thought away. He knew better than to be sucked into this love thing. It never went anywhere. Look where it had landed his mother. His father had never married her, choosing instead to stay in his rich world and send his love by check. As a child, Flex had thought they were married, though his father was often away from them on business. In Flex's young mind, his father had a secret job as an FBI agent or an astronaut.

When someone taped his father's picture in *Ebony* magazine's annual Bachelors of the Year feature to his locker at Hotchkiss Prep, any delusions he'd had were gone. From then on, their Martha's Vineyard summers were strangled with tension. Eventually, Flex's father only showed up occasionally for his mother's charity events. Her eyes had sparkled with expectation many times, only to have her hope dashed by his father's absence. No, real love meant pain. Weakness. What Flex needed now was strength.

The memory of his last conversation with his father made his biceps twitch. *"You're twenty-one now. Take the trust fund and use your head. Don't be dumb like I was. We're both free now."*

It was then that he'd learned of his parents' ill-struck bargain—that his father would provide their living expenses until Flex was twenty-one. There had been a trust fund for education too, but any access to it had required his father's approval. Five years and two moves later, getting the last payment out of his father had been a painful ordeal for both of them. Intent on making his own way, Flex had spent most of the money on a down payment for a new place for him and his mother to live.

Though Flex could hang his hat anywhere, years of luxury living hadn't prepared his mother for a Bushwick flat. Though she didn't complain, Flex felt that the loss of his father's provision was somehow his fault and that he needed to do something to make up for the care his father had abandoned. Though he and his father didn't see eye to eye on much, the man had drilled into Flex's head that he was always to look out for his mother.

Between trying to find a new place, getting his modeling career started, and writing the business plan for his own fitness business, money seemed to evaporate. That only made Flex more determined. Under no circumstances would he go groveling to his father. His big break was coming, and he'd be ready.

Fletcher Rayburn Longhurst II might not want Flex as a son, but God did. And he'd be the best son he could. He'd come to New York to make it big, but he and his mother had been reunited with Jesus Christ instead. Now if he could only figure out a way to prove himself to his father, make his mother proud, and please God at the same time . . .

It was a tall order. One that didn't leave room for blind spots. Or beautiful women. He swiped his tongue over his teeth, avoiding the nagging feeling that no matter what he did, he wouldn't be able to shake the storm of the woman in the building behind him.

He'd have to call Chenille later about this uniform thing. He was already in la-la land after the first meeting. It would never work—

"Watch it, now. I wouldn't want to touch you or anything."

Flex lifted his eyes from the pavement and leveled them in the direction of the voice. Megan's voice. With her sunglasses low on the bridge of her nose and her blond-streaked horsetail high on her head, she shot Flex a scornful look. Great. Just what he didn't need. Where was she going, anyway? Was Raya actually going to design that dress? Of course she was. Money made the world go around, didn't it? Evidently, even Raya wasn't immune.

"Hey, Megan. Sorry about the other morning. We'd love to have you back at the gym whenever you're ready."

He'd waited to hear the backlash from his boss about their run-in, but evidently she hadn't said anything. He was relieved at first, but seeing her again, he knew her silence was just another trick. He didn't like owing favors.

Megan grinned and took his hand, leaving a smudge of bronzer on his wrist. "It's okay. You don't scare me. I know how to handle men like you."

"I'll bet you do." He tried to force a smile, but he only managed to lift an eyebrow, a habit the photographers at the photo shoots he went to were trying to break him of. He allowed his hand to drift to his side instead of snatching it back like he wanted. "So you're going to see Raya about the dress? I thought you were kidding."

Megan tapped a black stiletto against the sidewalk. "I never joke about money. Between my mother's wit and my father's guilt, I get what I want—for myself and whoever I'm with."

Scary thought. Flex stuffed his hands in his jeans and sent

up a prayer of thanks for his bachelorhood. He wouldn't want to marry a woman like Megan, but the thought of having a daughter like her was even more frightening. No doubt she would train all her offspring in her oh-so-evil ways. He loved kids though. He'd even taken foster-care training, in hopes of adopting someday. By himself, of course.

"If your family will spring for it, knock yourself out. I'd rather have the money, personally. That much cash could help a lot of people. Seems a little selfish to waste it on a dress."

As quick as he'd said it, he was reminded of his own self-ishness. He could have gone to law school like his mother wanted instead of blowing his trust fund on moving back and forth from LA to New York following broken dreams. He could have married Brooke and been set for life, though it would have likely cost him his life. Maybe everybody had his or her own million-dollar dress, something desired in spite of the cost. He was all too aware of his own, but what was Raya's?

Megan shoved her sunglasses back up on her nose. "Waste it? That's easy for you to say. Longhursts don't have to prove anything."

"What?" Flex stared for a moment, letting her words sink in. *Longhurst*. He'd come to New York under Dunham, his mother's name and now his own legal moniker. Megan may have been new money, but she'd certainly hit the nail on the head. Or better yet, hit the man in the gut.

"You heard me. Do you think I came to that dinky gym and picked you out for nothing? You're cute, I'll admit, but it takes more than that." She curved her flamingo pink fingernails around her chin. "Money follows money. Don't let a pair of brown eyes make you forget that. Miss Thing doesn't have a dime."

All the better, Flex thought as Megan strode away. He walked too, in the opposite direction, his fingers laced behind his head. He turned his face to the sky. "I'm not ready for all this. Not at all." Things had been so simple until a few days ago, until he'd asked God to give him everything, anything he wanted him to have.

A pigeon tumbled down from the roof of the next building. At the last moment, it soared back to its perch. It wasn't the most eloquent of signs and probably not a sign at all, since Flex didn't put much stock in such things, but a peace settled over him as though it had been an eagle. The verse he'd painted on the wall of the new nursery fluttered through him as well.

"Those who hope in the LORD *will renew their strength. They will soar on wings like eagles; they will run and not grow weary, they will walk and not be faint."*

Okay, so maybe it was a sign. Pigeons weren't exactly eagles, but he was no super saint either. If he could just stay focused on Jesus, keep flying, everything would be okay . . . wouldn't it?

He cast a last glance behind him, thinking of Megan and Raya—so different except for the power they both had over him. One held his secret, and the other held his heart.

5

Even with the vent directly overhead, Raya's sweat beaded down the back of her neck and into her blouse. She stared at the numbers on the church uniforms for the third time. Instead of getting cheaper, the cost soared with every design element she tried to take away. All the fabric and monogramming discounts were linked together the way Gram had taught her. To exclude any of it—the embroidery, extra colors, and quality fabric—would make the price rise. If the order were larger, she could work around it, but for twenty pieces?

Flex's voice rang in her head. *"If you can't do it . . ."* She could and she would. She set the file aside and rubbed her temples. Her chest constricted. After living through LA smog with her asthma, Raya thought she'd overcome the ailment, but New York seemed to have resurrected the childhood illness. She pulled open her bottom file drawer and fumbled in her drawstring Coach bag, only to come up with an empty inhaler. Her last one. Health coverage, or her lack thereof, suddenly took on a new meaning.

Raya dug farther in the drawer for her emergency Coke, one of a number of cans of caffeine she stashed at Gram's, here at work, and sometimes in her purse—anywhere she might end up unable to breathe. She held her stomach at the thought of the hot pop, then tossed it back.

"There she is!"

A fine spray of brown liquid filmed Raya's computer screen as Megan's voice stung her ears like salt in a gunshot wound. What was *she* doing here?

"There you are, you little sneak! Why didn't you tell me about your new account?" Chenille held both hands in the air, her fingers yellowed with cheese powder. For the first time in weeks, a rosy glow instead of stress radiated from her cheeks. Megan was responsible for that joy. And Raya would be responsible for taking it away. "You were waiting until next Monday's meeting to announce it, weren't you?"

I was waiting for never.

"I think there's been some mistake," Raya said.

Megan shook her head. "So modest, just like she was in college. Don't worry, Raya. I took the liberty of telling your employer about our arrangement and the stipulation for payment. She has the utmost confidence in you." She stared down at her fingernail as if locating a microscopic chip in her polish. "As do I."

Too bad Raya didn't have the same confidence. In fact, right now she couldn't be entirely sure she wasn't about to reach out and grab Megan by the hair.

Gram was right. Megan and her mother's plan was total destruction of every aspect of their family. Prayer was the only weapon that could defeat them. The weapon of her warfare.

Father, help me. Keep me from falling. Prepare a table for me even in the midst of my enemies. Give me the courage to keep from slapping her.

Streams of cola ran down the monitor. Raya grabbed a wad of paper towel and shoved her keyboard out of the way. A few bubbles escaped but not enough to kill the keyboard. But this, Chenille and Megan smiling at her, that was enough to end Raya for good.

"Don't worry about the monitor, Raya. I'll get you another one when this is over. A laptop even. Think of all the kids we can help with this!"

Megan frowned and looked around the small, dim office. "Kids? I think you'd better worry about helping yourselves. Didn't you just tell me the firm is on the verge of closing?"

Chenille crossed her arms defensively. "Not exactly."

"Close enough." Megan's smile curved upward like the mouth on a pink jack-o'-lantern. "You've got to take care of home first, or someone else will. Right, Raya?"

"Wrong, Megan. There will always be thieves who sleep in castles, but in the end, they're still thieves." Raya formed a smile of her own. Her mother's smile.

Megan's lip quivered. "You think you're better than me. You always have."

"No, *you've* always thought you were better than *me*. I took you into my home, into my family, and you betrayed me in every way. No, I don't think I'm better than you. I don't think of you much at all." Raya stood slowly until she and Megan were face-to-face, or chest-to-nose, as Raya had a good five inches on her.

Chenille clamped her hand on Raya's arm. "As much as we value your business, Miss Arietta, I will not allow you to demean my employee. There's obviously more history between you two than sharing a room in college—"

"You've got that right," Raya said, shaking off Chenille's

grip. "The last thing we shared was the groom. No, make that my father. Are you happy now? You've got him too."

Megan's eyes widened. "It's not like that. I only came here because I wanted—"

"You wanted what you always want, Megan. Anything that isn't yours."

The two flights up to Raya's apartment usually wore her out. Tonight she savored each step, drank in each note of konpa music slipping into the stairwell. She paused on the landing, then moved toward the apartment where the sounds originated. Her hips swayed to the staccato flute and stout trumpet bursts issuing from the open door. The tall, dark man sitting just inside the door raised a hand as she approached. His wife's hearty Jamaican laughter laced with his soothing Haitian dialect echoed from within the flat.

"Bon après-midi."

"Good afternoon to you, sir." Raya smiled at the greeting from her downstairs neighbor.

She sampled the aroma of Mr. Vernet's fried plantain mingled with his wife's curry, jerk, and lime. Like their marriage, the couple's cooking joined all that was wonderful about the Caribbean. She'd eaten many gut-busting dinners in that apartment.

His brown, wrinkled hand extended into the hall, offering Raya a sack of what she knew would be ripe mangoes, the ones he kept next to his chair. "Thank Mademoiselle for that dress she made Lola. She looks like a dream in it." His voice was lush, almost green.

"I'll tell her." Raya took the bag and reached inside, nodding in agreement before heading upstairs.

The gift reminded her of the tailor from the subway. As

she prayed for him, she considered the many people's lives her grandmother's nimble fingers had touched. Gram knew how to capture a woman's flair and turn it into an outfit no one else could wear. Some said Raya had the same gift for design, but Raya disagreed. Her gift was more narrow. Gram could please anyone. The block kept her busy.

With a bag of blushing mangoes for company, the trip upstairs ended too quickly. She'd rubbed her dress a little too hard to get out the Coke stains, and the fabric bagged in places, but what worried her most was the hurt that would certainly show in her face. The last thing she needed was to recount the day, and that's just what Gram would want her to do.

An image of Flex swaggered through her mind, first in that Brooks Brothers look-alike suit, then in his workout gear, then today in those jeans.

Well, she'd tell Gram everything but that. Some things needed to die on their own. Didn't the Bible say that even a fool seemed smart if he kept his mouth shut? The same applied to a granddaughter who wanted to get some sleep. Raya inserted her key and twisted the knob.

A song of scent not so different from what she'd smelled downstairs echoed in the air. Notes of saffron and olive oil mingled with onions, black beans, and yellow rice. Raya crossed the threshold and stepped over neat piles of brocade and satin, all marked with turquoise squares neatly labeled with customers' names. Raya flinched, as she did every evening at the sight of the words on the edge of the blue tissues.

Aryanna and Darrell. Together forever.

The napkins from her wedding. It seemed strange to see them so often, but Gram had managed to retrieve them all. Paper was paper, she said, even if it had a bum's name on it. The woman believed in everyday luxuries, but a waster she'd never be. Raya sighed and let her purse dangle at her side. Speaking of Gram, where was she?

Two pecan-colored fingers lifted Raya's purse off her shoulder and slid it to the floor. There she was.

"Good evening, cherie."

"Adieu. How are you?"

"Blessed." Gram took the bag of fruit and placed it on the table. "From Lola and Jean-Claude?"

Raya nodded.

They chatted back and forth in ribbons of Creole and patches of English, stitching the words into a quilt of their own understanding and love.

Gram ran a hand along Raya's dress, her fingers going directly to each imperfection. "It's salvageable. Take it off and let me wash it by hand. Then I'll fix it."

Raya placed one hand on her grandmother's. "It's okay. Really." She kicked off her heels and considered adding that she'd only paid ten dollars for it, but that would only ensure that Gram would fix it.

The zipper buzzed down her back. "Lines, dear. You must always keep your lines. This was a fine piece." She stooped at Raya's ankles, waiting for her to step out of the dress. When her granddaughter obeyed, she held up the dress, pointing at the waist. "It's too big here now. And the neckline is stretched. Next time dab. Don't scrub. You know better. You must have been upset . . ."

The brain sucking had begun. Was there any use putting up a fight? Unsure, Raya walked to the hall closet and tugged on a robe adorned with salmon-and-seafoam-colored raffia, her first attempt at sleepwear so many summers ago. She watched in amazement as Gram disassembled her dress in seconds.

"Ruined?"

"No. I'll fix it. Not as nice as it was, but nice."

"Thanks."

Gram nodded from her seat at the sewing machine. "Now, are you going to tell me now or drag this out all night?"

Raya sank into the couch. There was no getting past her.

"You're tight as a drum. Something you need to tell me?"

Flex lay facedown on the couch with his hands crossed in front of him. His mother's karate chops whacked against his shoulders, pummeling the tension from his muscles.

Without looking back to see, Flex knew her eyes brimmed with questions, none of which he was prepared to answer. Sometimes working at the same gym with her had its downfalls. They'd designed their schedules not to overlap, but some days it was unavoidable. All during his session with an especially flirty actress today, his mother had been watching him like a hawk.

"Just say it, Mom. What's on your mind?"

Without answering, Angela Dunham switched from the lightning-quick edges of her hands to her tiny fists. With one final punching motion, she tapped Flex to sit up.

"You're working too hard, Fletcher." She caught herself and used the name he preferred. "I mean Flex. It still sounds like something from a cartoon to me, but I know it makes you feel independent from your father—"

"I have to be independent from him." Flex shrugged off her hands and turned to face her. "For both our sakes."

His mother gave him a peaceful look, the type that really made him crazy. "I'm already dependent . . . on God. I don't need you. Or your father." She patted his face. "Be still and know that."

The words from Flex's favorite psalm cut him to the quick.

Every time he mentioned his father, Mom spoke only of being still and making peace.

"There will be a time to be still, but it definitely isn't now. I've got to make a home for you and a business for myself. Have you heard any more about the new place?"

Her lips formed the elegant smile Flex had always cherished. Though she'd never complained about their Brooklyn apartment, her eyes danced whenever he mentioned the two-family home they were trying to purchase. Or was she laughing at Flex's efforts to take care of her?

"I still haven't heard. I can't believe you put down so much money. This place is fine—"

"It isn't, and I'm sorry. Things didn't work out exactly the way I planned." He'd made decisions, some right, some wrong. There was no use picking things to death now.

Flex pushed up from the couch in the living room. Though he loved his mother and wanted to look out for her, it was days like this that he wondered if the two of them moving to another place wasn't a mistake. Though a wife and kids might not be in his future, this mama's boy bit was played out.

Still, they'd managed to pull together a decent place. It was nothing like when they'd lived in DC or Boston, but the few visitors they'd had—a few friends from the gym and people from church—seemed to have been impressed with it.

Flex, however, knew how much his mother missed the mansion and servants she'd left behind. Though she'd never complained, she stared at the diamond ring around her neck that she'd never explained. The gold band that had once fooled him on her wedding finger now sported an oval ruby Flex had given her three Christmases ago. It was the best he could do.

"If I could, I'd take you back to Boston. Put you up in a wonderful place where you could invite your old friends."

He popped his knuckles one at a time and dragged himself to the kitchen. A banana would pump some potassium into his muscles. He'd pushed his body too far today.

His mother followed, her face creasing into fine lines he'd only noticed since they'd come to New York. Whether it was the city air or the absence of her regular Botox treatments he wasn't sure. He'd offered to pay for her beauty rituals, but she'd refused, encouraging him to get a manicure and haircut instead. "I've been keeping up this mask for a lot of years," she'd said. "I'm a little relieved to let it get some air."

She placed her hand on Flex's shoulder. "I don't know what's gotten into you in the past few weeks, but working yourself to death won't solve it." She paused, staring at the floor as if trying to decide whether to mention something.

Just say it already.

She squared her shoulders in front of him. "You've been a little unsettled since your session with that Arietta girl, the one from California. I've heard her father's name. They're new money. Name-droppers. You didn't tell her anything, did you?"

Trying not to choke on the banana he'd just bitten into, Flex took a deep breath. What would his mother say if he told her Megan knew all about him—about them?

"Megan? Is that what you think this is about?"

It *was* about her in a way. It was through Megan that he'd seen Raya again, learned her name. Now he couldn't forget her no matter how hard he worked.

"There is nothing between Megan and me, okay? We're at odds, if anything."

He could see his mother sink back into her skin. Flex smiled as her body deflated from the eased tension. He planted a kiss on her cheek.

"Why would I want some snobby little rich girl when I've got the prettiest girl in the gym right here?"

She whacked him on the shoulder, then reached into the fruit basket for an apple. "Well, I'm sorry for treating you like a teenager. Just be careful. I know her type. She's in heat, looking to get married. That kind of girl will . . ."

What? Get pregnant like you did?

Flex stared at his mother as she swallowed her words, ashamed at his thoughts. Would this ever get any easier?

She ran a hand across her mouth. "I sound like your father, don't I?"

Flex nodded. Twentysomething years of fear that he'd repeat her mistake was a lot to overcome, even for a woman as sweet and kind as his mother.

"He couldn't have said it any better himself."

Angela sighed and walked out of the kitchen, waving for Flex to follow. They sat in the breakfast nook, where his father's face smiled at them from the cover of *Men of Color* magazine. Flex cringed but forced himself not to get up and throw it out. For years he'd followed his father's venture capitalist career from one magazine cover to another. Not anymore. Tomorrow he'd cancel his subscription. He had his own life to worry about now.

His mother tucked her classic pageboy behind both ears. "I was wrong to say that about your client. I don't know her or her parents. In truth, it's probably you they'd think was trying to take advantage, considering the circumstances."

"True."

Flex's father was one of the richest men in America, but it didn't mean a thing. When Flex dropped out of Princeton, the checks had stopped, leaving only his now depleted bank account and a cloud of confusion he'd never understand.

One thing was certain though—he would never be accepted by his father.

Flex stretched his neck from side to side, uncomfortable with the lingering question in his mother's eyes, big and round like Raya's. The last time his mother had looked at him like this was when she'd tried to explain the deal she'd struck with his father to receive payments until he was twenty-one. Too bad she hadn't signed up for a love account too. Her gaze had showed regret that evening. Just like now.

"It's late, Mom. We both have clients tomorrow." He rubbed his eyes, hoping there'd be no more soul-searching. Tonight's prayer list was long enough as it was.

She tossed her apple core into the trash. "I have more I need to say. I don't deserve to, considering the way your father and I have handled things, but I need to." She looked as though she was going to cry.

Flex grabbed her hand. "What did he do now? Is he coming? Did he call?" He clenched his fists.

She cleared her throat. "Nothing like that. It's you. You're distant. Working too much. Not talking enough. I pray for you, but—"

Definitely time to move out. "What, Mom? Everything's fine. Honestly."

She frowned, digging into the pocket of her jazz pants. "Is everything fine? I was cleaning up in your room, and I found these." A string of foil packages connected by perforated edges dangled from her dainty fingers.

Flex felt the breath leave his lungs as he eyed the length of silver packets.

"Mom, please believe me. Those were from before. A while before. It's not like that now. I would never—"

Her sobs absorbed his words. "I shouldn't have gone into your room, but I needed to borrow your luggage. They never

67

did find mine at LaGuardia. And you've been so open about your celibacy . . . I just don't want you to lose what you have going with the Lord."

Or end up like me.

It was unspoken, but Flex heard the thought just the same. "How long have you had those?"

She shrugged. "A few days. Since the morning that Arietta girl came in. And then you left the gym that day and never came back. Since then you've been a little . . . well . . . touchy about things."

Flex dropped his head and caught another look at his father's smile, mocking him as usual, on the magazine cover. After that crazy day with Raya and Megan, he'd actually considered leaving New York City and starting over elsewhere. Even taken out his luggage, only to find the unsavory souvenir now in his mother's hands. He should have pitched them, but he'd shoved them back into his luggage, not wanting to deal with the part of his past they represented.

"The funny thing is, I kept them because I didn't want you to find them in the trash and freak out. And you found them anyway."

"I'm sorry. You're a grown man. You're probably thinking I need to get a life."

He shook his head. "It's okay. You were right in a way, just not the way you thought. There is something—someone."

His mother smiled cautiously. "I should have known. You're carrying that bag of rocks again. I haven't seen you with those in years."

"They're not rocks, Mom. They're beads." It was too goofy to get into. Best to stick to the story. "She works at Chenille's place. She's designing the uniforms for the boys at church. I'd seen her on the train before." He cracked his knuckles. "Something about her gets to me, you know?"

A knowing grin eased across his mother's mouth. Her gaze fastened on his father's image. Her eyes sparkled with sadness. Did she feel the same about his father? Still? It didn't seem possible.

He smiled at her, hoping he was wrong. "I can't say I haven't had my struggles with celibacy, especially at the gym all day. But gradually the Lord has become so real to me that things have become easier. Sure, I'd see pretty girls, but I knew they weren't for me. Not part of my destiny."

His mother tamed a flyaway hair. "But this girl is different?"

He nodded. He'd held his breath as Chenille and Lyle entered the sanctuary the past two Sundays, but so far Raya hadn't shown up. If he could just get through their meetings about the uniforms, he'd probably never see her again.

Yeah right.

"She's really something, Mom. Nothing like Brooke—" He cut himself off, regretting the words as quickly as he'd said them.

His mother looked wounded.

He sighed. "I didn't mean it like that."

His mother shrugged. "It's okay. I deserve that. I thought planning that wedding without your knowledge was a good thing, setting you up for the life you deserved. A life I couldn't give you anymore. I know now how wrong that was."

Flex stood and took his mother's hand. Wrong? You could say that again. "Don't think about it. It's over." In truth, he meant the words for himself, though it probably wouldn't be a problem. Tonight Flex was tired enough to sleep without thinking about anything, not his dead almost wife, not his father . . . If he got to sleep soon enough, Raya might even steer clear of his dreams for the first time since the day he met her.

Probably not.

6

"How's it coming?"

Raya swiveled in her office chair at the weariness in Chenille's voice and made a mental note to discuss a modified schedule with her later. "It's coming. I can't get the costs down or anything, but I think the boys will love it. I slanted the eagle—"

Chenille placed a bottle of cherry-flavored Tums on the desk. She scrubbed her palms together over the trash can. "The uniforms? That's what you're working on? You didn't hear a thing I said Friday, did you?"

Raya licked the Coke off her lips. Last week she'd been buried in choir robes and band uniforms for a Christian school upstate. The designs had taken all her attention, and Chenille's repeated appearances in her doorway hadn't earned more than a nod of her head. Had she missed something important? "No, I'm afraid I wasn't paying much attention. My mind was on . . . other things."

Flex Dunham. She stopped herself before she said it. She'd come to the Big Apple to get away from her mistakes, but in the short

70

time since she'd met Flex, there seemed nowhere to run. His words, now weeks old, wouldn't leave her alone either.

"God loves you."

She could still hear his coastal voice. Raya knew God loved her and was drawing her back to him. The scary part was that she felt he had plans for her to love again. And that she just couldn't do.

"What did I miss? Is there a new project?"

Chenille gave Raya a tired smile. Were those rings under her eyes? Something was definitely wrong.

"Raya, Megan called Friday. She and I had a long chat. She'd still like you to design the dress—"

"What?" Gooseflesh pimpled the back of Raya's arms.

Her boss swallowed a few more Tums and made a face, then put her hand on the back of Raya's chair. "I know it's a lot to ask. Too much. I only told Megan I would ask. When you said yes, I thought you'd heard me—"

"I didn't."

Chenille smiled weakly. "Okay. I guess that settles it."

"I guess. I don't know . . ." Raya sighed.

What kind of game was Megan playing now? Was this about Flex after all? She inhaled and offered up a feeble prayer. Though she'd tried to outrun God, her endurance had run out, leaving her faceup in the Father's lap. If only she knew what to do next.

Give me wisdom here. What should I do?

The voice that rang through her heart was neither small nor still. Instead, a clear, firm direction echoed through her.

Mercy triumphs over judgment!

"Forget it. I've seen firsthand the tension between you two. We really need the money, but more than that, I wanted to see you and Megan make some peace—" Chenille gripped her stomach.

Raya leaped from her seat, taking Chenille by the arm. "Chenille? Are you all right? The baby, is the baby okay?"

The terror in her employer's eyes answered the question. With her friend slipping to her knees, Raya grabbed for the phone. "Help! Somebody! Call 911!"

She could hear Jean screaming into the phone. Raya stroked Chenille's curls. "It's going to be okay."

Please, God, let it be okay. I'm sorry for the way I've been acting. Really I am.

Chenille moaned, clutching Raya's hand. Her face flinched in pain. "The dress. Call Megan." Still trying to wrap up loose ends in spite of the emergency.

"No need. I'll do the dress. Now take a deep breath," Raya answered without hesitation.

Jean crashed into the room. "They're on their way. I called Lyle at the counseling center. He'll meet us at the hospital." Her words blew out in strained breath.

Raya nodded. Chenille laid her head on Raya's knee. "Thank you," she said before closing her eyes. Her hands remained pressed to her belly as if to hold the baby in.

Tears stabbed at Raya's eyes. Tomorrow she'd regret agreeing to make the dress, but now only one thing mattered. Well, two things. Chenille and her baby.

He never took a breath.

Nathan Kyle Rizzo, born with ten adorable toes and one of his mother's red curls, never tasted the sweet breath of life. His mother drank in all the air he'd missed, in gulps and sobs, her face carved with sorrow.

Raya stared down at the little body, more muscle than fat

except for the plump cheeks, wondering how her mother had felt at her own birth. Though this baby hadn't survived, watching his birth had been a miracle. She stared at him, praying as she had through the night as they induced Chenille's labor. Again Raya willed the little body to move.

The babe lay still.

"Let's take some more pictures, Lyle," Chenille said in a whisper, adjusting the clothes she'd put on Nathan, a Precious Moments T-shirt and a pair of blue booties Jean had crocheted. Raya mustered a smile at the words on the fabric. No phrase could have been more accurate to sum up the last few hours. Precious moments for sure.

Lyle rubbed his balding head, glistening with sweat. He leaned down from his perch on the other side of the bed and kissed Chenille. "I think that's enough photos, sweetheart. We have to let him go."

Raya bit her lip. She'd been thinking the same thing for a while, but she dared not say it. How could she impose on a mother's love? Without having lived, this child seemed to have received more love from his parents than she'd ever known.

Chenille scowled at her husband. "This is my son. I am going to hold him, take pictures of him, and sing to him—" Sobs wracked her shoulders.

The nurse peeked in with a troubled look.

"We're almost done," Lyle said.

She nodded and shut the door.

"I will play 'This Little Piggy' with him if I want to. This is it. This is all I get. Why can't you . . . why can't they let me have that?"

For the fourth or fifth time in the last hour, Raya tried to ease away from the bed. She had no place here. Lyle cleared his throat. She turned back, only to find his pleading eyes. *Help me*, his eyes said.

Raya blinked away her tears and pulled up all her strength. "Chenille, may I hold him?"

Her friend looked confused but extended the stiff bundle to Raya. She surveyed her friend with narrow eyes. "Be careful."

Swallowing back a scream, Raya took the cold infant from her friend's arms. She stroked the soft shirt and then grabbed one of his toes, so much like gray little nibs of corn. "This little piggy went to market . . ."

Chenille moaned deep from her belly and broke out into the first good cry she'd had since the birth. Lyle dropped the rail on the side of the bed and let her fall into his arms.

"I am so sorry, honey," he said. "So sorry."

"It's not fair . . ." Her words muffled into her husband's shoulder.

Lyle wiped away a few tears of his own. "Nobody said it would be." He paused, closing his eyes. "I don't know why this happened, but I know God hasn't turned his back on us. He's still here, right now."

The door inched open, and the nurse tapped Raya's shoulder, then took the baby. Tears pooled in the neckline of Raya's dress. Was God here?

"Surely I am with you always, to the very end of the age."

Her heart pounded as her friends cried softly, speaking in the hushed tones of grief. She inched to the door, feeling a holiness permeate the room. God was here now. And he'd been there then. Sometimes it just didn't seem like it.

Help me, Lord. I just need more than a promise right now. Something real—

The door inched open again, hitting her in the back. She turned to face the intruder, Flex with swollen eyes. Before she could say anything, he gathered her into his arms.

Unable to be strong anymore, she let him take her from

the room. She leaned against his shoulder, and he propped himself up against a wall, stroking her hair. Neither of them spoke.

They just cried.

She felt like heaven.

Flex lifted his head from Raya's white, soft curls soaked with his tears. When he'd arrived at Garments of Praise for his meeting with Raya, he'd known immediately that something was wrong. Even the stern woman who guarded the desk looked ready to break down.

On impulse, he'd reverted to his mother's Dominican roots as he often did in despair. "*Cómo estás?*" he'd mumbled, scanning the sad faces.

"*Muy malo.*" The older woman had shaken her head and walked away unable to speak anymore.

An Asian woman with long, thin fingers had spoken kindly to him. "Raya is at Mount Sinai with Chenille." She'd paused, eyes downcast.

He'd dropped his briefcase then, thinking of Lyle, his prayer partner and only real friend. They'd prayed for that baby every time they met. The guy talked of nothing else . . .

God, please. He'd looked at the woman, scanning her face for hope.

She'd given none, offering the sober truth instead. "They lost the baby."

He'd raced to get here, winding through turnstiles and climbing stairs two, three, at a time, only to arrive as the nurse carried the dead baby out of the room. A boy it seemed, from the blue shoes. A boy with a wisp of his mother's red hair. Though he'd come knowing the child had died, the sight of the child had done him in. He wasn't a crying man, but to see someone so small, so helpless . . .

When he'd opened the door and seen Raya there crying too, he couldn't help but take her into his arms. She lay still against him now, her body spent of anguish but tears running still. He kicked the sole of one foot against the wall behind him to ease the tension as his body seemed to awake to Raya's presence. He'd felt this before, when he'd touched her hand during their first meeting. Then, as now, Raya's very life had seemed to course through him.

Get it together. This isn't the time.

And he did get it together. For about three seconds. His breathing slowed, and his heart beat at a normal pace. He was just about to let her go and say how sad everything was, when she looked up at him with those giant eyes.

"Kiss me," she said.

He foolishly obeyed, feathering his lips against hers. It was so much sweeter than he'd imagined. It was a tender kiss, the kind husbands give their wives at funerals. Safe but intense. His foot skidded to the floor as he took her face in his hands. She placed her hands on top of his. They pulled away from each other, engulfed by grief.

"Thank you," Raya said softly, walking away, though her hands remained in his grasp.

Flex released her hands, but she didn't move away. They stood staring at one another when Lyle pushed through the door beside them.

Lyle smiled in spite of his obvious pain. "Just the people I was looking for."

Forcing a smile, Flex watched with his heart in his throat as Raya walked back into Chenille's hospital room. His body ached at the sight of her. His mind and spirit should have been stronger than the grief that made Raya ask him to kiss her. Now it wouldn't matter even if he left New York.

He was hers.

Raya stared at the computer screen. The day's weather and news flashed by, but none of it made sense. Nothing did. Watching Chenille lose her son had changed Raya forever . . . along with those two insane words.

Kiss me.

What on earth had she been thinking? She hadn't been thinking at all, of course, but hurting. Hurting for her friend, for herself. Somehow in the midst of Chenille's tragedy, all her own tears, locked up over the past few months, had raged like a flood. And in the midst of it, there was Flex, holding her lightly. Gently.

She leaned back in the office chair. Chenille needed her more than ever now. She had to forget whatever had made her crazy enough to ask Flex for a kiss and him stupid enough to give it. If this business was going to make it, she'd have to come up with a design for Megan. Having shared a college dorm with Megan and watched her go through more clothes and men than a small nation at war, Raya knew it wouldn't be an easy task. But it had to be done all the same.

"There you are," Jean said, dropping a stack of pink message slips on Raya's desk. "Call her. Please. I'm tired of talking to her. She gives me fits."

Raya scratched her chin and eyed the stack of messages. All from Megan. All one minute apart. Could she handle this on top of everything else? She wanted nothing more than to run to Chenille's apartment and feed her chicken soup for the next six weeks. But that was Lyle's job.

"Thanks, Jean. I'll take care of it."

The older woman nodded and started for the door.

"And thanks for holding things down the past few days. The design you finished for me on those new choir robes was excellent."

The pause stretched into silence.

"Uh-huh." Jean's invisible mask lowered over her face. She grunted before moving on. "Just be careful. And get to work."

Raya gave Jean a salute as she left the room. She wasn't fooled a bit. Jean put up a brave front, but underneath all that, there was a tender heart. Flex said she'd been almost speechless the day Nathan was born.

Flex. Back to him again. He'd invited her to come by the gym for a free training session, said it'd help her keep from crying and focus on her work. It sounded like a good idea in theory, but the thought of a sweaty room full of half-dressed strangers didn't float her boat right now. Not to mention that seeing him again was probably a bad idea. She'd have to call and cancel. Maybe she'd take a run alone in the morning.

The phone rang beside her before she could figure it out.

"Hello."

"Hey, Raya. It's me, Megan."

Raya stared at the receiver. It sounded like Megan's voice, but where was the attitude? "Right. Sorry about the messages. I was just going to call—"

"That's okay. I just wanted to know if Chenille was all right. I sent some flowers to the hospital, but I can't get through to her room."

Had someone kidnapped Megan and replaced her with some sort of caring robot? "Um, she's resting, but doing better today. She'll go home tonight."

"Okay. I'm so sorry about her baby . . . and about what

happened before between you and me. Can we start over, maybe?"

Raya paused before answering. "Megan, we can start over. No problem. But I have to ask, are you all right? You sound—"

"Different?"

"Yes, different."

"Well, I've been thinking about some things. Praying even . . ."

Praying? Raya looked around the room, braced herself on the desk. Would the walls fall in next?

Usually this was the point where she'd dive in and share her own testimony, offer her help. Not today. She wasn't touching this one.

"That's great. Sounds like some wonderful things are happening with you. When do you want to consult about the dress?"

Raya wasn't comfortable on this chummy ground. She'd been burned by the likes of Megan too many times. Being softhearted had gotten her nothing but dumped and duped. Somebody else would have to help Megan work through her issues.

I have enough problems of my own.

It wasn't the godliest thought she'd ever had, but it was where she was on the whole thing.

"Tomorrow, maybe? Or do you need the groom too?"

Raya stood and walked to the window. "No thanks."

Megan laughed. "I'll bet."

"Just you is fine. We'll get his input next time."

"Great. I'll see you tomorrow. Say, around ten?"

Take a deep breath. It'll be fine.

"Sure. Ten." Should Raya start screaming now and get it over with?

"Smooches!" Megan said, sounding like her annoying self again.

Raya cringed. "Bye."

Lily entered as Raya hung up the phone. Sadness tinged her eyes, but her face showed its usual happy expression. "Megan?" she asked, holding up the pattern for the boys' uniforms to the light.

Raya marveled at Lily's patterning skills. Jean's cutting too. Where had Chenille found them? In all her travels in the fashion world—Paris, LA, New York—Raya had seen only a select few with such exquisite skill. Except Gram, of course.

"Yes, Megan. I'm going to try to make a go of this."

Lily's kind expression brightened. "Of course. I'm praying for you. Nothing is impossible with God."

The truth of the Scripture rattled in Raya's bones. Though her Christian life was marginal of late, her starving faith was growing, focusing for this battle, this assignment. Lily's conviction of her success buoyed her soul.

Focus.

Lily folded her pattern neatly and peered over Raya's shoulder at her latest mood board for Megan's gown. A swatch of sequined cloth and several sleek sketches of a fitted, glittery gown adorned the board. Lily frowned.

"Is that the new one? It looks like a snake."

Raya's shoulders slumped as she looked at the color image of a silvery, sequined gown fitted from head to foot. A snake for sure.

"You're right. I guess without my realizing it, some of my real thoughts about Megan came out."

"I can imagine." Lily took a seat beside her. "Big-time messed-up situation. Just don't allow the real snake to use you against her. Jesus died for her, you know."

Raya stared at her co-worker, surprised once again by her

straightforward manner on spiritual things. A caretaker for her elderly mother, Lily saw things in terms of dark and light, sin and righteousness. Raya had viewed the world through those same eyes not so long ago. Her heart struggled to do it still, only to see things in blurs faded by humanity's frailty. She took a deep breath.

"You're right, Lily. I'll try to see her as God sees her."

Lily nodded. "Look at her through the blood, girl. It cleanses all." She winked. "Even the pattern-cutter tracks up my arm."

Raya bit her lip, thinking about how she'd dodged into the hall with a pattern cutter her first week here. After she'd gouged Jean with scissors a few days later, everyone quickly agreed that Raya should stick to her design room. "Again, I'm sorry about that."

Lily smiled falsely, wiping away one of the tears they'd all learned to accept since Chenille's loss. "I know. Now cheer up and make something pretty. And be nice to Mr. Dunham. Methinks he is a man of God."

Me too.

"I'll try for the dress. I don't know about the other."

Lily shrugged. "I will pray," she said with finality, as if that solved everything.

And didn't it? Wasn't everything in God's hands? Raya wiped away a tear of her own. Had Chenille's baby somehow slipped through his fingers? As if in response to her doubt, the sweetness of the hospital room enveloped her again. No, God had been there, even in their loss. He hadn't dropped little Nathan. Rather, it seemed he'd reached down and drawn the infant to himself. Still, it hurt so much . . . and all she'd done was watch.

She opened a new digital art file, scuffing her elbow on a photo on the desk. She turned it over. Jay Andrews, smiling as though nothing had happened. Raya clipped the photo to her monitor. Jay was what this company was about, what Chenille was about. Raya would make this dress work. She lifted her stylus pen.

God, help me.

7

Business was good. A little too good. From actresses to art students, word seemed to be out that Flex was the personal trainer to have. He was "just plain fine," as he'd overheard two of his new female clients whisper when they signed up. For fun, Flex had tried to assign these two dancers to his mother instead. While they agreed that she looked good for her age, it was him they wanted.

And after that day with Raya at Mount Sinai hospital, all he seemed to want was her. They'd talked once since then, but neither had mentioned the kiss that had passed between them. Flex saved that agony for his prayers.

Today he had to be with Megan, who was showing her wares in a cocoa bodysuit. Every eye in the house was on her—except his. All Flex could think of was Raya looking divine in the coffee-stained skirt she'd worn at the hospital. That kiss had hijacked his mind.

"Lift a little higher," he said, pushing Megan's arm to a full extension. "Keep the tension on the biceps throughout the movement. Don't rest until the end."

Megan looked a little miffed but straightened her arm. "Whoa . . ."

"Exactly. Give me two more of those, and that's it for today."

Cranking out the remaining reps, Megan spoke in trickles of breath. "Are you done for today? I was thinking we could—"

"I don't think so." Flex smiled when he said it, trying to be as professional as possible, but she looked hurt all the same.

She lowered the dumbbells to the bench. "I understand. I've just been trying to get some understanding on this whole Jesus thing. It's sort of confusing, you know?"

Boy, do I.

"I'm glad you're trying to figure it out. I don't know if I'm your guy though. I'm still trying to get the answers straight myself. What about Chenille?" Immediately he realized that option wouldn't work. "Or Raya, maybe?" Not that he even knew where Raya was spiritually. Chenille had spoken about Raya's walk with God, but it all seemed to be in the past tense. He prayed for her more often than he'd like to admit, but their times together seemed to shoot right past talking and into places he'd vowed never to go again.

She definitely hadn't taken Chenille up on her offers to come to church, but he couldn't judge anybody on that. How many years had it taken him to get back there? There had to be someone else to help Megan though. His mother, maybe? No. Not with the comments she'd made about Megan before.

"I don't do so well with women," Megan said. "Don't worry about it."

He sighed, knowing he'd regret what he was about to do.

"Tell you what. Why don't we meet later at Man-O-Cure? They have a juice bar, and I have some friends there."

She looked stunned. "You have friends *there*?"

Flex laughed. "I do. Church friends even. I have an appointment Thursday at eleven. Meet me at ten."

"Can I get your home number?" She looked sincere. "You know, in case things change."

Now she was going too far. "Try the cell number on my card. That's the best bet to reaching me."

"Okay. See you then." She turned and shot him a flirty look before starting her obligatory hip sway for every guy in the gym.

They all gave him the "you getting that?" look. No matter how many times he explained his celibacy, none of the guys here believed him. He held up one hand and shook his head but laughed a little at the hidden guy language of looks and nods.

If women only knew . . .

His eyes fastened on his mother's face, across the room at the pec-fly machine. If there was one woman who knew the language of men, Angela Dunham did. Her relationship with Flex's father had versed her in things Flex would never understand.

She waved him over. "What was that about?"

Flex mopped the sweat from his brow and eyed the clock. "Nothing. She wants to talk . . . about God."

With a smile, his mother motioned to the heavyset woman on the machine. This lady was new but faithful and had already memorized the circuit his mother had designed for her. She moved quickly to the next machine.

"Talk about God, huh? I'll bet." Remorse flashed across her face. "Just be careful, okay? Please."

"I will."

Raya stood to stretch her legs and escape the stacks of unworthy designs littering her desk. Though she'd come back to New York City to save herself from herself, making a wedding gown for the woman who'd killed her dreams had never crossed her mind.

She kicked off her shoes and paced around her small corner of the building. Darrell was no dream, and Raya knew it. If she'd ever taken her love for him seriously, the thought had been shattered the morning her eyes met with Flex's across the train. Now, that man was a dream. Not one she could make a reality, but a dream all the same.

Her father's haughty voice on the phone this morning had scathed her ear. *"I'm sorry about your friend, but I warned you. This little mess she's calling a business would never have survived anyway."*

Though he'd thrown the insults at Chenille, Raya knew exactly what her father meant—that she'd never make it without him, or his money. She swallowed back her doubts and steeled herself with determination. She'd help Chenille save this place and probably save herself in the process. As for love, she'd taken her fill of it once, and that would have to last a lifetime.

She shook out her fingers and took a seat in front of the computer, setting aside all the designs of the day. She'd been trying to take components from past designs and piece them together, but that wasn't working. She had to start over from scratch. She couldn't hold back, protect herself. It was all or nothing, and nothing wasn't an option.

The phone rang, interrupting her wave of creativity. She ignored it, then considered it might be Chenille, even Megan.

"Hello?"

"Hey, you." A man's voice. *The* man's voice. For once she wished it were her father. Facing him seemed like nothing compared to this.

She gripped the phone. "Flex?"

"It's me. Just wondering if you're still stopping by the gym tonight. To work out, remember?"

Raya dropped her head. It was today. "You know . . . I've got a lot going on here. I don't think I'll make it. I'm working on Megan's gown, and it's not going so well." She'd stay here all night if she had to. "Besides, I'm sure you've got other clients—"

"I do, actually, so later is good. I know you're working hard. All the more reason to sneak in a workout. Come when you can. I'll be here."

"It probably wouldn't be until eight or so. Seriously. You don't have to wait—"

"I do. And I will. I'll see you soon. And one more thing." His voice turned firm.

Raya took a deep breath. "Yes?"

"Do you like sushi?"

Is this a D-A-T-E? "Love it. Why?" *Why am I spelling to myself?*

"It's a surprise. Oh, and if you still have that suit you had on the day we saw you running, bring that. It screams 'Let's sweat!' I love that thing."

Raya forgot to breathe. Was this the same reserved guy she'd kissed at the hospital? And that outfit? He loved it? She swallowed. The account had hated it, and Chenille had designed them an entirely new outfit. Nobody ever loved her stuff, except Gram.

"I think I can do that. See you in a bit."

"Make that a little bit. And don't work too hard. I'm praying for you. Bye." His words came in a rush, and then the phone disconnected.

Raya hung up and dropped to her knees in a pile of wadded paper.

"Lord, this is getting out of hand . . ." She stifled a squeal. "And I think I like it! Please, please don't hurt me. I can't take it. Not again."

Flex wanted to bang his head on the wall, but the place was too crowded for him to do it. It was 9:00 p.m., and he'd waited for Raya long enough. Thinking back to how desperate he'd sounded on the phone, he couldn't blame her. *I love that thing?* Had he actually said that?

Talk about corny. He sounded like one of those awful reality dating shows he hated so much. Flex rotated his neck in a circle and looked at himself in the mirror. Behind the new muscles lurked the same young man determined to find his own place outside his father's shadow. As long as he worked like he had lately, he'd soon have enough money to take care of his mother in the way she deserved and get his fitness business off the ground.

He had big dreams: a clothing line, fitness equipment, personal training services, all faith-based and targeted to the African American market, where health was a growing concern. Falling in love would just complicate things. He flung a towel over his shoulder, relieved Raya hadn't showed. He bent down to tie his shoe before heading for the shower.

"Here I am."

He eased upward and caught Raya's reflection in the wall-to-wall mirror. Her platinum white hair was now ash-blond and curled into tiny twists. Her eyebrows curved over her chocolate eyes in the same light color as her hair. Golden lip gloss on top of red lipstick finished the look as he'd seen the makeup girls do at photo shoots.

If he didn't know better, he'd take her for a model instead of a designer. But one look at the unitard he'd admired so much on her slim but strong body and he had to agree that design was her first calling. He'd never have put together colors in such a bold combination, having been raised in a world of muted beiges and grays, but on Raya the colors looked like the spark she was.

"There you are." He smiled and turned to her, trying not to act as goofy as he had on the phone. Before he realized what he was doing, he gathered her into a hug, invigorated as her skin touched his own. Nearby, a stack of weights clanged to a stop as one of the regulars stared in disbelief. Though his no-nonworkout-touching rule was unspoken, even the guys knew the deal. Already he'd played his hand.

Flex clapped his hands together, more to snap himself back to reality than anything. "Let's get started."

In contrast to the commanding businesswoman he'd encountered on his visits to Garments of Praise, this Raya was the fun-loving but somewhat shy girl who'd smiled at him on the train.

"Sure. Where do you want to start?"

He tilted his head toward the treadmill. "Let's do a few minutes of cardio first. Warm up the muscles."

Raya started to say something but nodded instead.

He'd been working with women long enough to know what that meant. Trouble. "What?"

"Nothing. It's just that—well, can we do the bike instead? Or the rowing machine? The treadmill is just so . . . well, boring."

He frowned. "Boring? Walking is the safest form of exercise

there is. Since it's your first time, let's keep it simple. We can always speed it up or adjust the incline."

Raya tilted her head a little. "I can walk anytime. I came here to work out. You're supposed to help me reach my goals, right?" Though the words spat like fire, the smile that came with them was worth the sting.

A pair of bodybuilders squeezed past the two of them, one guy eyeing Raya for all to see.

"Hey, man," Flex said to the sweaty monster. "How's married life treating you?"

The guy pulled his gaze from Raya and walked on. "It isn't all it's cracked up to be," he called back over his shoulder.

"I heard that," the other guy said, following close behind him.

Though Raya had seemed oblivious to the men's roving eyes, their words seemed to cut her the wrong way. Her face wrinkled up like his mother's did when something smelled.

"Those guys stink. In fact, this whole place stinks."

Flex laughed heartily and took her hand and headed for the rowing machines. "Sweat. It's an occupational hazard." And so was touching beautiful women, something that hadn't bothered him in the slightest until now.

"You don't smell like that." She took a seat on the machine and read the flashing monitor in front of her, where a little rower image smiled and encouraged her to press start.

"Oh no?" He stifled another chuckle.

He hadn't laughed this much during a session in the year he'd been here, and he wasn't sure he liked it. He obviously looked moronic, judging from the looks the guys around the club were giving him, much different from the casual nods they'd thrown him when Megan was in earlier. This expression, the "is that your woman?" look, was much more intense. Thank God his mother had gone home hours ago.

He ground his teeth, realizing why the guys had reacted so strongly. He was off his routine—not on the treadmill with a first timer. And while he'd usually have stepped back for the muscle heads to pass between him and a client, Flex had guarded the space between himself and Raya with narrowed eyes.

Watch yourself.

Raya looked flustered, fishing for words after her comment about his scent. Her golden brown cheeks flushed with color. "You . . . I mean. I meant that you . . . well, you smell good." She reached out and pressed the start button on the machine and started rowing like crazy, biting her lip all the way.

If that wasn't the cutest thing, Flex didn't know what was. He put his hands on her elbows. "Slow down. This machine is harder than it looks. You want to extend all the way. Bring the bar into your pecs. Push off with your legs." He let go of her arms, dropped into the rowing station next to her, and pressed the screen. "Like this."

Raya continued, following his instructions. Now and then she looked over at him with determination and sweat etching her face. Without saying a word, she matched her strokes to his. Realizing that he might be going too fast, he tried to slow down, but Raya shook her head.

Ten minutes later the exercise took its toll. "How much longer?" she said in one long breath.

Flex looked at the rower on the screen halfway across the river. "About two minutes."

"Let's go for it, then," she said with a weak smile.

He pressed on in silence, both intrigued and aggravated with himself. Under other circumstances he'd never let a client push this hard in the first session, but he had to admit it was refreshing. Fun even.

Since Raya had started first, her rower reached the riverbank first. Instead of stopping, she rowed on until Flex's guy reached his bank too. They stopped rowing at the same time and allowed their plastic seats to glide back to their original positions.

She swiped her forehead. "What's next?"

Flex crossed his arms, wishing for once that he were a little less conditioned. A bit of deep breathing could do him good right now. He'd invited Raya to train with him because he wanted to help her relieve some of the stress of the last week and the weeks to come. As it was, it seemed that she was training him. He tried to gather himself, to remember the program he'd worked out for her.

A wheezing sound stopped his thoughts. He grabbed Raya's hand. "Are you okay?"

She shook her head. "Asthma."

He clamped his teeth together. She'd pushed too hard, and he'd let her do it. "Inhaler?"

Raya shook her head again, with her eyes squinted in embarrassment.

He scrambled out of his seat and knelt beside her. "It's okay," he said in his calmest voice. "Breathe. I'll get you a—"

"Coke," she whispered as her brown eyes widened. "How'd you know?"

"I have it too. Not much now that I'm older, but now and again. Don't try to talk."

Flex swallowed hard as he stood and raced to the staff counter. He tapped the shoulder of a guy with a pink crew cut. "Tell me you've got a Coke."

Brad's, the receptionist's, head bobbed like a dashboard toy. "Always. Regular or diet? Cherry or vanilla? Warm or—"

"Would you just give me one? Make it cold." He looked over at Raya, now panting, sitting on the rower. "And regular."

The man leaned over and reached into a small fridge. "Here. Tell your girlfriend to drink it fast."

Flex snatched the can and started back to Raya. He'd have to clear the girlfriend thing up later—both with his co-worker and himself.

8

Raya gulped down the remains of the now lukewarm cola and took a much-needed breath. Flex's program had been a challenge, and she'd had to fight him to let her continue, but she'd made it. And though she hated to admit it, she felt better. Her mind was clearer, her head didn't hurt, and she'd sleep like a rock tonight instead of tossing and turning. In her mind glimmered a still sun, a long-past day when another kind soul had handed her a Coke. Many times she'd wondered what had happened to that gallant geek. Probably in management at some software company by now.

She turned to her current companion, who was anything but a nerd. "I still can't believe that day with Megan when I met you again . . . after the train," she said before taking another sip. "Didn't you recognize me? Why didn't you say anything?"

Flex shrugged. "What was I supposed to say? Remember that guy on the train who said God loved you? Well, that was me."

She laughed. "That sounds about right."

He sat down on the bench across from her in the almost-empty gym. "You would have thought I was nuts. And you and Megan were having some kind of weird *This Is Your Life* reunion."

"More like *You Wrecked My Life*."

"I'm not even going to touch that one," he said playfully, lifting both hands. "As it is, you didn't remember me, so I think I did the right thing."

She pulled her lips away from the Coke. Beautiful lips. "Excuse me? I did remember you, even though you looked quite a bit different, Mr. Businessman Turned Workout Guy." She patted his shoulder. His stomach took a dive. "You're the one who didn't recognize me."

"The hair pretty much gave you away, but once I heard that squeak—"

"Hey!" She punched him lightly. "Don't go there, okay?" She drained the last sip of soda and released the can to his extended hand.

He tossed the can behind the counter and rubbed his shoulder in mock pain. "I like the way your voice does that." He flashed a smile but stopped short of showing teeth. "It's cute."

Cute. Raya's grip tightened on the counter, resisting the urge to groan. He'd said it in a voice people used to describe little kids . . . or cats. What a fool she'd been to think he liked her. He thought of her as a friend or a sister, and a baby sister at that. Had she imagined the fire in their kiss or the passion in his voice on the phone tonight?

What difference did it make? She didn't have time to even be here, let alone have feelings for some man she barely knew. Raya looked around at the remaining Nike-clad crowd, with their perfect bodies and matching socks.

"This was fun, but this place isn't really my thing. They

need to hire somebody to Lysol this place," Raya said as she walked back to the rowing machine and picked up her towel. This little event had been humiliating enough. She didn't want to have to share sweat and germs too.

Flex did a sniff check under his own arm and peeked back at her from under his armpit. "I guess that includes me now, right? All my sweetness has surely worn away after the circuits we did."

She rolled her eyes and gave a sideways grin. "Not quite."

Probably not ever. Their rowing hadn't broken a sweat on him, and he'd moved through the other exercises beside her, hoisting twenty-pound dumbbells as if lifting bags of potato chips while she struggled with five-pounders. Sure, he wasn't shower fresh after their workout, but when he stood close to her, the usual mix of scents intoxicated her as always—Irish Spring, shaving gel, and that sweet sandalwood stuff.

"You always smell good. What is that you wear? I've been meaning to ask."

"Me too, Flex. Maybe it's lavender?" Male laughter echoed from an elliptical machine nearby.

Flex sucked his teeth. "You guys mind your own business."

He lowered his voice. "There's some vanilla in it. Sandalwood is that other smell, the musky smell I really like. And a drop or two of lemon essential oil, I think."

She nodded. Their close proximity during the exercises had afforded her quite a whiff of Flex. In fact, she could still smell him. She took a long breath as he leaned back. That stuff was better than Coke. Almost.

"I think I know what you're talking about. Weird. But I like it."

Silence hung between them like a veil. Raya's chest tightened, knowing all Flex's sweat-bunny friends were watching. It was one of those kissing moments, like in a chick flick.

Flex licked his lips. "I like it too. One of my clients got my fragrances for me when I was hurt. Now I'm hooked. A place uptown. Sweet Savour—"

"Is it after ten? I'd better go." The image of him soaking was too much. Raya shifted her weight to her other leg. "If I stay much longer, I'll need a soak myself."

"Right. We'll have to take a rain check on that sushi. Let me walk you to the train." Flex's towel dangled from his arm. "I'd love to work with you again." He crossed his arms. "Next time, though, bring your inhaler. One of these times you might have a bad attack that Coke won't remedy."

She frowned. He sounded just like her father, always telling her the right thing to do but providing no way to do it. Chenille provided no insurance, and Raya's father had just cut her off his insurance plan in a last-ditch effort to make her come home and work for him. The Coke had done the job so far, but Flex did have a point.

"I'll think about it."

And she would, about both the training and the prescription. Until lately she'd never known how much things really cost, especially medicine. And her salary was a joke. If she had to pay rent and utilities too, it'd be hopeless. How did people do it? She hadn't complained to Gram, knowing that her meager social security income and her habit of charging too little for the dresses left little to spare.

Raya's father had bought Gram's building in hopes that collecting the rents would give her some money, since she never told him her needs. Costly renovations, late payments, and a soft heart left things pretty much the same. Raya would have to tighten up more now, skipping even the sale bins.

"Thanks for your concern too. I'm fine. Really."

"Of course." Flex's eyes, brimming with doubt, bored through her. "I'm just glad you showed up today. Megan just returned for her second visit. A lot of my female clients don't—"

"I'll be back." How dare he compare her with Megan? Or his other female clients? Raya might be out of shape and stop breathing every now and then, but she wasn't some china doll.

He nodded as if not sure he believed her. "Okay. I look forward to that."

"I will be back. Really."

"Okay. I believe you. It's just that so many people start programs and never stick with it. I try to get people to stick it out for twelve weeks, hoping they'll continue on their own, but few make it through." He headed toward the locker room.

Raya followed. Was he giving her a challenge? "Design me a program, and I'll stick with it. I'll . . . wait, how much is your fee? I know you invited me today—"

"Nothing. Consider it a gift," he said before stopping at the fountain for a drink.

Raya bristled as he stood and smiled at her, so satisfied with himself. "I don't take gifts from strangers."

"Good policy. And a safe one," he said, taking her hand. "Good thing it doesn't apply to me. I know all about you, remember? God loves you and all that?"

She smiled bittersweetly, thankful he didn't truly know all about her. "I suppose you're safe enough." It was only twelve weeks, right? "I can take whatever you can dish out. Just tell me what to do."

Flex grinned until she thought his face would crack. "Just meet me here at 6:00 a.m. tomorrow—"

"What?"

He ran for the locker room. "And then come back Thursday, Friday, Saturday, Monday, Tuesday . . ."

She stared after him in despair, wondering if she wanted him to walk her to the subway after all. What had she gotten herself into now?

Instead of the usual whisper of dinner snaking down the stairs or the everyday buzz of Gram's serger, dark silence greeted Raya upon returning home.

She was grateful. She'd been up and down since Chenille lost the baby. And now there was Megan's design, her mistake of signing up for Flex's workout plan because of her rattled pride, and well, just Flex himself. Even the blast of a hot shower couldn't erase her confusion. She'd resumed her daily Bible reading after that night at the hospital, and prayers seemed to come from her like breath, but she needed more. And she didn't relish having to admit it to Chenille or to Gram. This Sunday she'd have to make another trip—to church.

Fluffing her twists with a towel, she quickly covered the short distance from the bathroom to her door, convincing her tired muscles to imagine the bed was long enough and begging her body to gift her with a good night's sleep. Listening for the even tone of Gram's snoring, Raya paused before going into her room. There was no sound except the whisper of *Masterpiece Theatre* on the radio. Gram had waited up for her.

With a smile, Raya tiptoed into her own room, not bothering to turn on the light. She dived into her little bed, thankful for her grandmother's love. When her body hit a firm, silky surface instead of a lumpy, too-short mattress, she skidded over the edge of the queen-size bed covered in what had to be satin sheets and clicked on the light.

When the room lit up, she whirled, gaping in surprise at

her new queen-size bed covered in white satin sheets and a matching comforter. The peeling wallpaper was stuck fast. Her grandmother sat in the wicker rocker at the end of the bed, the only original piece in the room. A convertible otto-man in bold stripes of teal, gold, and fuchsia that Raya had admired in a magazine sat against the far wall with a lava lamp beside it. She covered her mouth. The sofa was gor-geous, and she'd always wanted a lava lamp. The rocker was just comfortable. But that bed . . .

She stared at it again, waiting for her grandmother to say something. Anything. Like why she'd bought *white* satin sheets. She covered her face.

"I figured you're a woman now. It's time you slept like one," Gram said quietly. The Barbie set was folded neatly on her lap.

"Thanks, but the money. How did you—"

The old woman tipped up her chin. "Your father. It's one thing, the game he and I play, but you're his child. I told him you needed some things. You have a doctor's appointment next week. I hear you wheezing at night."

Her chest tightened as though she'd have an asthma attack right now. "Daddy? You called Daddy?"

Gram waved her hand as if swatting a fly. "There's a first time for everything. Pride goes before the fall, and it's time we all stopped falling. I'm too old for the bruises." She looked away. "And you're too young for them."

Raya smiled at her grandmother's wisdom. True enough, the foolishness with her father had gone on too long. It wasn't his money she wanted though. It was his love and his un-derstanding. To be treated like a daughter instead of the son he'd wanted, like a woman instead of a child.

"I figured you're a woman now."

100

A woman? More like a fool. Had she imagined the catch in her grandmother's tone? It was as if . . . as if she knew.

She stared at Gram, as if in question. Her steely brown eyes glared back, her face motionless. Raya didn't know how, but Gram did know something about what had happened to her, probably more than she knew herself.

Raya tried to breathe. Surely, she was imagining it. This was just a nice gesture. Nothing more. It would kill her grandmother to know that Raya had gone back on the promise she'd made, both to Gram and to God.

And to herself.

"Thank you, Gram. I don't know what to say."

Gram nodded, setting the chair in motion. Raya had loved the rocker as a child and delighted in sitting in it. She hadn't sat in it since coming back here. She stared at the floor. Would she ever feel like that again? Like a girl?

"Nothing for you to say but thank you. About the room, at least." Her grandmother patted the end of the bed. "Come here, and let's talk about the rest of it."

Raya gripped the bedpost.

"Sit." Her grandmother's voice left no room for negotiation. "I've already forgiven you—"

"What?" Raya felt the life leaking out of her. And she'd worried about going back to church. That'd be a piece of cake compared to this.

Gram pulled a single cuff link from her robe pocket and laid it on the new comforter. "I found this in the bridal suite when I packed your things. I have a feeling Darrell is somewhere missing it, like you're missing something he has. Something that he can't give back." She kissed Raya's forehead.

A mournful wail rose from somewhere deep in Raya's belly. She buried her head in the folds of her grandmother's soft robe. "I am so . . . so sorry."

Gram held a long, brown finger to her lips. "Hush. I forgave you long ago." She relaxed back into the chair and started a slow rhythm. "What hurts me is that you won't forgive yourself. Or accept God's forgiveness. That's a sin too, you know."

Another sin? Goodness. Was there any hope for Raya at all? She knew what her grandmother meant; she'd heard it many times before—the blood of Jesus is enough. It had sounded reasonable then, when she wasn't the one needing to have the blood applied, when she was the pristine girl, as chaste as these sheets. Now it seemed so much harder.

"I . . . I'm sorry." It was all she could think of to say. Raya slid off the bed onto her knees, her eye blurred with months of tears. She half screamed the words.

The rocker stilled as her grandmother joined Raya beside the bed. "I know. I'm sorry too. But you know what? You have to let it go. He died for this. Let him clean it."

Fists balled at Raya's sides. There it was again.

He died for this.

She looked at the door, wanting to run, but knowing there was no use. She'd come to New York for this conversation, but now it was too much. Her grandmother's needle-pricked fingers smoothed her hair, kissed her temples.

Tears flooded Raya's face as she crumbled in her grandmother's arms. "I tried. I prayed for forgiveness. Many times. But the bad feeling, the horrible feeling, it just won't leave. I know what the Bible says, but I still feel awful."

Strong arms hugged her tighter. The scent of talcum and lavender soothed her, calming her breaths.

"My darling girl. Forgiveness doesn't take away the pain. Or the scars. It removes the debt." She raised Raya's chin to hers. "And the wall." Another hug. "You asked for forgiveness, you say. Once. Twice. Both times it was granted. Yet you did not accept it." She closed her eyes.

Raya pushed up onto her knees, away from her grand-mother's grasp. She dried her tears and dragged herself up onto the bed. This was farther than she wanted to go.

Her grandmother shook her head. "Don't be angry, hard-ening your face like that. I'm not perfect. I'm an old woman with secrets and failures too. Things that make me cry at night. Things for which the blood is sufficient. Things that yet make the heart sick." Her accent thickened into staccato syllables.

Raya peeled her eyes open. "You? Secrets?"

For all her life, her grandmother had been like Jesus sheathed in brown skin and chiffon capes and satin hats. A beautiful, wonderful Christian who always did the right thing, said the right thing. What was she saying now?

"Don't look at me like that. I'm human too."

Raya pulled her hands from her grandmother's grasp, not wanting to imagine what Gram could mean. Her grandfa-ther had died when she was just a girl, but she could still remember his booming prayers and love-filled stares at Gram when he thought no one was looking. It was his love that had first given Raya the sense of something amiss between her parents.

Shaking her head and muttering in Creole, her grand-mother stood and started for the door. "Yes, I am a sinner, Aryanna. And so are you. And for sinners there is only one cure. A Savior. I have known for months of your choices. I forgave you immediately. It's time you forgave yourself." She pulled her robe closed and tightened the belt around her waist.

She patted the bed. "Now sleep well, my princess, and pray to your King. He longs for you with an everlasting love."

With that, she turned out the light, and Raya slid into the folds of the bright, white satin. Even in the dark she could see its brightness, like a blanket of fresh snow she'd seen once on a Brooklyn Christmas morning before any feet could spoil it. Clean. New. All the what-ifs of the past year assaulted her mind. What if she'd caught a disease? What if she'd gotten pregnant? What if—

I would have loved you anyway.

This time the hushed tones of her heart melted away Raya's questions, reducing her to a sobbing heap in a ball of white fabric. Something inside her broke, and she realized, as if for the first time, that she could never deserve God's love. Not if she'd stood pure in that white dress in June, and not now. She'd thought that if she was good enough long enough, the Lord would give her someone to love and someone to love her back.

Instead, he'd chosen to love her himself.

Fist in her teeth, Raya turned to the wall. "Thank you."

9

Flex's stomach growled like a tiger's.

"Okay, back there?" the cab driver asked, smoothing his full beard and looking into the rearview mirror.

"I'm okay. Just hungry."

Still distracted from his workout with Raya, he'd left his protein bars back at the gym. And now he was headed to see her again, under less pleasant circumstances. He mustered a smile for the driver, whose taxi had saved Flex's day many times before. Today, though, the fellow might be driving him to destruction.

I can't believe Megan pulled this.

She'd called just as he arrived at Man-O-Cure, asking him to meet her at Garments of Praise instead. She had an appointment with Raya, one she'd supposedly forgotten. No good could come of it, but what could he do? Besides being a paying client, Megan sent in one or two referrals a day. Only a few signed up for his services, but in the fitness business, a few made all the difference. Still, this was a bit much, and he planned to tell her so.

His stomach flipped as if searching for the expected nourishment. The six meals a day required to maintain his muscle mass and keep his body fat low was hard enough on a city schedule. Mix a beautiful woman in the evening with a crazy woman in the morning, and the result is one hungry man.

He'd counted on grabbing a protein shake at Man-O-Cure while chatting with Megan, but her last-minute change of plans left him rushing to the garment district in a cab. He'd had half a mind to forget the whole thing and keep his appointment for the "man power treatment" he so hated—manicure, facial, haircut, highlights, the works. He still didn't know why he had to look like a movie star to sweat with one, but so far every suggestion from Stan, his church friend at the desk, had hit the mark. Each treatment was followed by a surge in returning and new clientele.

Flex tried to tell himself his reason for agreeing to meet Megan was to reward her loyalty as a client, but it was the possibility that Megan's yearnings for Christ were sincere that made him put his own plans aside. What if his mother or Lyle had blown him off, too busy for his many questions over the past year? If there was even a chance, he had to try to help Megan, at least until Chenille was up and running or until he and Raya were close enough for him to suggest that she take over.

As the cab skidded to a stop, he recalled the tense words between him and Megan about his secret. Why did he feel a similar tension this morning, like he was entering an ambush?

"No weapon forged against you shall prevail."

The Scripture flew to his mind like fire. He'd spoken the verse to the church basketball team at practice the week before. He smiled at the thought of those eager-faced boys. He'd told them briefly of the new uniforms, but he'd held back on how great they would look. He planned to relish their joyous surprise.

"Here we are." The driver's voice tugged Flex's attention from the hunger seizing his middle.

"Thanks." Flex handed the driver a crisp bill, folded twice to hide its denomination. He hopped out before change could be given. He chuckled, listening to the horn blows forcing the cab on and the driver's shouts for him to return. Between his paying living expenses; buying the silly manicures, hair treatments, and clothes required to please his rich clients; giving to his church; and trying to plan his business, Flex's margins of excess were pretty slim. He always tried to give this man a nice tip though, even if it meant going without a meal later in the week. Wasn't that what protein bars were for?

The Chinese woman from his previous visit greeted him at the desk with a smile. What was her name? He'd talked to her about Beijing over the phone, laughing because he had been there and she never had. Li Li, her parents called her, she'd said. She had a more American name for herself.

"Good morning, Lily."

If his remembering her name pleased her, she showed no sign. Her smile remained a moment longer and then her eyes went back to the computer screen, where she stared at a difficult-looking pattern.

Flex rotated his head, trying to make sense of the pieces. It didn't look like any uniform he could think of. A choir robe, perhaps?

"She's there. Go on in," Lily said, nodding toward Raya's office.

Flex started for the back hall. The one condition of his meeting Megan here was that they meet before her appointment with Raya. But where was Megan now? Perhaps they'd started the meeting early for some reason. It wouldn't hurt to check . . .

Especially when you want to see her again.

He shoved his hands in his pockets and started for Raya's office. He did want to see her again, and that worried him. Today's workout should have been more than enough, but it wasn't. Even with the overwork and hours of crying that had played around her tired eyes, Raya had filled his sterile, orderly world with light and laughter. He hoped she would do the same today. But he doubted it. Megan had a way of putting a damper on things.

"Knock, knock." He tapped the file cabinet, surprised not to see Megan there. Raya showed no reaction to his entry, remaining hunched over her keyboard, typing furiously. Lines of concern creased her forehead.

Flex cleared his throat.

She jumped, almost smacking her head on a light clipped to her monitor. The joy in her eyes at the sight of him last night refused to appear now.

"What are you doing here?" She spoke slowly, as if weighing every word.

Whoa. He took one step back. "I'm here to meet Megan, actually." He checked his watch. It was 10:03. "Have you seen her? I missed an appointment to be here."

Raya's shoulders dropped. Her eyes looked as if they'd been covered with a coat of glaze. Something was definitely wrong. Flex pivoted slightly.

You know it, buddy. Run like the wind.

"Have a seat," Raya half whispered. "I'm sure Megan will be along soon."

He scratched his head, feeling his door of escape shut with every second her sad eyes stayed locked on him. He hesitated. Raya's melancholy glance flashed with anger.

He sat. This was weird. He'd managed to squeeze himself between Megan and Raya again. He laid his arm across the back of the chair, trying to relax the way he had during their first meeting. He shrugged off the lumps knotting his neck.

"What'd you think about the workout? Sore yet?" He sounded like an idiot.

"Great, and yes."

Like her co-worker at the front desk, Raya's eyes stayed fixed on the computer screen in front of her. This time Flex didn't crane his neck to see the monitor. Seeing her was task enough.

"Good. Glad you enjoyed it."

He considered giving some lame advice on the importance of hydration, but it sounded goofy even in his head. He gulped down the icy air filling the room, then stood. Megan was a valued customer and all, but she'd have to fend for herself on this one.

Raya blinked in his direction. It was enough. "Well, if Megan shows, tell her I came by, okay?"

The wheels of her office chair sped across the cement floor. Flex knelt and caught her just as she toppled out of the seat. He steadied her on one knee, trying to both ignore and memorize the warmth of her velvet skin.

"Be careful."

Raya nodded, leaping from Flex's touch as though it were able to sear her through. Flex tried not to take her reaction personally, but such actions didn't do much for a guy's confidence, especially a guy with half a can of mousse in his hair. How he longed to just let his hair alone and forget it. Like he was about to forget this. He stood again, then pivoted . . .

"Wait." Raya approached cautiously, thrusting a stack of deco-type drawings under his nose—wedding gown sketches.

Now she wanted to talk shop? I don't think so. "Nice. I'm sure she'll like one of them."

He hoped so, anyway. Too much longer on this project, and Raya might lose it totally. He wished he could offer some insight, but his metro-man image was only a façade. He was clueless when it came to such things. All the pictures looked the same to him. He turned to go.

Raya grabbed his wrist. "Which one? She didn't come, so I guess you can just pick and get the whole mess over with. She's already an hour late."

Flex straightened. "Me? Why would I pick Megan's dress?" It was all he could stand to pick her exercises.

The sweet-faced designer bit her lip. Then her nostrils flared. "Because you're the groom, stupid. Or are you going to play dumb about that too?"

"I'm the *what*?"

Jean poked her head inside with a scowl, but Raya waved her away.

"Is that what this is, some kind of prank?" Flex kicked a pile of wadded paper balls next to Raya's trash can.

She closed her eyes. Another beautiful day in the Big Apple.

Her legs gave way, and she dropped into the seat Flex had occupied minutes earlier. "You're not the groom, then? Just to be clear."

He narrowed his eyes to slits.

Raya nodded. "Okay, okay. I get it. Sorry."

"Humph." Flex rubbed that disarmingly cute fuzzy thing under his lip until Raya wondered if it would wear away. "You're not as sorry as she's going to be. Do you know what she used to get me here? God. She wanted to talk about God. Can you believe that?"

Raya's breath faltered as she recalled her talk with her

grandmother about God the night before. Could she believe that even someone twisted like Megan could have questions or be genuinely seeking God?

He died for that.

Absolutely. The same blood that was sufficient for her would work for Megan as well, if she chose to apply it. That was the part Raya had a harder time believing.

"Megan isn't all there. Just pray for her, that's all I can say." And it wasn't easy to think of, much less do, unless she thought of how she must look before a sinless God.

Filthy.

Only today, for the first time in a long time, she didn't feel filthy. She felt clean, like those ridiculous white sheets she slept on. Or at least she'd thought so until she laid eyes on Flex and her flesh came to life, betraying her determination not to be attracted to him.

As Flex turned to leave, a wide smile creased his mouth. "You were mad!" He lifted a finger at her. "You thought I was with Megan, and you were mad. You do like me!" He laughed like a raving schoolboy.

Raya stared at him, in both horror and fascination. "I do not! And I wasn't so much mad as confused. I thought you'd lied to me, and we're . . . we're . . ." Raya searched for the word every guy hated to hear. "We're friends, aren't we?"

Not best buddies or anything, but she thought it would fly. And it did fly. Right in the face of Flex's confident rejoicing. His lips pouted a little. "Yeah. Friends. Trying to be, anyway."

Raya forced a smile. Eleven more weeks, and she'd make sure never to see him, smell him, or endure his smoky charcoal eyes again. By the time she ran across him in the subway, he'd be married, following some Megan look-alike, and hugging her Prada bag to his chest. She gagged at the image.

"You should have known better though. I told you, I'm not marrying anybody." He shifted onto one leg.

"That you did."

He smiled weakly, staring at his surprisingly unmanicured fingers. Imagine that. Man hands. Megan, or whoever his rich dish really was, would be mortified.

"See you in the morning?" he asked on the way out.

And then there was that.

"Sure, Flex. See you in the morning."

Megan must hate us all.

She'd arrived unexpectedly three days later with no mention of Flex or the previous appointment. Too tired and sore to broach the subject, Raya could only watch as the bratty bride-to-be promptly discounted every one of the gown designs.

"Too short," she said, flipping through the pages like a child reading a picture book. "Too boxy." She held up another. "Cute, but lose the sleeves." She shook her head as she flipped through several more, then paused on the final one, leaving Raya's heart pounding.

"Nope. The waist is nice. Very clean. But what about my legs? I don't want a miniskirt, but have you seen my legs? They need to be able to see my calves at least."

At least.

Raya considered grabbing a bolt of satin from behind her and wrapping the fabric around Megan's knees and winding up to her head. Her mouth would be shut, and her legs would show.

Works for me.

But it wouldn't work for the firm. Or for Chenille. Everything was riding on this.

"I've noted your comments and hope to incorporate more

of your desires in the next set of designs. I will, however, have to invoice you for this set and the new sketches as well."

Megan shrugged. "Chenille has my information. Just get it right." Her voice sounded like a root canal during a rock concert. Loud and painful.

It took all of Raya's rediscovered faith to keep from hurling her shoe over the desk and between Megan's eyes.

Lord, help me. She is working my nerves like a banjo.

An idea pushed to the front of her mind. "That is our goal here, to get it right." She pressed the intercom. "Jean, do you have a moment?"

"For you, chica? Anything."

Raya chuckled at Megan's scornful reaction to her co-worker's endearing tone, and her own joy at being on the receiving end of it. Jean didn't call just anybody chica.

Sharing management duties in Chenille's absence, Raya, Lily, and Jean had shared quite a bit of latte and laughter in the past few weeks. Both women teased Raya kindly about her fateful ventures in the hallway with sewing tools. "Watch out for the slasher," Lily called playfully each time she emerged from the design room.

I hope we're still cool after this.

Jean appeared with a bright smile, which quickly soured at the sight of Megan. "I'm here," Jean said sternly. "Whattaya need?"

Raya strained to keep from laughing at the look on both Megan's and Jean's faces.

"Miss Arietta didn't find any of our designs to her liking. Take this, please?" Raya extended her bridal design portfolio from her last year at the Fashion Institute of Technology. Since Megan hated her new stuff, maybe she'd like the old.

Jean snatched the book, casting Raya a look that meant payback for sure.

"Let her look through that with you and discuss with her the best silhouettes for her body type. Let's do a first measurement and photo as well." Raya paused. "Please."

"No problem," Jean grumbled, heading out the door and showing just how big of a problem it really was.

Raya was already thinking of ways to pay her back. Without money, of course.

Megan remained across from her, with a stunned look. "I'm paying for you. Now I'm supposed to go with her?"

Jean ducked back inside. "Unless you're waiting for a limo, yes. Come on."

Jumping at the sound of Jean's drill-sergeant voice, Megan leaped to her feet and followed, casting a fearful look behind her as she shuffled out of the room.

Raya waited a few seconds and released a blast of laughter. Maybe they should have let Jean handle Megan from the beginning.

Hoping the day's events would get an elusive laugh out of Chenille, Raya made her daily call to her friend, trying to decide how much to share. Ringing echoed in the receiver before she'd made up her mind.

"Hello?" Lyle's voice sounded grim, a stark contrast to his usual optimism.

"Lyle? Is Chenille okay? You sound upset." Fear streaked Raya's voice.

Anguish stained his. "Chenille is fine. She's sleeping now, and someone from the church is here. I'm glad you called. I need to talk to you. Can you meet me at the church? Do you still have the directions we gave you?"

She didn't like the sound of this at all. "Sure. When do you want to get together? Tomorrow? I'm bringing dinner by—"

His voice cracked. "Now."

10

Raya clung to the desk in the children's annex of New Man Fellowship. Whatever had caused Lyle to call her here must be something impossible, something worse than what had happened already. And that she couldn't accept. Her parents' money had kept her from having many friends growing up. Chenille was one of the only people besides Gram who truly knew her, and now something else was going on with her friend. Something terrible. She could see it in Lyle's face.

"So what's going on?" Raya's breathing was as shallow as her hope that her misgivings were unfounded.

Her friend's husband swept a hand over his now totally bald head. She couldn't help but smile. Today he looked a lot more like that pudgy-faced boy back on the playground than anybody's husband. Even back then Raya had known they were perfect for each other.

Lyle stared at the door, then began. "First off, thanks for coming, Raya. As for my news—"

The door to the youth room swung open. Flex tumbled inside with a sports bag on his arm and a pair of sneakers in his hand. He froze at the sight of Raya, then extended a hand to Lyle. "Sorry, man. I came right over when I got your message. Had to come for practice anyway." They slapped hands. "What's up?"

She shook her head at the sight of him. Another problem. Tomorrow's workout would be interesting. For now, though, she needed to know what was going on.

Lyle hugged his friend. "I was just getting to that. Have a seat."

As if sensing the seriousness of the meeting, Flex slid silently into a desk beside her.

Lyle's face calmed. "As I was saying to Raya—and I think that's the best thing to do, just say it—the news is bad, but it isn't about Chenille."

Raya raised an eyebrow. Flex clenched both fists.

"It's about me." Lyle took a breath.

On instinct, Raya clutched Flex's hand for comfort as she felt the anguish of the hospital all over again.

Lord, they just lost a baby.

Strong fingers laced through hers. Flex's jaw tightened.

"It's stomach cancer. It doesn't look good."

A dreadful silence gnawed at Raya's mind. She tried to pull her hand away from Flex's grip, but he pulled her closer, tucking her arm under his.

He pummeled the desk with his other fist. "No. No!" His eyes blazed. "There has to be something we can do. Can't we fight it?"

Raya listened in a stupor as questions rifled through her mind like bullets. How could this happen? Why? She pried her hand from Flex's firm but gentle grip. Chenille was teetering on the edge as it was. How would she survive this? Bible verses sprouted in her mind like flowers, but she refused to pluck even one. There would be time for pat answers and cookbook prayers, but that time wasn't now. Now she was angry.

Lord, I don't understand. There's no way I can make her understand either.

Lyle grabbed both of their hands. "I called you here because I need you. And Chenille needs you. No matter how this fight comes out, I'm going to need your prayers, both together and separately, starting with tonight around nine when I break the news." He looked away. "She won't take it well."

Raya wiped her eyes. Who would? Raya and Lyle didn't say much besides casual greetings and holiday hugs, but the thought of life without him was too much for her, let alone his wife, to bear.

"Is any one of you sick? He should call the elders of the church to pray over him . . ."

She ignored the thought. Hadn't she prayed for their baby too? Raya shook her head. Her struggling faith had taken one blow already. Could it withstand this too?

Lyle eyed her cautiously. "If you two don't think you're up to this, I understand. Totally."

"We are." Flex answered crisply, casting her a sideways glance. "I mean, I am."

"Me too." Embarrassed, she settled back in her chair. "Prayer. Support. Food. I can even move in if it comes to that." She chuckled, but Lyle didn't return the humor. His eyes told her that it might come to exactly that.

He sighed with relief. "Thank you both. This is all a shock to me too. They had suspicions, but I didn't want to worry Chenille, her being pregnant and all." His lip trembled. "I got the call today. Both your names came to mind immediately."

Flex rose and went to comfort his friend. "If you want me to come with you tonight—"

Lyle shook his head. "No. This is just between us. Prayer is what we need. I wanted to get something in place before I talk to her. I'd appreciate it if you keep it quiet for now." He looked at Raya. "She hates pity, you know."

Raya nodded, sniffing. She and Chenille had that in common.

Silence blanketed the room like a fine mist, the raw grief robbing them of words.

Head resting on her fingertips, Raya watched as Flex placed a hand on his friend's shoulder. The eyes of both men closed in silent prayer.

This was quite different from the shouting, hands-laying-on prayer service where her grandmother had announced she had two pea-sized brain tumors. Each spring the ladies from the building celebrated Gram's health and prayed for another year of cancer-free living.

These guys exuded the same power without a word. How would Chenille react? Raya remembered her friend's stony face when baby Nathan emerged blue and still. *She won't cry*, Raya thought. *But she needs to. God, how she needs to.*

God himself would have to hold her up with his mighty hand, keep her from falling. Raya knew all too well how easy it was for trouble to derail a believer, even a strong one. She'd suffered enough at her own hands, let alone arbitrary trials. She sucked back a breath, realizing what she'd just thought.

Arbitrary? Didn't God hold all within his grasp? Perhaps it was easier for her to believe he didn't than to try to understand why he seemed to let some lives slip between his fingers.

Just be there for her.

When she raised her head, both Flex and Lyle were staring. Lyle waved her over and gave her a quick hug. "I don't know his plans for me, Raya, but they're good plans. Don't doubt that." He flicked away a tear. "He even let me see my son."

Raya opened her mouth to speak, but no words would come. Lyle's gratitude and praise splintered her anger and doubt. She didn't understand any of this, but Lyle was right. God was good.

Even now.

Flex patted Lyle's shoulder but said no more. Peals of laughter sounded outside the door, followed by knocking worthy of New York's Finest.

"Coach, you in there? Practice started ten minutes ago."

Flex banged back against the wall. "The boys—"

He shuffled forward, but Raya beat him to the door, eager to see the kids she'd imagined wearing the bright uniforms back in her office. She realized too that she was looking for something to lift the sadness in her heart. She was eager to forget Lyle's news, even for a moment. But nothing could have prepared her for what she saw on the other side of the door.

Jay Andrews, whose happy smile peered down at her from her monitor each morning, stood frowning at her, his too-big shorts riding below his waistline. Unthinking, she reached out to hug him, but he batted her hand away, anger seething in his eyes.

"Watch it, lady!" He hunched farther into his Knicks jersey as his peers broke out into laughter.

"Look at Jay. He's found himself a new mama."

Raya pulled her hands to her sides, feeling the heat of Flex's gaze on her. He stepped forward.

"This is Miss Joseph, guys. She's designing that cool uniform I told you about."

The laughter hushed as they eyed Raya with admiration. All except Jay, whose frown had turned into a scowl. "I

119

hope the uniforms turn out, then." He snatched a ball from a cornrowed boy next to him. "'Cause she's messed up."

Raya didn't know whether to laugh at the kid or slap him. For the past fifteen minutes, through passing drills where no one caught the ball and dribbling exercises that looked more like a geriatric soccer competition than a team maneuver, Jay had been making faces at her—rolling his eyes, grimacing in disgust, and anything else he could think up.

I'm the one who should be making faces. He plays worse than all of them.

Raya settled down on the sideline, reminding herself that she was the adult. Why, then, did she feel so angry? Was it the aftermath of Lyle's terrible announcement or her disappointment that Jay wasn't the sweet-faced little boy from the photo?

Jay cut his eyes at her before squaring up and shooting another wild shot that boomeranged across the gym. No matter how wide he smiled for pictures, this boy was still hurting.

"Stop! Come on, guys, I know you can do better than that." Flex winced at the sight of their aimless wanderings around the half-court on what should have been a basic play. "Let's try it again."

At first he'd seemed restrained by Raya's presence, but now his frustration diminished any previous inhibition. When the boys botched the play a second time, Flex kicked the ball down the court. "Aren't you guys listening? Come on. You're better than this."

No they're not. And neither are you.

Raya stood, knowing it was Lyle's cancer Flex had kicked, along with the realization that although he had skills and know-how, he wasn't as prepared to deal with this group of project boys as he'd thought.

She looked down at her tank top and knee-length skirt and her midheeled loafers. Both gave enough comfort to move.

She approached Flex. "Give me the ball."

The whistle dropped from his lips. "Not now." The words were strained.

"Yes, now." She snatched the ball, not waiting for his reaction before holding it over her head. "Aiighht. Y'all been getting over on Coach. Let's see what you can do with me. Line up." She narrowed her eyes at Jay. "You first. Right here, in front."

The boy looked at Flex. "You've got to be kidding."

The coach blew the whistle. "You heard her. Line up!"

After a chorus of teenaged complaints, the boys made the line.

Raya nodded, still holding the ball in the air. "When I slap the ball, you break."

They stared at her, uncomprehending.

"Don't play me, okay? Break. Like on the playground. I got five dollars for whoever can take this ball from me." She smiled at Jay. "And no fouling."

Metal scraped as Flex took her chair. His eyes lit with hope for the first time this afternoon. "That's right. And don't hurt her."

"Hurt me? Please. I'm worried about hurting them." She jerked around. "Break!"

The boys scattered like fallen leaves. Raya dribbled between her knees and behind her back. Jay ran toward her with determination. She paused to lure him, and just as he dived for her, she shook him with a quick pivot and cut toward the basket. Aiming toward the box on the backboard and lifting off with one foot, she leaped into the shot and hit the ground as the ball fell through the hoop.

The laughing, complaining boys peeled themselves off the gym floor and started toward her, murmuring in various dialects of court slang.

Jay leaped to his feet. "Again. We'll get you this time."

"Yeah, guys get her this time." Flex waved a five-dollar bill of his own from where he now stood, surprised and smiling on the sideline.

Raya chuckled. Flex wasn't so different from the boys. Neither knew how to lose.

"Okay. I'll give you another chance, but we've got to even things up. There's too many of you and one of me. I need four players on my team."

"Not me," Jay grumbled under his breath.

Definitely you.

"Let's see. Mr. Mouth here." She pointed to Jay. "You, you, you, and . . ." She paused, smiling at a tall, plump boy hiding behind a few of his friends. "And you. Yes, you, right there." He'd make a great center if she could get him moving.

"Aw, man . . ."

Flex clapped his hands. "Is that any way to act? Come on, guys. Hands up. Look alive."

Nodding earnestly, the team fanned out, raising hands lagging during previous drills. Their eyes blazed as she threw the ball into Jay's hands. Flex watched in amazement as the boy snatched the ball and paced across the half-court line.

Raya jogged behind the boys, shouting out encouragement and direction. "Block him out," she called to a wiry boy settled in at the forward spot. "Move out of the middle," she encouraged the heavyset center who'd set up camp in the middle of the floor. The ball made the rounds, finally releasing from Jay's hands and into the basket.

Jay pumped his fist and ran back downcourt, his hands flailing up for defense like a brown flag of victory. "Come on, Miss Raya! Get your hands up. That's the first basket I made all year. We're going to beat these fools."

She picked up her pace at his command, forcing a serious look to her face. Fools? They'd work on that later. "You got it, partner."

As she backpedaled to guard the six-foot eighth grader rumbling toward her, Raya caught a glimpse of Flex.

"Thank you," he mouthed.

She nodded and turned to catch a rebound. She couldn't please Megan or her mother, bring back Chenille's baby, cure Lyle, or erase her own past, but teach a few stubborn boys how to play roundball?

That she could do.

11

"Hey! What are you doing?" Flex ran from the locker room to the weight bench where Raya lay alone, without a spotter, pressing ten pounds more than usual. Though he had to admit that she seemed to be able to add weight quickly, this wasn't safe.

"I'm working . . . out," she managed between gasps, pressing up the shaky bar with all her might.

Flex jumped onto the spotting stand and thrust himself over, catching the bar just as it broke from Raya's grip and plummeted toward her face. The coarse metal scraped his gloveless hands. Blood threaded down his forearm as he clanged the bar into place.

The cut hurt a little, but the thought of what might have happened hurt him more. Why did she always have to go against everything he said? No wonder she got along so well with the boys from the church—she was just like them. Hard-headed.

Raya's hand smoothed over his, wrapping his knuckles in a towel. "I'm so sorry. Really."

Though he wanted to give her a lecture about equipment safety, the squeak in her voice made him want to laugh instead. What was he going to do with this woman who drew blood from him one minute and a chuckle the next? She could keep a guy in stitches—literally. He pulled the towel to his chest and fought against the smile forming on his mouth. He lost.

"You could have been seriously injured. Not to mention you'll be wiped out for the rest of the workout. What's with the Ms. Olympia bit?"

Raya looked at her feet, her auburn cornrows shining in the morning light. Flex tipped his chin down to survey the new hairstyle, an intricate design of braided swirls, leading up into an afro puff. How did she do that? Reinvent herself every week. Maintaining the rich-guy image was killing him, but Raya seemed to switch her appearance like breathing, with each look more fetching than the last.

"It was the boys, I guess." She looked up with a cautious smile, her eyes squinting. Did she still think he was mad? "Practicing with them those few times really got me going. More than my sessions with you, I'm afraid. Not that you're not good or anything—"

"Right." He crossed his arms. She always made her insults sound so endearing.

"It's just that working out with them means something, you know? It's not about being pretty or anything. It's about being strong and smart and . . . and . . ."

He leaned against the bench press. "Caring about somebody?" Why did that come out so softly? He cleared his throat.

Raya sat back down on the bench. "Exactly. Caring about somebody."

In the pause that followed, Flex was sure they were both

thinking about the same somebodies—Chenille and Lyle. He'd talked with Lyle every day since that meeting at the church, and the prognosis remained grim. Flex knew that praying was the most powerful thing he could do in his own strength, but still he felt helpless, as though there was something more he could do.

Even with work, church, the basketball team, and all the appointments in between, he'd almost gone crazy considering the possibilities. He sighed, realizing Raya's feat this morning was a product of the same frustration. He sat beside her. "How's Chenille taking it?"

Raya's chin sagged. "She's not taking it. She's in total denial. Says we don't understand. Don't believe. God has healed him, and that's that. She won't hear anything else. I don't want to hear anything else myself."

His heart thudded in his ears. Hadn't he reacted the same way when his father revealed the true nature of his parents' relationship—a business deal rewarding his mother with twenty-one years of wealth and him with the task of asking his father for every dime he needed? Flex took one of Raya's long, slim fingers.

"I hope Chenille is right. I pray she is."

Raya sighed, then pulled away. "I hope she's right too."

A short guy in a blue bodysuit leaned over the spotting stand. "Sorry to interrupt you two lovebirds, but some of us want to work out." He frowned at Flex in jest and then broke into laughter with another man, tall but corded with muscle.

Flex's bicep vein pulsed as he led Raya to the warm-up area. She'd most likely skipped her warm-up again today. He'd long since stopped trying to defend his relationship with Raya to this early-morning crowd. There was no point trying to reason with those guys once they got something in their heads.

Especially when it's true.

He jumped on the treadmill next to Raya's elliptical machine and clicked on the Christian music option he'd talked the owner into installing. Flex had purchased the initial CDs, but now there was both a Christian radio station and a growing CD collection. People seemed to love the new choices. He clamped on the headphones and dived into Donny McClurkin's *Live in London,* skipping right to "Victory Chant."

Flex ran on, forgetting Raya's presence as the worship cradled him, drew him in. When the conveyor slowed to indicate the end of his run and he yanked off the headphones, he heard his own voice singing the refrain. "Hail, Jesus, you're my King—" Realizing his volume, Flex's eyes darted around the gym.

"Was I that loud the whole time?"

She winked at him. "Louder. I enjoyed it though. You have a nice voice."

Flex swallowed. She did things like that arbitrarily—a wink or an arch of her silky eyebrows—things that made him want to drop to his knees for a proposal. Crazy things. "Yeah, well, I'll let you sing next time."

She shrugged and took off for the shoulder press, the first in a series of exercises for the chest, shoulders, and back, all of which showed diamonds and circles of fresh muscle through her dark velvet skin.

Cut it out.

Flex tossed the thought away, wandering back to the problem he'd had when he'd left home this morning. A problem he'd need Raya's help with. He watched as she slipped the pin into place. Forty pounds. She was pulling out the stops everywhere. Especially his heart.

Raya let the weight click on the final rep. Her body screamed in response to the increased weight on all her exercises. Though sweat poured off her, she'd needed something to distract her today. Flex's every move twisted like a knife in her heart. Their grief-stricken kiss at the hospital still haunted her, always swimming on the edge of her thoughts. And worst of all, she needed to ask him something and didn't know how.

Maybe I should just forget the whole thing.

She slung a fresh towel over her shoulder, trying to forget the bloodied one somewhere in the trash. For health reasons, any Heavenly Bodies laundry with blood had to be disposed of. AIDS. She sighed at the memory of a worse risk, one she'd taken. She'd never be that foolish again. Not with—or for—anybody. She was back on track with God, with her family, and even with that scraggly bunch of little boys worming their way into her heart. She couldn't let her feelings for Flex derail her. Whoever that fool back in LA had been, Raya never wanted to be her again.

Determined to be more careful with both her words and her feelings, Raya headed back to the elliptical for a five-minute cooldown. When Flex plopped down on the bike on the other side of her, she stared straight ahead, trying and failing to ignore his thighs cycling in and out of view. She averted her gaze to the treadmill on her other side, where an elderly man with kind eyes eased up the incline. Still, Flex remained fixed in her thoughts as the broken notes he'd sung earlier wafted back to her. She'd been truthful about his voice, clear and rich with plenty of carry. It was the brokenness in the tone that had surprised her, a brokenness she heard at night in her own voice. The catch in his throat said more than a million words and made Flex even more attractive—if that were possible.

You're falling for the guy, just face it.

She couldn't face it. She wouldn't. Every man she'd ever known, from her father to her almost husband, had abandoned her, left her behind. This was no time to go extending her heart. Chenille needed her. God wanted her. There wasn't room for anything else.

"I guess that's it," she said as the lights dimmed on the keypad in front of her.

Flex looked panicked. "I guess."

A blast of rock music strangled away the quiet. Raya stood and waved good-bye.

Flex grabbed her arm. She blinked, trying not to melt at his touch. There was no condolence in his eyes this time, only . . . what?

"Y—Yes?"

He inched closer, avoiding the music. "I need a favor," he shouted over the blaring chorus.

Realizing it was need she'd seen in his eyes and not desire, Raya braced herself, wondering which was more dangerous.

"How can I help?" She cupped her ear with a hand.

He put his bandaged hand around his mouth, creeping closer than she could handle. "I said, I need you—"

The song stopped suddenly, leaving his words hanging in the air. Silence crackled in the gym as everyone's eyes fastened on them. Flex bristled, but he didn't turn around.

"I need you to do me a favor."

With Flex this close, the only favor that crossed Raya's mind was kissing him until his lips fell off, and she doubted that was what he needed. She met eyes with his next appointment, a glamour girl who looked ready to meet any of Flex's needs.

"What is it?"

"The boys," he continued. "They've enjoyed working out with you these past few weeks. They—" Flex looked left, then right as if about to reveal an embarrassing secret. "They say they won't practice unless you come back."

A giggle escaped her lips. "You're kidding."

Flex snorted. "I wish I was. The little traitors. They won't do a thing for me. Jay went as far as to say he's not coming back unless you're there. Can you believe that? After how he treated you?"

She smiled, remembering Jay's initial reaction to her. He called her Miss Raya. They'd certainly come a long way, but how would she fit in the late practices with the boys, the early workouts with Flex, Megan's dress, the uniforms, being there for Chenille . . . And hadn't she decided to start back to church this Sunday?

"I'd be honored to practice with the team." The words were out before she thought it through. Her own need, though, the thing she needed to ask Flex for, pricked at her mind. "I'll do it on one condition."

Flex shook his head. "I knew that was too easy. What is it? A day off from the workouts? Letting you beat me in front of the boys?"

She frowned. *Letting* him beat her? He could be so arrogant sometimes. "No. Something for a mutual friend of ours. Megan."

Anger clouded his face. "No way. She only has three sessions left. I don't want anything else to do with her. She tried to—"

"What? Marry you? You should be flattered. It really doesn't matter what she did. The bottom line is I have to design a dress she wants and get the thing made. The firm needs the money, and I need this to be over." Her voice rose. "Now, can you help me or what?"

Flex slanted his eyes. "Hold it down, okay? What do you need me to do? Just tell me, Ray."

Ray. Her father's old nickname for her stopped her cold. She scanned Flex's eyes for a minute, finally realizing he had no idea what he'd said. She'd tell him later never to call her that again.

"Megan liked a few of the sketches, but she couldn't make up her mind. She invited her fiancé to pick, but—"

"But he never showed up. She's predictable, if anything. Or did the chauffeur show up in his place?" He leaned back into a stretch.

"The groom didn't show, but he did call. He's a doctor, evidently. Couldn't get away. He actually sounded legit."

Flex scratched the minibeard under his bottom lip. "Well, good for her. I'm glad she bagged somebody."

Was that anger in his eyes? Jealousy? Raya didn't want to know. She needed his cooperation and to get far, far away from this gym. "Anyway, Megan wants me to start over. I worked hard on those sketches, but she doesn't like any of them—"

He stiffened. "Why do I think my name is about to be mentioned here?"

Smart guy. "I asked her boyfriend's height, his weight, his tastes . . . He seemed a lot like you. I talked her into letting you pick a dress—"

He opened his mouth in disgust. "Aw, no, Raya. No way."

She smiled, squinting her eyes. "And told her you'd come to the formal shop to try to pick some matching tuxedos. You know, make sure everything coordinates and they have it in his size."

Flex braced himself against the wall next to the water fountain.

A bronzed beauty sporting an entire tube of lipstick on her frowning lips tapped him on the shoulder. "It's 7:09," she said in an agitated voice.

He didn't turn around. "I'm sorry. Go ahead and get on the treadmill. I'll be right with you."

Not that there was anything left to say. Flex's set jaw said it all. He wouldn't do it. She'd been a fool to ask. The only thing Flex cared about was himself. She was just another pet project for him. The boys too. She'd probably end up practicing with them anyway, but right now she needed to do what Flex was so good at—look out for number one.

"Well, looks like the deal's off. See you in the morning? Or is that off too?" Hmm . . . that came out snippier than she intended.

He grimaced. "Wait. I'll do it. I'll hate it, but I'll do it. Don't say I never came through for you." He spun and jogged to the treadmill before she could respond.

Raya paused for a drink of water from the fountain, watching him trot away. She could kick herself for making such a fuss. It was important, but more than that, she'd wanted, needed, him to come through for her. Again. Why hadn't she left things alone and used this whole thing as an escape? The truth, that she didn't really want an escape, bit into her mind. Already she was weakening, getting needy. Still, he'd come through.

So did you.

Also true. There were a lot of things Raya and Flex could say about each another, but neither could ever say that the other wasn't a good friend. Ironically, they'd been there for each other in the past month more than anyone else had.

"I know I'm going to regret this." Flex allowed the wind to push him along as Raya led him into the formal shop. He'd already spent an hour staring at drawings of dresses while Raya explained the differences in each. Long sleeves, strapless, wedding points, embroidery . . . just thinking about it all gave him a headache. How did Raya keep all that in her head?

And the drawings. Everything he'd seen from her up until now had been computer aided. Those images had blown him away too, though he hadn't let Raya know it. But these sketches of hers had a rhythm, a heart to them. The something that made her different from everyone else, the something he was starting to . . . love?

Yes, dummy, love.

There it was, out in the open. Love. Now what was he going to do about it? Go shopping, that's what. The last thing in the world Flex wanted to do. The last time he'd been dragged into a formal shop was for his own wedding, a farce planned by his mother to pair him off properly. Little had she known that the sweet Christian girl she'd picked out for him would be dead from AIDS three years later.

Raya smiled wide. "Don't look so glum about this, Flex. You'll regret this, of course, but with fond memory. Just hang in, we're almost done."

His heart melted at the sight of Raya's smile. Wedding shopping was the last thing he wanted to do with any woman, especially her. She was the first person who had made him give more than a fleeting thought to the idea. Her down-to-earth personality defied the fake relationships from his past. When he looked at her each morning, he dreaded the moment when their workouts would end. What would it be like to wake up to a woman like that every day, wondering whether she'd look like a runway model or a basketball star?

He'd help Raya today, then get through her workouts and the boys' basketball season, but that was it. He had a business to build, his mother to take care of. His father had made a fool of him long enough. Flex refused to go crawling back to him for money again. And once the business started, he'd have to devote every second to it. Failure wasn't an option. There was no use starting something with Raya that he couldn't finish.

No marriage. Ever.

It had been his mantra before coming to Christ, before he knew sex was designed for a husband and wife. Celibacy started off as a cramp in his style, then became the thorn in his flesh.

"Here we are."

The brightness of the beads, veils, shoes, and purses almost blinded him as they whisked past racks of gowns in every shade. "Red? Who would wear a red wedding dress?" He groaned. Some of the dresses were pretty at best, but none held the sparkle of Raya's designs.

"Some people might not feel comfortable in white. Ever think of that?"

Her sharp answer surprised him. He hadn't thought of that. What if guys had to wear white tuxedos? How many men would qualify? Certainly not Flex.

You are already clothed in white, my son.

He took a breath as he always did when God seemed to impress something upon his mind. The concept of hearing from heaven was a bit much, but he couldn't deny that sometimes God's voice rang out in his mind. This time, as always, he was grateful. Sometimes his guilt overshadowed God's grace.

"I see your point, Ray."

Raya paused as if she was about to say something but thought better of it. "Good. I called over a few choices in your size. Go over there and try them on. I'll pick a coordinating gown and see how we look together."

"Together?" He hadn't meant to say it so loud, much less make it sound like a root canal.

She stormed off toward one of the racks. "I know I'm not Megan or one of those Barbies you train, but this is no picnic for me either. Let's just get it over with."

Now you've done it.

"That's not what I meant."

And it wasn't. The thing that frightened him most about being dressed in wedding garb with Raya was that he'd run to the nearest church. Battling back his growing love was hard enough in street clothes.

"Just get dressed."

So he did, or at least he started to. With the salesman's help, he tied the bow tie, straightened the cummerbund, and was about to put on the straight black jacket when he caught his image in the mirror.

I look just like him.

Minus about thirty pounds and plus a head of hair, the image that stared back at Flex was one of his father preparing for yet another of his mother's charity dinners. Though he'd endured the functions and Angela's faith, Flex's father had always spent his dressing time, time when he looked like this, expressing his displeasure. "Always trying to save the world. She'd do better to save herself." As if on cue, he'd turn and stare at Flex. "If it weren't for you . . ."

The words came to Flex now as he ripped off the tie and yanked the shirt out of the tuxedo pants. He changed back into his own jeans and T-shirt, leaving the formal clothes in a heap. The salesman called after him. "Where's the tux? It looked so—"

Flex raised his hand, requesting the man's silence. He paced the bit of tile in front of the dressing room door, deciding whether to stay. What difference would it make if he left now?

You look like him, and now you're acting like him too?

Flex bounded back to the dressing room, edging around the attendant and picking the clothes up off the floor. "I've got it." He shoved the shirt on a hanger. "Sorry."

The man smiled. "Weddings can be stressful, especially for people as in love as the two of you." The man ran a hand through his gray hair as if remembering his own wedding day. "I think it's wonderful that she's letting you see the dress. Tradition is great, but you kids today put a spin on the rules."

Too stunned to speak, Flex managed a few words. "We're not—"

"Don't sweat it. Every man feels this way. You, me, and our fathers before us. It seems like it's a lot of fuss, just for the girls and all, but as time passes you'll be grateful for the memory."

"Right." There was no use arguing with the man, bent as he was on making Flex's imaginary marriage an event for old times' sake. He watched as the old guy puttered off with a knowing smile.

Why was it that everyone who saw him with Raya assumed they were together? Were his feelings for her that evident? Flex shrugged off the thought along with a passing thought of his parents, who'd never had a wedding day. Was there ever a time when Fletcher Longhurst II had loved the beautiful dancer he'd gotten pregnant on vacation? Or was Flex's entire life the lie his father made it out to be?

A knock sounded at the dressing room door. Probably the attendant with another story from his own trip to the altar.

"Come in." Flex dropped into the stuffed chair swallowing much of the room. No use being uncomfortable and unhappy.

Instead of the gray-headed storyteller, the door opened to reveal Raya wearing a dream in white with cupped sleeves and roses embroidered on the front. The skirt was covered with that gauzy stuff his mother put nuts in for parties . . . tulle. And it held a treat this time for sure. All the gowns had seemed identical on the hanger, but on Raya . . .

This one looked heavenly.

"Stunning."

It took all his restraint to keep from jumping from his chair and kissing her. What did they do, put some sort of love dust in the seams of those gowns? Love dust? If the salesman had walked up with a Bible and a ring, he'd have married her on the spot.

What am I thinking?

She cleared her throat and stepped forward, fingering the lopsided tuxedo on the hanger and then her gown. "You like it?"

"I love it." Did he say that out loud? Oh well. He stood and took her hands in his. Lost in the moment, he stepped closer. "The dress. I love the dress, I mean."

"Of course." She bit her lip in that cute way of hers. "I think she'll like it." She paused. "What happened with the tux?"

Flex felt his chest tighten. The walls seemed to close in. How could he explain how hard all this was for him, how it made him think of all the things he'd run from?

"The tux was fine. It's me. I can't do this. Coming here was a mistake."

He tried to squeeze past Raya to get out of the dressing room, but the train of her dress swallowed his feet. He fumbled forward, then stood. Dress picking was one thing. This was torture.

"Flex! Are you okay?"

He wasn't, and he'd never be again.

"I'm fine," he said, jerking open the store's front door and hobbling into the street. "Just fine."

12

She'd done it again. No matter how Raya tried to keep things simple, easy, something always went crazy. She squirmed through a cluster of dog walkers, surveying the address scrawled on a piece of paper. She'd gone by the gym to find Flex, to apologize, but he wasn't there. The guy at the desk, whose hair color changed more often than hers, had scribbled down his address. "Just stop by. He won't mind." Flex's friend had kept a straight face when he'd said it, but now Raya wondered if the joke wasn't on her.

It didn't matter. She pressed ahead, remembering the pain in Flex's eyes before he'd run from the formal shop. After seeing him in all those suits he showed up in periodically, she'd had a hard time deciding who was the real person—the manicured gentleman or the cotton-and-denim guy. His jeans and T-shirt self had won out today. And that wasn't all. Something about weddings, about marriage, had hurt him. Raya paused on the sidewalk, comparing the numbers on the buildings to the digits scribbled on the paper in her hand—4952. She was getting close, just a few more up.

She took a deep breath, steeling herself for whatever would come next. She wouldn't go inside, even if he offered. She'd decided that on the train. No matter how much she went on about not acting on her feelings for him, in person she seemed to fail the test.

On the next block, she found she'd crossed into a new area. A building something like Gram's but smaller and more melancholy loomed before her. She looked around to gather her bearings. Bushwick. Bushwick? She never would have guessed. The building number was the same, but what apartment? She unfolded the note completely and saw "3A" scrawled in the crease. *This is it.* Raya climbed the stairs quickly, then lost her nerve at the door.

She shoved her purse back on her shoulder and rapped lightly at first, then harder as the seconds ticked by. Finally she accepted he wasn't home, her relief mixed with disappointment. She fished in her purse for a pen and a piece of paper to write a note.

> Flex,
> Sorry about today. I didn't mean to upset you.
> Thanks for picking the gown, and for the
> compliment. See you at the gym.

She paused trying to figure how to sign it. "Sincerely" seemed too formal, but anything else seemed too casual. What had she told him that day at the gym? They were friends. It sounded seventh grade, but the whistle of September cold singing against her scalp and ears convinced her it was sufficient.

> Your friend,
> Raya

She folded the note and scribbled his name, then tucked it into the mailbox mounted next to the door. Her feet beat a hasty exit against the stairs as she fled, suddenly wishing she'd taped the note to the door so it could blow away.

"He's not here," a voice called behind her.

Raya turned to see a distinguished older woman in gray wool with a blunt bob and a strand of dime-sized pearls. Real ones. A Caribbean flavor, like her neighbor's jerk seasoning, peppered the woman's voice. A West Indian voice. Raya sifted through the dialects in her building, trying to place the lilting flow. A Spanish rhythm. Dominican, perhaps? Whatever the woman's ancestry, she looked too young to be his mother and too old to be a friend.

I'm an idiot.

"Thanks. I'll check with him later."

The woman crossed her arms, locking Raya in her gaze. What was that in her eyes? Jealousy? She moved onto the porch and down one of the front steps. A tight smile braced her mouth.

"He's a busy man. He doesn't have time to play," she said in a low tone. "I would just leave him alone, know what I mean?"

Raya forced her legs to move but gave a slight nod. She knew just what the woman meant. The tone—and the implication—were quite familiar. It was a rich woman's way of saying, "Get lost. You're not good enough," without spoiling her dinner. Only her mother could have said it better.

He wasn't prepared. Flex had spent much of the past month praying about his friend's illness, but as Lyle stood before the church to give an update on his condition, Flex's stomach lurched. Though Lyle was facing death, his face exuded the same hope and faith as on the day Flex had met him. And Flex had been wrecked by the sight of a wedding dress. Who was he fooling? No matter how many years he studied the Bible or attended church, he'd never be able to accept something like this with the peace his friend possessed. He was barely sure of his own salvation some days, especially since he'd stormed out on Raya in the formal shop. She hadn't been the same toward him since. Some mighty man of God he was turning out to be.

"Nothing new this week. Things are the same. In the natural, anyway. In the Spirit? Well, we need everyone to pray for us during this time, both for my healing and for our marriage." He kissed Chenille's cheek.

Chenille remained silent at her husband's side, but she clutched Lyle's hand at the mention of their union. Even in her pain, her strong faith showed through.

Flex's mother gasped next to him, as she did every time she mentioned the situation. "I just love those two. They were some of the first people who talked to me here. And their marriage—I mean, they're so open, just asking for prayer like that. I can't imagine."

"Lyle says that's their secret, keeping everything up front. Not letting things slide. I'm sure it might not work for everyone, but he swears that the little foxes spoil the vine."

His mother nodded. "He's right. So young to be so wise. Oh, Fletcher. I am so sorry for them. That young man has been so kind to you. We must pray for them more." She squeezed the clasp of her purse in determination. "We shall pray for him each morning. Early, okay?"

"I'm sort of doing that already . . . with a friend. Maybe in the evenings? Just pray for him whenever you think of it." He stalled, thinking of Raya, his prayer partner and 6:00 a.m. client. He'd doubted she would return to the gym after the way he'd acted at the bridal shop, but she had come. Part of her, anyway.

"Fine. Perhaps it doesn't have to be a time, just thinking of them, bringing them before God often." She smiled and turned away.

Music ebbed to a soft flow as the pastor called the congregation to the altar to pray. Lyle and Chenille remained in the midst of the crowd.

His mother, uncomfortable with the press of so many strangers, kept her seat but reached out for Flex's sleeve as he stepped into the aisle. "Pray for your father. He's hurting."

It was only respect for his mother that kept him from pulling his arm away. Instead, he nodded, knowing how hard it would be to pray for his father sincerely. So many times he'd forgiven that man only to allow his heart to fill with anger again.

Flex staggered forward in the crowd, thankful that they'd sat close to the front. As usual, New Man Fellowship was filled to capacity, though many more of this morning's churchgoers had come for the dinner after the service than the daily bread. The pastor didn't mind. "Many times the way to a man's spirit is through his empty stomach," he often said.

Flex smiled at the thought as he allowed a man in a tattered suit into the aisle. The compassion and generosity toward others that had drawn him to this church eased his grief at the sight of Lyle's drawn face.

As Flex reached the front, different people took turns praying into the microphone. He didn't recognize any of them from his old cell group, the children's ministry, or the other programs he'd worked in before life got too busy. He listened intently as people blessed his friends and offered up requests for physical and emotional healing of their own families. After a brief pause, there was another prayer, one that stole his breath.

"Father God, I place the Rizzos in your hand, knowing that your grasp is sure and your grip faithful. I thank you for the time I spent with their son, Nathan, and for their friendship." The voice, Raya's voice, trembled.

Flex pressed his lips together and followed the voice until he spied her across the room, like a ruby on a sea of sandy suits and dresses. Her eyes met his.

"Most of all though, Lord, I pray for those like me, who have families, mothers, fathers, and have taken the relationship for granted. Turn back the hearts of the fathers to their children and the love of mothers to their little ones. Life is short and precious. May we not waste one second hurting one another instead of loving. The time cannot be given back."

The microphone thudded as she passed it to the next person, but no one else spoke. A hush fell over the sanctuary as the pastor retrieved the mic and whispered the Lord's Prayer. Flex kept his eyes on Raya, but she never turned his way. He focused on her words instead, digesting the truth of them. Regardless of the horrible things his father had done and said, he too needed forgiveness.

"And when you stand praying, if you hold anything against anyone, forgive him, so that your Father in heaven may forgive you . . ."

Whispered prayers danced around Flex's head as he yielded his anger toward his father. His knees buckled, and he let them cave, holding on to the pew beside him. Like the many others on their knees and faces in the cramped space, he cried out to God as though he were alone.

"Father, forgive me. For I too have sinned."

After a blur of time, Flex rose and returned to his seat,

turning back periodically in search of the sparkling beauty with doe eyes and burgundy hair.

She was nowhere to be found.

He squeezed in next to his mother, whose eyes were red and wet with tears.

"I need to tell you something," she said, taking his hand.

Not now. He'd just cleaned his hands, his heart. "Whatever it is, don't worry about it." He took her hand but steadied his gaze on the cross at the front of the sanctuary. Whatever his mother had to say would have to go down front with the rest of the stuff he'd just dropped there. "Whatever it is, he'll take care of it."

He hoped so, anyway.

"I hate it."

Raya stared first at Chenille and then at Megan, who held the design Flex had picked an inch or two from her face.

"You're kidding, right?" Raya felt the strength ooze out of her.

Megan turned to Chenille, pointing out the roses embroidered across the dress's tunic. "What are those dots in between? They look like bird poop."

Chenille, back to work for the first day in weeks, cradled her face in her hand, her elbow propped on the corner of the table. She smiled. "They're sequins."

"That's what I thought." She shook her head. "What am I, a Vegas showgirl? I'm getting married for goodness' sake."

Raya's mouth dropped open as she suddenly realized what Megan was saying. Did this miniskirt maven want a conservative dress, traditional in every way? It sure sounded like it.

"So let me get this straight. No sequins or fitted skirts?

You liked both in the first set." She shuffled for the set of prior sketches.

Megan shrugged, sitting back into the chair. "The doctor —the guy I'm marrying—his mother is a bit old-fashioned. Traditional. And the more I think about it, I want that too."

She reached in her purse for a check and handed it to Chenille. "Here's the installment on the first sketches." She paused, lowering her voice. "I'm glad to see you back." She looked back and forth between Raya and Chenille as if searching for something. Probably looking for Jean.

"Well, I still have the measurements and consult you did with our, um, specialist last time. I'll change the design aspects you indicated to something more conservative. What about the roses? Do those go too?"

"No. I want the roses somewhere in the concept. I sort of have a thing for them . . ."

Her thoughts wandering from the meeting room, Raya's mind fixed on the woman that day at Flex's house. From her perch in the balcony, she'd seen the same woman with him at church. Their embrace had chased away the last of her suspicions. She'd considered asking Lyle, even Chenille, to be sure, but it was obvious from her friend's pain-stricken face that such things weren't a priority right now. For all Chenille's bubbly matchmaking before, she hadn't asked Raya about Flex, or anything else, since returning to work.

Chenille steepled her fingers. "Well, Megan, we're certainly glad to have your business, but I have to ask at this point if this is the best route for you. You seem to be somewhat unsure of what you want—"

"I want her." She slipped back in her chair and pointed at Raya. "We've just been miscommunicating is all."

At least somebody wanted her. The wrong somebody, but somebody all the same.

"I see." Chenille looked through the two previous sets of designs again. "There are many beautiful concepts here, and I see from the notes that they were all designed according to specifications you gave. As much as I appreciate your business, we may need to lay down some guidelines here. Just how long do you expect this part of the process to take? We'll need to make a prototype—"

Megan turned to Raya. "His mother is coming in three weeks. I'll need a sketch by then. Can you do it?"

Chenille's need transmitted across the desk in her steady, somber gaze. She'd lost enough already and was fighting for her husband's life. She couldn't lose her business too.

Raya took a deep breath. "Sure, Megan. It'll be done. I'll give you a call." Right after she pulled off the prototype for the team uniforms, rescheduled the doctor's appointments she'd canceled to get these sketches done, and finished all the other work she'd set aside in the past few weeks. Sure, she'd get it done.

Megan's corkscrew curls bobbed like an accordion as she rose. "I know this is a bit out of element for both of you. Thanks for trying so hard. You'll get it." She turned to Raya with an icy smile. "I know you will."

Raya didn't smile back, choosing a short prayer instead. Hadn't Flex said Megan wanted to talk about the Bible? Other times too, in college, she'd seemed receptive as they'd spent long nights talking about guys . . . and God. Even with all Megan's tricks, a part of her seemed to want to know God, to love and be loved by him. The last time they'd discussed it, a week before Raya's wedding, Megan had turned away, her eyes wet with tears. Like King Festus speaking to the apostle Paul, Megan had tugged her heart away as it raced toward Jesus. "Girl, be quiet," she'd said. "You almost make me want to be a Christian. To give up everything." Maybe through all this ugliness, some good could still come.

A smile eased across Raya's face. It was good to be back to her old self, even if she might lose it ten minutes from now. Even if she couldn't have the most wonderful man she'd ever met. As painful as it was to see Flex with his sugar mama, or whoever she was, it was wonderful to be in with other Christians again, to let the worship blow through her, to pray, to be able to let comments like Megan's slide off instead of cutting through her.

It was good to be back.

"Lord willing, Megan, I'll get this right." She stood and pushed in her chair. "Pray for me, will you?"

He couldn't fight it anymore. Tapping the numbers with his freshly manicured fingers, Flex did something he thought he'd never do again—call his father. Though he'd tried to get away from it, Raya's heartfelt prayer and the cry of his own heart had led him to try to restart the communication between the two of them. He gripped the receiver, hoping Fletcher Longhurst II would be too busy to answer as he'd always been before.

"Hello?"

Flex stared at the phone, surprised at the lingering sadness in his father's tone. "Dad?" His heart skipped a beat. What would he say now? All the things he'd planned to say—I love you, I forgive you, I'm sorry—seemed to melt away at the sound of his father's voice. "Hey. How's it going?"

"Not well for you, I presume, or you wouldn't be calling." His father's voice changed in tone, echoing the superiority Flex remembered so well. "How much and what for? I knew you'd run out of money again."

Flex swallowed back the anger pooling in his throat. Why did it always have to come to this? And to think he'd actually considered telling his father about the team, even thought of asking him to sponsor the boys' uniforms. His mother seemed so sure his father was hurting, that he'd changed, but Flex heard the same obnoxious gloating in his voice.

"No, Dad. I haven't run out of money." *Yet.* "I called because Mom seemed to think I should, that you were lonely—"

"Is that Angela?" A woman whispered in the background just loudly enough for Flex to hear. He recognized the voice immediately. One of his mother's freshly divorced friends.

"You're really something, Dad."

"Wait, son. It's not what you think! Earline was praying with me." The cocky arrogance drained from his father's speech and was replaced with an urgent repentance. But it came too late. "Don't tell your mother. You've got to believe—"

Click. Flex placed the receiver back on the base and banged his fist on the kitchen table, thankful that his mother had gone out for a run. He dropped into a chair at the table, grabbed a banana, and devoured it in a few bites. Miss Earline had met with his mother for Bible study as long as he could remember. How could she? And even worse, how could his father? And praying together? What a lame excuse. Why did everybody have to blame everything on God?

The same reason you do.

The thought drew him up short. What was that supposed to mean? Sure, he'd kept himself from expressing his feelings to Raya because he needed to build his business, but it was spiritual too. Though he'd come a long way in the past year and grown closer to Christ, he wasn't husband material. And the Bible made it clear—sex was meant for marriage. Flex knew all too well that the feelings he felt around Raya, the way his blood had boiled when he'd kissed her . . . where all that could lead. It was bad enough that he had his past to deal with. He couldn't risk hurting Raya too. Hurting himself.

"To him who is able to keep you from falling . . ."

He sighed as the verse copied onto a card in his pocket marched through his mind. For a while God had seemed to totally ease his weakness to temptation, even in the gym. Then he'd met Raya. From the first day of their workouts together, he'd carried Bible verses in his pockets, even in the bottoms of his shoes. Now none of it helped much.

Even his father's disrespect couldn't push Raya out of his mind. Not that the older Fletcher was off target about his son's finances. With the last chunk of cash he'd been allotted spent on living expenses, Flex had little to show for his move to New York—except his compounding feelings for Raya Joseph—an investment he never meant to make.

13

Thursdays had become his favorite days. Raya didn't make every practice now, and the boys were okay with that. But she always came on Thursdays. And although she'd canceled yet another uniform consultation with him, she'd assured Flex that today she'd bring the prototype for the uniforms. She'd sounded a little gruff though, so he wasn't sure what to expect. He'd grown used to her aversion to him, but anything to do with the kids usually cheered her up.

"She's here!" Jay waved to Raya from the window where he'd been posted as sentry.

Flex followed, smiling at the boys' eagerness . . . and trying to hide his own.

"Does she have it?"

"I think so. Must be in that bag."

"Ooh-wee, those rich kids we played over the summer won't have anything to say about us this year. They won't be able to touch us."

Raya made it to the door but no farther as twenty pairs of expectant hands reached toward her.

"Get back, guys. Let her in." Flex sliced through the little group and escorted Raya in with a wave of his hand, a hand that wanted desperately to run its fingers through her copper afro, down the arm of her patchwork leather jacket . . .

Stop it, man.

"So you got it done, huh? What'd you end up changing? To get the price down, I mean."

She took Jay's hand and started for the bleachers. They creaked as she sat. The boys crowded around. "About that," she said. "I wasn't able to pull that off, exactly." She shrugged, then unzipped the garment bag slung across her lap.

As Flex's mind raced in confusion, trying to figure out what Raya meant, the boys' eyes lit up like Times Square on Christmas.

"It's the bomb." Jay got to it first, lifting the silky blue jersey for all to see the flame burning up one side. "New Man" was in the center, with the number 01 below it.

She'd definitely changed the design, but it seemed just as spectacular. And expensive. What had she meant by not pulling off the discount exactly?

"Turn it over, man. Let's see the back."

Jay flipped the jersey over and stared at his own name, while the others complained at the sight of "Andrews" spelled out in gold on the back.

"Aw, man. No fair. You get the first one."

Jay beamed but looked sad for them as well. "It's cool, right, Miss Raya? You'll bring them one too next time?" He leaned over and whispered to her. "Thank you, but take this back until they get theirs. I wouldn't want anybody to feel bad."

Flex smiled as he overheard. Jay and Raya had formed a special bond, one he'd envied as recently as last week. But now being close to Raya wasn't his concern. What had she done? These kids couldn't afford these uniforms, and neither could he, not before the season started. He fingered the invoice in his pocket. A thousand dollars. Mother used to spend that much on a luncheon.

Raya spoke softly. "I'm going to hold on to this one until everyone has paid for theirs—"

Jay reached down, pulled a twenty from his sock, and thrust it forward. "I got mine. And legit too. Been carrying groceries and cleaning off stoops. I even watched somebody's baby. Changed a diaper and everything."

Flex felt his chest squeeze, both at the thought of Jay watching someone's child and at the boy's determination. How could he let the kid down easy? He stared down at his smooth hands, then clapped them together, revolted at the sight of his own skin. All the money he'd spent on stupid manicures and treatments could have made these kids' dreams come true.

"Hold on to that partner. It seems the uniforms are going to be a little more than that—"

"But you said . . ." Jay's wall of protection rose like a shield around a spaceship. "How much more?" he asked Raya.

"Thirty dollars more, I'm afraid." She looked stricken, as though the reality of what this meant to the team had finally sunk in. Her eyes narrowed at Flex.

Is she mad at me? She's the one who did this.

Jay's hands hung at his sides. He shook his head. "I knew it was too easy."

The other boys followed as he climbed out of the bleachers.

"Wait, guys! We're still having practice. We'll get the uniform thing figured out." Flex pleaded with them, all the while trying to figure out where he could get the money.

His father was out of the question. His mother had saved money over the years but had given it all away long before now. His last check from his father had gone straight to the mortgage company as a down payment for the new place. Maybe if it fell through in the next few weeks . . .

"You just don't get it, chief. There won't be any more practices. We've got to go make some money." The pudgy center held up both hands in defiance, his eyes desperate.

Flex glared at Raya. How could she have done this, destroyed everything he'd tried to build with these kids all in one day? Wasn't it bad enough she was destroying him?

"No, son. You need to stay here. It may not be in time for the first game, but I'll find a way to get the uniforms—"

"That's what you said all summer." The boy waved him off. "Underneath all that fancy talk and nice clothes, you just like us. Nothing. We can't let those rich kids disrespect us again. You wouldn't understand." The boy paused, then turned to Raya. "And you should have understood. We out."

Raya ran behind them. "I'm sorry." She looked at Flex, again with anger in her eyes. "We'll . . . I'll get the money. Just come back."

The boys kept walking.

"Jay!" She kept after them, reaching for the boy's shoulder.

He brushed her hand away and never looked back. He'd made his crew believe in her, and she'd let them down. For twenty boys with single moms, grandmothers, or two struggling parents, the thousand dollars that evidently seemed so little to Raya after pondering Megan's million every day was a thousand too much.

She let her hand fall away and stood still, her face so different from the gorgeous grin she'd worn when unveiling the surprise. Had she thought Flex was kidding, that he had the money and just didn't want to pay? Why would she put him in this spot with the kids and then act like it was his fault? He took a deep breath. Maybe he'd been wrong about her after all.

Maybe he'd been wrong about everything.

Toe food. It was her grandmother's description of tofu, the choice item on Raya's current menu, besides a large serving of steamed crow. She should have known when Flex remained silent as the boys cheered that the extra money really did make a difference—just like he'd said it would. Had she just assumed from his coiffed hair and manicured hands that Flex would be able to foot the bill?

Not unlike her father, Flex reminded her that just because someone had money didn't mean anybody else was getting any of it. The gear and maintenance were probably just gifts from his woman friend anyway. The horror on his face at the practice made her wonder if he had a dime.

She swallowed and moved on to the next aisle in the uptown bath and body shop where she'd come to browse. As she rifled through the fragrances, the men's section caught her eye, and she realized she'd subconsciously come here because of Flex.

"One of my clients got my fragrances for me when I was hurt. Now I'm hooked. A place uptown. Sweet Savour," he'd said.

Raya walked to the other side of the room and picked up a bottle with an olive and tan cap. Worshiper. She uncorked it but didn't lift it to her nose. She didn't need to.

It was him.

Lemon, sandalwood, vanilla—it was all there, sweeping over her in a flood of memory, bringing with its subtle notes images of early morning workouts when he'd positioned her hands correctly, jumped on the bench press to spot her

. . . Like a potion, Flex's scent begged to differ with all the things she'd convinced herself about him lately. Maybe she had him all wrong.

But that woman . . .

"May I help you?" A sleek saleswoman in a fitted suede skirt and peasant top appeared out of nowhere.

"I'm just looking . . . well, sniffing."

The woman smiled, revealing a cover-girl smile. "This one doesn't do well on everybody. But the ones who can wear it? Oh my." She held her hand to her mouth. "There's this guy at my gym—"

"I get the idea."

Raya returned the bottle to the rack and fled the store before the girl could say anything else. How could she have ever let herself feel anything for Flex? From the moment she'd seen him with Megan, and even before that on the train, she'd known what kind of man he was—too rich, too handsome, too much trouble. Hadn't the fiasco with Darrell taught her anything?

She stalled on the sidewalk, allowing October to whip around her, thrashing to an end. She couldn't, wouldn't, let the boys down, even if it meant asking her mother for the money. Those kids' hopes had been dashed enough.

She brought her hands to her face to warm them, inhaling the enticing smell instead. An image of Flex and all his selves: the suave style of the spiky-haired businessman, the casual cool of outstretched legs and an easy smile, and finally, the sweaty intensity of his tousled curls and bulging biceps. Which one was the real guy? She'd probably never find out.

The only thing she knew about Flex for sure was the name of the earthy sweetness staining her fingers.

Worshiper.

He was that, if nothing else.

"I'm afraid of God." Chenille leaned back in the chair and crossed her legs. A blue and white granny square filled her lap. A stack of like projects was piled on the corner of her desk. She'd taken three blankets to the hospital and showed no sign of stopping. Raya wished she'd paid more attention to Gram's lessons so she could help too.

Chenille looped the yarn around the hook twice. "I know that sounds bad, but I'm just being honest. I feel like one of those animals in Narnia, you know? He's scary, but he's good."

Raya chuckled. "I do know. In fact, you don't know how relieved I am to hear you say that, to hear you say something."

Lyle went in for countless treatments. On Sundays he recounted the failure of most of them. Still, Chenille showed up at work more days than she should have, silent and sullen. Today, though, she hurt enough to actually talk. Raya thought she'd come to her friend's office to talk about the uniforms, but it was also to hear about these faithful fears so seldom spoken.

Chenille pushed the finished granny square across the desk and crossed her legs at the ankles. *Beautiful ankles. Even Mother would have to admit that. Why do I think silly things at serious moments?*

Her friend nodded, as if reading her mind. "I know you haven't known what to say. Lily, Jean, you—all of you have been great. Praying for me. Covering for me. I'm sorry—"

"Don't be." Raya patted the seat beside her. "There won't be any apologies here. No politically correct Christian guilt. Sometimes there's just nothing to say."

She slid forward in the chair and let her head fall over onto Raya's shoulder. "I just finally gave up and told God everything. That I was mad, scared, hurt. I expected lightning bolts, but I found grace instead. Things don't look good."

"I'm sorry." Raya tightened her grip on her friend's shoulders. She'd thought Chenille's changed mood meant something good. She dropped off dinners and notes routinely, but Chenille rarely came to the door. Usually someone from the church care group opened the door. Raya stared down at her friend, remembering summers of double Dutch and bad sewing, of girl talk and first loves. Now Chenille was losing hers. "I'm so sorry."

"Thank you." Chenille wiped her eyes. "I want to say don't be, but I thank you for being sorry, even though right now I'm basking in gratefulness for the opportunity to have loved this man, to have carried and birthed his child, to have been his friend . . ." Her shoulders heaved with sobs.

Raya felt herself crumbling, both in grief and in . . . envy? Would she ever know a love like that? Working out with Flex every day reminded her how close she'd come to true love. Would she ever have what Chenille and Lyle had?

God, help me not to run from this. She needs me to hear it. I need to hear it.

She squeezed Chenille more tightly. Her friend turned to face her, and they stared at each other for what seemed like forever.

Chenille wiped her eyes and broke their embrace. "Cute shoes," she said, pointing at Raya's purple Mary Janes. "Nice collarbone too. Still working out with Flex?" She wiggled her eyebrows.

Raya smiled, feeling guilty about discussing shoes or men at a time like this.

Chenille nodded again. "It's okay. I just told you I'm scared of God. You can tell me you're scared of a guy . . . and of me. Spill it. What happened?"

Raya exploded with laughter. "I messed up everything. The uniforms cost too much, and I thought he'd pay—"

"He told Lyle you thought that. Flex doesn't have any money. He just looks like it."

Tell me about it. Same here.

"I couldn't cut much cost from the original design. I didn't want to bother you. Megan had me all mixed up, and I guess I just thought it would be okay." She stopped and took a breath, reading Chenille's face.

Like a true friend, she'd absorbed it all and, from the look on her face, was considering the possibilities. "You started at fifty, right?"

Raya nodded.

"A grand shouldn't be that hard to scare up. I don't have it right now. The church doesn't either, not with the AIDS hospice and all, but we can get it."

Raya sighed. "Before the first game? It's Thanksgiving, I think."

"I don't know. That's a couple weeks away." Chenille's voice faltered. "A lot could happen between now and then. I'll try."

"Forget it. I'm sorry for even bringing it up." Why was she such an idiot?

"Don't be sorry for needing me to do my job. Flex told Lyle about it anyway. I was going to drop by your office later." Chenille propped her legs up on the desk and let her head drop back into her hands. "I know a lot's going on, but don't feel like you can't talk to me about things. I need you to talk to me. It distracts me. If it comes down to it, we'll ask Megan for an advance on her dress. Speaking of Miss Thing, how are things coming there?"

Raya paused, wondering how much of this story her friend already knew as well. Flex hardly said a word to her each morning, but he certainly had no problem spilling his guts to Lyle. How embarrassing. Best to stick with the facts.

"Megan agreed to let Flex pick her dress—"

"Right. That was the one she hated the other day, right? The one he picked? I'll have to check the notes on that again. How did that go, anyway? I couldn't believe you got him to do it. Whenever I've mentioned weddings to him before, he's turned to wood."

"I made a little bargain with him about practicing with the boys. He wasn't pleased, but he did it. Even went in to try on the tux to go with it. But something set him off, and he ran out of the store."

"So is that it? Are you mad that he left? Is that why you're not talking to him?"

Raya stared at Chenille. Even with all her friend's tragedy, she was still doing it. "That's not it. That woman—"

"What woman?"

The words came out in a rush. "I went to his apartment to leave a note, and some beautiful old-but-young woman, the kind whose age you can't be sure about unless she tells you, answered his door and pretty much told me to get lost."

An irritating grin eased across Chenille's mouth. "A Dominican lady? Wearing pearls?"

Dominican. So that was it. It hadn't occurred to Raya that Chenille knew her too. She felt like a fool. "Yes, that's her."

"That's his mother, silly." Chenille doubled over laughing.

Raya's heart dropped to her feet. "Why didn't you tell me?"

"You didn't ask." Chenille recovered slightly, simmering down to a giggle.

"It . . . it couldn't be. She's older, but not mother old. He told me he was twenty-six—"

"She's forty-three, I think. I remember because I was shocked too." Chenille stroked Raya's hair. "So this is why you've been giving him such a hard time? They've been wondering."

Raya rolled her eyes. "They?"

"Flex and Lyle. Flex comes over, they study and pray, and then they try to figure out why you're mad at him. Of course, I'm called in as a material witness. Usually Lyle and I have been fighting about something else, and I end up biting both their heads off. I told Lyle to stay out of it, but he's determined to be a deathbed matchmaker—"

"Chenille . . ." Humor was one of her friend's ways of coping, but it cut Raya to the heart.

Chenille dropped her feet to the floor and leaned across the cheap desk. "Laugh with me while I'm laughing, Raya. It might be a while till it happens again."

14

Raya took Flex's medicine ball, glad to see a spark of her old self back in the gym. In the week since she'd returned to normal, neither of them had mentioned it. They were trying some new cardio. Something to break up the monotony of the bike. He looked hard at her as if he sensed something was wrong. Again.

"What's the matter?"

Raya heard Flex's voice, but she didn't know what to say. She was having one of those days. A guilty, horrible, why-did-I-do-it day. Something she'd never be able to explain. She threw the medicine ball back at him instead of trying.

He held the ball and waved her over. They weren't alone in the gym, but the morning crowd was scattered. He put an arm around her shoulders. Why did that feel so good? She should have moved away, but she didn't. He let go instead. "Talk to me."

She dropped onto the mat. "You ever feel like you blew it? Like you know you're forgiven and God loves you and everything but that what you did just broke everything forever?"

Raya sighed when he didn't respond immediately. Of course he didn't understand.

He plopped down beside her. "Oh yeah. I feel like that at least once a day."

"A day?" She stared at him in disbelief. She had this kind of day once a week now maybe. But every day? "Man, what did you do?"

Flex laughed. "Lots of stuff. Things with my parents. My job here. Things in my past, mostly."

His past? Why did the thought of what that might mean make her flush with anger? "I don't want to know."

He smiled. "Good. This is about you anyway. I was just agreeing that, yeah, I feel like that. A lot. If I'd been on the straight and narrow all my life, I guess it would be easier, but I wasn't. So the head games are part of the package."

Head games. That described it exactly. "So what do you do?"

"The same thing that got me saved—I accept, I believe, and I confess."

"Sounds too easy."

He scratched his head. "Not easy. Simple. There's a huge difference."

Wasn't that the truth? "So what do you accept, believe, and confess? That Jesus is alive? That he bailed you out?"

Flex shrugged. "Sometimes. Mostly it's stuff about grace and being clean. Moving my sins from the east to the west. That kind of thing. I read it, agree with it, pray it in faith, and then say it out loud." He sucked his teeth. "Sometimes I have to go in the shower and scream it."

Raya turned on her belly and cranked out a few push-ups for no reason in particular. After about ten she sat up. Some session this was. Usually he'd have her sweating her head off by now. Sometimes a spiritual workout was even more important.

"You actually scream it?"

He nodded. "Not trying to get TV preacher weird on you or anything, but there's something about vocalizing. For me, anyway. 'Speak to this mountain and it'll be cast in the sea,' you know? I've got a lot of mountains." His voice told of rock cliffs and crags as well.

Raya's eyes narrowed as she thought of what haunted her. She dared not think of all the things that poked at Flex's mind.

"I guess I never thought you dealt with this kind of thing."

He nodded. "Why? Because I'm a man? That Christian Superman myth. Don't buy it, not even for a minute."

"You guys using this area or what?"

Raya turned and shook her head. "Have at it." She probably should have asked Flex, but he smiled in agreement.

"Let's just hit the bikes and do a quick circuit. Then we'll pray for Lyle and get in a quick Bible study. Maybe it will help both of us. What do you say?"

I say you scare me.

"That'd be great."

"I need your help." Flex barely looked at Megan when he said it, but not one word he'd said missed her attention.

She crossed her arms, leaned back against the front of the treadmill, and shouted over the whir of exercise bikes. "Need me, huh? I knew you would. What's the matter, figure out that love without money just isn't enough?"

Flex sighed. She was going to make this much harder than

he'd thought. He wiped his hands on a towel and turned, motioning for Megan to follow. She didn't. This was almost as bad as dealing with his father.

He approached her again, this time coming closer than he'd dared before. Her face lit up at his closeness. He didn't look around at what he knew would be the questioning faces of his co-workers. No time to worry about that now.

"Come with me. Out front." When she only batted her eyes, he added, "Please."

She ran her hand up his arm. "Was that so hard? That's all you had to do. Say the magic word." With that she squeezed past him and swayed to the gym's front door.

He rubbed his jaw. This was a bit more than even he could swallow. He could always just go to the locker room and forget the whole thing, but it wouldn't matter anyway. He'd never live this one down. Might as well try to make it productive. Waving away the grunts and sober looks of his friends, he followed the path Megan had taken, not surprised to find her waiting in front of the glass doors, where everyone could see.

"Can we step over here?" He motioned to the storefront next door.

Megan shook her head. She smiled flirtatiously. "Nope. I need witnesses. And no touching, remember?"

Flex sidestepped her verbal jab and dived in. "Okay. It's no big deal, really. It's just that I coach a basketball team, a few kids from the church—"

"So? Do you want a medal?" Megan looked annoyed.

Flex threw back his shoulders. "Let me finish." He paused. "Please."

That earned a lopsided smile. "Go ahead."

"Anyway, they need uniforms for the league. Chenille's firm designed some great ones—"

"You mean Raya designed some great ones, don't you?" Suddenly she looked very interested.

"Well, yes, I guess so. That's not the point. The outfits are a little out of the players' price range, and there's no time to get something else before the first game. I think Raya thought I could cover it . . ."

Megan's eyes turned to ice. "And you can. Call your father. Don't be a fool like her."

"Like who?" What was she talking about? Raya may have gone to Stanford and kept a mean hairdo, but she was just as broke as Flex. Megan had said as much herself.

"Never mind. Look, how much do you need?"

She didn't beat around the bush, did she? "A thousand. Give or take."

Megan shrugged. "That's all?"

Her tone made Flex's biceps vein twitch. All? That was almost a month's rent and a lot more than he had right now. The nerve of her.

"Yeah. That should do it."

Anger ripped through him at having to be in this position. Why hadn't Raya just listened to him? Their talk this morning came back to him. She had other things on her mind, things that kept him up at night too.

"Wondering what Cinderella will have to say about this? I can see it on your face." Megan gave him a seductive look that almost made him laugh out loud, but he had to control himself and get this money for the kids. She could be so ridiculous sometimes.

"She's not my Cinderella, okay? It would be nice if you could just keep this between you and me though. I wouldn't want her to think—"

Megan's eyes widened. "Think what? That there's something between you and me? That you're trying to fix her mess

166

behind her back? No, we can't have that. Tell you what. I'll do you one better. I'll make it two grand and give it to her. Make her think she saved the day."

Flex smelled trouble. "You don't have to—"

"I insist. Maybe it'll get her going on my dress. Everything so far has been atrocious. I don't know what's wrong with her." She cast Flex a sidelong glance. "On second thought, I know just what's wrong with her."

Me? "Hey, we're just friends." At least he hoped so. She and Lyle were the only people he really talked to. "I don't have anything to do with that."

Megan snorted and started back inside the gym. "Yeah, right. And she has nothing to do with you out here begging one of your clients for money either, huh?"

Flex stiffened, following her eyes to the second floor of the gym, where his seldom-seen boss stayed sealed in his office. "You wouldn't."

She bumped the glass door open with her hip. "I would. But not this time. I'll play along for now. Raya needs to concentrate on my dress anyway."

He swallowed, suddenly caring less about his job than about having Raya find out why Megan had suddenly decided to give her two thousand dollars. And what if she decided to spend it on something else?

She won't.

"You don't scare me, Megan. I'll share with my employer the little tricks you've pulled with me and the rules you've broken. I'm coming to you on a personal basis. What I have to know is that you won't tell Raya what we've discussed here today."

"Of course not." The lie wafted toward Flex just as the door shut.

His stomach wrenched at the contempt flickering in Megan's voice. He'd known going in that dealing with Megan would be a devilish deal, but he couldn't think of what else to do.

"Faith is being sure of what we hope for and certain of what we do not see."

Yes, faith. That's what a good Christian would do—believe. But lately he wondered if there was any goodness left in him. Lyle's sickness had brought in a cloud of doubt that seemed to cover Flex wherever he went. Hadn't he prayed his entire life for his father to marry his mother, to respect her, to . . .

To accept me? To love me?

He shook at the thought. He'd long since accepted that Fletcher Longhurst's love was something he'd never attain. Why these feelings now?

Because he was in love. And the siren who'd just walked away with yet another of his secrets would make sure that love would never bloom. Megan would tell. And when she did, Raya would never forgive him.

He walked back into the gym and was surprised to see Megan waiting just inside the door. She stepped toward him.

Megan's voice lost its edge. "You really like her, don't you?"

He sighed. "I do."

"What is it with her? Is it the Jesus thing? I just don't get it." She wilted a little.

"The Jesus thing? That's part of it. Well, all of it, but not. There's more. Don't get me wrong, Megan, you're beautiful—"

"I knew you thought so." She sprouted up like a daisy.

Flex shook his head. "You didn't let me finish. There was a 'but' coming. That beauty doesn't go deep enough. Not for me, probably not for that guy you're trying to marry, and definitely not for you. Not that I'm one to talk. I have a lot of ugly still lurking in here." He paused, waiting for a quick comeback.

Instead, Megan squeezed his hand. "Thanks, Flex. Thanks for being honest with me. It's not often that people take the chance. I'm still not sure about God and everything, but there has to be more than . . . than what I've got. It's just hard to believe there's something more. I feel like I've wasted my life—"

"No. God never wastes anything. Look at me. You seem to know my story. I could be dead right now. Easily. But he gave me grace, another chance. Maybe so I could be here right now talking to you."

Her head bobbed. "My boyfriend has been talking to me about some of these things too. It sounds different coming from you though. And about your secrets, they're safe with me. I'll put up the money too."

Flex held up a hand. "Forget it. I'll talk to my father."

Megan smiled and stared at the door. "You should do that, but not about this. I've got it. Don't let Raya get away, huh? If she's half of what you guys think she is, she's really something. Oh, and thanks again."

His hand stuck fast on the door. If Raya was a hundredth of the woman he'd made her out to be in his mind, Flex was in trouble. Big trouble.

Raya pulled her coat around her, gathered it at her neck to fight off the fall chill. This was no LA, that's for sure. And the Brooklyn summers of her childhood hadn't prepared her for this kind of cold. Her body had stirred early this morning, her limbs throbbing and hungry for movement. Without thinking, she'd gathered her clothes and started for Q station, started for the gym.

"Morning, Miss Joseph."

Raya waved to the receptionist. His hair was green today, but in a much more flattering cut than last week. Her own hair, now chestnut brown, dangled from her crown in yarn-wrapped strands. She paused at the sight of herself in the mirror, then continued removing her jacket as she went.

To him.

Flex waited at the bench press, as he had for many Mondays. Chest, shoulders, and back today. Legs, biceps, and triceps tomorrow. This weekend marked the halfway point of her training. What would she do when there was no tomorrow?

"Hey, you." Flex laughed and flashed a boyish grin.

Training or not, she'd be back. "Good morning."

He loaded the weights, two twenty-fives. Her heart still raced at the sight of those weights . . . and at the sight of him. There was a gold ring on his pinky, one that hadn't been there before. Her throat tightened.

Probably another "gift" from one of his groupies.

She put her jacket and bag down next to the bench press. No sense going to the locker room now. "Still want me to do cardio? I know I'm late."

Flex shook his head. "Let's just go for it. You're warm, right?"

She nodded. "Yeah. I ran from the train."

She flattened herself on the bench, looking up at him. Even upside down, he looked, and smelled, incredible. "I think I'm going to have the money for the uniforms. If I can make Megan happy, that is. Pray for me, would you?"

Something flashed in his eyes. Anger?

"I pray for you every day, but I'll add that to your list." His voice was flat.

Raya tugged on her weight gloves and took her place. She gripped the bar and pushed the weight up with shaky hands. "*My* list? You've got a whole prayer list just for me? I can just imagine what's on it."

"You have no idea." Sadness showed in his eyes. His hands shadowed the bar as she eased it back to her chest and then pressed up again, trying to ignore the tingling in her toes from being this close to him.

You've got it bad, girl.

Their eyes locked, and the intensity of feeling seemed to add another fifty pounds to the bar. It seemed like lead in her hands. What number was she on, anyway? Flex had stopped counting. He was staring at her . . .

"Eight, nine . . ." Raya strained out the words and the motions. Flex moved from spotting the bar with his out-stretched palms to taking a light grip on the bar and helping Raya lift it.

She shook her head. Did she come every morning for this? To feel Flex pull her love to him and push it away?

"One more, come on. I'm with you."

Yeah, but for how long?

No, she needed to do this herself. To push up, to push Flex away from her mind for good. The metal pressed against her ribs as she paused for a moment. Then she shot the bar up with a jerky blast.

"Hey! Hold on!" Flex said, trying to catch the bar, which had been level at first but now was crooked as Raya's strength gave way.

"Ouch!" she cried as something in her wrist burned and seemed to snap. Her hand went limp. Flex grabbed the bar just as it crashed toward her face.

Raya rolled off the bench and onto the floor, holding her right wrist. Her drawing hand.

Flex put the bar in the rack and stood over her like a guardian angel. He touched her hand gingerly, immediately knowing her concern. "Your hand." His voice emptied out, like water swirling down a drain.

The other trainers huddled around, shooting out questions, but Flex ignored them, gathering her in his arms. "It's going to be okay."

His eyes begged her to believe him. She buried her face in his shirt instead. How would she ever get Megan's sketch done now?

Her wrist was sprained, not broken, the doctor at the walk-in clinic assured Flex, wrapping it neatly. "She'll be fine in a few weeks."

He'd make sure of that. He'd insisted on bringing her home. Though he'd known what to expect, her building, with its clean hallways and enticing breakfast scents, delighted him. His *abuela* would have loved this building. He took a deep breath. She would have loved Raya too.

"Let me help you with that."

Gently he took the key from Raya's fingers and placed it in the lock. After opening the door and replacing the key in her hand, he stood on the threshold, drinking in the sight of lavender-scented material draped everywhere. Like a room full of curtains, only better. Unsure whether to stay or go, he watched as she fumbled to put the key on the table. Pain shot across Raya's face, though she tried to cover it up.

That look was all the invitation Flex needed. Concerned about further injury to her hand, he helped her to the couch. It was covered in piles of green fabric. Taffeta, he recalled from Raya's descriptions at the formal shop. He looked around the room for somewhere to prop her up, but there was nowhere.

"You do an awful lot of sewing. I don't see anywhere to put you."

She shook her head. "Not mine. My grandmother's. Put me in there." She pointed toward a door down the short hallway.

Her room? Flex hoped she couldn't feel his heart beating against her. He could tell by her reluctant tone and the look in her eyes that she wasn't quite sure about it either. He took a step. He was no teenager. He was a grown man. A Christian man. And this was an emergency.

"Sure."

They got to the room all too soon. He almost gasped as he put her down on the bed, silky with white. A room fit for a princess. Only a crown was missing.

To avoid her beauty and his response to it, he gazed around the room, then stopped at the arrangement of picture frames on top of her dresser. One photo in particular caught his attention, one with Raya and a nerdy, slim boy who could have been him ten years ago. A cluster of black and white balloons floated over their heads. A smile tickled his lips.

"Don't look at that!" Raya half shouted as Flex reached for the photo.

He batted her hand away for a closer look. A whistle hissed through his lips. "That dress. Wow . . ."

"Yeah. Wow. That's what people always say. It's a polite way of saying, 'What in the world?'"

Flex frowned. "I mean what I say." Didn't she know that by now?

Raya tried to pry the gilded frame from his fingers, only to pull her hand back in pain. He tucked the frame under his arm and kissed her hand, lowering it tenderly to her side. He surveyed her as he lifted the photo again.

She shook her head. "Go ahead. I'll close my eyes."

"Good." He pulled the frame out again, marveling at the dress, the skirt in full bloom with some kind of flowers. Her hair was done up in a chignon. Pearls graced her ears. Breathtaking. "This is the most beautiful thing I've ever seen." And he'd seen a lot of things. He squinted. "Seriously. What kind of flowers are those?"

Eyes still closed, Raya groaned. "Lily of the valley. And believe me, no one thought they were beautiful. When my date saw me, his eyes dilated a good inch or two. My mother thought I'd been attacked by a tree."

He sat down and looked closer at the white border around the photo. Someone had scribbled "Raya's first texture" in the margin.

"Wait. You designed this?"

She lifted her arm and moved it onto the pillow beside her. "Unfortunately. I was quite the renegade back then."

"And now?" Flex tugged his gaze from the picture and fastened his eyes on hers.

"And now, I don't know. Nobody gets it. Nobody wants it . . ."

I want it. I want you.

She fumbled with the quilt with her good hand.

He lifted her chin with his bad hand, sore from wrenching the bar away this morning. "You amaze me. How you see things that aren't there and make them into something. That's a gift."

He followed her eyes to pictures of a man and a woman, both of whom looked familiar, probably because of Raya's resemblance to them. Her parents. In separate frames.

"Sometimes it doesn't feel like a gift. Sometimes I wonder

why God didn't just make me the same as everyone else. It's hard to always be so . . . different. I try to be normal. To be safe. But—"

"Shhh." How he longed to kiss away her words. No sense starting something neither of them could finish. Not with her enveloped in that white satin, looking so beautiful with those swollen eyes.

"There's no such thing as normal, Ray. And if there is, I'm glad you're not it." A hug wouldn't hurt, would it? He pulled her to his chest, tucking her head under his chin. She received the embrace but seemed afraid to return it. As well she should be.

He pulled back, reading the fear in her eyes. *Will you hurt me? Are you safe?* her gaze seemed to ask. He let her relax against the pillow. She was right. There was no safe place. None but Christ.

He stared over at the solemn face of Raya's father, posed in a stance Flex knew well, the prideful hunch of a workaholic. His father stood erect in photos to hide the same stance. His father. That man certainly wasn't safe. Even though his mother had confirmed the innocence of the situation between her friend and his father, Flex wasn't sure if he bought the whole thing. His parents' relationship seemed like a trap, something that snapped shut on them the moment they acknowledged their love. The same trap he'd fall into with Raya if he wasn't careful.

Raya settled against her headboard, ignoring his eyes the same way she had that first day on the subway. That day that had changed his life. Maybe being trapped wouldn't be so bad after all . . .

Flex leaned forward, breathing Raya's powdery scent mingled with antibiotic ointment. Closer and closer he came, waiting for her to move away, to run from him, but she stayed, eyes locked on him. His heartbeat monitor blared, breaking the moment. He kissed one of her eyelids and rolled onto his back, hands over his head as he tried to turn off the out-of-range heart alarm. He had to laugh as he read the output.

"Out of range. I've never gotten my heart rate up that high sitting still." Leave it to Raya to give him a workout just looking at her.

She pressed a palm against her chest. "It's a good thing I wasn't wearing one. That was almost the big one, like Fred Sanford." She giggled softly.

He sat up and shook his head. "You're crazy, you know that?"

And I'm crazy about you.

Something snagged against the back of the pillow as he pulled his hand away. That stupid ring Megan had left him at the desk. He palmed it. Why hadn't he locked it in the gym safe? He'd meant to, but someone had asked him a question, and then he'd started loading Raya's weights . . .

Hopefully, Raya hadn't seen it, but he'd tell her about it anyway. Soon. Come clean about everything. For now, she had his complete attention.

She slid her prom picture back into its frame. "So I've been told. Look, I'm sorry for all that I said before. Especially the part about God and how he made me. I mean, who am I to say who I should be? I don't even know who I am—"

"You know who you are. You just don't want other people to know." He waved around the room at the boas draping the closet doors, the mannequins in different poses, the easel by the window—

He froze.

She did too.

Both of them sat, eyes fixed on the easel.

Raya turned away. "Who knew you'd bring me home?"

"God knew."

Flex turned the easel toward him, facing her sketch of him. Well, it seemed like him, but much better: honest eyes, cheekbones a half-inch higher than his, and lips a supermodel would beg for. The dab of hair under his lip, the one every photographer in town begged him to cut, tapered into a perfect *V* all the way down to his chin. He stroked it now.

"Very nice. I might cut it like that."

"It's just a—" She scrambled to get up, but he moved first.

"Shhh." With a finger to his mouth, he smoothed her cheek, eased the pillow with her sprained wrist closer to her. "Calm down. You'll hurt yourself." They hadn't discussed the ramifications of her wounded hand, but Flex knew she couldn't risk injuring it further.

Nodding, she closed her eyes again, only this time she pinched them shut.

He crept back around the bed and unclipped the sketch. The paper dangled from his fingertips as he brought it to his lap. Her designs had been one thing, but this? She was an accomplished artist as well.

Though she made no move to open her eyes, Raya protested from where she was. "It's just a line drawing. Subconscious mind, I guess. Doodling. Sometimes I—"

"Talk too much." He looked up from the page with a smile. "May I keep this?"

The front door slammed in the distance. Keys crashed against wood. "Cherie? Is that you? Is that a man I smell?"

Flex was already on his feet, both jarred and charmed by the sound of the woman's voice. Raya's eyelids peeled back as she fumbled to get up. Flex restrained her gently with one hand as he stood instead.

"Mademoiselle?" he called out.

Like an angel, his favorite client appeared in the doorway, her white afro skimming the low doorframe like a cloud. Her alarm became joy.

"Trey? Is that you?"

Flex nodded, swallowed by the old woman's strong, spindly arms. Hopefully, Raya hadn't noticed the nickname she'd given him, one only his grandmothers, both now deceased, had called him. Trey. Fletcher Rayburn Longhurst III. He'd tried to get her to call him Flex, but she'd refused, asking who he'd been born as.

Question marks danced in Raya's eyes. "You two know each other?" she whispered to no one in particular.

"I taught an exercise class at the community center last summer. This lady was front and center. And I see her at church showing off her beauty."

At seventy, the age she thankfully proclaimed to anyone who would listen, the old woman made heads turn wherever she went. Her beauty went deeper than makeup or clothes. It was the heart-deep elegance of a woman at peace with herself. Raya had it too.

Mademoiselle turned him aside as she saw the bandage around Raya's arm. "Cherie! What happened?"

"An accident. Flex-Trey was kind enough to bring me home. I apologize for not calling you."

So she had heard the name. Oh well. After today, it was time to explain anyway. That picture . . . Flex held up a hand. "And I apologize for staying so long. I—"

Raya's grandmother—or was she an aunt?—waved him away. He looked again at the man's photo. Definitely the grandmother. Paternal.

Mademoiselle surveyed Raya's arm. "I trust my grand-

178

daughter. I thought thieves might have been about. Next time just stay in the living room, if you don't mind."

"Yes, ma'am." He cracked his knuckles, feeling like an idiot, but the sweet smile she added took off some of the edge.

She shook her head, turning her attention to Raya. "And so it has come to this, eh? You would not dream, so you cannot work. Broken."

Raya gave her grandmother a wide-eyed look. Flex started for the door, but the old woman grabbed his forearm, and he knew from training with her that she wouldn't let go easily. He'd often joked to the class that Mademoiselle could have been one of the famous strong women of old. Skinny as ever but with the grip of a lion. They didn't make women like that these days. He looked at Raya. Well, not many of them, anyway.

"Gram, it's not broken, just sprained. It's not too bad." She held up her wrist and lowered it again, denying the pain of even the smallest movement. She cut her eyes at Flex, daring him to say different.

"Not your hand, cherie, your spirit." Gram turned on one heel, displaying the trail of pink chiffon behind her, a cape covered with roses the size of cabbages. "She designed this, you know. But now she refuses to dream."

"Gram!"

Flex backed up in the direction of the doorway. It was definitely time to exit. "I should go. Forgive the intrusion—"

"Forgiven, on one condition . . ."

A knot bobbed in his throat. "Name it."

Gram whisked by him, her chiffon trellis sending a flutter of roses across Flex's gaping mouth. "Don't hurt her. She loves deep, my cherie. If you care for her, don't be afraid to show it." She smiled. "Help me get her some ice."

Raya hiccuped behind them as Flex followed the white-haired beauty out of the room.

"I know I embarrassed you, talking to Trey that way, but don't look so glum." Her grandmother's white afro shook as she whipped the last stitch around a sleeve of her New Year's Day wedding dress. "Some folks just bring out the chatter in me. That boy is one of them. Hand still hurting?"

Gram reached down and lifted the edge of a length of ivory satin draped over a chair. Raya's eyes glided down the length of the fabric gathered in her grandmother's hand.

She looked down at her bandaged wrist. "Not so bad."

Gram looked over at Raya. "Is that about five-eighths? I don't have my glasses."

Raya nodded, and her grandmother sheared off the section in one deft movement.

Gram motioned to a hutch made of cherry wood across the room. "You've had a long day. Why don't you eat dinner while I run you a bath? I'll even grab your dream book for you to look at. It'll make you feel better. It always does."

Raya shifted her weight on an overstuffed wing chair she shared with a bolt of pink taffeta. "I don't think so, Gram. I've got . . . a lot on my mind." Her voice peaked an octave.

She fingered the ring in her pocket. She'd found it wedged between her pillows. From the inscription, she knew it was a gift from Megan. How could she have been so gullible as to let Flex in this apartment, let alone her bedroom?

Don't rush to judge. You know Megan has fooled you before.

"I think I'll just turn in." Her voice squeaked the last word.

"Mm-hm. I was wondering when you'd get to *him*." The old woman added the satin to a pile marked "New Year's Day wedding," then dropped her measuring tape and scissors into

a bowl on the table. She retreated to the kitchen, no doubt to turn off dinner.

Raya crossed her arms. She'd planned to keep her mouth shut about everything, but it looked like she'd end up spilling it all. She couldn't get anything past Gram.

"Am I that obvious?" she called.

"Just to me. What's going on?" Gram's glasses slipped off her nose and hung on the chain around her neck as she reentered the room.

"This." It was all Raya could do to keep from throwing the ring, a lion's face in eighteen-carat gold, across the room. It was the inscription that cut across her heart.

Thanks for everything. M.A.

Megan Arietta.

Raya cleared her throat, trying not to think of Flex's clean-shaven face and that little bit of fuzz under his lip. Or the way he'd lean back sometimes and stare right through her. And that cologne . . . She shook her head. Only a few men could get away with wearing vanilla. Enough said.

"That girl's a cunning character, but I wouldn't read much into it." Gram's lips curled into a sly smile. "Trey is a good man."

It wasn't the "good" part of him she was worried about. It was the "man" part of Flex that concerned Raya. Sometimes he seemed like a rock to her—spiritually and physically—but in truth, he was only human. She knew firsthand how weak a man and woman could be.

Raya took a deep breath, remembering the sound of his voice during that heartfelt discussion earlier in the week. "Speak to the mountain," he'd said. Had all of that only been an act? She wasn't willing to take the chance.

"It doesn't make any difference, Gram. It has nothing to do with me."

"Right." Gram set the ring on the table and placed her glasses on her nose. She turned to the row of hutches and wooden armoires behind her. She stopped at the tallest one, gleaming with a deep red-brown color, and reached onto the top shelf. Patterns and thimbles rained down to the floor. She ignored them and kept on searching, sticking her hand into the corners until she retrieved a dingy sketchbook with "Dream Designs" on the cover in chunky cursive. A handful of charcoal pencils resurfaced next.

She dropped the booty in Raya's lap. "Take this. And don't worry about that man. Or Megan. She's just mad because she doesn't have the strength to be what God made *her*. It's easy to seem successful, Raya, but it's hard to be yourself." She sat in her chair at the table and forced two pieces of jade satin through the sewing machine.

A Christmas wedding, no doubt. The buzz of the needle almost drowned out the rest of the old woman's words. "Your father gave up being himself to get rich, and he hasn't been right since."

Raya let the pencils and paper slide to the floor. Pierre Joseph take the easy road? Never.

"Daddy's doing what he always wanted to do—make money. And he says if I want to be any good at it, I'd better stop dreaming and get serious. This is serious. Chenille needs me. If I'm ever going to make it in this industry, I need the experiences—"

"Sounds like a whole lot of other folks' wants to me. What about what you want?"

She shrugged her shoulders. Did it even matter anymore? "What good is dreaming if no one understands your dreams? If it doesn't pay the bills?"

Though Gram wouldn't take a dime from Raya's father besides his purchase of her building and the rents she seldom collected, Raya had a few redecorating plans of her own. As

much as Raya loved the building, it could use a new touch here and there. She might not be in a place financially to do anything yet, but she hoped to be able to surprise her grandmother someday soon.

The sewing machine stopped. Gram lifted the metal foot and rotated the fabric. She started again. "I understand your work. How many brides have you and I made happy over the years? Why, when you were ten, you drew me that starburst dress for Betty Oluwe. Remember that?"

Raya groaned, wishing she could forget it. That shapeless tent was more of a nightmare than a memory. "That dress was horrible, Gram."

"Not to her. Or her husband. You drew that woman's personality. You create from the heart. True, it's not for everybody, but the people who it is for never forget it. Don't ever lose that, eh?"

Raya's hands covered her face. Be humble, but don't let anybody walk over you. Be thankful, but don't be afraid to tell people what you need. Do as you're told, but do what your heart tells you too. Be angry and sin not. All Raya's life, her grandmother had been speaking in riddles. God too. She'd never truly understand either one of them, though she dearly loved them both.

"I hear you," Raya said in a low whisper.

She stared down the hall toward her room. What she needed now was sleep, not dinner, and definitely not dreams. No time tonight. She had to come up with a plan, a way to somehow finish Megan's sketch with a bum drawing hand. She could almost see Chenille's pleading eyes every time she thought about the situation.

Playtime would have to wait. Deadlines didn't leave room for dreams.

Gram stopped moving—stopped cutting, measuring, tapping her foot to the Tabou Combo album drifting up from the apartment downstairs. Her glasses dropped around her neck.

"I didn't want to have to do this, but I guess I'll have to," she said, standing. She walked over to the overstuffed floral sofa and stepped onto its cushions, reaching for a small square in the ceiling.

Raya pushed aside the slippery fabric beside her. The attic? She hadn't seen Gram go in there since, well . . . never.

"What are you doing?" she asked as her grandmother's head disappeared into the small space.

"Getting this," she said, lowering her tall, lean frame, so much like Raya's own, down to the couch again. She held an oversized plastic bag bundled and bound like a pirate's treasure. Undoing all the tape and knots, she unearthed the bag's contents, a dusty easel. Tubes and brushes littered the few inches of coffee table free of patterns and pins.

"This is what your father loved. Not the money. He probably thought marrying Vera would bankroll his painting, but—"

"He loved mother." Raya frowned.

Her grandmother's words held more than a little truth, but in Raya's dreams, her parents still loved each other . . . and loved her.

Still, to know that Daddy had given up his art to take a job with her mother's family firm and secure Raya's future turned her heart a little. She rubbed her hands across the easel, sending a flutter of dust into the air.

"Careful, baby. Your asthma."

Raya nodded, her breathing already short. Yet she couldn't pull herself away from the easel or the watercolor painting still clipped to its base. The corner was torn, but the image unmistakable. The vulnerable stare and smiling mouth were a sight Raya had never seen, but the high brow and the mole made clear the model's identity.

Vera. Her mother.

Warmth flooded over her. They had loved each other once. Truly loved each other. She'd always known it, but seeing the painting and the loving strokes that created it cemented the truth in her mind. Since her own mismatches at love, she'd given up her fairy tale of her own family, but now something fanned the embers of her heart. Could her parents love again?

Her mind traveled back to the ring Flex had left behind. *I may as well pray for them. There's no hope for me.*

She smiled up at her grandmother. "Put this back, Gram." She gathered the tubes and brushes. Her gaze skimmed over her mother's image, faded but bright with a youthful hope Raya wished she'd seen in person. She slipped the easel and her Dream Designs book into the same plastic bag. "Keep this too, please."

Her grandmother's narrow shoulders slumped. She dropped onto the sofa. "Baby, don't. Please. You're so good." She clapped her hand over Raya's. "And I'm not just saying it. Is it because of this Megan? The wedding?"

"No, Gram. This is what I want."

The older woman eyed her suspiciously, lifting her glasses to her face for a closer look. "You've got a good eye. You bring passion to it. You're as good as anybody in the district now. In a few years—"

Raya shook her head. She'd heard it all before. Talented. Wonderful. One day. A day that never came. And never would come. She'd spent her entire life waiting for the fairy tale to begin, for her parents to love each other, to find a place where she could design from her heart, to have a family of her own to love . . .

Where had all those daydreams gotten her? Dumped a day short of the altar, stuck in the middle of her parents' nasty divorce, and robbed of the most precious memory of her life, except for a motel key and a man's cuff links?

Her personal life had flatlined, and now her professional life took a dive too, leaving her doing meaningful work she had little aptitude for. And when she did get a chance to do what she was good at, design evening wear, it turned out to be a gown for the woman who'd wrecked her life. What use was a dream book?

Unless they were just going to be a preview of what would come next on the market, her scribbles had little value. Every sketch in that old pad had ended up on the cover of *Vogue* or *Women's Wear Daily* with someone else's name. Vera always called them copies, though she knew Raya had drawn them months before. Gram always thought it was funny. Her little fashion prophet, the old woman used to call her. She'd say, "Want to know what they'll be wearing next season? Ask my cherie. She always knows."

Raya swallowed back tears and padded down the hall to her room. The freedom during her summers here had saved her sanity when her father refused to let her draw at home during the year. Raya complied to keep the peace, only to empty her mind of nine months' worth of fringes and beads onto a grubby sketchpad Gram refused to throw away. Her grandmother believed the Lord gave ideas out to anyone paying close enough attention—even fifteen-year-old girls and sixty-year-old fools. Raya chuckled, thinking about tonight's conversation. Ten years hadn't changed Gram's mind.

Raya was tired of being disappointed. Weary of trying to keep her parents together, Raya had found a love of her own, Darrell Fagan. A son of her father's biggest patron,

186

Darrell had swept Raya off her feet during her last semester at Stanford. Elated, her father had rushed to merge the two families—and their money. When the wedding flopped, her father made use of the crowd, announcing plans to divorce Raya's mother and move in with Frances Arietta.

Was Raya ready to start shopping for love again too? The flutter of her heart every time she saw Flex seemed to say so. A flutter that could only bring back the ripping, tearing pain she'd left behind in California. Though he always had excuses, Flex had the same strange coincidences with Megan that Darrell had. Though she could forgive, her memories, raw and fresh, refused to be denied their voice. She couldn't afford to let herself lose control again. Her father, Darrell . . . men just used her as it suited their purposes. She had to protect herself from herself, from that little girl inside still looking for a happy ending. The image of her mother's portrait flickered in Raya's mind. What about that? Wasn't that love?

Probably. And look how that turned out.

Raya walked into her room, stunned as usual by its brightness even in the dark. Without turning on the light, she slipped into the cool sheets. Her eyes fixed on the back of the rocker at the foot of her bed. Was it moving? The creak of the rocking chair at the end of the bed gave Gram's presence away. Knowing she'd been detected, Gram spoke. "Don't, Raya. I know that look. They're done, your parents. We prayed and prayed and prayed for them. Some people are broken and don't want to be fixed. Let it go. You've got your own problems now."

You can say that again.

"But—"

"No buts," Gram said. "If you're giving up dreams, you might as well give up on your parents. You know I'm a praying somebody, but your mama and daddy can try even an old woman's patience. Twenty years of praying is enough." She took a long sniff. "For both of us."

Raya fingered her own cropped curls. Twenty years? Had it been that long? The summer before her kindergarten year, her first vacation in this apartment. When Raya had asked for her parents, questioned why she'd been sent away, her grandmother's answer was always the same: "Let's pray, baby. Let's just pray."

And so they had. Raya had prayed in the morning with Gram, during her art classes at the community center, and before bed. After all those years of prayers, just when Raya thought everything would finally turn out right, it had all fallen apart.

"Gram, growing up, when I said I couldn't draw the things in my head, what did you tell me?"

In the shadows Raya could see her grandmother frown. "Don't turn things around, girl."

"Come on. What did you say?"

Raya slipped out of bed and walked in front of her grandmother and put her arms around her waist.

"With God . . . anything is possible—"

"Right. Let's just leave it at that." She gave Gram a squeeze before getting back in bed. She'd get her dream book down again once she'd helped Chenille get the business back on track . . . once Mother and Daddy were in love again. Once . . .

"Good night, cherie," Gram said and lit out of the room in a sleek stride.

"Good night," Raya whispered, turning her back to the door.

Gram sang her song of corners and close work. Raya's lullaby. Their love song.

"Lord, lift me up and let me stand. Lord, plant my feet on higher ground." The pace of the machine quickened as Gram's voice filled the air, choked with seldom-shed tears.

Raya smiled, thinking of the lucky winter bride. It would be a beautiful dress.

15

"It looks like he's going to be okay. For now, anyway." Chenille looked dazed. "I'm so thankful, but it's so hard wondering every minute I'm away from him if . . ."

"Don't be away from him. I'm here. My hand is better. Go home. Now." Raya gave her friend a sympathetic but unyielding look.

Chenille wiped her eyes, then picked up her crochet hook. "How can I? Your hand isn't that much better. With you unable to draw, we're going to have to let you talk us through it. Put something together as a team. Lily does a great sketch, and Jean can tell immediately whether a piece will flow. We have Megan's mannequin constructed and the muslin patterns for the designs Megan rejected. Who knows, maybe we'll end up with a bridal collection out of this."

Not if I can help it.

Raya turned away, staring at the gold lion ring on her desk. She'd spent most of the night rolling the cruel circle between her fingers. Even now her eyes burned as she read the line of curved script one more time.

Thanks for everything. Raya wasn't sure how much everything was, but it was definitely too much for her to endure. No matter how much Flex . . . Trey . . . or whatever his name was proclaimed he had no feelings for Megan, something was going on. Well, he could have her. They were meant for one another.

"No bridal line, Chenille. I don't think I could stomach it."

Chenille swiped her thumb over her mouth, for once free of any cheese substance. "You never know. Anyway, I'm going to call the girls in. We need to do something. Megan's business has helped, but we need more money to keep the doors open. You guys really held down the fort for me, but my absence threw things off."

Raya frowned. "Your absence? You make it sound like you had a cold or stubbed your toe. You lost your son, honey." She paused. "And your husband isn't well. I'll get with Lily and Jean. You go on home."

Chenille stood straight, but her legs trembled. Red, white, and blue yarn trailed behind her. "I can't . . . I need to—"

"It's okay." Raya rounded the desk.

Chenille's body heaved. "He's better, Raya. Better. Why do I feel like this? Every second I'm not there, I'm terrified. When I am there, I don't know what to say. Am I cutting him off now? To protect myself? Dear God, I don't want to. I love him so . . ."

"I know you do." Raya pulled her friend's cardigan around her shoulders. When had Chenille's collarbones and shoulders grown so thin? By now she'd met most of the people on the New Man Fellowship care team and had considered becoming one herself. The phone rang each team member in order, going on to the next if it detected a busy signal or a cell not turned on. She didn't understand the system, but in times like these, she was grateful for the computer skills volunteered by whoever had come up with the system.

"Hello."

Raya grabbed the desk. Flex's voice wasn't what she'd expected. "Hi, it's me. Raya."

"Hey, you're feeling better! I'm so glad." He took a breath. "One thing though. Did I leave—"

"I need you to come and get Chenille and take her home or call someone on the team who can. I'd do it, but I've got to figure out how to finish an important project. Thanks in advance." She hung up before he could respond.

Chenille squinted her swollen eyes. "That was a little rude, don't you think? What gives?"

Raya's teeth grated. More explanations. One last look at the ring, hidden from Chenille's view, gave her the logic she needed. "I can't trust him, so the best thing is to stay away."

"Whoa? Trust him? When did things get this deep? And what did he do to make you think he can't be trusted? Flex is one of the most honest guys I know."

Raya tapped her stylus on the electric pad with her left hand, wishing she could draw with it as deftly as she'd dialed the phone. "His name is Trey, actually, and I don't want to talk about it. You just relax here. I'll gather our team, the 'girls,' as you call us, in the conference room."

"Trey must be a nickname. Never heard him mention it."

"Gram called him that."

"That explains it."

A whisper of laughter played between them and hushed all too quickly.

A weary smile played on Chenille's lips. She looked toward the opening to her office and wished, not for the first time, that she had a door instead. Sometimes it'd be nice not to have to worry about laughing too loud.

"Jean loves that name, doesn't she? The girls. That's what you all are to me. My friends. My girls. I hope I don't have to lose any of you."

"Is it that bad?" Raya slid down in her chair.

Chenille nodded. "I haven't wanted to say, but yeah. Megan's payments would have really helped, but with me not out and hitting the pavement and phones for new accounts, well . . ."

Raya licked her lips. "I've got a crazy idea."

"Spill it."

She took a deep breath. "I could give her my dress."

Chenille's mouth opened slightly. "Huh? Who? Megan?"

Raya nodded. "I still have the design for my wedding dress. I could show the sketch—"

"I wouldn't ask that of you. Of anybody."

"You didn't ask. I'm offering."

"You're serious? I mean . . . well . . . didn't she see it at the wedding?"

"No. I was totally secret about it, even with her. I guess I should have kept Darrell under lock and key too."

"Raya . . . don't do this. Really. It's in God's hands. Maybe it's time for this wonderful ride to end. I'm okay with that."

"I'm not. I'm not ready to give up yet. Besides, I'm starting to think showing her the sketch at least will be healing in a way. I keep thinking I've let go of it, but there's always a little more dirt under the rug, if you know what I mean."

"I do. Well, I won't stop you. She'd probably want some changes, but if she could just accept something . . . Do you still have the actual dress?" Chenille blew out a breath.

"I do, but I'm not ready to offer that. I know she'll make enough changes to the sketch to make it different. I don't know why giving her the dress seems so much different. It's the same thing."

"I know why. There was so much buildup to that moment. I probably couldn't even do the sketch. One of Lyle's old girlfriends called to RSVP to our wedding at the last minute. I erased the message."

"You? Are you serious?" Raya was too shocked to laugh.

"Yes, me. Everyone has a weakness, and Lyle is mine. I really admire you, Raya. You've handled everything that's happened about the wedding remarkably well. Now, the stuff with Flex? That could use some work."

Raya swallowed hard. "Unlike him, I don't feel comfortable discussing it with you. Let's just say things continue not to add up."

"Like with his mother?"

A growl burned in Raya's throat. Between Gram and Chenille, it was a wonder she didn't have a nervous condition. "Look, I know I got that wrong, but some things are, well, just more plain."

"Did you ever talk to him about the thing with his mother?" Chenille stood and leaned over Raya.

"Well—"

"I didn't think so. And this, whatever it is that's got you riled now, why not ask him when he comes by? Just talk to the man. What's so hard about that?"

Raya's head hung. "Everything."

Chenille's arms circled hers. Tears wet Raya's neck. This wasn't the time.

The boss collected herself first. "Well, call Megan in and buzz me later. If she hates it, we'll go with plan B, which was plan A." She held her head. "Are you confused?"

Raya smiled. "Nope. Got it."

She reached to the back of the file cabinet for the sketch

she'd abandoned. Her mother's notes and initials still marked it in several places. Good thing she hadn't burned it like she'd planned. Raya would scan it and clean it up, make it like new. She stared at the gold lion roaring with lies on the desk in front of her. For once Megan might get the seconds.

"I've got good news and better news."

"Not now, Mom." Flex stared into his mother's sparkling eyes, too radiant for such a dim evening. First he'd found an envelope from Megan in his box apologizing for how she'd acted about his request for the money. She'd been praying, she said, and felt honored that he would choose her to confide in. She'd even sent a ring as a thank-you gift.

He'd slipped it onto his pinky, turned backward, so it wouldn't get stolen at the gym . . . and then Raya had showed up and had her accident. When he'd shown up to pick up Chenille, Raya had pushed the ring onto his finger without hearing a word he said. In the old days, he'd have called this negative square one, something that set a relationship back to a place past the beginning. Only God could fix things between them now. If his mother had good news, that would be wonderful, but he was too emotionally spent to care.

"It can't wait, Fletcher."

He tried to read his mother's face. What he found there shocked him—love, and not for him. It was a look he'd seen many times in his youth, his mother's eyes glazed with love for his father. His shoulders tensed.

"What now?"

She sank onto the sofa beside him. It was brown leather, in good condition, but not her taste. She never said it, but in all the time they'd lived there, she'd never sat on it. Until now.

"Well, first of all, our application for one of the two-family homes was accepted—"

"Are you kidding?" Flex stared in shock.

Thousands of people were scrambling to get into the new family homes going up around Brooklyn. He'd put up the last of his inheritance and all of his savings in hopes of having a place for both himself and his mother, but in his own name. All the money he'd spent on clothes and cars, women and airfare, came back to haunt Flex on his credit report. He hoped to have it cleared up soon. He was almost there now. He wanted to look out for his mom, but he was a grown man, and he was getting a little tired of explaining his actions every evening. Maybe the day could be salvaged after all.

"They want you to move in right away. Next week."

He made a face. "They want *me* to move in? Just me? And next week?"

He looked around his crowded apartment—workout equipment, clothes, music, his computer, modeling portfolios. And the magazine collection. Forget it. That alone would take a week. Maybe he could sell it on eBay . . .

"That's the other news, darling. I won't be moving with you to the new place." She extended her left hand, which until now, he'd been too exhausted to look at. A diamond the size of a sugar cube gleamed at him. "Your father has asked me to marry him."

Flex hopped to his feet and prowled the room, circling first the couch, then the recliner. "Marry him? Now? Why now? Is he dying? I mean, all my life he could have done this, and now, when I'm old, he wants to do things right? No way. Give it back."

She smiled a sickening sweet smile. "I will not."

He stopped short. They'd always been close, his parents, in an estranged, volatile way he'd never understood. His father hadn't minded passing his name on to Flex, but the man's heart had been the off-limits area. And now his mother was smiling like a schoolgirl at the possibility of getting the crumbs of the man he'd once been. New house aside, this day was one long, cruel joke.

"Why on earth would you marry him now? He doesn't love you. He can't. If he did, he'd have married you long ago. You had a child together. What could change things now?"

Angela Dunham smiled like the long-legged dancer in the scrapbook of photos under her bed. Though his mother was stunning at forty-three, Flex had always wondered what had happened to that girl in the picture, to the fire in her eyes, to the laugh in her mouth. It was all back. She laughed long and hard to prove it, then held a hand to her mouth, smudging her lipstick.

Flex gasped. Who was this woman?

"The money. It was always the money. Who can have that much? I couldn't. He wanted to marry me from the first. But when I saw it all—the houses, cars, boats—I was afraid, even angry. How could one person have so much when others, good people, had so little? I was young and couldn't get comfortable with it. I felt guilty. I know it's silly, but I couldn't live that way, so cold and silent. I begged him to take me back to the Dominican Republic, but he wouldn't. And so we stayed. Here in the States . . . and apart."

No more pacing. Flex felt dizzy. "It was you? You told *him* no?"

She nodded. "Many times. He was a different man here. Like ice. Like metal. In the Dominican Republic, he had music and warm hands. We sang together. Danced. Here he was too rich for that. Too much responsibility." Her eyes sparkled. "But not now. Now he's giving it all away."

Finally the truth of what she said registered. "Giving it *all* away? All of it? I know the guy doesn't owe me anything, and it's not like I want it, but all that money? What's he going to do with it?"

She stood, her hips moving to an unheard beat. "We have started the Agape Foundation for AIDS research and support of AIDS orphans in America and abroad, especially in Africa."

The words struck him like a slap. That much money could really do something. Change something. "And he's really doing this? I mean, it's in writing?" This didn't sound like anything his father would think up.

"It is. He'll keep some for us to live on. Off the interest mostly. And there's a provision for you and your family as well."

"I don't want—"

"Fine. Then it will pass to your children. But don't think harshly of your father. Money can be an alluring mistress, drawing men to forsake all to get it." She walked to the table and fingered the lion ring he'd left there. "Sometimes they don't even realize it until it's too late." She eyed him knowingly.

He shook his head. Raya hadn't listened to him, and neither would his mother. There was no point trying to explain. "Mother, I'm working hard every day and then some. Photo shoots, casting calls, the gym—"

She nodded. "Contests? Someone called from the Mocha Man competition today."

Flex lunged forward. The Mocha Man. He'd almost talked himself out of entering, knowing how it sounded, even to him. But the $100,000 grand prize, modeling contract, and media connections overcame his fears. He'd gone to the preliminaries a couple months ago, not expecting to hear anything back. Some of those dudes had been cuter than girls. Way farther than he was willing to go.

"About that, Mom. It was just a—"

"You made it to the next round. The next competition will be here, Thanksgiving weekend."

His body tensed. "The boys. They have a game."

She smiled. "I wish I could help, but I don't know where I'll be. Sounds like you have a dilemma. I'm sure you'll figure it out." She started for her room. "Just don't take as long as your father did."

As the shock of having to move alone settled in, Flex released his parents to their happiness and decided to try to see if there was a chance for some joy of his own. By doctor's orders, Raya hadn't yet returned to the gym, and after their last exchange, he wasn't sure if she would. In a last ditch effort to talk to more than the voice mail on her cell phone or Lily or Jean saying that Raya couldn't get to the phone, Flex took a detour to her subway stop, the same one where he'd first met her. He made her out quickly, a pink rhinestone sparkling against the crowd. Her eyes widened when he approached, and her mouth trembled. Was that a smile?

"Just listen for a second." Flex watched his words swirl in the cold, praying that Raya wouldn't freeze him out too. "You didn't need to give me back that ring. I just sent it to Megan. It's hers. There's nothing between us."

"And what is there between *us*?"

She'd said it. What he'd been thinking every day, every hour. She had guts. One more thing he loved about her. Could he spill his now? Tell her he loved her? What if she didn't feel the same?

He stepped closer. "What do you want there to be between us?"

"Let's not do this. You have a friendship with Megan. Stick

with that. There's nothing else to talk about." She turned away from the train platform and started in the other direction.

He ran behind her, took her gloved hand. "There's everything to talk about. Please. Megan was thanking me for talking to her about something she was dealing with. Now, please, tell me we're okay. I can't have you thinking something that's not true."

"I don't know what to think."

I think I love you. I know I do.

The train zoomed by, leaving a chasm beside them. Many people had fallen to their deaths on these tracks. Until today the danger had never seemed real. But with her here, her eyes deep enough to dive in, to drown in, the idea of falling forever was all too real.

Lord, help me.

Flex sank his hands into her hair and spoke softly. "Well, I'm going to tell you what I think. I think you're the most beautiful . . ." He kissed her temple. "Intelligent . . . " He kissed her nose. "Maddening . . ."

His lips devoured her mouth; his fingers dug into her hair. A soft cry escaped Raya's mouth. This was no kiss of grief, but it held the same emotion, the same trust. Her hands found his cheeks, shadowed today as on the day that she'd met him. She returned his kiss with equal intensity, as if hurling herself off the edge of something wonderful, something beautiful . . . something that would leave her with another broken heart.

"I can't do this." She pulled away.

And she couldn't. Her body, which had once stood the warmest of Darrell's kisses, responded to Flex in a grown-up, strong-willed way. God kept sex for marriage for a reason.

Once you woke up the beast that was desire, it demanded to be fed. And Flex looked like a ten-course meal.

He held her hand, and she felt her pulse threading against him. "I'm not going to hurt you, Ray. I promise I won't. We can call Megan right now. Force her to tell the truth. I don't want her. I want you."

She threw her head back in frustration. "Why do you have to say things like that?" If he only knew. She wanted him too, but not in a way she was proud of. How could she make him understand? "Look. It's not about Megan. There's something about you that makes me . . . it makes me . . ."

"Yeah." He let her hand go. "You make me crazy, girl." A blustery wind blew between them. "I mean, look at me, kissing you all in the subway. Mademoiselle would have a fit."

"And then some." Raya took a deep breath. Since coming to New Man Fellowship, many guys had asked for her number, invited her to church events. Nice, safe guys. Why couldn't she have fallen for one of them?

Flex shrugged. "You've got to admit, though, it was good."

She nodded, twisting her wristlet purse around her arm. "Ridiculously so."

"So we're cool? No Megan confusion?"

"We're cool." She whispered the words.

Flex sighed like a teakettle, making no effort to hide his relief. He lifted one eyebrow. The same way her father did. "Want to try it one more time? For the road, I mean."

Raya agreed with her mouth, caressing Flex's lips with her own a second time in cold, crowded Q station for all to see.

It was safer that way.

16

The humidifier fogged across Chenille's living room and into the nook, where she, Lily, and Raya huddled together. Lyle's breathing, less ragged than during their last visit, sounded like music. Raya hadn't wanted to come today, hadn't wanted to intrude, but Chenille had asked them, begged them to come in. And now, seeing the light in her friend's eyes, Raya was glad she had.

"I can't believe she took it." Chenille stared at Raya in disbelief.

Raya shrugged, not so sure herself. She turned to Lily, who had also been present for Megan's little acceptance speech after seeing Raya's original dress design. Lily nodded, confirming she'd heard it too. There were a few buts here and there, but with Megan that was to be expected.

"She hasn't exactly accepted it yet," Raya said. "She said 'with modifications.' That could mean ten prototypes like before. And we don't have time for that. Unless . . ."

"What?" Lily leaned forward between

Chenille and Raya, whose eyes were already locked. "Tell me."

Chenille blew out a breath, then peeked into the other room, where Lyle slept. A beep sounded, then dimmed. His vitals. She stared away from the girls, then, sure that all was well, turned back to face them and their problem.

"I know what you're thinking, Raya, and I won't have it. I'd never ask you to do that, not for any amount of money. This has gone on long enough."

Tell me about it.

"Will you please tell me what you all are talking about?" Lily's voice climbed.

Lyle coughed in response.

Chenille jumped to her feet.

Raya followed, ignoring Lily's plea. She'd explain to her on the train.

"It can't get any worse. Really. If necessary, I'll be the live model, wear my dress for her. I always knew that might be a possibility." Maybe Raya should have burned her wedding dress like she'd considered.

Lily gasped. "Your wedding dress?" She spat the words. "That won't do. That thing with the ring was bad enough—"

"What thing with the ring?" Lyle's voice was weak but peaceful. "If you're going to wake me up, let me in on the secret too."

All three women covered their mouths. The few other times they'd come in, they'd talked around Lyle, and he'd coughed, rolled over, and even smiled, but he'd never woken up. In fact, Raya hadn't actually talked to him in weeks. Evidently, Flex kept some things to himself. Chenille too.

"I'm so sorry," Raya whispered. "Chenille, I'll call you later. We should go."

Lyle waved them off. "Nonsense. It's good to be awake

and well enough to talk at the same time. Besides, I want to know about the ring." He wiggled his eyebrows. "Is it from any guy I know?"

Raya shook her head. "No, but it was given to that guy. By another girl."

"Bummer. Well, I just coach him. I can't be held responsible for his actions."

"Or yours." Chenille gently pushed him back onto the bed and then pushed a button to raise it higher so he'd stop straining to see them.

He smiled. "And it's good to see you, Lily. And I do see you hiding over there."

Lily emerged from behind the aquarium. "Sorry we were so loud."

"Loud? Please. These two don't know the meaning of the word *quiet*," he said, pointing to Raya and Chenille. "And if it's not them, it's that other little bird, who conveniently forgets the good parts—except how beautiful a certain fashion designer is."

Warmth rushed to Raya's cheeks. What had Flex been telling him? "Sounds like a big lug instead of a little bird. Don't believe a word he says."

Lyle patted Chenille's hand. "We don't have to, right honey? All we have to do is look at the two of you."

"I told you, Raya. Flex might be the one." Lily looked pleased with herself.

Chenille smoothed her husband's scalp. "I don't know, Raya, that bird usually talks some pretty good stuff when he lands here. I'd listen if I were you."

If only all I wanted to do was listen.

Raya scratched her scalp between her new microbraids, so much heavier than the last time she'd worn this style. She and Flex were getting too comfortable. Since that day at the platform, the lines had blurred into lingering hugs and here-and-there kisses. And most dangerous? The looks they gave one another. Looks that said . . .

"So the bird's been telling you good stuff about me, has he? We'll see."

In truth, she could already see. Attending biweekly practices and resuming her daily workouts had made her closer to Flex than ever. Each day it grew more difficult to keep her guard up. They'd have to have a talk. Soon.

At least she had the money for the uniforms. And now that Megan had accepted a design, it'd be a job getting the uniforms done in time, but she'd make it happen. Then she'd let Flex take the team from there. Soon her twelve-week program would be over as well. Whatever was growing between them would have to end too. She couldn't disappoint God, or herself, again.

Chenille took down the handrail of the rented hospital bed and sat closer to her husband. How much were they paying for that? The nursing care for the few hours Chenille came to the firm or to church cost a tidy sum already. So much that Chenille refused to discuss it at all. Raya had to help, even if it meant revisiting her worst moment.

She joined Lily on the lonely brown sofa jammed in beside Lyle's bed and equipment. Chenille lost herself in Lyle's eyes. Lily and Raya smiled at each other, then opted for small talk.

"I checked out your father's TV channel. Quite a setup he has there." Lily tried to sound cheerful.

Raya cringed. "It's not his anymore. They kept him on, but he's just a figurehead. Sorry for anything you might have seen."

Lily stared at her with questioning eyes. "It's been inspiring, really. My mother likes it. I can't take the videos, but some of it is very good. There's a modeling contest and a scholarship drive. Very hopeful."

Hopeful? Raya couldn't hide her shock. The Mocha Man modeling contest had been the final straw in her decision to quit Nia. To her, the contest was as degrading and stupid as the similar shows for women.

"Are you serious? You liked that?"

Lily nodded. "I did. Many of the guys were Christians. Just trying to catch a break. Hardworking." She lowered her eyes at Raya. "You should check it out."

"I doubt I will, but you never know."

Well, she did know, but there was always the off chance that a TV might drop out of the sky and attack her. That's about what it would take. What foolishness would the new executives come up with next?

Lyle coughed again. "Did I fall asleep? Sorry."

Chenille offered him another blanket. "You'd better rest, honey. You have an appointment in the morning. I'll show the girls out."

He barely accepted the extra layer of covering before nodding off again.

Lily and Raya tiptoed to the door, leaving their boss to her real job. When she tried to rise, they ran outside into a driving wind.

"Oh yeah," Lily said, before turning to go in the opposite direction. "This was delivered for you. I knew I'd see you tonight, so I brought it along." She waved and disappeared before Raya could ask more.

Not that she needed to. The Nia Network's heritage seal and chocolate-colored stationery told it all. The Nia ball. Thanksgiving Day and here in New York. How was she going to get out of this one?

"You don't have to do this, you know." Flex's breath steamed in the winter air.

Raya pulled her coat tighter, careful not to step on a patch of ice lurking beneath the snow. "I wanted to help. Both for you and for Jay. I think it's great that you're renting part of your place to him and Miss Bea. Maybe this can be a new start for him."

And an end for us.

She adjusted her arms around a box of magazines marked "Black Enterprise 1992–95." It was the fifth box she'd lugged to the U-Haul so far. How many magazines did Flex have? And why? What did a personal trainer need with *Money*, *Forbes*, and everything in between? She was afraid to ask.

Each day it seemed she learned something new about Flex—his love for Central Park hot dogs in spite of his rigid fitness diet and his uncanny ability to recite all of Sugar Hill Gang's "Rapper's Delight." He even liked her staple, Vanilla Coke. It didn't taste bad on him either. She sighed, knowing already that the talk she'd planned to have with him wouldn't happen tonight. They would have to discuss this "friendship" though. She couldn't take much more.

As quickly as she thought that, he wrapped his arms around her shoulders.

"You really didn't have to come, but I'm glad you did. Thanks for sharing this with me." He flashed her favorite smile, the one that made her stomach hurt.

She escaped his grasp. "It's nothing," she said, pretending her heart wasn't flipping. Since those kisses in the subway, every look from Flex made her feel like that old Roberta Flack tune. He was killing her softly. And he didn't even have a song.

Jay emerged from the house and cleared his throat. "I know she's cute and all, Coach, but it's cold out here."

Flex laughed. "Right. Right. I don't want to leave Miss Bea at the new place alone too long. Let's get on the road."

And so they did. With a van full of clothes, books, and magazines waiting to join the furniture and workout equipment at the new place, they set out together, Raya, Jay, and Flex, smelling his usual lemony self.

Raya stretched her new muscles, barely strained after moving boxes that would have killed her two months ago. It was her mind that needed a workout now, a workout in God's Word. Only nothing would come to mind.

Lord Jesus, keep me from falling.

Flex reached over the sleeping boy between them for Raya's hand. "I've been doing some thinking. We should—"

"What happened to your mother? I thought she'd be here today. I know she's not moving with you, but—"

"She's busy." Flex released her fingers. Anger seasoned his words.

Jay snored on the seat between them, breaking up the tension. He was faking, but it was cute anyway. Especially when he tricked himself into going to sleep for real.

Raya let the silence envelope her, wondering whether to pick up the subject of Flex's mother again. She hadn't meant to bring it up at all, but when he started in on things between the two of them, fear rose up in her, scrambling her words. Didn't she want to talk about things? Not now. Later, when they were alone. That tightened her throat. No, they didn't need to be alone. This was just fine.

Though they didn't discuss their families much, both Raya and Flex shared similar hurts with their parents, hurts that didn't require explanations. She'd gathered from their conversations that most of Flex's anger was directed at his father, especially regarding his parents' reconciliation. That she just didn't get. She'd give anything to have her parents back together. Well, almost anything.

Should she ask more? Did she dare go there with him when she hadn't been forthcoming about her own family? It would only complicate things to tell him about Daddy, about the network.

Complicate things for whom? You or him?

It was easier to keep things on his turf. "Are you mad at her? Your mother, I mean?" A week ago, he'd relayed the news of his parents' marriage like a crime on the evening news. "I'd think you'd be happy."

He gripped the wheel but kept his gaze fixed straight ahead. "You'd think? You have no idea what my father is about."

This was a bad idea. "But I do have some idea what you're about. Or at least I'm starting to know. I also know how it feels to need forgiveness and not receive it. If I recall, it was you who helped me with that."

It was his turn to sigh. "That was different. You couldn't forgive yourself for . . . for whatever it was you thought was so terrible."

She held her breath for a moment. Would they ever become close enough for her to tell him everything? Not if she could help it.

Then why are you trying to be his counselor? Mind your own business.

The van rolled to a stop in front of the new place. Raya smiled at its cheery exterior and sunny windows. If funds had been tight for Flex before, they certainly would be even tighter now, even with tenants.

"What you told me made good sense, Flex. Accept, believe, and confess. It's what saves us, what keeps us. Accept your parents' marriage, believe that God is working things for your good, and confess your anger." She reached across Jay and touched Flex's jacket. "Tell your dad—both down here and up there—why you feel the way you do."

His jaw set into a line. "Why not try that with your father? You won't even talk about him."

Raya pulled back her hand. How long would it be before Flex found out who her father was? What would he think of her then? She'd thought that Lyle, Chenille, or especially Megan would have done the deed of telling him by now, but they'd left the job to her. Only the right time hadn't come up. Until now.

"My father? I . . . I don't know. It's a long story."

"I like those kind." Flex eyed her patiently. She looked away.

Jay poked his head up between them. "Let's go in. A guy can't even sleep around here."

Flex nodded and gave the youngster a little jab with his elbow. A troubled look passed over his face. "One more thing, Raya. What are you doing on Thanksgiving?"

"How are you going to pull it off?" Lily's voice was calm but concerned.

Raya stared at the tickets for the Nia ball and a scathing but predictable note just delivered by courier.

None of your designs, dear. Please. There's a dress reserved for you at Donna Karan.

Lily frowned. "Donna Karan? Don't get me wrong, DK is amazing. I'd do almost anything to wear one of those dresses, but it just doesn't seem . . ."

"Me?" Raya had to agree.

"Exactly. Don't tell me, your mom's dress is from there too."

"You know it. I don't know how I'm going to pull this off. Whenever I'm around Vera, I get totally goofy."

"I hear you. My mother practically waits by the door every night waiting for the husband to follow me in and the baby to drop out. You're being pretty ambitious, I've got to say. The ball and the basketball game too? How's that going to work?"

Raya dropped into her chair. "I don't know. I have no idea why I told Flex I could cover the game. He still won't tell me what's so important that he has to disappoint the boys." Especially after he was so intent that she not disappoint them with the uniforms.

Admiring the network's signature chocolate-colored invitation, Lily shook her head. "Who knows? Probably trying to surprise you with something." Her fingers traced the twenty-five gold stars embossed around the edge of the stationery—one for each year of the network. One for each year of Raya's life.

"You like that? My father must have insisted they at least keep the original invitation design. People look for it."

She wanted to think so, anyway. The more probable truth was that the new Allied Media execs were too lazy to come up with something new. Nia was just another name in their portfolio now. And her father? Just one more name on the payroll.

"I do like the invites," Lily said. "And you can make the game and the ball, but you'll need a plan."

Raya nodded. "That's why I came to you. I envision the ideas, but you make them happen. Maybe you can *pattern* a way for me to be a baller and a beauty all in one night?" She squeezed Lily's arm.

Her new friend's lips slid sideways. "It'll cost ya."

Raya's mouth flooded with laughter. "Anything." She

clutched her patchwork leather bag. "Within reason. I'm too broke to get another one of these."

Lily narrowed one eye, and Raya knew she'd answered too quickly. "Your shoes. The high pink ones."

Raya gulped. "The Via Spigas? You gotta be kidding—"

"I'm not." Lily made a pouty face, then smiled. "You can make it on your own, you know. Seriously."

Maybe, but Raya wasn't willing to take the chance. Things weren't the greatest between her and her parents, but she didn't want to disappoint them either. She'd done enough of that.

"The shoes are yours. Not that you can wear them until spring anyway."

"Tights, girl. Get with it." Lily drove a hard bargain.

"Wait, what size do you wear?"

Lily slammed her boot up onto the desk. "Eight and a half. Hoping I had some tiny Asian feet you saw in a movie?"

Raya held on to the chair as laughter overcame her. Salt wound down her cheek, the first happy tear in a long time. "You're too funny." She took a breath. "I didn't even think you noticed those shoes."

"I notice everything. Speaking of which, exactly what is up with you and Flex? We all want to know, but I was nominated to find out the details. He sure calls here enough."

Raya wadded up a piece of paper from her sketchpad and tossed it Lily's way. "So that's what y'all do behind my back, huh? Send the pattern chick to get the goods? Talking about him is off-limits, remember?"

If only thinking about him was . . .

"Raya!"

Both women turned slowly, hoping they'd only imagined the sickening whine. There was anguish in the voice this time, but it wasn't any easier to listen to. It was a tone they'd both come to dread in the past few weeks.

Megan's voice.

Before Raya could respond, Megan launched across the desk and grabbed her by the shoulders. Noting the distress in Megan's eyes, and realizing that it could be something about her father, Raya fought the urge to shake off her grip.

"Megan, what is it?"

The young woman nodded, then shook her head just as vigorously, making no sense at all. After a gulp of air, she motioned toward Lily. "Can she leave? Please?"

Raya gripped the desk as hard as Megan held her shoulders. What kind of trick was this? She couldn't take any chances. She eyed Lily, who crossed her legs and sat back in the office chair in response.

"She stays," Raya said, hoping she wouldn't regret it.

Megan's eyes flitted back and forth between them, each glance pleading. Finally she fixed her stare on Raya alone. Tears streamed against her foundation in fingers of beige.

"It's my mother," she whispered. "She's HIV positive."

17

"Did he call yet?" Raya tried not to let her desperation come through in her voice. Since Megan's dramatic revelation, Raya had been calling her father night and day. Vera wasn't picking up either, though she managed daily email reminders about the Nia gala.

Gram wound the measuring tape tighter around Raya's waist. "Did who call? Trey?"

"No, Dad. I'm waiting to hear from Dad."

"Good luck with that. You know his attentions are divided these days. This dress will get him though. Your waist is so tiny it's sickening. I'm going to have to go on the program Trey has you on."

Raya looked away without responding. She'd gladly let Gram have her slot. This morning on the bench press, always an awkward exercise after she'd sprained her wrist, she'd looked up at Flex and seen his eyes as though for the first time. Those naturally arched brows and long, glossy lashes . . . the most beautiful eyes she'd ever seen. And then he'd laughed, asking what was wrong, making his eyes laugh too. Even now she shuddered at the thought. When her program was over, they'd have to take a break from seeing each other, maybe permanently.

If not, she was going to fall like a rock for him, and she couldn't do that, especially not now. "The Body for Christ program is no joke, Gram, but I'm sure you'd love it. I'm looking forward to my plan ending though."

Gram pulled a section of pink satin tight around Raya's middle, then took a pin from her mouth to mark the closure. "Something tells me your 'program' might not end as easily as you think."

Tell me about it.

"It will. And you know what? Let's just quit with this trying to rush and make a new dress. The last thing you need is another dress to make. I'll just pick up the clothes Mother picked out—"

"No. You are not your mother, nor should you dress like her. You will arrive in an original." She poked another pin into the fabric. "An Aryanna Joseph original."

Raya's breath caught at the sound of the phrase, one she'd doodled, whispered, and played but never said aloud. A tear veined her cheek.

Gram wiped it away. "What are you doing with your hair?"

Raya fingered the wavy synthetic hair sewn in over her own natural braids. The micros had driven her crazy. "I was thinking of another weave. Something like this but with cornrows in the front. Daddy always likes that one."

Gram unpinned the satin and threw it on the table. "What do *you* like, cherie? You're a woman now. Stop apologizing for the beautiful, creative person you've become. This is a ball, not a funeral."

Raya stared at the still-silent phone. If Megan had been

telling the truth, a funeral might be more of a reality than she was willing to admit. How much longer could she keep it from Gram?

"I need to tell you something—"

The shrill ring of the phone cut through her confessions. Gram walked back to the kitchen, leaving her to the call. Raya lifted the receiver, her eyes pinched together in anticipation. "Hello?"

"Hello, sweetheart. It's Dad."

"And Mom."

Raya's heart surged with relief . . . and confusion. "You're calling me on three-way? What—?"

"No. I'm at your mother's." He cleared his throat. "Visiting."

What kind of craziness? "But, Dad, what about Frances? You didn't—"

"Your father has told me all about that, dear. Thank you for your concern. We've both been tested."

"But you'll have to do it—"

"Again." Her father's voice was pierced with regret. "We must test again. We know."

Silence swallowed his next question, one she knew he would ask the next time they were alone—how did Raya know? They'd always thought her the strong one, as though she were the parent. Well, she wasn't always strong. Sometimes she crumbled and God had to gather the dust.

Instead of asking why Raya might need to know about such things, her father continued with his explanation. "I haven't been with Frances in over a year intimately. I let her move in to make your mother jealous, to make myself feel justified. It didn't work. Even before her diagnosis, she'd moved out. Your mother and I have been . . . talking for a while now."

So that's why Raya hadn't heard from her mother. "I don't know what to say. Why didn't you tell me?"

"We didn't want to disappoint you. We know our rocky relationship has taken its toll on you. It's one reason we wanted you married so badly, so that you could see that there is such a thing as real love, even if we didn't model it for you."

Raya pulled the phone away from her face. So many years of praying, hoping . . .

"So that's it? You're back together just like that?"

Her mother's voice broke. Was she crying? Unbelievable.

"That's not all, darling. Even though we've both been tested, there's a very real possibility that one or both of us could be positive or even have the virus."

Raya gripped the receiver and turned away. "But you, Vera, you're not in danger." She said it more as a question than a statement.

Her father answered. "This is awkward, princess, but yes, Mother is in danger. We were, uh . . . talking before I learned of Frances's news."

Raya pressed the back of her hand to her eyes. Was everyone insane? If only her father had stayed where he belonged—in Costa Mesa with her mother, at the network, in her life . . .

"Daddy . . ." She could say no more.

He choked up. "I know, Ray. I know. I've been praying, and I see I've made a lot of mistakes, with you, with your mother, with the network . . ."

Praying? "We've all made mistakes, Daddy."

"Yes." To Raya's surprise, her mother agreed. "Our first mistake was trying to change you. Can you forgive us?"

Raya's tears drained down her wrist, pooling at her elbow. Onions sizzled in the kitchen behind her. "Yes, I forgive you."

"Good. It's a start. We'll see you at the gala. Wear whatever you like. And, Raya?"

"Yes, Vera?"

"Call me Mom. Talk to you soon."

Raya replaced the phone on its base and wandered into the kitchen. She wrapped her arms around her grandmother's narrow waist.

Gram folded yellow squash into the golden onions. She paused to pat Raya's hands clasped around her. "You had something to tell me?"

Raya rested her cheek against the purple silk stretched across Gram's back. "You remember my first texture, Lily of the Valley?"

Her grandmother stopped stirring. The squash browned, then began to burn. Gram didn't move. "The Lily." She whispered. "I made a cape to go with it, you know. The Lord gave me a dream about it. It was for your birthday a few years back, but you stopped coming around."

"I'm sorry about that. I'm here now. Maybe this is what it was meant for." Raya let go of her favorite seamstress and reached for the spatula. Her birthday was three days from now. As usual, the gala had swallowed it whole.

"Maybe," her grandmother whispered in a way often followed by Gram's final words on everything—"Let's pray." This time, though, she said nothing more.

Knowing it was probably because Gram knew she was hiding something from her, Raya built up the nerve to tell her what was going on with her parents.

Gram blinked a few times and wiped away a few tears, but otherwise remained unchanged. "And the lily? You must wear it now. It will cheer them to see it."

Raya agreed, though she'd decided to wear it anyway. "Thank you, Gram, for everything. I'll lay out the old dress, and we'll hook it up. I'm going, so I might as well go as myself."

"She's a keeper."

Flex looked up in surprise at Roxy, his favorite manicurist. She dropped by the gym regularly, and lately, in the morning. She stood enamored as Raya chatted with some of the other regulars. Her laughter rifled through the place, hollow with morning. As hollow as his heart. This was their last workout together. Twelve weeks had passed all too quickly. He should have said six months instead. A year even. He followed Roxy's eyes to Raya.

"She's something, isn't she?"

He held up a punching shield for Roxy to pummel with her gloved hands.

She swung with determination. "I wanted to get with you. You know that." Another punch. "And when I saw her the first time, I was like, 'Who does she think she is?' But she's not what I expected at all. She's a people person. You need that."

Flex didn't comment, bracing instead for Roxy's next hit. Raya had come early this morning, brought gifts for the staff and some of the morning crowd. New Testaments for some. CDs for others—Donnie McClurkin, India.Arie, Kanye West, Jill Scott. Each musical selection reflected what she'd observed about the individual. He'd watched as they'd opened their gifts and her personal notes. Even the muscle-head guys looked touched.

"Ooh." He rubbed his temple where Roxy had just connected a left hook.

"You all right?" She dropped her fists.

"I'm fine." He smiled and dropped the shield as Raya approached. "See you later." He didn't even look back.

Roxy laughed behind him. "You got it bad."

Worse than that.

Raya waved to Roxy, then punched Flex on the shoulder. "You ready for the final workout, Mister Man?" Her smile lit the dim room.

Rock 'n' roll bellowed through the speakers. Flex took Raya's hand and started for the bikes, trying to ignore the last gift bag, still in her hand. She stopped at the bicycles and set the bag down with her keys.

He released her hand and shuffled through the box of praise CDs near the cardio station. Usually he tried to start the music in the morning, but a newbie had beat him to it today. And rightly so. Raya looked quite distracting. This week brought a new hairstyle, slanted cornrows in the front and wavy afro in the back. At one time he'd achieved the same effect by untwisting his shoulder-length natural hair, but he'd opted for a shorter style after his first manicure. Long hair and pretty fingers were too much. His mother had been beside herself with joy.

He'd been relieved too. That hair had attracted a lot of attention over the years, all from the wrong kinds of women. Now he was with the right kind of woman and had no idea what to do.

He pointed to the bag. "You sure you don't want to put that in the locker room? I'll walk it back for you."

Raya shook her head. "No, I'll leave it here. It's for you."

"Really?"

He popped a CD in, Margaret Becker's *Falling Forward*. That's what he needed to hear today. Falling forward, not falling back. Lately his past haunted him more and more. Glimpses and whispers of women, some who'd hurt him and others who'd been hurt by him. God cleansed the sin, but the wounds remained. He hopped on a bike and pedaled like crazy. Raya did the same, her eyes flashing.

He hadn't come this far to fall back now. He'd let his guard down with Raya, and soon one of them would be hurt, if it wasn't too late already. Maybe this parting was for the best, even if it didn't seem so in his heart.

"I got you something too. For your birthday." He had to shout a little over the music, and he hadn't planned to tell her until the session was over, but her gift sort of put him on the spot. Not that he'd been able to give her what he wanted. It was a stupid gift the more he thought about it, but at the time it had seemed appropriate to send the message he wanted to send—that he wanted to continue their friendship. Maybe one day, when he'd become a man worthy of her, he could offer more. Flex tried not to even think about it.

She stopped pedaling. "My birthday? Who told you?"

Flex rode on, afraid to look at her. For all his ability to turn to stone with everyone else, he melted at the sight of Raya. "You said something one morning about your birthday being two days before Thanksgiving."

"You remembered that?" She pedaled again, slowly now.

"Of course I remembered. It was important." *You're important.* "Chenille's hints over the weekend didn't hurt either."

He grinned but hurt at the same time. With all that his friends were going through, they were still praying for Flex. And for Raya. How was it that Lyle was walking through the valley of death and Flex still couldn't deal with his own life?

Thinking of the man he'd been, the man he could be again, Flex wondered if he'd ever be able to be with someone, stick with someone. He pedaled faster. "For the weapons of our warfare are not of the flesh, but divinely powerful for the destruction of fortresses." He mumbled the words, glad for the blaring music, which quit all too soon. He paused and looked at Raya, for a moment considering forgetting all his plans and proposing right there . . .

They moved to the bench press in silence. Instead of lying down on the bench, Raya sat on it. "I know we're supposed to be working out today, but if you don't mind, I'd like to give you your present now."

"And get yours, I'd bet." Great. Why had he even mentioned it?

She smiled. "How'd you know? You got a girl's curiosity up."

"It's nothing special. I probably shouldn't have mentioned it. I—"

"It's okay. Anything from you is special. You've already given me the sessions. It was a wonderful gift. Who knew how out of shape I really was?"

Nobody. You were gorgeous then. Now . . .

He turned away, not wanting to even think about it.

"Be right back."

He made it to his locker in three strides and snatched the small bag covered with lilies. He'd searched all over the city for something to go with his strange gift. A stupid idea. Maybe he should ask her to wait and try to get her something later.

Just give it to her.

He was stuck. On his way back to Raya, he passed the leg press, where one of the bodybuilders squinted at the little flowered bag, then pushed upward with his monstrous thighs. "It's perfect, man. Good looking out. Don't let her get away, okay?" The big guy's voice lowered. "She's been talking to my wife. Things are really turning around."

Flex nodded and walked back over to the bench press. He'd seen Raya talking to a number of women after her sessions in the morning. Actresses, models, bodybuilders. Beautiful women who weren't exactly looking for a Bible study. Somehow Raya's flair and self-confidence set them at ease. But marriage counseling? He'd have to pay closer attention. She was definitely a team player. Something a loner like him could use.

"Like I said, it's not much, but I tried." His voice felt raw and scratchy as he spoke. "Here."

Raya took the bag from his outstretched hand. Her smile was tender. She patted the bench beside her.

"Lilies."

He sat, reeling as she leaned into him. "Yes. The Lily of the Valley. That's what you are to me. It's like a lot of bad stuff has happened lately with Lyle, the team, my family, but in the midst of the downtime, there you were . . . blooming."

Her hand brushed his face. "If all you gave me was this bag and what you just said, it would be a beautiful gift."

"Open it." He mumbled something else, incoherent even to himself. As she drew the silver frame upward, he turned away.

She gasped. "You . . . you drew this?"

Her fingernails dug into his arm, but he didn't pry her hand away. Did she like it? It seemed that way. He turned, staring at the drawing, a sketch of her in the prom picture he'd admired at her apartment. Chenille had provided him with a similar shot to draw from.

"I'm not as good as you or anything, but I wanted to thank you for being my . . . friend." He wanted to say more, but he stopped himself.

Raya rubbed her finger across the word engraved below the freehand sketch.

Forever.

Her eyes looked moist. If she cried, he'd want to kiss her, and he'd done enough of that. Too much, in fact. He rubbed his temples.

"Forever?" She whispered. "What does that mean?"

That I'll love you until my last breath.

223

"That even if we don't see each other as often, we'll always be friends. Or at least I hope so."

"Oh." The word escaped her mouth like air from a deflated balloon.

Maybe she didn't like it after all. Why weren't women simpler? The iron he faced every day made its expectations clear. Did she want more? If she really knew who he was, the things he'd done, she'd feel differently.

"Chenille helped me get those little silk flowers on there. That was a nightmare. And the oil crayons . . ." His words all ran together the same way the prayer was melting together in his mind.

Help me, God. I'm sinking here. Big-time.

She gave him a kind but reserved smile. "It's beautiful." With that, she deposited it back into its little bag and then bounced to the cardio area and returned with her bag, a large gold one. She held it out to him.

Flex took a deep breath and stuck his hand inside. He touched cloth. A team uniform, maybe? He tugged up a wad of silky material. Nope. Definitely not. A running suit similar to the one Raya had worn that day they'd run into each other hung from his fingers. Only this suit was larger, with a hood. The colors were just as bold, but the mustard yellow was a more golden color. When he held the fabric up to the light, the faint outline of tiger stripes showed at both sides of the suit. He'd probably never wear it anywhere, but it was amazing.

"Wow."

One corner of her mouth turned up. "Is that all you have to say?"

He searched for words, but they wouldn't come. "I . . ."

"You don't like it. I told them you wouldn't." She tried to snatch the garment back.

He held fast while she stretched the fabric across the gap between them. Flex tugged it back gently. "Wait. Give it back. You're going to mess it up. And who's them?"

"Jean and Lily." She let the suit snap back into his hands. "I told them you'd hate it. You're never going to wear it. I can tell by the look on your face." Her voice rose a little.

Roxy rocked forward on tiptoes on the elevated boxing platform behind them. He ignored her. Without meaning to, he'd hurt her feelings. Again.

"I love it. Seriously. Isn't that what I told you about the other one?" He took her chin in his hands.

His boss was certainly monitoring the floor and would have something to say about this little gift exchange, but he had to let Raya know he appreciated her gift. And her presence. Her father hadn't looked very friendly in the photo, but on days like this, Flex thanked God for Raya's parents. They must have been in love once. Only love could create someone as special as her.

She shrugged. "I guess you did say that."

He smiled, tucking the outfit back in the bag. "See? And you know why I love it?"

Raya's eyes rolled upward. She shook her head. "Here we go."

"'Cause it makes me want to sweat!" He jumped on the spotting rack on the back of the bench and struck a pose, growling the way Raya did during a grueling set.

Raya snorted and slid onto her back, raising her hands above her. He checked the pins on the plates. She pushed her gloves down between her fingers, grabbed the bar, and pushed up with a roar like the one he'd just let loose.

Lord, I love that sound.

"That's it. Give me fourteen more." *Years, that is. Days. Hours. Minutes. Anything.*

Somehow he had to make this session last forever.

"C'mon, Jay. Get your shoes on." Flex called after the boy for the third time before climbing the stairs to his own apartment. The place was all his, down to the furnishings, but Miss Bea, Jay's aunt, couldn't handle the stairs, so he slept up there. Thankfully, Miss Bea enjoyed having a huge kitchen at her disposal. He had a bit more meat on his frame to prove it, most of it muscle. For all his metabolic calculations, he never imagined the endurance greens and corn bread could provide.

"Is Miss Joseph comin'?" Jay emerged at the top of the stairs, wearing a smile and the bright basketball uniform Raya had designed. "Or is she meeting us there?"

Flex smiled too, taking notice that the boy had started calling Raya Miss Joseph. For all Jay's rough act, the young man seemed to both admire and respect Raya quite a bit.

"She's meeting us at the gym." Flex heaved his garment bag over his shoulder and grabbed a second bag containing his shoes and accessories. He stuffed his keys into his pocket. "She'll drop you by here after."

Jay shrugged. "Whatever. I just want to make sure one of you actually shows up for the game. I know we're just a bunch of kids and all."

Flex checked Jay's neck for the key he'd given him on a chain. He tried to ignore the sting of the boy's words, but they'd already hit their mark. "Look, we've been through this. I'd be there if I could—"

"Right."

Flex wondered himself if the words were really true. Did it even matter if he went to the contest now? The way he'd bulked up over the past month, he'd never have a chance at winning anyway. Still, he had to try. That hundred-thousand-dollar grand prize could help him launch his fitness business and show his father there was more to Flex than being Fletcher Longhurst's son. If he could get his head out of the past for more than five minutes, maybe the winnings could secure a beginning for him and Raya too. No, he had to go.

"Come on." Flex led the way downstairs.

Fumbling with his bags, he motioned for Jay to open the door. "It's just something I have to do. When you get older, you'll understand," Flex said.

"Will he?" The female voice caught him off guard.

Flex pivoted on one foot to find Raya standing like a sculpture at the front door. Her hair, a giant fro with a pink rose tucked behind one ear, made him want to drop his bags and set off for the game with her and Jay.

Like a family.

"Hey. I thought you were meeting us at the gym." He tore his gaze away from her and that dreamy afro, sandy brown at the roots and gold at the ends. He reeled his heart in, forcing himself to deal with facts, not fantasies. They weren't a family, no matter how much it seemed so sometimes. And he was in no position to change that. If he didn't win tonight, he might never be.

Raya stared at a piece of paper she'd taken from her pocket, then refolded it and stuck it back in her pocket.

"That was the plan, to meet you there, but I wanted to wish you well for your . . . whatever it is. I know it must be really important for you to miss the game." She eyed his bags curiously but didn't ask more.

His shoulders relaxed. He leaned over to kiss her lips but went for her forehead instead. No more of that. She rewarded him with a peck on the cheek, which he made no move to wipe away. Her plum lipstick, his favorite, would go with him all the way downtown. He'd have to cleanse his face before the first-round judging anyway.

"People! We have a basketball game, okay? Enough with the kissing already." Jay squeezed by them and walked slowly toward the subway station. He looked thoroughly amused and disgusted.

Raya tried to pull away.

Flex held her. "Let him go. He does this every morning. He'll stop at the corner." That rose, the biggest one he'd ever seen, brushed against his face. He fought the urge to kiss her—and not on the forehead. "Thanks for the encouragement. And for understanding. And thanks for all our talks. I'm really going to miss you at the gym."

She smiled in a way that let him know that she'd miss him too but that she'd be glad when it was all over, including tonight. The look in her eyes didn't hurt him. He understood. She both thrilled and terrified him.

Best to steer things back to safe ground. "What you said the other day, when we were praying for Lyle, it really got to me."

"About the fellowship of Christ's sufferings?" She traced the edge of her lips for runaway gloss.

He smiled, tapping his cheek. "You don't have to worry about that. I think I got all of it."

She smiled. "It looks good on you."

A knot formed in his throat. So much for safe ground. "About that suffering thing though. It's easy to always concentrate on the blessings, you know, the good stuff. But this thing with Chenille and Lyle is really challenging me. Taking me deeper."

He could have easily added that this thing with Raya was challenging him spiritually too, like no relationship ever had before. The more he felt for Raya, cared for her, the more he realized how wrong his previous connections had been. He realized what had really been exchanged and how he was tied to those women too, in a mysterious, horrible way.

One flesh.

And now here he was, wanting to be one flesh again, only in the right way, with the ring and the dress, everything. Maybe if he told her everything, she could wait. No, he couldn't ask that of her, and he couldn't take his father's money either, whatever was left of it now that he was saving the world and all. The checks came without Flex asking now, but knowing his father, one argument between his parents could cut that off. He couldn't expect Raya to live like that. He had to let her go. Each night he vowed not to fall deeper for her, but every dawn found him sinking farther into love's quicksand. What would he do when he stopped seeing her altogether? He'd be done for.

The flower sagged over Raya's earlobe, undone by a flurry of snow. Jay stood like a snowman on Slim Fast at the corner. Flex tried not to wonder where the flower had come from. Probably a birthday gift from some rich cat. So much for the goofy picture frame.

Forever.

How corny could you get?

"I'll walk you to the station," he called after her as she walked away, motioning for him to follow.

He pointed a finger at Jay. "Stay there, son. We're coming."

He cleared his throat. He hadn't meant to call Jay "son" and was grateful Raya hadn't made note of it. His mother used the phrase intermittently toward him, but his father never had. It had always been "Fletcher." Somehow, hearing it, even from his own lips, warmed Flex's heart. In truth, wild little Jay and sweet Aunt Bea, Lyle and Chenille, and even Raya were all becoming part of his family.

As they reached the corner, his leather gloves intertwined with Raya's suede ones. This time it was her hand that took his. He smiled in surprise, both at her grasp and at the gift she tucked inside his jacket pocket.

A half-frozen pink rose.

"That was awesome!"

Raya shook her head at Jay, who was still floating on air after his first basketball game. She sighed.

"It was a good game."

The boy craned his neck at her. "Good? Did you see how I flew through the air like Jordan? And that three-pointer? Ooh-wee! I was on tonight."

She rolled her eyes. "Yes, you were on, but you threw the team off. If you'd followed the plays, it would have led to opportunities to actually win the game. That's the goal, you know. Next time pass to Juan and let him draw the fouls, get their big man out of the game."

Jay shrugged. "We'll win next time. I'll really be on then." The boy kicked a snowdrift into the street.

It was hopeless to try to make him understand. No wonder he and Flex got along so well. She checked her watch—6:30. The ball started at 7:00, but her father seldom turned up before 8:00. She trotted up the steps behind Jay, watching as the boy turned his new key in the lock. She stepped slowly to follow him inside. After treating the brokenhearted team (except for Jay, of course) to ice cream after the game and waiting for Juan's mother to show up, Raya was way off Lily's schedule. But she could still pull it off if she could just—

"Miss Raya!"

Raya pushed her way inside and saw Miss Bea sprawled

out on the rug she'd given Flex as a housewarming gift. A ribbon of blood trailed from the old woman's lips.

With Jay hugged to her side, Raya reached for the phone. As she did, a wad of paper, her agenda for the day, fell from her fist onto the floor.

18

The lights burned his skin, but Flex smiled anyway. He'd made it to the set of the contest, held on a side stage at the Nia Network's annual ball. A guy reeking of baby oil and looking like a copper-colored seal slithered by, his feet slapping against the oak floors of the Metropolitan Pavilion, a wonder at any time of year with its twenty-foot ceilings and early 1900s decor. Though Flex didn't agree with all of the network's programming choices, somebody knew how to do things right.

With his stomach rumbling and his too-tight jeans cutting into his flesh, Flex felt pretty much like a sellout too. It was a meat market, this contest. The dressing rooms reeked of hair mousse and body wax. Man-O-Cure must have made a killing in the past few days. Problems with Jay and Miss Bea's doctor's appointment had made Flex miss his last few appointments. In preparation for today, he'd done nothing more than shower and clip his nails. If he was going to do this, he might as well be real about it. Sometimes it seemed as if his entire life had turned into a lie.

"Can you step over here, please?" The producer didn't bother to look up at him from where she stood below the stage but looked toward an *X* taped near his feet.

Flex took a few steps, then froze when she tossed a shiny bikini swimsuit his way. He was just another steer, no doubt about it. For all his hopes of winning the Mr. Mocha, trotting around in a Speedo wasn't part of the bargain. The yellow slip of spandex dropped to the floor. He made no move to retrieve it.

Anger creased the producer's face as she climbed onto the stage, picked up the swimming trunks, and attempted to hold the horrid things across Flex's waist. He backed away.

She frowned. "Nobody likes ice, no matter how cute it is. If you want to keep placing, loosen up a little." She stretched out the ridiculous getup a second time.

Flex retrieved one of the registration forms from the music stand behind her. He'd received a similar one in the mail. "I brought my own stuff. Just like it says here, see? Activewear." He pointed to his mesh shirt and jogging pants hanging on the rack nearby.

She laughed in his face. "You're kidding, right?"

He banged his forehead with the heel of his hand.

Lord, I'm so sorry. I missed the boys' game . . . for this?

"Seriously. That's what I'm wearing."

The lady shrugged, dragging her tapered fingers down the clipboard until she found his name. She drew a line through it with permanent marker.

"If you want to lose, that's on you. Your call-in votes were high, but all the other guys will be in these." She held up the poor excuse for a suit. "What you have over there is plain, black, and flat. It won't pop under the lights." She shrugged. "You'll be a wash."

Heart in his throat, Flex scrambled off the stage and

grabbed for his bag. He tossed out the shoes and ties he'd meticulously placed there hours earlier in search of something he'd stuffed in there and forgotten. Something that would pop—the unitard Raya had brought him.

She'd dared him to wear the outfit around the gym, even saying she'd have spies watching out to make sure he did. He'd laughed but promised himself not to do any such thing. Ever. He dug like crazy to find it now. Compared to that yellow horror of a swimsuit, Raya's outfit looked like the tuxedo he'd chosen for evening wear.

His hand slipped under the piece of cardboard at the bottom of the bag. A cool, stretchy something touched his fingers. He shook out the spandex item, thankful for every bit of the added fabric in the man's version. Flex was especially thankful for the hood. Too bad it couldn't hide his face. Not that Raya would ever watch Nia. She'd made comments about it on more than one occasion, and he was ashamed to say that he still watched it sometimes, that he'd even come back to the Lord after watching a program during the gospel hour.

Even though she wouldn't be watching, there were always all the people at the gym and probably some of the kids on the team. Suddenly only a win would make being here worth it. A win that seemed impossible, according to the producer. He'd have to call on some of Raya's nerve. Lord knows she'd be able to pull this off—wearing the suit, winning the contest, all of it. Though she got down on herself sometimes, in the end, she always came up fighting. Flex would too.

On his own terms.

"Is that it? Hmm . . . I don't know. I still think you'll lose." It didn't seem as if the woman had looked up, but she had somehow.

"Look, I didn't come here to go home a loser, but I didn't

come here to be a stripper either. This is what I'm wearing. Let me put it on, and you may think differently."

The whistle blew backstage as the aromas of turkey and dressing whipped through Flex's nose. He ignored the scents, focusing on the no-holds-barred dinner Miss Bea had promised later. He'd tried to talk her out of it, but she'd insisted. And he wasn't complaining.

After this foolishness he'd need more than a good meal. It was as if every guy who'd ever beat him out of a modeling job was here. He followed the crowd, including an annoying pair of twins he'd met at a Ralph Lauren casting call a few months back. They'd tried to convince him to go out for the *Ebony* bachelors spread. The memory of his father's face in that lineup so many years before ruined any possibility of Flex trying for that layout. He'd tried to explain, but the twins had somehow misunderstood. Today they'd snubbed him at every turn. The taller brother snorted and adjusted his emerald green Speedos.

"He must be kidding wearing that," the other brother whispered loud enough for all to hear. "No experience. He'll make us all look bad."

Flex grabbed the rail of the makeshift stairs, thankful for the side curtain. Those guys didn't need anyone to make them look bad. They were doing a great job all by themselves. He took a deep breath and closed his eyes. Raya's soothing voice filled his mind. *"Accept. Believe. Confess. You can do all things through Christ."*

Raya had taken to having the boys recite the words during practices, and Flex thanked her for the ritual now. If she'd had the heart to make this outfit, he was going to have the guts to wear it well.

The aggravated producer tapped him on the shoulder. "Is there anything you want us to say about that . . . that thing you've got on? It's a little, well . . . interesting. That hood . . ."

"This is an original design from Garments of Praise Fashion Design. Real clothes for real men."

Flex steeled his shoulders and tightened his muscles until the blood pumped into his new, larger frame. It was a photo shoot trick, and he hated to use it, but it was all he had.

The woman's eyes widened. "I like that." She held a narrow finger to her lips. "Step up. You'll be on soon. Who knows . . . maybe they'll like it."

Flex climbed up onto the landing, thankful the light blinded his view of the audience. Whether they'd like it or not, he couldn't predict, but millions of people were about to see the real him, covered by the handiwork of a good woman and the blood of a Jewish carpenter.

Gasps followed them inside the pavilion. Raya allowed herself a small grin when one of her mother's society friends covered her mouth and another spilled her champagne at the sight of her.

A ramrod-straight man in tails offered Raya a glass of water with a lavender bud floating in it. Daddy was always full of surprises.

"Maybe later," Raya said, still watching the reaction at each gold-lace-covered table she passed. The chairs were covered as well, in ivory and chocolate linen, two of each at each table. A man in a tweed sport coat gave her an empty-eyed stare.

"These people don't know what fashion is, coming to a ball with their behinds hanging out. When I came up, folks used to dress at things like this. At least your father will have on his tails," Gram murmured.

Raya nodded, adjusting the long white gloves Gram had insisted on. She'd fought the idea, but when she'd put them on, she had to agree that it was just the right touch. She'd even worn her tiara. Gram had stuck the crown so far into Raya's scalp that she might need brain surgery to get it out, but who could resist being a princess, if only for one night?

"Do you think we should call and check on Jay?" Raya asked through clenched teeth, ignoring the wave of whispers as they passed the rows of round tables on both sides of the ballroom. Raya avoided the sign marked "Interviews and Live Tapings." Her father had always insisted someone else do the celebrity interviews each year, though as a teen, Raya had longed to spend time with her favorite stars. He didn't have to worry about her walking in that direction tonight. Leaving Jay with neighbors after rushing Miss Bea to the hospital had soured Raya for any fun. She'd stay long enough to see her father, and that was it.

"Jay's fine," her grandmother whispered. "Jean Claude and his wife will take good care of him. He's probably still eating. They'll call if they need us."

"But the hospital—"

"The pastor is still with Bea, remember? He has your cell number. Now stop worrying and walk like who you are—the princess of this monstrous kingdom."

Raya made no reply. She knew from Gram's furrowed brow that she also worried about Miss Bea's health. Young people, Gram said, shouldn't think too hard on such matters. Maybe that had worked when Raya was younger, but with all that had happened lately, she didn't feel young anymore. God was calling her into an adult faith, a faith that faced death and embraced life, a faith that saw sin and turned from it, knowing how dangerous it could be.

If only she'd turned away from Flex more often instead of indulging his kisses and touches, each one only serving to bond him closer to her. And for what? He'd made no mention of any hope of a relationship. He'd made it clear from the beginning that he wouldn't be marrying anyone. Though her desire to help the boys and improve her health had been sincere, spending so much time with Flex had been foolish and misguided. Too much like how things had started with Darrell, and look where that had led.

"At least they kept the decorations." Gram shrugged, looking around the pavilion.

It was one of Gram's favorite locations. While still on staff at Nia, Raya had heard that the gala would be at Jay Z's nightclub, but the old-school crowd had opted for classic over trendy. A year ago Raya might have been disappointed to miss out on the antics of some of her favorite performers. Tonight she was glad for the pavilion's stuck-up simplicity.

From the tasteful African cornucopias on each table to the vibrant watercolors, the signature Nia decor remained. The twenty-foot-high African mask with eyes worthy of the best flash shot was a new addition, probably chosen by someone at Allied Media, an up-and-coming black firm owned by some of the richest men of color in the world, a group of venture capitalists known only as the Alliance. The annual ball had always been a private, subtle affair except for the live tapings. It was her father's way of giving back to the community that had made him.

She shivered. Not this year. They'd all be paying homage to something else altogether. Big business with big money. The five-hundred-dollar ticket price would still go to charity, but the message was clear—this was just another media opportunity for Allied Media and their subsidiary businesses, whose logos hung from the ceiling on banner ads worthy of a sporting event.

One banner in particular, off to the right of the room, caught her attention: the Mocha Man Contest. The script was maroon with gold flourish, and the banner sported the silhouette of a broad back and narrow waist. Raya hung her head, trying not to think of the man who fit the profile dead-on. When she saw him again, she'd have to cut off their friendship, relationship, whatever it was. Or face the reality that one day she might not be able to pull away when his kisses ended.

Gram lifted Raya's chin. "It's a nice night. Have a good time. I'm going off to find some people I actually recognize." Gram frowned before moving off. Her touch lingered on Raya's gloved hand. "Watch yourself. There are wolves about."

Raya turned as Gram's hand slipped away. What was that supposed to mean? One look behind her said it all. A tall man with hazel eyes took her right glove and kissed it. Raya's blood iced in her veins. His locks were gone and his goatee shaven, but there was no mistaking this guy's identity. She'd know him anywhere. The groom who almost was.

"Hello, Darrell. Good to see you." It wasn't exactly, but he didn't have to know it.

He let go of one hand, only to take the other and kiss it too. "Aryanna." He spoke with the same delicious tone he'd always used with her, though then he'd called her "baby doll" and "sweetness." She waited for the leap her heart had once felt at his voice, at his touch, but neither surfaced. Though her mistake still haunted her, she'd thanked God for keeping her from marrying this man as many times as she'd kicked herself for becoming intimate with him, for giving all her treasure to a fool.

"You look surprised to see me. I sent the roses on your birthday. I figured you'd know that meant I'd be here."

Darrell's code of gifts. She'd forgotten it already. The flowers had been pretty though. The biggest roses she'd seen in a long time. Shame they'd come from such a bum.

She gently tugged her hand away. "I didn't put the two together, sorry."

Darrell held up both hands, then dropped them at his sides. "Your dress is breathtaking. It was so late that I thought you weren't coming, and then I heard my mother whispering about 'that dress,' and I knew it had to be you. And the tiara is . . . fitting. I suggested you have one for the wedding, remember?" He tugged at his crisp, white sleeves.

She nodded. "As you can imagine, I'm trying to forget. Now if you'll excuse me, I need to find my father."

Though she did need to see her father and leave, Raya's mind was split between Jay and Miss Bea. Seeing Darrell made her realize just how far she'd come from his rich, pampered world and just how far she wanted to stay away from it. Already she was tired of his bourgeois banter.

"Aren't you with someone? I'm sure she's looking for you."

Darrell gave Raya a puppy-dog look, the same one she'd fallen for before. She could still hear his words. *"We're getting married in a few days, what's the big deal?"* The thought turned her stomach. How had she ever let herself become so weak?

"I'm alone, Raya. I came to see you."

"How unfortunate for us both."

Where was Megan when Raya needed her? Probably with her mother. Raya balled her left glove into a fist. The possibility that she too could lose her parents was shoved so far back in her mind that she didn't dare let it come up for air.

240

She wheeled around on her pumps and started back down the main aisle. She'd have to look for her father later.

Immune to her effort to ditch him, Darrell followed, matching every one of Raya's strides with his own long legs. Faced now with a gawking crowd on the right, an exit into the snow in front of her, and the dreaded Mocha Man set to her left, Raya had only moments to make a getaway. The crowd, surging toward the contest, made the decision for her.

Darrell didn't miss a step. "Is that tiara real? Diamonds, I mean? I doubt it at a thing like this. But I'd like to give you something, a gift for all the trouble I caused."

"No thanks."

Why did men like Darrell think gifts fixed everything? True enough, it didn't hurt, but it didn't heal anything either. Only God could do that. She moved closer to the pulsing beat behind the curtain, not pausing to say more. She'd never asked for any explanation from Darrell. She didn't want one now.

He jogged behind her, his tux slapping against a few chairs as he skirted the edge of the aisle to catch up. He grabbed her hand, allowing himself to be dragged along as she pressed forward. He tapped her shoulder, but she stared straight ahead. Corked by the crowd, he was stuck next to her.

Darrell started right in. "Okay, look. Enough with all this. I messed up, okay? I'm sorry for what I did to you. I know that no words can make you believe me, but I'm different now. I got . . . I got saved—"

"What?" The words stopped Raya cold right at the edge of the stage. Why did everybody have to pull the God card?

He shook his head. "It wasn't all lies. I knew you were too good for me. Scary good, you know?"

Raya blinked. She did know. Just like Chenille had said about God—like Aslan from Narnia. She lifted her eyes to the man who had betrayed her and realized, not for the first time, how badly she'd betrayed herself.

"Scared? You were afraid of me?" She shouted over the music.

Darrell nodded. "You're the kind of woman who could make a man lose himself. I wasn't ready for that." His eyes blazed into her. "I'm ready for it now."

Oh, please.

"I'm glad to hear that, Darrell. And I hope you find the woman you're looking for. Right now I need to find Daddy and say hello so I can get home." *And check on Miss Bea and Jay.* "I doubt that a few months has really made that much difference for you."

Hasn't it made a difference for you?

She ignored the thought, partly because of a bronze man sauntering onto center stage in a scant piece of green spandex, the kind of outfit that kept her off the beach these days. She jerked her head away, thankful that the lights again blocked her view. She scanned the crowd for her father. What kind of mess was he putting out now?

Darrell smiled, looking a bit crushed but not dissuaded. "I know it's hard to believe. I'm having a hard time believing it too, but it is what it is. Actually, Megan had a lot to do with it—"

"Megan?"

The music swallowed their words. Raya walked closer to the stage, forced to choose between the parade of pinup models and Darrell's incomprehensible words. Maybe Megan was truly seeking Christ after all. She'd certainly need him now. They all did. She made a note to call Frances and wish her a happy Thanksgiving.

Her pursuer refused to give up. She turned to face him. Darrell smiled. "Those roses were just a flash of what's to come. I know you don't think there can be anything between us, but if you could just let me call you . . ."

The announcer's voice doubled in volume. "And here is the contestant with the highest call-in votes from the first round, wearing the latest in activewear from . . . Garments of Praise Fashion Design."

Raya spun around in time to see a body she knew all too well walk onto the stage. The man's face was shrouded by a hood, only intensifying the effect of his piercing eyes. On the downbeat, Flex threw the hood back and paced across the stage like a hungry tiger. The crowd went wild.

"Flex Dunham, personal trainer and budding entrepreneur, is a representative of a new trend in fashion. The triple C man—clean, crisp, and cut. The votes will tell whether he's the look of the future or just another pretty face. This piece says it all. Real clothes for real men. No sissy Speedos for this guy."

Applause echoed off the rafters. Flex responded by striking a biceps pose. As he did, the lights shifted to follow him, leaving him and Raya face-to-face. He paused as though his feet were nailed to the floor.

Raya tried to run, only to turn into Darrell's chest.

Darrell looked down at her with an understanding glance. "Need to go somewhere and talk?"

"Anywhere but here." The tears she'd vowed not to cry tonight snaked down her face.

19

He had to find her.

"Wait, Mr. Dunham. There's more to winning Mocha Man than shaking a few hands. You still need to meet the choreographer for your video."

Flex stared at the producer, then shook his head. Video? Were these people losing their minds? "I take this contest win very seriously, and I mean no disrespect, but right now I really need to find somebody."

He smoothed his tuxedo against his heart, as if to hold it in. Where was Raya? And what was she doing here? The look in her eyes had cut him to the marrow.

The producer held fast to his arm.

Flex sighed. "See that guy over there? The one with the purple hair? He's my manager. Send the choreographer to him."

The woman's face brightened. "You've signed with someone already? Maybe you're not as green as I thought."

He groaned as she shuffled away toward

the gym's receptionist. Poor guy. Flex would have to take him to lunch next week. Though, knowing Brad, he'd probably eat it right up. Who knows how he'd snuck in here anyway. It seemed all of New York was poking around. Flex would be happier to see Raya than any of the stars milling around in the pavilion, in spite of the tall, dark, and handsome stranger who had led her away. In the time it had taken him to get dressed, he'd lost sight of them both.

Flex pushed through the crowded aisle to the center of the room, where he saw the golden-eyed brute holding Raya's hand. An ocean of people separated them, but nothing would stop him now.

"Excuse me." He weaved in and out of stale conversations and unsipped drinks. "Pardon me," he said, moving closer to the center of the room, only to lose visual on the evil woman stealer. Raya's eyes had told him that all was over between them, but he preferred to focus on the moment when they'd first locked eyes, the instant when joy and pride flashed across her face. Anger had clouded her eyes too quickly for him to be certain, but he'd seen something there before she'd run off with that man.

"Watch it, buddy!"

Flex made a quick apology as he almost toppled a waiter's tray. He moved more slowly now, realizing the enormity of his task. There were too many people. He'd have to wait it out. The crowd would thin sometime. He could only hope she'd still be here.

Why hadn't he just told her in the first place? Sure, he was a little embarrassed about the contest, but was it really that big a deal? She'd looked so hurt, so betrayed . . .

And why? Just for something so silly? Well, not anymore. If he found her tonight, got her away from that big, pompous-looking guy, he'd tell her everything—who his father was, how he felt about her—even ask her to marry him. There was no time for any confusion. He'd make himself plain.

As he came to the decision, still wandering through the maze of tables, he caught sight of a wonderful dress, a floating garden covered with . . .

Lilies.

His lilies.

He paced to the edge of the aisle and started climbing chairs. She wouldn't get away from him. She couldn't.

Lord, please help me explain. Help her to understand.

"Look at him. He's so eager to meet me that he's climbing the furniture. Come on over here, young man." A man's hands, manicured and perfumed, hooked Flex's arm and pulled him to the head table.

The stupid contest. Why couldn't people give him a few minutes' peace? Right now anybody except Jesus would have to take a number. He tried to pull away, but the man's grip held. "Nice to meet you, sir." He turned to his captor, scanning the gentleman's familiar face. He couldn't place the name. Was this the casting director or the acting coach? "I look forward to working with you." The crowd swallowed the lilies, every last one.

The older man released his hold, leaving Flex to consider this strength that matched his own, perhaps even exceeded it. He studied the determined face before him, the eagle eyes. He squinted. Could it be? It was. A masculine version of Mademoiselle's face, the same face from Raya's nightstand. Her father. The eyes had a few more creases, and the hair was sprinkled with white, but it was definitely the same man.

"You look forward to working with me, huh? Handsome and ambitious? Most men are scared of that, but I like it. That's how I was. That's what got me here."

Flex followed the man's eyes to the top of the mask suspended from the ceiling. Between the eyes was a picture of this man. Flex read the words below it aloud.

"Pierre Joseph, founder and CEO, Nia Network."

The words stabbed him. So Raya was—oh, goodness, what had he been thinking? And here he was worrying about his secrets.

"That's me. Now let me show you around. I have a feeling about you. You've got a look. Something fresh. You may be around Nia a long time."

Mr. Joseph's words fell on Flex's ears like lead. The crowd he'd fought to get through melted like butter to greet them, making a line on either side. Raya was first on the right. Her crown and necklace flashed in the light as they approached. Raya's father relaxed his titan grip. Flex suddenly wished for the old man's stubborn squeezing. It had kept his blood flowing at least.

"This is my daughter, Aryanna."

Raya kissed her father's cheek. "We've met, Daddy. We're . . . we're friends."

The other man, the one who'd escorted Raya away, cleared his throat, but Mr. Joseph acted as though he wasn't there. He kissed his daughter's hand and placed it in Flex's unsteady palm.

"Any friend of yours, princess, is a friend of mine."

Flex tried to breathe. Friends? Some friends. How could she not have told him about this? She must think him some kind of fool. The truth twisted like a knife in his chest. She'd done it to him the same way he'd done it to her. They were both fakes. The truth didn't make it hurt any less.

Raya flinched as though his touch cut into her flesh. Her terse smile fooled others, but Flex felt the tension in her wrists and fingers, even through her gloves.

247

"How'd Jay do? The boys? Did they win?" he asked, unable to say more until he could get her alone.

Her eyes clouded. "They lost, and something happened to—"

"Hey, man! Where'd you come from?"

Flex turned from straining to hear what Raya was saying about Jay to standing face-to-face with the man he least wanted to see.

His father.

Raya's father looked all too happy to see Flex's old man.

"And this, you two, is somebody I invite to these things every year, and he never shows up. Why he's stooped low enough to dine with us lowly millionaires tonight I have no idea. Fletch, meet my Ray and her friend, our new Mocha Man."

With a curtsy and a distracted smile, Raya responded to the introduction. Flex had no chance to respond before his father grabbed him into a hearty embrace and then pulled him back for a long, proud look.

"You did good up there," he said. "Good job declining on the Speedos. Horrible, those things."

The receiving line went quiet. Raya's father looked confused.

Flex willed his body not to shake. Why would his father choose now, in front of all these people, to give him the first praise in God knows how long? It didn't matter. As usual, the man hadn't acknowledged their relationship. Neither would he.

"Thank you, sir."

"Congratulations . . . son." Fletcher Rayburn Longhurst II leaned forward once more. Coarse lips brushed Flex's cheek.

As Flex struggled for breath, Raya pulled away. He knew

as her hand escaped his grip that there was no point in run-ning after her. She was gone for good.

It was too good to be true. She should have known that from the beginning. Raya clutched her head, now bare of her tiara. Even with all Gram's careful placement, when Raya heard the ocean waves in Flex's father's voice, saw that fa-miliar spray of freckles across his nose, when she realized who Flex was and what that could mean, she couldn't do a thing but run. And even then he followed, in her heart, in her mind. Darrell had surfaced on the edge of the crowd and tried to grab her hand, but he couldn't hold her.

Even now she imagined Flex standing beside her in that ivory tuxedo, making every man in the house besides her father look ridiculous for having attempted to wear one. As the limousine circled the block again and again, she saw him emerge from the crowd like a dove, only to be swallowed again by the somber silk pigeons and satin-lapelled penguins. Even from this distance, Flex made the entire room, stars and all, look as though they were committing a fashion crime. Raya suddenly realized that his crime had been commit-ted ten years before on a sandy Hawaiian beach when he'd stolen her heart.

Her breath fogged the glass.

Can it really be him?

It didn't seem possible. On the last-chance love vacation she'd planned for her parents, an argument had erupted despite her best planning. Raya had buried herself in the hotel pillows and sheets before running down the unending flights of stairs and onto the beach, barely able to breathe. As the limo pulled off again, the snow on the ground dissolved into sand, into memory. The freezing night gave way to an afternoon sun, a sun that beamed down on two young hearts, a sun that stood still just long enough for promises.

Forever promises.

That sun hung over her mind, along with a memory she'd thought long forgotten . . .

Her throat tightened as she groped along the beach. Too bad she hadn't brought her inhaler down like her grandmother had advised. Instead, she'd fled down the hotel stairs with other things—a headache, a broken heart, and unfortunately, an asthma attack. The teenager paused, her shoulders caving, her head buzzing. Her prayer was simple as she slid to the ground—*Lord, send somebody to help me.*

"Breathe," a voice said.

Raya looked up from between her fifteen-year-old knees. A pair of huge brown eyes beamed at her through a pair of thick glasses. Old, wise eyes trapped in a teenage boy's body.

"Huh?" she asked in a slip of breath.

The rail-thin boy stood beside parents as long and brown as himself. He knelt on the sand beside her and inhaled deeply, as if willing her to imitate him.

"That's it. Now try again."

His mother joined them. "Do you have your inhaler, son? She doesn't look good. Perhaps we should call the—".

Raya shook her head. She'd felt the attack coming on and had gone back to the room to get her asthma medicine, only to find her parents in a fight to end all fights. And her grandmother, who usually remedied such situations, was nowhere to be found.

"I'm fine. Left . . . my . . . inhaler up in my room. Give me a . . ." Her chest wheezed out a breath. ". . . minute."

She tucked her head between her legs again, more from a desire to avoid the strangers gathered around her than from her inability to breathe. Though it probably looked bad to them, it would pass, just like always. Her inhaler wasn't all she'd left behind in her hotel suite. Her parents' voices, even louder than usual, still rang in her head. This vacation was supposed to remind her parents how much they loved each other, but it had only served to make things worse. Now they were fighting again.

About her.

"Come on." The guy pulled her up with a strength that contradicted his frame. "Mom's right. You don't look so good. Let's get a Coke. Sometimes caffeine helps."

She struggled to sigh but couldn't gather enough breath to speak. Nodding instead, she allowed him to take her hand. His strong but gentle grip surprised her, as did his determined look as he tugged her along like some stray dog in need of rescue.

"Two Cokes, please," he said to the man behind the cart.

Raya shot a grim smile at the man behind the counter, who wore a turquoise Hawaiian shirt and a pink lei. He looked happy, like her parents were supposed to be. She gasped, now wishing she'd braved her parents' argument to grab her inhaler.

A gentler grip squeezed her hand. "In through your nose. Out through your mouth." He pulled a bill from the pocket of his shorts and handed it to the drink salesman.

The man narrowed his eyes. "A hundred? Got anything smaller?"

The boy reached across the counter, took a soda and peeled back the top. He held the can up to Raya's lips. His face reddened. "Nothing smaller." He pocketed the change the man gave him, a wad of ones, fives, and tens.

She accepted the cold drink and stared at him. A hundred-dollar bill? On the beach? Who was this guy? He'd looked at the vendor as if he didn't know denominations less than a hundred dollars existed.

And I thought Mom was bad.

He lacked her mother's snobbery though. Something about him was . . . real. Though tall, he couldn't be much older than her. Sixteen at the most. His chest was caved in like someone had hit him with a wrecking ball. And those glasses? They looked like they were made of bulletproof glass. Even so, he had a handsome way about him. And he was a gentleman. She thought of the things her father had said to her mother as she'd fled the hotel room moments before.

"Feel better?" He smiled.

Nice teeth. Must have done the braces early. She rubbed her tongue over her own silver set. "I do. Sorry for just plopping down to die beside you and your family like that. It wasn't as bad as it looked. I get worked up sometimes, but it usually passes . . ."

Her words drifted into silence. She couldn't say what she'd started to say—that her asthma attacks usually coincided with her parents' fights. How could she explain to this stranger, with his Leave It to Beaver mother and freckled, smiling father? He'd never understand.

Tangled in her thoughts, she started off along the sand. Her good Samaritan followed but didn't speak.

The bubbles in the soda tickled her nose as she downed another sip, cold and sweet. She clutched the can with both hands and looked up at the hotel climbing up out of the beach like a concrete palm. If Mother somehow looked down and saw her holding this can of liquid sugar . . .

She's on the fifteenth floor. Besides, they're arguing about you, not looking for you.

"You're cute, you know that? And not, you know, stupid or anything."

Raya froze for a moment. What was she supposed to say to that? This was still a stranger, even if he did seem nice. Best to play it cool.

"Thanks. I think."

He laughed, then waved at his parents as they walked away. "See what I mean? Most of the girls I know would have dived into flirting 101 for the likes of geeky me." With that, he pulled off his bulletproof glasses to reveal a pair of dazzling eyes.

Wow. No geek there.

No wonder those glasses were so thick. Hiding those eyes was a feat. She took a step back and stumbled over a rock in the sand. The beaded edges of her wrap clanged together.

As if aware of the power of his gaze, the handsome stranger whisked the frames back onto his face before steadying her elbow. He leaned in closer to see the fuchsia and tangerine bulbs lining her cover-up.

"Nice. Are those things glass?"

"Plastic." She froze. He was asking about the clothes. She hadn't planned to wear this, but Gram had switched her clothes . . . as always.

"Great colors. It looks good on you."

It was her turn to blush. "Thanks. And thanks for the Coke." She lifted the can. "Your parents are probably looking for you. You'd better get back."

"No rush. I know you don't know me, but if you don't mind, I'd like to hang out with you. My parents are busy, and well, sometimes I just know that something is important and I need to concentrate on it."

She lifted an eyebrow. "And I'm that something today?"

His breath came as deep as Raya wished hers would. "I didn't mean it like that. It's just, well, sort of a knowing I get about things—my dad's stocks usually. Never a person before. Let me shut up. I'm just making it worse."

She smiled and took his hand. She knew this knowing he spoke of, though to her it was more than that. It was God, whispering, tapping her shoulder. He was doing it now.

"It's okay. My parents won't miss me either. Maybe we can just walk down the beach?"

"I'd like that." A wide smile told just how much he'd like it.

They walked hand in hand, talking about everything from Beethoven to beat boxing, with her companion even pausing for a poor rendition of the throaty sounds so much like a beat machine. From there, conversation shifted to Picassos and PSATs, even their somewhat skewed views about God. The elephant in the room, their parents, mocked every pause in the conversation until they changed the subject again. After a treatise on the Harlem Renaissance and Donny Hathaway, they both stopped short, amazed.

"Will you marry me?" he said, his breathing much shallower now.

Raya frowned. "Boy, please."

"Not now, I mean, but someday. Maybe if this God of yours is real, he'll bring us together again. I can't imagine meeting anyone more perfect . . ."

Perfect? The sun must be getting to him.

Besides, they didn't even know one another's names. And she wasn't about to offer hers. He seemed just as reluctant. "Maybe God will do that. Maybe he won't. Let's just take today as a gift, a still sun like God gave Joshua."

The story of how the sun had hung in the sky for one full day at Joshua's request hadn't made much sense when she'd read it with Gram that morning, but somehow, after an afternoon of peace, of hope, of deep breaths, it did.

"What? I thought he brought down the wall of Jericho, like the song." Dude looked seriously puzzled.

"He did. Don't worry about it. I was just thinking out loud." She stared back at the hotel, knowing that Gram would come looking for her soon, if she wasn't already. "We'd better turn around. We've gone pretty far."

She clutched the can of soda, now hot and sticky in her hand. She'd meant to throw it out several times, but the lively conversation had made her forget it altogether.

He nodded as they started back down the beach. The sun dipped below the horizon like a lemon cookie in a bowl of rainbow sherbet. Hues of melon and pink spread across the sky as though God was painting by number.

"My parents aren't looking for me. No doubt they're

arguing right now. I'll walk you back, but I'll probably stay out here."

Raya's beads knocked together as she stopped short beside him. "Your parents? Arguing?" She squinted across the beach at two tall mahogany figures among the evening silhouettes scattered along the edge of the tide. Their smiles from before were noticeably absent, even at this distance. "But they looked so—"

"Happy? It's all an act. People meet, fall in love, and then hate each other for the rest of their lives." He walked faster. "Except for us, maybe, right? We won't be like that." He held her hand to his lips and kissed the top of it.

She dropped her can and jerked away. Was this a serial killer in training? They got their starts young . . . Still, his words burned her heart more than his tender kiss. Tepid Coke spewed out and oozed between her toes.

And his.

She leaned down, tried to clean up the mess. "People forget how much they love each other sometimes, but they can make it right again."

The guy nodded, his Adam's apple bobbing like a turkey's gobble. "Oh, the vacation of love, is it? How's it going so far?"

Her eyes widened. How did he know? Were his parents trying to patch things up too? "It's going . . . fine."

"Is that why you were down here not breathing and they were up there fighting?" He picked up the can and tossed it into the trash. He took the wad of money from his pocket and bent down, wiping her feet.

Was he crazy? Wasting good money like that? She was too upset to care. She wiped her eyes before the tears could escape.

"They'll be fine. It's me. I'm the problem. If I stop drawing and making clothes, things will be better."

She ran a hand down her swimming suit and wrap. It had been so fun to create, but now she wanted to snatch off every bead and throw it into the sea.

He stopped wiping. "Making clothes? You made that?"

She nodded.

"And they're mad about it?"

"Daddy says I should stop doodling and get serious about something. Mother says—"

"Maybe if they stopped talking about you and started talking to each other, something might change, but other than that miracle, you can pretty much hang it up."

He wadded the soggy money back into his pocket without wiping his own sugar-glazed toes. Instead, he stepped away and dipped his feet in the ocean.

Duh. Why hadn't she done the same?

He returned as quickly as he'd come, pulled a dollar and a pen from his pocket, and scribbled his number on the bill. He tucked it in her hand.

"Call me."

Her heart pounded. "Okay."

He moved closer, within kissing range. A second before she raised a hand to push him back, he lifted her hand to his lips and kissed it instead.

"Promise?"

Was this light-headedness the feeling all her boy-crazy friends always talked about? Or was she dizzy from a lack of oxygen?

"Sure. I promise."

They were almost back now, the music rising to meet them with the smell of roasted pork. There would be a luau soon, but the beach was clearing as people went to change for dinner. In the days they'd been here, she'd seen the pattern repeatedly.

But she'd never seen anything like this boy—man— whatever he was. A few steps more and they seemed almost under the perfect sunset, the end of her still sun. Agreeing that this was indeed an important something, she held his hand, caught a few last peeks at those gorgeous eyes, and wondered if Gram would appear with a tiki torch any second. She didn't, and Raya wouldn't have cared if she had.

Why she was so captivated with this guy she wasn't sure. Her friends would have laughed if they'd seen him—hundred dollar bills or no—but she felt drawn to this stranger. Even his hand on hers felt safe, like he was a sure bet. It was good to be sure about something, even for a moment.

She sat down, knowing their time was spent. He smiled, kneeling on one knee now and closer than ever. He tried to keep the talk going even at the cost of going where she wanted least to go. "Now, back to your parents . . . You making clothes is not destroying their marriage. They're way gone. They're making up stuff now. Don't quit creating. It's not about you. It's them. And you'll need something to get you through when they break up—"

Raya kicked at the ground, sending a wave of sand into his face. He shook off his glasses and spit the grainy residue out of his mouth. She hadn't meant to do it, but she couldn't take any more of his doom and gloom talking. Things were hard enough. Hope was all she had. Maybe he wasn't such a nice person after all.

"Hey! What was that for? I was just telling you the truth."

She grabbed the fringe of her cover-up and tugged, sending fuchsia and cantaloupe spheres bouncing along the shore. Along with her heart. "It's not the truth. The only truth is that love is hard and sometimes people need a little help." She hung her head. "Lord willing, I'm going to keep them together." She turned to him. "I'll be praying for your parents too."

He swiped the last of the sand from his eyes. "Don't bother. They enjoy aggravating one another too much. Sometimes . . . I wish they would—"

"You don't mean that."

"I do." He knelt and picked up the beads from where they'd dropped in the sand. He shoved his glasses back on his face and looked up at her. "If you're going to pray for something, ask that God of yours why he lets people who hate each other have kids who get stuck in the middle." He stood, staring into her eyes from close range this time.

"Ask him yourself," Raya said as she tried to run, but the sand swallowed her steps. The bill stuck to her toe as she ran out of the sand and onto the pavement.

His number. And she'd promised to call. She ran faster, trying to forget both the guy and his digits. Raya stared up at the hotel. Right now other promises had to be kept.

Forever promises . . .

"It can't be him," Raya whispered into the New York night as the memory faded.

It couldn't be, but it was. Who knew that string bean would turn into such a hottie? And why he was playing poor she'd never know, except that, same as her, it had something to do with his parents. What was God trying to do, drive her insane? After the way things had turned out with Darrell, was she supposed to believe Flex was her destiny, her knight in a white tuxedo?

Yes.

"Lord, I can't. Maybe back then I could have accepted it, but I'm not even sure about that. Now, well . . . that's just too easy. And things aren't easy anymore, if they ever were."

What an understatement. In the time following Flex's debut on the stage, she and Darrell had had the chance to sit down and really talk about their time together. Though she'd been looking for something to keep her mind off of Flex, Darrell had given her a little too much to chew on, sandwiched between his repeated apologies. "One more thing," he'd said so softly she could barely hear. "A few lady friends of mine have turned up HIV positive of late. I'm testing again. You probably should too. Not to worry though. I look healthy, don't I?"

She'd almost thrown up on his healthy self. First Dad and his mess, and now this. And then Flex turning out to be the prince instead of the pauper. Her heart thudded as the driver made the turn toward the pavilion again. If this was going to happen, why hadn't God warned her, told her not to get with Darrell and ruin everything? She wadded her lily-covered shawl into a pillow and lay down in the back of the limo, wondering if Daddy was putting a horrible missing persons photo of her on Nia. He could be weird like that, not talk to you for months and then explode with concern just when you didn't need it. At least she'd outrun Darrell. He'd followed her in a cab for twenty minutes before giving up. Flex hadn't come after her. Had he seen her too?

She hugged herself, grieving Flex's whispers and kisses, little things she'd never have again. Her cell phone buzzed. Daddy probably. She picked it up and checked the number. Her mother. She'd spied Vera as she sped away, confident that her mother wouldn't risk her silk stockings for a chase. Through the night air, Raya could make out her mother's words—"The indignity of it all."

True enough, but tonight Raya was too frazzled to be dignified. The phone gave one last buzz, then was still. Raya held it, thinking of Jay. When she'd called to check on him, he was already sleeping and there was no word from the hospital. It looked like the only person in danger of dying tonight was her. The image of Flex's father, so distinguished with his midnight and silver beard and dancing eyes, slashed through her mind. It took only a moment to recognize him as the man on all those magazine covers, the ones she'd hauled out of Flex's Bushwick apartment. Remembering where she'd first seen him had taken a few minutes more.

When she'd curtsied to him, Mr. Longhurst had dipped at the waist, his eyes surveying her quickly and completely, a skill her father was also proficient in. Much worse were the dollar signs she'd glimpsed dancing in her father's eyes, just as when she'd become close with Darrell. How could she go through it all again?

The limo stopped in front of Gram, who stood ready on the curb. She grabbed the door and climbed inside.

Ashamed, Raya sat up. She stared out the window. "Sorry if you were waiting long."

Gram said nothing. She placed a bent tiara on Raya's lap. She reached across Raya for the carafe of steaming water Daddy always kept on hand for tea. Her lashes fluttered like a butterfly's wings, curling in a haze of steam. She retrieved two mugs from inside the back of the seat in front of them. She reached into a refrigerated compartment and took out a white-chocolate-covered strawberry for each of them and placed them on china saucers. Daddy had done all the small things, things Raya had loved as a little girl, things that had kept her quiet while he worked his life away. Raya watched as Gram ate the first strawberry, but she shook her head when one was offered to her. She had no stomach for her favorites tonight.

"It can't be that bad." Gram poured a stream of tea into one of the china cups and set it next to her granddaughter. Raya didn't take it. Even mint tea was powerless against this.

But Jesus isn't.

"It's better . . . and worse than anything," Raya whispered.

So many nights she'd wondered what had happened to that skinny boy who'd acted like a man, proposed to her as if love were simply a prize at the bottom of a box of Cracker Jack, something to dig up, play with a while, and discard later.

"Tell me." A string of honey, also from the compartment behind the seat, dripped into Raya's cup from Gram's spoon.

Raya stared at the blue pattern etched into the china, tracing the loops with her eyes. She held it up to her face. "These lines would be beautiful screened onto silk, don't you think?"

"Aryanna."

Raya's breath quickened, but her mouth refused to form the words.

Gram pulled out all the stops, turning down her own seat to retrieve the cranberry muffins and turkey sausage she'd brought along for family breakfast that followed the all-night affair each year.

Raya shook her head. "That's for Daddy. His favorite."

Gram shrugged. "He's a big boy. His wife will feed him."

She swallowed, watching her grandmother sip quietly while peeling Raya like an onion with her eyes. The Bible, the one that she'd tried to talk Gram out of lugging to the ball, would come out next. A trusty sword in the hands of a skilled warrior. Raya turned away, but she heard the thin pages turning.

The older woman turned furiously and then paused, savoring a passage as though it were a confection. She turned again and put down her tea.

"What is it? A sin problem? If so, I've got something for that—'If we confess our sins, he is faithful and just and will forgive us our sins and purify us from all unrighteousness.'"

"Gram. Don't."

The pages turned again. "Our great God and Savior, Jesus Christ, who gave himself for us to redeem us from all wickedness . . ."

Tears poured out of Raya like rain. "Please."

"And to purify for himself a people that are his very own, eager to do what is good."

A sob escaped Raya's lips. These were her Scriptures, the ones she'd recited on mornings when she awoke to find accusation instead of mercy, guilt instead of joy. The words had comforted her then. They pierced her now.

"It's him. The money boy from Hawaii."

Gram took a sip of tea. "The fellow with the hundred-dollar bill from the beach? Here? Who?"

Raya snorted. "Flex. He's the boy."

"Trey? Why, even a woman as old as me can see that he's not a boy. Speak plain, girl."

Raya closed her eyes. She wanted to go to sleep for a very long time. "Gram, Flex is the one, the guy from Hawaii."

The cup froze at the old woman's lips. "Oh my . . . I prayed, but mercy, the Lord outdid himself. What did you run off for? This is good news, eh? Wonderful news!"

Raya fluffed the lump of flowers next to her. "I don't know if it's good or not. I'm just being honest, Gram. I'm not where I was. My faith is . . . is different. It's not that I don't believe that God could do something this wonderful, it's just that—"

"You don't think he wants to do it. You're still looking for punishment instead of mercy, for a setback instead of a setup. I know things haven't gone like you've planned, Aryanna, but you just have to trust. Don't be afraid. Let yourself fall—in love, in life. God will catch you. He wants to."

Raya didn't know what to say to that. It was too reasonable. Too true. Too scary. "Darrell told me to get tested again. Seems a few of his girlfriends have turned up HIV positive. And then there's Mom and Dad, Miss Bea . . ." She collapsed against her grandmother's shoulder. "Oh, it's all a mess. It's too late. Flex isn't that boy on the beach anymore. He's not looking to get married, and neither am I. I've got to make my own happy ending. Maybe if I'd met Flex a year ago."

Clucking her tongue, Gram let Raya cry. Wetness ran down Raya's neck as her grandmother shed some tears of her own.

"If you'd met the boy a year ago, he'd be dead. You would have killed him with your pious religion. I'm sorry that you lost something precious, but I'm thankful that it brought you down to earth. You were getting on even my nerves."

Raya sat up straight. "Really?"

Gram nodded. "You thought everything was so simple, so black and white. I knew a testing was coming for you. It had to. You were too smug about your faith. Now I fear you've gone in the other direction, forgetting the power of the cross. Whatever is going to happen, we'll get through it. There's medicine here for everything that ills." She tapped her Bible and flipped through it again, only a few pages this time. She looked down over her glasses with her finger marking the passage. "You want to read the next one? Or should I?"

Raya stared down at the worn page. Many tears had stained the note-filled margins. If she didn't read it, she'd have to listen to Genesis through Revelation before it was all over. She lifted the book onto her lap.

"The Son is the radiance of God's glory . . ." Her voice creaked like hundred-year-old wood.

"Come on," Gram said in her talk-back-to-the-preacher voice.

Raya's eyes dragged across the page, blurring the words together. "And the exact representation of his being, sustaining all things by his powerful word—"

"Umph. All things?"

Raya scowled, pulling the book closer.

"Go on."

She paused. This was the hard part, but the good part too. "After he had provided purification for sins, he sat down at the right hand of the Majesty in heaven." She closed the book and pushed it away.

Gram had her there. Raya slumped against her shoulder.

"Okay. You're right. It's done. Christ is seated. He's over all of it—Flex and his rich father, Darrell and his roses and HIV, Daddy, Vera, Megan, Jay, Miss Bea. All of it."

Gram nodded, temporarily satisfied.

Raya kissed her grandmother's cheek. The smooth-looking skin gave way as her lips pressed against it, releasing the scent of lavender.

"I know Jesus is seated, Gram, but I can't help but think Jesus should get up this time."

Gram tightened her grip. "Not even for popcorn, baby. His standing is done. It's our turn to stand. Go ahead and fall, baby. He knows the beginning, and he knows the end."

Raya buried her face in Gram's shoulder. She'd seen the end too. And she didn't like it, not one bit.

20

Flex looked outside his apartment window. Nothing stared back at him but dirty snow and the long, terrible grooves left by the ambulance that had taken Miss Bea away. Not only had he probably lost Raya forever, but he hadn't been here to help the woman who'd become so close to him.

Now he and Jay sat alone, silent after returning from the hospital. Miss Bea hadn't been conscious to hear his mumbled prayers or feel his feeble kisses on her wrinkled cheek, but Flex hadn't cared. After picking up Jay from Raya's neighbors, he'd fled Raya's building as if escaping a fire, but now he wished he'd climbed the next flight and somehow persuaded her to come along.

Though he hadn't meant to, Flex had allowed Raya to partake of something he'd denied everyone else of, even his mother. The fellowship of his pain. From that first day with Chenille's baby, the news from Lyle, the situation with Miss Bea and what might happen to Jay if she didn't recover . . . The mess with his father was the final stronghold, and now she knew about that too. From the look on her face last night, the truth had cost him more than he could afford. He'd needed her this morning. Jay had needed her too. The boy stared at him now, waiting to hear that everything would be all right. Flex turned away. Six months ago he might have said that, but today? He wasn't so sure.

"So how'd your thing go? We lost the game."

Jay's eyes were red, and his stomach bulged from the Thanksgiving feast Mrs. Vernet had prepared. Raya's kind neighbor had sent them home with a king's portion to boot. Flex had scarfed down most of it in the waiting room.

"My 'thing' went well." He paused, recalling the bitter victory. He'd won the contest and lost Raya all in the same night. "It was a contest. The Mocha Man—"

Jay shot up off the couch, now extended into a queen bed. "The Mocha Man? I saw that on TV—"

Flex narrowed his eyes. "When? You know you're not allowed to watch Nia anymore." His head hurt thinking about the boy's reenactment of a rap video in the school cafeteria just before Jay and Miss Bea had moved in. Though frail in body, Miss Bea had put Jay back in line with her quick mind. Flex could only hope to do half as well. Though the boy's aunt, and Flex's new favorite cook, was stable this morning, it didn't sound like she'd be coming home anytime soon. A diabetic coma was the latest diagnosis.

"I saw the commercial for the contest before I went on punishment. I haven't been watching videos. Especially not now . . ."

"Right. Go back to sleep. We'll head up to the hospital later. They tell me you stayed up pretty late last night."

The boy nodded, already fading away. "They had some cool music and lots of books. Ever heard of a cat named Claude Brown?"

"Yeah," Flex whispered as the memory of his introduction to Black literature flashed in his mind. *Manchild in the Promised Land*. A more appropriate title couldn't be found. "We'll read it together."

Jay answered with a snore.

Flex paused, looking down on Jay's sleeping form, trying not to choke up. Here he was worrying about losing Raya when this kid had lost it all. Still, the sound of Raya's tiara hitting the floor ricocheted through his heart. His pain was small in comparison, but wretched. And only one cure could heal it.

Jesus.

Flex's muscles creaked. Running around the city last night looking for Jay after hearing Raya's grandmother's message on his cell had worn him out. He'd been on his way there anyway to try to talk to Raya. After hearing about Miss Bea and seeing the fear in Jay's sleepy eyes, he'd come home instead. He looked around, thinking of Miss Bea and the room she'd quietly occupied. Usually as he entered the house, he could hear her singing. Would he ever hear it again? He prayed so. After Chenille's baby, Lyle . . . he couldn't take any more losing.

He rubbed his biceps, aching from all that silly posing. He had Jay to think of. Though people from the church would be at the hospital, it wasn't the same as family. Jay . . . and Flex were all the family Miss Bea had left.

The church was having a Morning of Thanks service today, but it didn't look like they'd make it. And to be honest, he wasn't sure if he wanted to make it if Raya would be there. He stopped beside his bed and scooped up the brownish pink mound of rose petals he'd dumped from his pocket this morning. He pressed a few petals into his hand. She had given the rose to him yesterday. He hadn't imagined it.

Bible in one hand and pad and pen in his other hand, Flex started for the dining room. Another snore buzzed from Jay's lips.

Flex shrugged. Definitely no service today. Jay had been through enough. He set his NKJV *Men's Devotional Bible* down on the table. He had his own Bible study schedule, but today he'd do well just to read the day's devotional.

He scanned the heading quickly. *Touch Means So Much.*

"It is good for a man not to touch a woman."

"You got that right." He buried his head in his hands, talking to no one in particular.

The verse was all too familiar. He'd wrestled with it many nights during the course of his celibacy. It had been his cardinal rule before—hands off. Why had he relaxed his standards with Raya?

Not long ago he'd found himself in this spot, confused and regretful, scraping this passage down to the original Greek. The word *touch* meant more than a hand upon skin. It meant the kindling of a fire, the awakening of urges that only physical contact could bring. Even now Flex could almost smell her soft, light scent . . . taste that Bonne Bell lip gloss . . .

He pressed his palms against the table in front of him, smudging the dark wood Miss Bea had polished so carefully. He'd done it again. Gone too far. Broken the rules. Let his heart lead his hands. Only this time he hadn't even realized it.

Lord, help me get over her.

Even as he thought it, Flex knew it was impossible. He'd never get over Raya. He could only pour that love into Christ, where it should have been in the first place. He rose and walked back to the living room, taking the side of the sectional opposite Jay.

Sleep called to him. Peace came in a dusty haze as he

closed his eyes. Maybe he couldn't fix things with Raya, but Miss Bea and Lyle needed him to be strong. To stay focused. To pray.

If he didn't, there'd be no hope for him at all.

The doorbell rang, cutting Flex's nap short. Jay rolled over, but Flex shook his head. "I'll get it." If it was news about Miss Bea, no need for the boy to be first to hear it.

Flex reluctantly pressed his eye to the peephole. If it was anyone other than Raya or their pastor, he didn't want to talk. Two smiling faces filled the glass circle. Standing outside were the people he needed most and wanted least to see.

Jay sat up, rubbing his eyes and wearing the same expectant expression he reserved for his favorite TV shows.

"Go back to sleep, man. It's my parents." He pulled back the chain and keyed the deadlock.

He mustered a smile as he pulled back the door. "What brings you two to my neck of the woods?"

His mother kissed his cheek. "We came to check on you and wish you a happy Thanksgiving. Sorry we didn't make it over sooner." She stepped inside, but his father didn't move.

Back to that, were they? Flex ignored his father's aloofness as best he could, focusing on his mother's eyes instead. They'd been holding hands when he opened the door, standing close . . . His mother was—his parents were—happy. Maybe one day he'd catch up to them.

How about today? Invite him in.

His chest tightened. "Come in."

It wasn't mushy or anything, but it was the best he could offer.

His father shook his head. "Are you sure? I told your mother we should have called—"

"Get in here, Dad."

Flex took his father's hand, shocked at what he'd just said. Not since he was a boy had he used such terms, and then always in hopes of hearing the corresponding affection.

The door slammed shut. His father smiled and removed his hat, the same color as his silver-splashed beard.

"Thank you, son."

Son.

Unsure how to respond, Flex gave a quick nod. All this warmth from his father was creeping him out. What would come next, a group hug?

His mother chatted softly with Jay behind them, but when silence choked both father and son, she spoke up. "I heard about the ball. About Raya. I'm sorry—"

Jay's forehead creased with concern. "She heard something about Miss Joseph? What happened, Coach? I just saw her last night . . ." Jay's brave armor cracked, and the events of the past twenty-four hours showed on his face.

Flex stepped away from the awkward nearness of his father and gathered Jay into a hug, one they'd shared at practices, after church services, and of late, in the hall outside the principal's office when Flex escorted Miss Bea to meetings about Jay's behavior. He grabbed the boy's face with both hands.

"Nothing is wrong with Miss Joseph. We've just had a misunderstanding. It'll be fine."

At least she'd made it home safe. Flex hadn't been able to resist calling from the hospital. Mademoiselle had assured him that Raya had made it home safe.

Flex's parents closed in around their son and the boy he'd grown to love. His mother smoothed her hand over Jay's braids.

"Do you remember me, honey? From Sunday school?"

The boy nodded and allowed himself to be pulled away from Flex and led to the kitchen, where he'd no doubt get another bellyful of consolation.

The two men who remained locked eyes, realizing too late they were alone with nothing to say. Flex suddenly felt hungry too . . .

"Stay, son."

There he went with that son business again.

"Okay."

The elder Fletcher took a seat on the sectional as though he were accustomed to sitting on cloth furniture. He didn't wait for Flex to sit down before starting in.

"Does that bother you, me calling you son? I can see where it would."

Flex gripped the couch as he took a seat next to his father. God was cleaning house this holiday. He'd waited for this moment for too many years, practiced what strong words he would say when this day came. Now his might was gone, leaving only his weakness and God's power behind.

Jesus, I can't do this.

"I guess I'll get used to it . . . when I'm ninety or so."

His father laughed. "If God lets me live to see it, I can work with that. Though it's just more wasted time, I'm afraid." He rubbed his beard. "I thank you for the privilege of calling you son. I've been a fool, Fletcher."

Flex licked his lips. It would be polite to refute his father, to make him feel better, but nothing came to mind.

His father nodded. "Your mother would have stopped me there, but you're honest. I like that. I wish I'd been that way. I was so caught up in the bad feelings between your mother and me—"

"Forget it."

The couch groaned as Flex got up. He didn't like where this

271

was going, where it would have to go if they were going to move on. Maybe in a week he could have this conversation. Maybe in a month. But not today.

His father's sleeve slipped over his wrist as he stood, revealing the Rolex Flex had seen so often on magazine covers. He hadn't seen the timepiece up close in years and never understood how anyone could spend that kind of money on a watch. But seeing it again, he had to admit it was beautiful. He pulled his eyes away.

Cool metal touched his fingers. "Take it."

Flex gritted his teeth. "No thanks."

Not taking no for an answer, his father pressed it into Flex's hands. His stomach knotted as he considered the value. He could probably start a business off the resale of this item alone. But he'd never sell it, that much he knew.

His father smiled and shook his head. "It's amazing. Your feelings about money are like your mother's, yet you're a lot like me. You think I'm trying to buy you off. I can read it in your eyes."

Flex's pulse raced. Like his father? Never.

The memory of himself in the bridal shop knifed across his memory.

Well, maybe. Just a little.

"I've got to admit. I don't know what you're up to. I mean, why marry Mom now? And last night? Hugging me up in front of all those people?" He would have said kissing, but he was still trying to convince himself that he'd imagined that part.

His father nodded. "Right. And all just to disrespect you. To make you angry, right?"

Flex eyed the kitchen door. This would be a good time for his mother to reappear.

His father touched his shoulder. "This isn't about your

mother. It's about you and me. In truth, I was jealous of you."

Flex searched his father's face, his eyes. How could this man who had everything be jealous of him?

"But why?"

His father nodded toward the kitchen. "You had her."

This time Flex summoned the strength he'd thought was gone, the bitterness he'd tried so desperately to excise. He grasped at the last blade of it, only to have it wilt into pity. What kind of man would envy his own child?

Dropping back to the lumpy sofa, his father cast him a knowing glance. "I know it sounds crazy, but I was crazy. Crazy for her, the one thing money couldn't buy. I told myself that once you were born, she'd marry me. Hmph." He closed his eyes. "She wanted no part of me then. She had you. I had nothing. The only reason she ever spoke to me was for your sake, or so I thought. All I knew was that every year you grew older brought me closer to losing her forever."

"So why did you have her sign that stupid document to release us when I turned twenty-one?" Flex's voice was rising, his heart pounding. When the day came to ask these things, he was supposed to be calm, quiet. His vocal chords defied the plan.

"I thought she'd never sign it, that for you at least, she'd cave and marry me. But she didn't. She went to church . . . and I went to sea."

Flex bristled, thinking of all the clippings of his father's travels, the nameless beauties at his side. He'd always thought his father had abandoned his mother and him, thrown them away . . .

He turned the Rolex over in his palm to check the time: 10:23 a.m. It was always good to know the exact moment your mind went bad in case anyone ever wanted to know. It was a horrible story, much worse than the one he'd concocted in his head, but what if he'd lost Raya gradually, along with their child? Their son? Without Christ, how much better could his father have handled it? Flex was having a hard enough time with God's grace.

His father's voice brimmed with pain. "I know that you might not ever forgive me, but listen to me at least. Whatever you do, don't let that Joseph girl get away." He took a deep breath. "You'll regret it forever."

Flex absentmindedly slipped the watch onto his wrist to busy his hands against the truth his father spoke, a truth he couldn't deny. He shoved his hands into his jean pockets.

"Tell me something I don't know."

21

Sunday came without Raya's permission. She'd spent days on a sleeping-turkey-eating circuit that would put even Flex's program to shame.

Flex.

There he was again, just as sure as she'd opened her eyes. She ordered him out of her brain every night, chased him away with her earnest prayers, only to find his face waiting in her mind each morning. She'd heard Gram whispering with him on the phone but hadn't dared to take his calls. What could she say? Where could she begin? It was all too jumbled now.

It's impossible.

Having Jay think she'd abandoned him or his aunt did bother her though. Raya had talked with Miss Bea briefly several times and planned to visit after today's service. Maybe she could see Jay alone at church somehow. During Sunday school, maybe? That would work . . .

Gram entered the kitchen in a floral silk

robe. If she was surprised to see Raya up, dressed, and brewing the morning tea, she didn't show it.

"Morning, cherie. You look well."

"Thank you." Raya poured a stream of hot liquid into a cup. She reached to move the *Times* off the table and replace it with Gram's Bible.

"Leave it." Gram pulled the newspaper out of Raya's hands and turned purposefully through its pages.

Raya stared, puzzled. Gram never read the *Times* before her Bible. "Are you okay, Gram?"

Wise eyes peered down over the edge of the paper. Slowly Gram turned the page around, revealing an article with a curious title: "New Firm Clothes Mocha Man."

The words, and their impact, bounced around Raya's mind and then settled into the creases of her thoughts. Garments of Praise was the firm the writer mentioned. She leaned in closer to find her name front and center, next to Chenille's. She covered her mouth.

Gram opened hers into a wide grin. "Looks like you made it, baby. The big time."

"I guess so." Raya stared at the page again. She'd dreamed of this kind of exposure, but not under these circumstances. Raya hugged her own shoulders.

The phone rang—both in her purse and on the wall. Raya chose the call she could screen. She scanned the number, then pressed the button, watching as Gram picked up the olive-colored phone across the room.

"Hey, girl."

"Did you see it?" Chenille shouted.

Raya cringed. "I did. Gram showed it to me."

How had Gram even known? She'd have to ask later. She sighed. What was the point in even asking? Everybody seemed to know what was going on except her.

"You couldn't have seen it. You're too calm. Did you read it all?"

"Well . . . not exactly."

"They want a line, Raya. A whole line!"

A line? They? She backed up into the living room. "Slow down. Who? What line?"

Gram huddled over the house phone, speaking in hushed tones. Flex, no doubt. This madness with Chenille suddenly made the situation with him fade. For the moment at least.

"Reebok, girl! They want a full activewear line—swimwear, fitness gear, the whole thing. They want to call it Flexability—"

"Great." Raya felt sick. She held her stomach. If she'd known this was coming, she'd have held off on some of that turkey from Miss Lola.

"He's the spokesman. I thought you'd be excited. You two seemed so . . . Wait a minute. Your dad's party. You never called me. What happened?"

Raya rolled her eyes to the ceiling. "Nothing happened, nothing at all."

The worship skipped along at the edges of Raya's brain, eroding the fortress of the past few days. Like a sick person force-feeding herself medication, Raya pushed a hallelujah past her lips. God met her on every note. Lyle was there, holding hands with Chenille. Except for the thinness etched into his face, he looked well. Content.

Raya considered that. In the face of his own possible death and the death of his son, Lyle was content. Peaceful. From her conversations with Chenille, Raya knew he wasn't always happy and didn't profess to understand any of it. He'd even thrown a few fits over the months. But still, he was here, praising God with today's breath.

And where was Raya? Mad at God for keeping his promises when she couldn't keep hers. Upset because he'd brought her the love she'd always wanted and she was too afraid, too broken, to accept it.

Her stomach lurched at the thought of Flex. His seat—right side, third row, on the end—was filled by a stranger this morning. Jay was absent too. They were probably at the hospital, where she'd be soon if she could manage to slip through Chenille's grasp. Her friend's sideways glances indicated she wanted to chat more about the proposed activewear line. Raya's line. Something Raya wasn't so sure about.

Soft strains of piano wound around her like a blanket, the Comforter, as Gram had explained it so many years ago using a bedcovering as an example. *You know how Linus has that blanket on Charlie Brown? The Holy Spirit is like that but better. He teaches you too. Talks to you about Jesus. An amazing thing.* Today she knew the words were true. How else could she be standing today? Without him she was nothing.

"Before we get started this morning, there's a family emergency."

Many in the crowd looked around.

The pastor cleared his throat and smiled. "Not your family, our church family."

Raya nodded in agreement. She'd been meaning to get more involved in New Man Fellowship. Today she would sign up to help with something besides the basketball team. Flex didn't need her anymore.

But I need him.

She wiped the thought away, leaning closer to hear the pastor's plea.

"Jay Andrews, one of our youth, has been staying with

Sister Bea Wells. She went into a diabetic coma over the holiday and won't be able to care for him for some time, if ever."

Ever? Was it that serious? One thought burrowed into Raya's mind: what would happen to Jay?

"A foster parent in the congregation has stepped forward to care for Jay until something permanent can be worked out, but help is needed for after-school supervision. This is basically a single-parent situation at this time."

Raya simmered, holding on to her seat. Flex had turned Jay over to someone so quickly? True enough, maybe ACS hadn't given him a choice, but why hadn't he contacted her? Why hadn't he—

Because she'd been acting like a fool, that's why. She rested back against the wooden pew.

Still, she realized she was angry at Flex for not following her, for not wanting to know what was wrong. For not being here today, waiting for her, praying for her, the way he had all these months.

You can't have it both ways.

She sniffed. Fair enough. "Excuse me." She slid out of the pew as the congregation lapsed into a few minutes of informal greeting time. Though she shook hands along the way and wished Gram hadn't insisted on sitting so close to the front and then wandered off to the bathroom, Raya pressed on until she reached the foyer. She scurried to the hospitality counter and placed her name first on the list to help the caring single woman who'd taken Jay in, whoever she was. Flex's name should have been there too, but there was no point worrying about that now.

That was over.

The air was too still. Raya had thought so ever since she entered the hospital. Gram's pace, reticent instead of her usual we-gotta-pray hospital tempo, scared her too. She picked up her own step, finding Miss Bea's room quickly. The nurse's station directly across from the room was empty. Raya's insides twisted as she paused outside the door.

Father God, I trust you. No matter what.

Before she could enter, the door opened and Flex slouched into the hall. He looked past her, past Gram too. Jay followed, his hair matted and his eyes swollen.

Raya backed up against the wall. Gram pushed around her and went inside, where Raya heard the voices of many people. One in particular. "Time of death. One nineteen."

"No . . ." The word rolled from her mouth like low-pitched thunder.

Jay scrubbed his eyes and flopped onto the couch. He put his head down on a table stacked with three-year-old issues of *People* and *Time*.

Flex moved slowly, to Jay first, giving him a squeeze on his shoulders, and then to Raya. He walked directly to her, then wound himself around her as if to keep the biting wind of death from blowing across her, pouring into her lungs.

He was too late.

Her chest began to heave, each time sinking deeper than before. Flex loosened his grip and leaned forward, pressing his forehead to hers. More than any other time in her life, she was grateful for her height.

And his.

She stroked his face, stubbled with more shadow than she'd ever seen on him. Shadow earned by sleeplessness, from the looks of his bloodshot eyes. If he felt her touch, he didn't show it, making no motion except to move back a little.

His eyes closed for a moment, then opened again. He croaked in anguish, "Kiss me."

Raya's mind denied the request.

Her lips complied.

Flex wanted to hold her hand, but he knew that part of their relationship was over. Raya's kiss, gentle against his cheek and warming to his heart, had confirmed it. The electricity underlying the comfort of the kiss they'd shared when little Nathan had passed was gone now. At least her smile remained.

He watched as she carefully combed through Jay's hair, all the while careful not to wake the kid. Amazing. The boy snored like a baby. And Flex was grateful. Things wouldn't be easy from here on.

"I want him to look decent when they come and get him," she said, picking through another braid with the end of one of the array of combs in that purse/backpack/kitchen-sink thing of hers. If she pulled out an elephant, he wouldn't be surprised.

"Right."

What she meant he didn't know, but he was too fried to care. ACS had assured him that his foster care certification and prior relationship with Jay were enough to qualify him for custody. Unless somebody told him different, he was taking Jay home to stay. He just wanted Raya to keep talking, to keep smiling at him.

"Your hair looks good." She gently maneuvered a knot.

Your everything looks good, he thought.

He pushed the thought away. "Thanks. I'm letting it grow."

She shrugged. "They've got weave for guys too, you know."

The comb in her hands dragged through Jay's cotton-candy hair, making a straight part.

Flex stuck out his tongue and pulled it back just as quickly. "Hair weave? For guys? That's just wrong."

He'd seen suspect dos on some of his photo shoots but tried to convince himself that no self-respecting man would do such a thing. He looked down at his ragged cuticles and sighed. Personal care. A slippery slope. One day manicures, next day a guy could turn in to a hair bear with a wig.

Raya smiled, but it was too perfect. Flex knew she was trying to keep the tone light for Jay's sake. He was trying his best to play along. She made another part. "That hair of yours would be hard to match anyway. So curly."

Match? He had no clue what she was talking about and didn't even try to figure it out. Only the curly part made sense.

"I guess. I'm amazed how you change your hair up all the time. Just when I think you can't surprise me, you do."

"Speaking of surprises, I guess we never talked about our fathers and the whole money thing. I wish I'd been up front. We probably have a lot in common." She paused to pick a snarl from Jay's hair but peeked up at Flex. Her eyes squinted as if trying to read something on his face.

Was this some sort of code? Something she didn't want Jay to know? If so, Flex was too sad and tired to figure it out. As for what they had in common, he wasn't so sure. Money or no, his helter-skelter childhood was probably nothing like Raya's tranquil environment. Her father had treated her like a princess at the party. Flex's father had given him his first hug in ten years.

"I guess."

Jay tried to straighten his head. "I'm almost done," she whispered, then turned to Flex. "Were you in Jack and Jill?"

He nodded before he realized it. At least they could talk about this kind of stuff now that they knew the truth about one another. "You?"

She smiled. "Yes. I did my time in J&J. It was okay. A bunch of snobs. Girls like Megan. They all went off to grad school, and I went to Fashion Institute. Lost touch with most of them." She focused on Jay's hair, winding her long fingers in an overlapping pattern. "Their wedding invitations all seem to find me though."

He slapped his knee. "Tell me about it!"

He'd made a few friends in Jack and Jill, a service organization for up-and-coming young people; Al-ka-pals, a teen group from his mother's sorority; and all the other usuals—but the memories of the torturous tuxedos made him shudder. Now he didn't mind them at all.

"Were you a deb?" he asked.

Her eyes glazed over. "A debutante? I was. And an escort."

"Me too."

"Cotillion?"

He nodded. "Beautillion?"

She finished the last braid and slid Jay onto the couch beside them, then hugged her belly. "You know it. I was dial-a-date. My mom had the dresses on a revolving rack. I just walked to the closet and let her tug them over my head."

Beautillion. The mention of the male coming-out ball sent a shiver down his spine. That was the night his mother had first started talking of "strategic unions" and other such nonsense. He knew now that marriage and all the things leading up to it were nothing but hostile takeovers. If only they'd had debutantes like Raya back then, things might be different now.

"So tell me more. About your childhood, your growing up." She covered her mouth. "Not like I was trying to pry or anything."

283

"Dad didn't live with us, but he sent nice checks." Flex ran his tongue over his teeth. "We did all right. Nothing spectacular . . ."

Unless you counted the house in the Hamptons, the summer place in Martha's Vineyard, Dad's plane, Mother's mansion. Nothing spectacular indeed. He was backing himself into a corner for sure.

Lord, help me out here. I don't want to get into this money business.

Raya was the first woman who'd ever gotten close to him for who he really was. Flex. A regular guy. Not Fletcher Rayburn Longhurst III, heir to the Longhurst millions. He flinched at the thought of his father's name, once his own, though he'd changed it legally as soon as he could. Nobody knew Dunham, but Longhurst? Longhursts were bluebloods, and he'd wanted no part of them. Or their money.

He looked down at his watch, upset that he'd forgotten to lock it in the small safe his mother had given him before the move. After the way his father was acting lately, Flex didn't know what to think. He could barely think at all, knowing Miss Bea was in the next room on a hospital bed, the bed where she'd taken her last breath. He felt the tears behind his eyes, but after so much hurt, they seemed afraid to surface. Flex knew this feeling well. He'd depended on it all his life, and it had only evaded him when it came to Raya.

Numbness.

"Yeah, growing up was something," she said. "I look at the kids on your team and think I had it a lot better than I remember. Sure, dressing up for all that stuff was a pain, but my parents were trying to do what they thought would help me." She stretched.

Flex stayed still and let his mind do the stretching. Once again Raya had a point. Maybe he'd been too hard on his parents. Though they hadn't been very nice to each other, they'd always tried to do the right thing for him. And until a few years ago, they had done the right things.

"I know what you mean. The grass always looks greener on the other side, I guess. I'm sure those kids would love to have the families we had, and we would have loved to run around and get our clothes dirty."

Raya's mouth opened and released a flow of bubbling laughter. "Why do you think I design clothes? That was the closest I could get to picking them out, let alone dirtying them. My Barbie had more wardrobe designs than grown women do."

He nodded, thinking of how he'd longed to run with the kids when his family drove through Roxbury in Boston or down the side streets in DC, how he'd dreamed of taking off his shoes and jumping in the stream of a fire hydrant. Challenging the boys to a race. He could only imagine what he must have looked like, face pressed up to the window of a limo in wonder.

"If I ever have kids, I won't be like that. I'll let 'em run . . . and pick their own clothes. Maybe even make them some clothes." He winked at her.

She didn't wink back. "I'll have to remember to pass this info to your wife."

His wife? Why did she have to rub it in? He stood, allowing the wound of Miss Bea's death to flare again and the realization of the truth to sink its teeth into his heart—Raya was moving on.

Without him.

"Yeah, well. I doubt there will be anyone to tell." He gritted his teeth. "My boss told me to tell you that you can work out for free until the New Year. Says he's tired of everyone asking what happened to you."

"It's only been what—a few days?"

Flex nodded. His boss was so tickled with the Mocha Man publicity that he'd thrown in unlimited free workouts for Raya if it would make Flex look any happier. "You are the Mocha Man after all," he'd said. What a joke.

"It doesn't take long to miss someone."

She nodded.

What did that mean? He refused to read anything into it. There were brick walls enough around town to run into.

"Will you come? My mom even asked about you."

Raya focused on the door to Miss Bea's room, which Mademoiselle still hadn't emerged from.

"Sure," she said. "I'll stop by."

Raya returned to the gym more quickly than he'd expected. Faster than he could handle. Unable to come in early most days lately, he'd arrived at 8:30 a.m. after dropping Jay off at school and chatting quickly with the school counselor. The late hour had relieved his fears about running into Raya.

And yet here she was, looking like a sad puppy, like a lot of stuff had hit home for her—namely, Miss Bea's death. She walked straight to him, checking first to see if he had a client. He looked too, hoping someone, anyone, would arrive. No one did.

She came closer, stopping a breath away. "I can't believe she's gone. I mean, it's not like we were that close, but still." Despite the clang of iron plates in the gym, Raya spoke softly.

"I know. I can't believe it either." Flex swallowed, restraining himself from taking Raya into his arms to comfort her as seemed to be his pattern. It seemed that everyone he prayed for ended up worse off than before.

Raya tossed her towel over one shoulder. "Did you know that they've placed Jay with someone from the church? A foster parent?"

He scratched his head. Did he dare tell her he was that someone? That he was in over his head and needed her help desperately? No. God would be his help. He'd asked too much of her already.

"I knew about that."

She stared at the floor. "Did you sign up to help? I thought sure you would have been there Sunday. Lyle came."

Flex's head jerked up. "He did? How'd he look?"

Raya sniffed. "His smile lit up the whole church. Chenille looked radiant."

He tossed his head back against the wall next to the bench press. "Thank God." At least something was going to turn out right. He reached out for her on instinct, but he grabbed his neck instead.

"I was surprised to see you here so soon."

She slid onto the bench. "Me too."

"You missed it, huh?" He smiled, thankful he hadn't said what he was thinking, what he was hoping—that she'd missed him.

Raya lifted the bar off the rack. "I did miss it." Two tens graced the bar instead of her usual twenty-five plates. "I feel like my body is going down quickly. Already I'm weak."

He smiled and stepped up onto the spot rack, both thankful and sad to see her again.

"Your strength will come back quickly."

The question was, would his? Between this Mocha Man foolishness, his new relationship with his father, and Jay's affairs, his own training had slipped in both intensity and frequency. If not for his clients, he might not be training at all.

The bar pressed up toward him but didn't return.

He leaned forward in concern. "You okay?"

"I am," she whispered. "Thanks for your help, but I've got it. My partner should be here soon."

"Right. Sorry. Just habit, I guess." He stepped down, wishing he could go right through the floor. It was more than habit, and they both knew it. As for her "partner," he couldn't bear to stay and see that golden-eyed goon from the ball show up. He'd learned from Mademoiselle that the character was Raya's ex-fiancé, the guy who'd gotten caught with Megan and messed up their wedding.

Weddings only brought thoughts of bad news. Sometimes he wondered, if he had married Brooke, would she still be alive? Would he?

No use going there, partner. It's done.

As always, Flex sucked it up, tried to throw the memory away. He was forgiven, but it still hurt. How could he even think he was man enough to love Raya? At least she was up front about whatever haunted her from her past. He'd done little more than stick Bible verses on his wounds. It was all the power he had. All the power he'd needed. Until now. Now the pain rose to meet him, fresh and bloody. Pain from wounds of foolishness, moments of weakness.

Maybe now would be a good time to head over to Jay's school and hash out some more details about the boy's study schedule. Even with only a few more weeks until Christmas vacation, Jay's teacher said the boy was so far behind that he'd likely repeat the eighth grade. Flex had been given only temporary custody, but he had to do the best he could for Jay, even if that meant less than the best for himself. Suddenly, "making it" didn't seem to matter.

He walked away, allowing himself a half smile at Raya's grunting, the sound of going further than one's body intended but short of where one's mind seeks to go. A sound Flex knew well. Her strength was low today, but her grit was at full power. Maybe he needed to start making some noises to pull the weight of the silence between them. They were talking all right, about Jay, about Miss Bea, but not about what mattered. Not about that night at the ball or the feelings between them. He got the feeling it wasn't open to discussion. At least he'd have this again, these mornings of mercy.

"Come on, two more, girl. Work with me now," Raya said to herself.

The self-talk was kind but firm. The same tone he'd used with her so many times. She'd always responded. Never complained. When things got rough, she'd just talked to herself, like now, or whatever it took. Once, during squats, she'd let out a scream that could have curdled anybody's blood. She didn't care who was listening. The gym had collectively paused, looked, and resumed working out. Smiles lit up all around. That morning they'd accepted her as one of them. From the moment he'd seen her, Flex had accepted that Raya was part of him.

Let it go.

On his way out, he noticed that his mother and not the Bad Guy had joined Raya for a workout. "Mom?"

"Morning, Fletcher." His mother added two more twenty-five pound plates before sliding into Raya's place on the bench.

He paused to watch the two women he loved most doing what he loved most. Why did it scare him so much? A month ago, with all his mother's concern about his relationships, she and Raya would have been an unlikely pair, but now they greeted one another with kind words. Both women paused to stare as he passed by.

Flex shuddered as he pushed into the locker room. What did this mean? Would his mother tell Raya he was the foster parent caring for Jay? That he was crazy about her? He'd wanted them to get to know one another better, but now he wasn't sure if it was such a great idea. Trying to be friends with Raya would be torture enough. If his mother got close with her . . .

He slammed the locker door. The tables had turned between the two of them, but somehow he was still on the outside.

22

Raya swayed forward. Her chin jerked as she awakened.

"Glad to have you back." The head of the Reebok concept team sat across from her, wearing three-and-a-half inch heels and a red power suit. She wasn't smiling.

There was no point in trying to explain. Not at this level of play. Raya dug her nails into her palm instead to keep herself awake. Chenille talked in animated tones with someone else from the team and didn't seem to have noticed Raya's little nap.

She stared at the clock. It was 2:30, and she'd agreed to pick Jay up from school today. Whoever his foster parent was, Raya couldn't let her down.

"I'm going to have to leave now. I have all the specs—"

"Leave? You just woke up."

Raya ran her tongue over her teeth. Two months ago she would have given everything for this. Maybe even anything. But not now.

"I do apologize, but I must go all the same."

The woman raked a hand through her short blond hair. "Well, I can say one thing for you, you're not desperate. That's new. Where are you going, if you don't mind my asking?"

She shrugged. She didn't mind. It was just too much to try to summarize. "School pickup."

Light shined in the woman's eyes. "Your kid? Why didn't you say so? Here, take my card and we'll lunch over the rest next week. What you've worked up looks great. I'm sure Flex will look great in it too."

"I'm sure." Raya mustered a smile. That part of the equation didn't bother her a bit. Flex would look good in a potato sack. "Now if you'll excuse me . . ."

Executive Lady, whose name suddenly escaped Raya, slid back her chair. "To be honest, I guess I can go and pick my kids up too. They'll be shocked to see me."

Raya sighed, debating whether to clear up the misunderstanding. Her rumbling stomach made the decision for her. She'd tell the whole story when they "lunched" later in the week.

She slipped Chenille a note of reminder that she was leaving early, not wanting to interrupt her boss's dynamic conversation. Her employer smiled and waved her on with the same amount of enthusiasm Flex had shown this morning when she'd tried to talk to him about Jay. Approaching him had been a mistake, but she couldn't take him pacing around every machine she went to. She'd hoped he would sleep in now that they didn't have a standing appointment anymore.

Tired of thinking about him, she crossed the Fashion Walk of Fame, not bothering to look at one name. What was the point? The walk to the train, the ride to Jay's school, all of it blurred before her.

As much as she tried to blame Flex for not responding to Jay's situation in the way she would have liked him to, she hadn't been fair to him either.

She strode purposefully to Jay's class and waited outside. Right now her mind was focused in only one direction.

Jay Andrews.

Flex rested his head on the door before letting himself in. Four new clients had signed up today, and he'd worked out with them all with a weary mind and an empty stomach. Thank goodness someone from the church had volunteered to pick up Jay from school. How he would make it through the next few weeks was more than he dared consider.

Call your parents.

It might come to that, but not yet. He'd try to pull it off through Christmas, let them enjoy their newlywed status. He braced himself for a dark, cold house. A warm, bright room dancing with unfamiliar but wonderful music greeted him instead. And onions . . . lots of onions. The memory of Miss Bea's lined face stabbed at him. God rest her soul. Had the Lord seen fit to send another church mother to take her place?

"Jay?" He called out a few times, but the boy didn't answer.

With a playful smile, he headed toward the kitchen, toward the music. Too late he realized where he'd heard the tune before—at the gym, leaking out of Raya's headphones.

She stood at the stove, stirring something wonderful in his biggest pot. His barbeque apron was wrapped twice around her waist. His knees almost buckled.

Jay sat behind her, staring intently at a schoolbook Flex had never seen before. He looked up with questions in his eyes. Probably math. "Hey, Coach! Look who's here."

Flex swallowed. "So I see." He wanted to say more but waited to see how Raya would respond.

She raised her head. Her face was streaked with tears.

Without thinking, he ran to her and wrapped his arms around her, kissed her hair, wiped her eyes.

She turned to ice in his hands. "It's nothing. Just the onions."

What an idiot he was. "Right."

Flex backed away from her, feeling awkward and clumsy, like a stranger in his own apartment. He glanced at Jay, who was watching them closely, as if waiting for the next disaster. Flex waved his arm to encompass the kitchen, "Well, thanks for all this."

She lifted the apron to her eye. "Thank you. He told me about what you've done with his school and everything. I didn't know . . . I'm sorry for what I said this morning about you needing to do more with Jay. I didn't know—"

"It's okay. I didn't expect you to be the helper either. I didn't even know you'd joined the care team. I appreciate the help though." He almost added, "Thanks and come again," but he caught himself.

Jay picked up his book and left the kitchen. Flex tried to stop him, but the boy shook his head, giving a thumbs-up as he escaped.

Flex froze, not having a clue what to do.

She kept stirring. "This should be enough for a few days. Do you have any cumin?"

"I'll check."

He went to the cabinet with a frown, knowing no such seasoning was there. With Miss Bea's cooking, he'd never gotten around to stocking the kitchen upstairs. With her gone, Flex stuck with using this downstairs kitchen. Miss Bea had required only salt and pepper, and his own cooking skills were limited to egg-white omelets and flaxseed oil salads. Lemon pepper was the height of his culinary knowledge. It went with everything. What was in that pot anyway?

"Sorry. Don't have it. Want me to go out for some?"

Her fresh, soft smell taunted him, even in a room thick with the funk of onions. The few seconds he'd held her brought all the wonder of her flooding back upon him. He needn't have worried about kindling any fires in Raya. It was his own flame he should have doused.

"Would you mind?" She stared down into the pot as if all life depended on its contents.

From the smell of it, he felt inclined to agree. His stomach squealed its assent.

"I'll be right back." He grabbed his keys and peeled out of the kitchen before she could comment on his talkative digestive tract.

Jay waited with a hopeful look beyond the kitchen door. He held up his palms. "Is she still mad at you?"

"Mad as ever. And she'll be madder if I don't hurry up and get something from the store for her. You wanna come?"

The boy's eyes brightened, then dimmed. He tapped the book. "Can't. She said I'm coming down with a cold and that I need to finish all of chapter 5 tonight. Can you believe that? The whole chapter."

Flex scowled. He appreciated Raya's help and all, but who was she to come in and take over everything, with her cumin and onions?

"She wants you to catch up all your math tonight? And what cold?" He felt the boy's forehead. "You're fine. Grab your coat."

As quick as he'd made the offer, Jay was at his side. As they stepped onto the porch, a burst of freezing wind and a covering of angry clouds greeted them.

"You think we should wait?" Jay asked sheepishly. "It looks like a storm. No use making her madder."

Make her madder? How could anybody do that? No, she could get her little seasonings and go back to her own house. He appreciated her picking Jay up, but this was more than he could deal with.

"No, buddy. I'm in charge of you, and I say we go for it. It'll be fine."

Even as he said it, Flex knew it wouldn't be fine.

But he went anyway.

They'd scared her half to death. When the doorknob finally turned, Raya struggled to escape Flex's recliner, which had sucked her in as if trying to provide some comfort. Flex jumped inside the door, half dragging Jay. She gasped at the sight of them, watching as half of New York's snow and ice slid off their clothes. She jumped up and took Jay's shivering form into her arms. The boy was freezing. And soaked through. She stared up at Flex.

"Are you happy now? Are you? I didn't even know that you'd taken him. I didn't know what to do."

Flex's eyes widened. "I thought it would be okay. It wasn't that long . . ."

"No, but it was long enough." She palmed Jay's forehead. "You're burning up. Why didn't you listen to me and do your homework like I told you?"

Too wet and weak for games, Jay stared at his coach and guardian but didn't say a word.

Raya took a deep breath. "Jay, go and change into some clean clothes. I'm going to go, but Mr. Longhurst will take care of you."

Jay frowned and started to speak but sagged against her instead.

Flex looked stricken at the sound of his real last name. He grabbed her elbow. "Calm down, okay?"

She was trying to calm down, without success. It was silly, her even being here, and even crazier that this upset her so much. It wasn't her place or her business. It shouldn't matter. Not this much. But it did, mainly because Jay was cold and feverish because of the mess between her and Flex. He shouldn't have to pay the price for the mistakes of adults. He'd done enough of that.

"You took him to show me, didn't you? To prove me wrong—make me the bad guy."

Jay reemerged in a clean sweat suit and socks. Raya helped him onto the couch and tossed a wool throw over him. She wanted to do more, to put his head in her lap and watch over him, but she'd gone too far already.

The boy placed his hand on hers. "It's not his fault, I . . ." Jay's voice trailed off.

Flex pulled the cover up around the boy's shoulders but refused to look at her.

She walked in front of him, staring him right in those beautiful eyes. "Well there's no way he can finish his math now. The teacher gave him one more chance to pass the course this semester. Evidently, she's been sending home notes with no response. I explained the situation."

He gulped. "I somehow missed that part of the explanation." He made a face at Jay, who only shrugged in response. "I did get your cumin though." He held up a wet brown bag like a pot of gold.

I could kick him.

"Thanks."

She remembered her morning Bible study. Do all things

without grumbling or complaining. Die. Be weak to become strong. It is in the times of weakness that we are the strongest. If that were true, she'd be a favorite for the Iron Woman competition.

Though she wanted to leave, she wanted to finish the meal she'd started to prepare. She wondered if teriyaki chicken and chickpea soup were any match for the pneumonia both Flex and Jay had probably contracted in the night's cold. Once she'd finished the meal, she'd go. For good. She heard Flex whispering to Jay behind her. "I'm sorry, man. Didn't mean to make you sick or mess up your math. You sleep and we'll do it in the morning, okay?" Was that a kiss she heard against the boy's forehead? She pushed into the kitchen and clutched her own face.

Lord, forgive me. I'm not perfect either. I shouldn't have stayed.

"Do you have any tea?"

Flex walked into the kitchen like a guilty schoolboy and pulled a box of Earl Grey, still in the package, from the pantry.

"Here. And I'm sorry. Really, I am. I don't know why I took him out in that. It was stupid. The whole thing."

Raya clicked on the burner, gulping down her thoughts, hoping the water would boil quickly and hide her expression in a cloud of steam. They'd been coming to this. Too bad Jay had to pay for it.

"You know exactly why you took him. You have to be right. You're the trainer, the teacher. You know how everything works best. Well, sometimes you don't know what's best . . . Fletcher." She pulled a mug from the cupboard. "Sometimes none of us does."

His hand covered hers. "I know that. I wasn't just trying to one-up you. I was a little . . ." His head tilted slightly. "Jealous? I guess he's sort of all I've got right now."

She bowed her head. "Me too." What was she doing? This was his house. She was truly going crazy. "Give him some tea with honey and lemon. Call Gram if you need—"

"We need you." Flex's calloused palms brushed her face. "I've spent a lot of time convincing myself that I don't need anybody. I was wrong. Jay needs both of us."

He moved closer, his eyes so near hers. She paused for a moment, dazed. At times like this, Flex seemed as strong a man inside as he was outside. Until she remembered that he'd just taken a child out into the snow. She smiled, imagining how Jay would react if he could read her mind. Being called a child would have him on his feet for sure. Still, Flex was right. Jay needed more than any one person could give.

"I'm not good at much besides making clothes, but I'll try. When I can do something to help somebody, I do."

Her own breath, honeyed from the chamomile tea she'd found and tried to calm herself with, wandered up her nose. She inched back.

He stepped forward.

"I know. That's what I love about you."

Love? He didn't mean that. Figure of speech. Raya stared at the clock on the stove. She'd stayed far too long. She pushed down on his arms, wrapped around her like the treads of the snow tires skidding against the street outside. He didn't budge, unless you counted his lips. They kept yapping.

"You don't have to know the right way, the perfect way to do something. You just try it with your heart. And it works." He smiled.

She sighed. It was supposed to be a compliment, she knew, but all her heart heard was that she did things the wrong way. Things like coming to New York, thinking she could be a designer, thinking she could help Jay . . .

She closed her eyes and then peeled them open when an

unexpected kiss landed on her mouth. A sweet and soft kiss, followed by an even softer voice.

"I'm sorry. For everything."

In that moment the last cord of Raya's heart was broken, and it floated away from her into his hands. In that instant it seemed she should trust him with anything, everything. What would he say if she told him they'd met before? He probably didn't even remember. They'd only been a few years older than Jay, and they'd barely met. Still, it had seemed so real—

A moan sounded from the living room. "Owww . . . my head."

"I'm coming." Raya pushed Flex out of the way and made it to the boy in three strides. She might not do things the right way, but at least she did something.

23

"Are you sure you're going to be okay?" Flex hated to leave Jay alone, but he had an appointment he couldn't miss. He'd tried to arrange with someone from the church, even his parents, but with the holidays approaching, no one was available. Even Raya, who had come through every time he needed her despite the tension between them, couldn't change her plans.

Jay sucked on an orange and clicked the remote to the Cartoon Network. "I'll be fine. What am I going to do, run out and cough on somebody? I can barely move. And after all that math and history homework, I can hardly think either. I'm fine. I'll call if I need you."

Flex looked doubtfully at Jay, knowing that for all his endearing personality and hard work lately, the boy had a streak of mischief the size of New York State. At least Flex had separated him from most of his crew by moving here. Not that it would stop them if they had a mind to get together.

"Maybe I should cancel." He'd changed the date twice already, but if he had to, he'd do it again.

Jay sucked the juice from the orange. "Will you go already?"

It wasn't as if he had much choice. He needed to follow up on this. Such things had to be done. "Okay. I'll call to check on you. You know the signal."

The boy shook his head. "Yeah, yeah. You and Miss Joseph and your signals." He clicked off the TV. "I'm going to sleep before one of you comes back and puts me to work on something."

"Put the chain on before you do."

Flex chuckled as he shut the door. The team was on a break until after the New Year. Jay had been home sick for the past five days, and Flex and Raya had taken turns tutoring him. The kid would probably never want to be sick again.

Not that Flex was feeling 100 percent himself. He was sure it was from that night in the snow, but usually vitamin C and rest shook stuff like that. For him anyway. Whatever this was had him in a daze, not unlike how he felt seeing Raya almost every day. Jay had suggested she move into Miss Bea's room, but they'd both disagreed. Vehemently. He didn't try to figure out her reasons, but he was honest with himself about his own:

No matter how much he went to church or read his Bible, he was still a man. A man who sometimes made very bad decisions, committed sins against his own flesh, as evidenced by the appointment he was going to now.

He reached the office quickly, thankful that his lack of health insurance hadn't kept him from getting care. His father had added Flex to his plan, but Flex would rather his parents not know everything about him. His mother had a way of getting chatty with nurses. He appreciated his father's concern and, in truth, the money that turned up so often lately. With Jay to think about now, Flex couldn't put off taking care of his own health any longer.

The nurse slid back the glass as he signed his name. "And what are you here for?"

Flex paused and looked around the waiting room. No one he knew. "Test results. Confidential."

She nodded. "Someone will be with you shortly." The glass clanged into place.

He took a seat and rummaged through the stack of *Sports Illustrated* for a financial magazine. He found none. He pulled a pocket-size New Testament from his jacket instead. The reality of what he'd come for weighed on him as he fumbled for an encouraging passage.

"Fletcher Dunham?" A slight nurse opened the door and called his name before he could find the passage he'd had in mind.

He stood and followed the nurse down another hall, past a sign with red letters an inch high.

Sexually Transmitted Disease Unit.

He felt sick.

"A little farther. Back here."

Flex slid into the seat, barely hearing as the woman explained that his second test was also negative and that it was very unlikely he'd contracted AIDS.

"You were lucky this time, but I wouldn't count on that. This is a killer." She slid a bag across the table.

Knowing its contents, Flex slid it back. "Thanks for the news, but I won't be needing those."

He was only here to follow up on the test he'd taken after hearing the news of Brooke's death. That time in his life seemed a world away.

The woman rolled her eyes and crossed his name off her

list. "Don't tell me, you're going to pray yourself celibate or some such thing."

He raised an eyebrow. "Something like that."

Obviously, he wasn't the first fallen saint through the door. He considered taking the lady's package to make her feel better, but he couldn't.

"Everything that does not come from faith is sin."

That part of Flex's life was over until God saw fit to change it. He couldn't think, with Raya, of the possibility of being with anyone else anyway. He stood.

"Thanks again."

Flex breathed a sigh of relief as he turned the corner, ignoring the bright, big letters. A bathroom door opened into him as he passed it by. He was so deep in thought, the impact barely registered.

"Sorry."

The voice pulled him up short. She walked on, not looking at him, but she didn't have to. He knew Raya's voice anywhere. He ran behind her, banging open the door to the waiting room. She'd been in the bathroom in the same unit he'd come from. What was she doing there?

The same thing he was?

No. It couldn't be. He recalled the hurt in her eyes that October morning when she'd said she couldn't forgive herself. He tightened his jaw, and he lunged out onto the sidewalk.

"Raya!"

The thought of another man put his brain in a vise. That Darrell fool. Maybe on her wedding night—

He dropped to one knee as if shot. Her wedding night? He fought for breath. But they didn't get married.

Raking through his freshly twisted hair and running to catch up, a memory licked across Flex's mind like a flame—

the beach and a girl with soft, dark skin and a honey voice that squeaked as she ran away.

The last fuzz of his memory cleared, and he remembered how she'd run from him then, her eyes blurred with pain.

He sank to his knees.

"Raya."

"Flex!" Without thinking, Raya ran toward him, bent over on the ice in front of the doctor's office. Was he hurt?

She slowed as she reached him. The look in his eyes frightened her. She gripped her bag for her cell. Was it Lyle?

"What is it? Come on, get up. You must be freezing."

He pressed her hand to his face. "Do you remember a day on a Hawaiian beach? Walking with a tall, skinny boy?"

She gasped. Somehow he'd remembered. "I . . . I do."

His lip quivered. Joy colored his cheeks. "Don't you get it? Don't you see? That was me. God did it. He brought us back together."

She was shaking now. "I know."

He shook his head. "Wait. You knew?"

"I recognized your father at the ball. Otherwise, I never would have known. You were so . . . skinny."

Flex's smile faded. Whether it was because of her comment or the realization that she'd known since Thanksgiving, Raya didn't know. He licked his lips.

"Skinny as a twig, I was. But I'm not the only one. You've thickened up some yourself since then."

People in the waiting room stared at them through the glass. How this must look, having a reunion outside the clinic. She took Flex's hand and dragged him onto a bench outside the office. As they sat he let her hand drop as he stared into the distance, still absorbed in his thoughts. She swallowed hard and opened her purse, digging into the side pocket for the mangled corner of a dollar bill. The numbers were faded, and some were missing, but "call me" was still intact. She pressed it into his wide, cold palm.

His eyes widened, but he didn't look at her. Instead, he pulled the tattered money to his face. "You kept this? You really did remember."

Raya nodded. "Of course. I went back for it. How could I forget you? Or your parents? I've been praying for you and for them all these years."

He wiped his eyes. "Are you for real?"

She bit her lip, letting the tears sheet down her face. Why did this silly childhood memory make her cry like this? They were grown-ups now. Things had changed. She was certain of that.

"For real. I prayed for your family every night. For health, for safety, for salvation—"

Flex took her hand. "For one still sun."

Raya let out a little sob. "Yes. Maybe I should have been praying that for myself."

He kissed her nose and dug into his pocket, retrieving that little velvet bag she'd seen him fumbling with so many times. As he pulled the string and dumped the contents into her lap, her breathing stopped. A handful of orange and pink beads. Her beads. She buried her face in her hands.

"I can't believe this."

"Me either." He blew out a breath. "But what I really can't believe is that you knew and didn't say anything. I mean, this was big, Ray. What happened to you? That girl I met, the girl I've been carrying around with me for all these years, she was so certain true love existed. I was the one who didn't believe. What happened to that girl?"

She nodded toward the clinic. "That girl died a few months ago."

His eyebrows gathered with concern.

"Not literally. Don't worry. I'm okay. Um, what are you here for?"

He didn't even blink. "An AIDS test."

The cold wood slats met with her back, holding her up. "I thought you were celibate."

Flex snorted. "I am. Two years now, but one of my . . . partners . . . from before, the girl I was supposed to marry, actually died a few months back. Brooke Ashton. You might have heard of her."

"The model? Wow. I heard about that. I met her a few times. She seemed so sweet. We talked about the Lord even. I'm sorry."

He covered his mouth, dragged his hand down over his goatee. "Me too. We never loved each other, she and I. We talked about the Lord a lot too. Unfortunately, we didn't walk that talk. Besides that day on the beach and every moment since I found you again, I've never been in love." He lifted her chin as if to get a closer look but moved no closer.

She stared at him. The usual lemon and vanilla emanated from his skin, but now she could almost smell something else too. The scent of the ocean. She'd smelled it only once before, then with her feet in the sand and her hand in his.

"Don't say that. Please."

His voice sank into his jacket. "I'm not Darrell, Ray. And you're not Brooke. This is a miracle. Don't turn it away."

"No." She stood and backpedaled toward the doctor's office. Her lips pressed together. "I can't deal with this. I know how it ends—babies die, people get divorced, they lie to you, leave you. God knows I love you, but—"

A kiss swallowed her words. Flex leaned down, pressed his forehead to hers. There seemed no more strength in him.

"I've let you treat me crazy, but this is too much. I'm just a man. If you walk away from this . . . don't try to come back."

"I'm sorry," she said, scrambling through the snow, trying to forget those beads on the ground, careful not to drop the crumpled shred of money in her bone-cold hands. With every step her resolve withered, her need crashed to the surface. At the corner she turned back, started running . . .

But Flex was gone.

"What is wrong with you two?" The head of the Reebok team walked off the Flex-ability set in disgust. He turned to Chenille. "Can you handle this, please?" The angry blond marched off the stage.

Chenille trapped Raya and Flex as they both tried to get away. "What's going on, guys? You're barking at each other. Flex, you're missing your marks. You need to . . ."

The words bounced across Flex's eardrums but, like everything else he'd heard for the last few days, didn't penetrate. He crossed the room and went out the door into the hall, where he grabbed the biggest chocolate donut he could find.

She was the one. And she hadn't wanted him.

He'd even been thinking of proposing to her once he knew the test was okay, putting his dreams on hold, and diving in heart first. Thank God he hadn't gone that far. Still, his mind played tricks on him, running through what he could have done differently. If he'd loved her so much, why had he waited so long to tell her?

Because she's nuts. And so am I for thinking about this again.

If he wasn't careful, he'd end up like his father. At least

they didn't have any children. Jay's face came to mind, but he forced it away, walking back toward the set, where someone had called his name. The music started again, and he pulled the ridiculous hood over his head for the fiftieth time. The videographer shouted suggestions, but he walked down the runway with a blank face.

"Cut!"

Chenille's face looked strained. "Let's take five. I need to get back to the firm, but I'd like to have this nailed first. Lyle? Honey, what are you doing here?"

Flex stumbled. Lyle? He waited for some emotion at the sight of his friend, but he'd spent it all this week. There was nothing left.

"Hey, man. Good to see you. You look good."

"You don't." Lyle kissed his wife and walked carefully toward Flex. "What gives?"

Flex wanted to blurt it all out, but he didn't have the heart to go through it again. It was bad enough dealing with the phone calls from his mother and Raya's grandmother asking if the two of them couldn't somehow work things out. During their last conversation, Mademoiselle had added details about how Darrell kept the apartment full of flowers. His fists clenched. He'd like to beat that guy down with a few of those roses. Better yet, with just the thorns. Flex walked with Lyle to a nearby chair, wishing his friend hadn't come at all.

"I've got some stuff going on, man. I'll tell you about it later, when you're feeling better."

Chenille shot a worried glance between the two men and shot off after Raya.

Lyle came closer. "Whatever it is, Flex, you need to just give it to the Lord. Raya too. It's eating you both up. He can cleanse everything, even the really bad stuff."

Flex shook his head. "It's nothing like what you might

think, but it's rough. You're right though. I need to give it to God and leave it alone. I hope you didn't come all the way down here just to tell me that. You need to be in bed."

Lyle steadied himself on the edge of his chair. "Don't flatter yourself. I came for the redhead."

"Good." Flex chuckled and stared at the ceiling.

Lord, I don't know how to let this go. I can't even be in here with her. But I'm just giving this to you. Raya, my heart, all of it.

Nothing felt much different, but with each second a quiet peace came over him. A peace beyond understanding.

Lyle nodded. "That's better. Now buck up, man. No weapon formed against you shall prosper. If she's for you, you'll have her. If not, we'll all have a good cry later." He hit Flex across the back of the neck. "Right now you've got work to do."

Flex nodded, ashamed that a man who'd been walking the edge of death for months had to spend his energy to give him a pep talk. Whatever the case, he felt like himself, if even for a moment. He cleared his head, preparing to do the shoot again, the way it was supposed to be done.

Raya's voice cut through his thoughts. "It's Jay," she said softly, her cell to her ear. "Said he tried to call you, but your phone is off. Child Services is there. Seems someone called and reported that he's alone. They're taking him away."

He didn't look back to see if she was coming. There was nothing else he could do for her right now. For them. But he had to save Jay.

Flex ran for the curb and piled into the sedan his father had bought him. The gifts seemed outrageous until he needed them. Without a word, Raya piled into the passenger's side.

"Buckle up."

He pulled into traffic without looking her way. How had he managed to have his phone off? He'd never done that. This mess had him turned inside out.

Raya pressed buttons beside him.

"Who are you calling?"

"Gram. Maybe she can go down and get him or at least sit with him until we get there—"

We? "I'm his guardian, okay? Temporary, true enough, but his guardian still. You can come along, but stay out of it."

He's all I've got. Leave me with something, Flex thought.

He sighed. How he'd loved this woman. Still did. He could never let her know it though. Not after all that had happened. She wasn't the only one who could turn to ice. In the rearview mirror, Flex eyed his face, each day looking more and more like his father's. Hiding his feelings grew easier each minute too. He'd been taught by the master.

"Maybe we should compromise on that. Your guardianship, I mean. After this, we're . . . you're going to lose him. Maybe if I took him—"

"You? No way." Flex slammed the horn with his open hand. "You've been a great help and all, but you've got work and . . . and . . ."

"And what?" She looked past him at the big, cold building Jay had described on the phone. "Turn in here. I think this is it."

Flex slid into a space and jumped out of the car, feeling for his wallet. Raya's boots clicked behind him. He didn't wait.

At the desk inside, the clerk looked amused. "May I help you?"

"Jay Andrews. I'm here to pick him up. I'm his guardian."

The woman smiled. "Oh yeah. That kid is something else. He's in the back."

"Thanks."

Flex whipped around the corner with Raya right behind him. They both ran down the hall toward Jay, who was sitting on his knees in front of a video game, pressing buttons like mad. When he saw them, he dropped the controller.

"Mom! Dad!"

Flex looked at the boy like he was crazy. "Jay? Are you all right?"

The boy winked at him, nodding to the man behind the desk. "Yeah, Dad." He practically screamed the insinuation. "I'm fine."

The social worker tapped his pen on the desk. "You can cut the act, Jay. I know that Mr. Dunham isn't your father." He stared coldly at Raya. "And you are . . . ?"

"Raya Joseph. I go to church with Jay and Mr. Dunham. I also help coach his basketball team and talk to his teachers, help with homework . . ."

"Ah yes. Miss Joseph. I've heard a lot about you today." The man turned back to Flex and then to a paper on his desk. "Sounds like you're doing quite a bit of Jay's care. You've both done well. Jay has really made a turnaround in spite of the tragedy of his aunt's death."

Flex had to agree. "She helps me with him. Most every day. He's only been alone a few times lately because he's been sick. Otherwise, we bring him along. Usually one of us is there."

"I see. And what is the relationship between the two of you?"

Jay held up his hands like two birds. "They're in love . . ."

Great. Now he'd done it.

"We're friends, sir." That was a stretch at the moment, but it was truer than any other explanation.

The man surveyed the files in front of him. "Jay has been shuffled around enough. He seems very attached to both of you. It's a shame you aren't 'in love,' as he puts it. If you were married, that would make things much easier."

"Really?" Raya looked ashamed.

Duh.

"At any rate, I think it's great that Miss Joseph is such a help to you, but if you're not making any commitment to one another, I think it's best that Mr. Dunham find a way to take care of Jay on his own—"

"But . . ." Raya and Jay both tried to interrupt.

Flex stayed quiet, trying to figure out how he was going to add yet another knot in the already fraying rope of his life. As Lyle suggested, he cast the burden heavenward, hoping it wouldn't come crashing down on his head.

"It will be difficult, but I'll make it work, sir. I'll ask my mother to help. I'm applying to adopt him through the AIDS orphans program."

"Excellent." The man closed the file. "Too bad this happened. I wish you'd let us know. Perhaps we could have arranged something in your area. Now he'll have to stay here for the time being. Although Jay is now thirteen, it is still considered unwise to leave children under eighteen at home alone."

"Are you serious? I stayed home by myself from eleven on—"

"You can't do that now. Not in today's world. Though it seems a small thing, you'd be shocked at what can happen."

Raya stiffened beside him.

Jay ignored them both, retreating into the shell they'd spent the past few months painstakingly removing. He pressed play on the game and started slamming buttons.

Flex knelt down beside him. "I'll get this worked out. I—"

"Yeah. Thanks, Coach. For everything. You too, Miss Joseph." His voice was flat.

The social worker stood and walked them to the door. "He has a court hearing next week. But it may be held over until January. They often are."

A building exploded on the TV screen. Jay cheered.

Flex exploded too. "January? He might have to stay here for Christmas?"

The man shrugged. "Possibly, but don't worry. He knows the drill. He'll be fine."

Flex closed his eyes. Jay would not be fine.

Neither would he.

24

December crawled in, bringing none of its usual joy. It was a week before Christmas, and Raya hadn't bought one gift. Her parents were in the clear for now, but Frances had advanced into full-blown AIDS. Jay still wasn't at home and Flex, well, he was barely talking to her. And who could blame him?

Whenever thoughts about what she'd given up crossed her mind, Raya pressed Jay's face to the forefront. She had to find a way to get him out of that place before next week. She lifted her cell phone to her mouth and spoke into the microphone. "Flex Dunham."

It was funny, now that they were estranged, his number was first in her vocal address book. They talked more about Jay than they ever had about one another. Though before Flex had always tried to draw her out and get her to talk more, now he shut her down as quickly as possible. Only for Jay did he have open ears—and arms. Despite the opinion of ACS, Raya knew Flex would be a good father. One who listened.

She hoped he'd listen to her now.

"Hello?"

"Any luck, Flex?"

"No." He sounded annoyed. "I can't talk now. I'm with a client. If Dad's lawyer calls with news, I'll call you."

The phone clicked in her ear. Hard to believe he'd changed so much in such a short time. It was as if they'd switched places. As if after so much trying, Flex's love for her had dried up.

In a way she was glad. It made things easier. Though the words between them were short at times, she could see that this hurt had brought about more light in him. More caring. She could see it in his interactions with everyone but her. And if she'd just stop calling and butt out of the situation with Jay, she'd probably see it toward her too, but she just couldn't. She'd already quit the gym, unable to endure his mother's sad looks. But she couldn't abandon Jay.

The intercom buzzed. It was Jean. "Your friend is back. And don't call me in."

Her friend? Besides Lily and Chenille, did she even have any?

They were supposed to be friends forever. At least . . . At most . . . Well, she couldn't think about that either.

She swiped at a tear, no longer caring about the mysterious visitor. It wasn't him, so what did it matter?

Megan stepped in minus half her ponytail and a whole lot of makeup. Raya stood to greet her. So far Raya's father had tested clear, but her mother's results hadn't been returned. It was a technicality, but every time she saw Megan, it worried her.

"How are you? And your mom?"

Megan smiled. A sincere smile. "We're not sure what's ahead, but we're going to fight it."

Raya squeezed her hand. They weren't quite friends, but they weren't enemies either. "I'm so sorry."

"Me too, but that's not what I'm here for. I'm here about my dress."

Raya rubbed her forehead. "We hadn't heard from you so—"

Megan's eyes glittered with anger. "Did you think because Mother's sick that I can't pay?"

Well, not exactly, but now that she'd mentioned it . . .

"That wasn't it at all. There's just a new line, and—"

"I heard. That's why I'm here. I figured all these things were drawing your attention away from my dress. I put my order in first, you know."

Would they ever get past this petty stuff? "Yes, I know."

Megan raked her eyes down Raya's body. "Good, then you won't mind that I've scheduled a showing for my bridesmaids and some other friends."

Raya rubbed her hands together. "A showing of what?"

Megan laughed. "Why, my dress, of course."

Good thing she'd had that dress cleaned. If it fit, Megan could just have it right now. Raya had no use for it.

"So you're going to wear your wedding gown in front of the wedding party?" *Weird.* "When?"

"Tomorrow night, at the Ritz Carlton. And I'm not wearing the dress. You are."

It was a perfect fit. Even though she'd quit the gym, all those workouts had paid off. Her wedding dress lay against her like an old friend. Well, Megan's wedding dress now.

No, it would always be hers. It had started out as her mother's dream, simple and strapless. But Raya's wide skirt and beaded bodice had given the dress her personal flair. She despaired now at allowing anyone, especially Megan, to wear it, but she knew the many changes Megan would require would change it totally. Still, her hopes and dreams were stitched in the seams of this gown, her best bridal design.

Oh well. For a few more minutes, she could dream. She might not ever be a bride in reality, but in her head she was a princess forever. That's what nights like this were all about.

A curtain of red velvet hung in front of her. Soft piano played on the other side, sifting between the hushed tones of a small group. She couldn't guess their number. Megan's voice rose over the others, giving sharp commands.

"Please be seated, everyone."

Chairs scuffed against the carpet. The ruby-colored veil fell away. The crowd gasped.

Raya did too.

Though the others were seated, one man stood directly in front of her. A man with dancing eyes in an ivory tuxedo. Megan's groom. He existed after all. And he looked familiar, like she'd seen him somewhere. The hospital, maybe? When Chenille was there? A small, bronze woman in the front row nodded in approval. His mother, no doubt.

The guy took Raya's hand and guided her across the floor as Chenille described the fabric, beadwork, everything except the gown's ugly beginnings. The man's hand upon hers felt strange and clammy. She wanted to stomp his foot for picking that ivory tuxedo. No doubt Megan had seen Flex's photos from the ball. Though this guy was handsome, it took more than looks to carry off that suit. This guy just couldn't do it. Megan seemed to know it too as she scribbled furiously on a pad in her lap. Why the boyfriend even had to dress up was beyond Raya, but that was how Megan did things. Large and in charge.

She felt the man's nervousness through her gloves, her

own heart pounding as she stared through the small crowd, thinking of Jay and of Flex. As beautiful as this dress was, it held nothing to that Hawaiian afternoon, to their tear-stained kisses and heartfelt hugs. She'd known Flex forever and just met him all at the same time. Suddenly she knew that it would always be that way, even when he was married to someone else.

Someone else.

How had that possibly slipped by her radar? No matter what Flex said or thought, he wouldn't be able to stay alone forever. His quick attachment to her had proved that. And likewise for her. What would she do when she saw Flex strolling down the beach one day . . . with his wife! And not to mention Jay, who felt as much her son as if she'd given birth to him.

Megan's fiancé tugged her hand. "Are you all right?"

For once she gave an honest answer to the questions she'd grown to detest. "No, I'm not all right."

He motioned to Megan, and the music stopped. Raya pulled away before the last beat sounded. "Thanks."

Chenille followed her to the dressing room, helping with the stays and zipper. "That was rough, huh? I could tell."

Raya spun around, yanking off the veil and scraping her hair into a ponytail. "What? The dress? Oh, it was fine. I just need to go. I've got a run to make."

Chenille tugged the gown over Raya's head. "To see Jay? Have you heard anything more? I know Lyle said he might come home today."

Raya shrugged. "There was a chance he might come to my place, but they didn't call. And Flex isn't returning my calls . . ."

She tugged on her jeans. Where had she put those socks? There.

Chenille helped Raya pull her sweater over her head and picked up her friend's purse and gloves and held them out to her. "I'm sorry about how all that turned out."

"Don't be."

Raya was already at the door.

She mounted the stairs to Flex's home with determination. Each step seemed higher than the last. Up, up, up to Flex's flat, a place once as familiar as his scent or his touch. All of which she'd missed. Tonight she'd put an end to that too. Now, though, she needed to see if Jay had made it home. She knocked at the door with a firm rap, for once not ready to bolt at the thought of him answering.

No one came to the door. Raya knocked three more times, then took a deep breath and tried the knob. As impossible as it was, the doorknob turned. The door swung open, but still no welcome came from inside.

"Flex?" Raya forgot herself and marched inside, stepping over the pizza boxes littering the floor. Another step brought her to Jay, curled up on the couch with sunken eyes and a drawn expression, even in his sleep. She reached for him but hugged his elbows instead, not wanting to wake him.

Thank you, Lord.

Jay's arms reached out in his fitful sleep. "Mama," he said in a hoarse voice. "They don't want me. Nobody wants me." The boy's arm hung over the side of the couch. His finger grazed the floor.

Raya covered her mouth with her hand. She'd prayed for months to know what was going on in that boy's head. And now she knew. He had the same problem she and Flex did. Rejection.

"Hey."

She stumbled and caught her breath. Had he been standing there long? She should have smelled him coming. Unlike the house, he smelled just like always. But she couldn't make out his face in the shadow. They'd drawn every blind.

"Flex?"

"It's me."

He stepped from the darkness. Raya gasped. His eyes were bloodshot, and a shadow, hours away from becoming a beard, shrouded his chin—and it wasn't sculpted like the one he'd had the day she'd met him. There was a place the size of a coin with no hair at all. No wonder he always wore the rest of his face smooth. He looked like she felt. Was Jay not there to stay?

"What happened? Are they taking him?"

"No." Flex brushed past her and stretched out on the couch opposite Jay. "I'm adopting him, as a matter of fact."

Her shoulders slumped at the singularity of the statement. He'd been clear that day at the clinic—if you walk away now, don't come back. And here she was. All she could do was hope and pray. Their being together had seemed such a God thing. She'd have to hope it still was.

"Oh. That's . . . that's great."

Flex sat up and perched his chin on steepled fingers. "Great? Is it? I don't know. I can't do this alone. That boy needs a mother, Ray."

Her heart flipped. *Ray.*

She sank to one knee. "A mother, huh? Does that mean you need a wife? I know you're not marrying anybody and everything, but if you've changed your mind, I know someone who'd really like the job."

Flex's jaw dropped open. "Are you proposing to me? To us?" He looked as though a snake had bitten him.

Jay tossed and turned across from them.

"Shh . . ." Raya said. "Yes, I'm proposing to you. To both of you. He needs a mother. I want to be his mother—"

"But do you want to be my wife?" He shook his head. "I appreciate the offer, Ray. But we need something real, something for the long haul. We need somebody who isn't afraid to love us."

Ouch.

This fellow definitely needed further convincing, maybe more convincing than she could do. She sighed. At least she'd given it a shot. She could go on knowing that at least. As she stood, though, she knew a shot wasn't enough.

"Look, I messed up, okay? You win. Just give me another chance. Please."

He pointed to the floor and his face. "Do I look like I won something? I'll give you a million chances. Just tell me that you mean it. Tell me—"

"That it's safe and I won't hurt you? Sorry. That falls under the scared-to-love category. Can't help you there."

"Oh, I think you can help me." He stood, feathering her cheek with his finger, then tipping up her chin. His smell, mingled with something else, dilated her nostrils. Eucalyptus. He smiled. "Vick's Vapor Rub. He came back with a little cold. I remembered what you said to do the last time . . ."

She fought back tears. "I love you, Flex. I mean it. And I do want to be both your wife and Jay's mother—"

Before she could say more, he cradled her face in his hands and kissed her like she'd never been kissed. Even better than that smack at the train station, if that was possible. Was any of this possible? She couldn't consider it now. She buried her hands in Flex's hair, meeting his kiss with all the love she'd held back from him. From God. And from herself.

"Say yes already, will you, Coach?" A strained voice echoed between them.

"Yes. A million times yes. And stop with the Coach bit. Call me Dad," Flex said, breaking his lip-lock with Raya just long enough to get out the words.

As laughter burst from all three of them, Raya and Flex collapsed back against the couch.

Tears poured into her mouth. "Jay? Have you been awake all this time?"

The boy opened one eye. "Long enough. Now ask her . . . Dad . . . so I can be sure this is a done deal before I go scrape some of this vapor rub off me. He practically painted me with it!"

Fletch tossed a pillow at his new son and pulled Raya closer. "The kid's got a point. What'll it be, Stretch? Take me for the long haul?"

Raya let herself rest on his chest. "Do you want to shave and let me think about it?"

"No." He pinched her side.

She rubbed the stubble on his chin. "Good. I sort of like that patchy look."

"You would. Just don't draw any pictures of it, okay?"

"I can't make any promises—about that, I mean."

Jay moaned. "So is that a yes? My skin is on fire."

"Well . . ." She lifted Flex's shirt to her nose and made a funny face. "Do I have to wash these too?"

Flex looked down at her with an impish grin. "If you're lucky."

Her stomach tumbled. Megan could have all the million-dollar gowns she wanted. This was priceless. She kissed him again.

"I'll take the job."

"All right!" Jay shot up off the couch and reached for

both of them. "We're a family." He stared up at the ceiling. "I knew you'd come through. It wasn't what I expected, but it's good."

Raya closed her eyes. She couldn't agree more. It was good, and getting better by the second.

Acknowledgments

Thanks to Christ for this opportunity.

To my family for enduring late night mumbling from the closet for months on end and untold amounts of Chunky soup.

To Jennifer Leep, my wonderful editor, for believing in me and Kelley Meyne, my fearless and talented copyeditor, for tackling this manuscript.

To Claudia for helping me find my voice again.

To Jessica Ferguson for reading every book I write and always finding something wonderful and kind to say while telling me when the words don't work. You are a grace.

To Beth Ziarnik for reading the proposal for this series and Nancy Toback for the wedding dress idea and your friendship.

To Wanza McInnis for answering all my Flatbush questions.

To Amy, Jen, and Staci, the ladies of the Threshing Floor for mentoring the mentor.

To Lisa, Heather, Bobbie, Angie, and Bonnie for blogging me to the other side.

To Gail for teaching me how to think pink again.

To the *Word Praize* family for enduring my absences.

To my mother for never giving up on me.

Dear Reader,

Thank you so much for sharing *Pink* with me. I hope that this book will lead you to pray for AIDS victims around the globe and in America as well. Black women currently make up 72 percent of females diagnosed with this disease. May every woman who reads this book discover what Raya discovered about herself—strength in weakness, power in purity. May God show himself strong to you today and for always.

For more information about AIDS throughout the African Diaspora, visit www.balmingilead.org. The Balm in Gilead is a Christian initiative against the devastation of this disease. For more information on AIDS orphans in New York City, please visit www.aidsinfonyc.org/orphan.

Join me in praying for AIDS victims and their parents. Thanks for being here. I appreciate it.

Blessings,

Marilynn

Discussion Questions

The questions below are intended to enhance your personal or group reading of this book. We hope you have enjoyed this story of strength in weakness, power in purity, family, love, and faith.

1. What do you think is the most important lesson in the story for Raya? For Flex? For Megan?
2. Why do you think Raya has run away from her privileged upbringing in LA? Is she weak, or is she empowering herself? What have you run away from and why?
3. How does God use the pain of child loss, disappointment, and suffering from disease to get to the heart of Chenille and the other characters in *Pink*?
4. Megan is seen as the antagonist throughout the story. Why does she try so hard to create havoc in the lives of Raya and Flex? What is she searching for? Does she ever find it?
5. How does Raya come to terms with her struggle to please people and live up to their expectations of her?
6. Father-daughter relationships are so important in the development of self-esteem. Why does Raya run away

from her father? How does coming to terms with him actually help shape her future?

7. Does your circle of friends reflect a multicultural array of women? If not, how can you broaden your circle of women friends to include other women of color (Hispanic, Asian, etc.)?

8. Is Flex using his mother as a crutch to avoid facing his issues with his father? Is she enabling him to do so?

9. Megan is out to get Raya. Or is she really? When competition threatens your professional and personal life, how do you respond?

10. Megan is searching for herself in rich men. How can she find and create strong friendships with the women in her life to help her become a woman of destiny?

11. How can you and/or your local church community address the AIDS crisis in the African Diaspora? Why are African Americans afraid to address the issue of AIDS in the church and among heterosexual women?

12. How do Raya and Flex deal with their choice of celibacy? Do they choose celibacy out of fear of AIDS or because of their relationship with God?

13. Do you pray for AIDS victims around the world? Their families, parents, friends? If not, why?

14. What do you think is the most serious issue in the church today? For women of color? For men of color?

15. If you knew your current spouse, a friend, or a family member had a personal encounter with AIDS, how would you respond?

16. What is the importance of Jay's story in the lives of Raya and Flex?

17. What are your predictions for Raya? For Flex? For Megan? For their parents?

18. Part of *Pink* is about forgiving others and yourself,

strength in weakness, and power in purity. How do Raya and Flex apply these themes to their lives? Who or what are you afraid to forgive?

19. As you were reading, did you believe Raya and Flex would give in to temptation and lust or honor their commitment to God, celibacy, and themselves? What allows them to honor these commitments when it gets tough?

20. Compare and contrast Raya at the beginning of *Pink* to the Raya who emerges at the end. Does she change? Do people ever truly change?

21. How does each character in *Pink* resolve or respond to his or her parent(s) and/or friend(s)?

22. Raya's relationship with her grandmother is pivotal throughout the novel. How has it shaped Raya? How does this relationship affect Raya's relationship with Flex? Her relationship with her father? How has it shaped her views about God, religion, and relationships?

marilynn griffith

jade

Coming in June 2006

Excerpt from **Jade**

The envelope held Lily Chau's future. And she held a letter opener, running it under her fingernails for the remnants of her present. After skimming under the nail of her ring finger, she snagged what she'd been going for—a hunk of prunes that had lodged under her nail during the chop-and-puree fest once known as breakfast. Breakfast that her mother had returned as quickly as Lily had spooned it all in, leaving Lily standing in a puddle in her best shoes.

"Jump in the shower. Grab the black pants. Your wrap blouse is clean. I saw it the other day," her neighbor Pinkie had said, arms going in every direction. "You don't know how to feed her, Lily. You should have waited for me."

Lily had tried to wait, but her mother wasn't in a waiting mood today. The guilt over leaving her hungry mother with their neighbor had sent her into a chopping and blending frenzy that had ended as such things usually did, by seeping into her shoes and staining her best skirt. But that was okay. She'd put a barrette in her mother's hair and fed her breakfast. Where God chose to store that breakfast was up to him.

Lily's days of being a fashion plate were long gone anyway, despite her job in the clothes industry. The pants she wore now were turning into her work uniform. But her mother was still alive, her boyfriend was still dropping hints about their inevitable wedding, and she grew closer to God each day. Things were good, with hopes of getting better. Becoming stable.

So why was she holding the letter opener in both hands? Lily ran the point of it across the envelope, tracing the letters in the return address: The Next Design Diva Show, Nia Network. Lily slipped the blade into the envelope's back flap, then slid her finger against the instrument's edge. She pulled upward slightly, ripping the corner, and—

"Are you sleeping in here?" A husky voice laced with laughter echoed in the hall before its speaker reached Lily's office. Jean believed in giving people warnings of her impending arrival, even her friends. Since her bittersweet personality could suck the oxygen out of any room, the announcement was usually warranted. For everyone but Lily, that is. Lily saw through Jean's fast moves and loud talk . . . to her heart. She hoped her friend wouldn't see through her just as quickly today.

"Can't you ever stay in your office during the creative hour? We've got thirty more minutes. Take a nap, why don't you? Or color in a coloring book like that guy over in production."

Though Lily chided her loving workaholic friend for coming to visit when they were all supposed to be spending time alone to refuel their creativity, the interruption was a gift. For a moment she'd let herself consider something impossible. Something still forked on her letter opener.

Jean whisked into the office just as Lily swept the letter into her desk drawer, where it would accompany her secret copy of *Modern Bride* and a cigarette she'd found after quitting and hadn't thrown away.

Pausing to push Lily's huge fossil doorstop into place, Jean gave her friend a lingering glance. "Oh my. Now she's cramming things into that drawer again. Or are you peeking at those silly ten-dollar wedding magazines that all say the same thing? Or were you dreaming of that picket fence on Long Island with your doctor friend?"

Warmth rushed to Lily's face. "Neither. You need to stay out of my desk, you nosy thing."

With a laugh brewing in the back of her throat, Jean approached Lily like a lioness in a good suit. "Listen, honey, nobody needs to be nosy to know anything around here, especially when you stuff that drawer so full it won't shut. I can't tell you how many times I've had to come in here and pick all that mess up off the floor since you ran the custodian away from here."

"Here you go with that again. I told you. I did not run the custodian away. He can still clean in here . . . when I'm here."

"Uh-huh." Jean shook her head in pity.

"He was stealing my rocks!" Lily banged the letter opener on her desk, wanting to shove it into the drawer too, but now she was too afraid of what might come flying out if she did.

"Listen to what you just said. Stealing rocks. Now, I admit you've got some of the best pebble and bauble collections I've ever seen, but you've got to let it go."

She reached around Lily and yanked out the drawer. The

magazine unfurled as if she'd pulled the string on a parachute. Fabric swatches, neon note squares, and office supplies spilled over the sides and onto the floor.

Jean stuck her hand toward the back and came out with a pitiful excuse for a Virginia Slim. "You've got to let this go too. You haven't smoked in almost two years. What are you doing, planning a slow suicide sometime in the future?"

"I . . . I . . . just give me that, okay?" Lily reached for the cigarette, peeled back its skin, and emptied the tobacco guts into the trash while trying not to get too much of the smell on her fingers.

As she considered what she'd really saved up for later, disobeying the voice of God, Lily became much less concerned with Jean and more concerned with her own heart. Sometimes it seemed like she'd come so far, but there were still those little secrets she tried to keep, parts of her life she tried to stuff in a drawer. And God kept having to come and pick up the pieces when it spilled over the side.

She grabbed a wet wipe from her purse and scrubbed her hands, only to realize what dangled from Jean's fingers.

The envelope.

The rumpled magazine had covered it, but as usual Jean had left no stone, or mangled bridal magazine, unturned. She looked as though she'd caught a tiger by the tail.

"So they did pick you! I knew they would. They had too. I told Raya I was going to call her father myself if they didn't."

Lily froze. She'd carried the envelope around in her purse for two days wondering why the show had written her. She'd considered submitting sketches several times, but each time, something had happened with her mother's health to make her forget it. There was also the quiet that had come over her every time she'd prayed about it. She felt as though she

333

was supposed to wait and see the salvation of the Lord, that what God had would come to her through another way. Now it seemed that her other way might be from the office down the hall.

"What did you do?" she asked.

Beads from Jean's bracelets jangled as she shook her wrists. "Nothing much. I took a few sketches from your book and scanned them. Sent that robe you designed for that stupid boyfriend of yours—"

Lily clenched her fists. "The kimono? That was Ken's Christmas present. I've been looking everywhere for it. How could you?"

Her friend smiled. "Easy. Now hush and open the letter. At least I don't try and match you up with men. Not that you couldn't use some help there too . . . Don't look at me like that. I care about you."

If this was caring, Lily didn't want to think of what uncaring might feel like. She pried the letter from Jean's fingers and placed it in the drawer, now empty except for a star-shaped paper clip in neon pink and a pencil with no eraser. Lily's sketching pencil.

She stared up at the ceiling. "Why couldn't I have regular friends who don't care about me so much? Goodness, Jean, how could you? I mean, sure I'd love to have my own line, my own show, but I can't—"

"Here we go again. You really should have been a Catholic, you know. You're a natural at the guilty martyr thing." Jean dropped into the chair a few inches away. "We've been over this a gazillion times. You can do this. None of your excuses hold water, especially your first one—that you're not good enough. Knowing that means you are good enough. Everybody has to start somewhere. As for your mother, she can go wherever you go."

It was Lily's turn to laugh this time, though there was little humor in it. "Like the way your grandkids could go wherever you go, Jean?"

Her stoic friend grabbed the desk with a white-knuckled grip. "Okay, you got me. I still think you should open it. Just to know."

"No thanks," Lily said, taking the letter from the drawer and ripping it to shreds. "Whatever I need to know about myself isn't in this letter. It's in that," she said, nodding to the Bible in the bookcase beside her.

Jean's jaw tightened, but she turned for a quick glance at the Bible Lily had motioned to. She turned back quickly, sweeping the torn bits of paper into the trash with her cupped hand. "Once again your future depends on your faith. I guess that'll always be the difference between you and me."

"I sure hope not." Lily stilled her friend's hand by gripping it with her own.

Marilynn Griffith is a freelance writer who lives in Florida
with her husband and seven children. When not chasing tod-
dlers, helping with homework, or trying to find her husband
a clean shirt, she writes novels and scribbles in her blog. She
also speaks to women at conferences and prayer gatherings.
To book speaking engagements or just say hello, drop her a
note at marilynngriffith@gmail.com.